S0-AZP-397

20th, November, 201[illegible]

Thank you!

Love,
Meghan
&
Jonathan Millea

The Lasting

Jonathan S. Millea

This is a novel is a work of fiction.

Library of Congress Card Catalog Number: pending.

~ ***For Meghan*** ~

A dear friend for whom I shall forever have a special place in my heart.

Special Thanks to ***Mr. John F. Millea****, my wonderful father whom without his help, this book would not have been possible. Thanks also to* ***Mrs. Karen Yash****, my editor and good friend.*

The Lasting

Jonathan Sheridan Millea

I

The heat of the summer evening was unbearable on Manhattan when she stepped out of the taxicab. She immediately unbuttoned her collar and brushed back her shiny red hair as she walked up the steps to the rundown apartment building in Greenwich Village. It was now almost nine o'clock and it had been a very long day. Quite frankly, she was glad to be home.

Emily Shanahan, at only a little over twenty-four, worked as the Deputy Director of Public Relations for a local newspaper. The week at the office had been plagued by accusations of libel material printed about a corrupt factory in Newark two months ago. She had scrutinized every single word in the alleged article only to find all the facts stated were perfectly true. Nevertheless, the lawyers hounded her like a pride of hungry lions after a baby zebra. With the matter left unsolved, next week wasn't looking any better.

She punched in the security code and went inside the musty old building. As she hurried up the dimly lit stairwell to her second-story apartment, she felt the sweat begin to run down her face. When she unlocked her door and walked in, she exhaled with a pleased smile.

Air conditioning! she happily thought. She slammed the door and tossed her briefcase on the couch. "David!" she called, kicking off her high-heeled shoes and making her way towards the kitchen. She opened the refrigerator and looked around for something that hadn't yet spoiled and grown a jungle of mold on it. "David?" she asked again.

David Shanahan rushed down the hallway, dressed in his fancy suit pants and crisp white shirt as he dried his soaking hair with an old towel. "Hello! How was work today?"

Emily gave a low growl. "Guess."

"Monday's going to be trouble?"

"Yepper," she said, pulling out a tub of cream cheese. She grabbed a box of crackers off the counter and sat down on the table, snacking ravenously on the food. She was a beautiful woman with a slim, sexy build and deep blue eyes to match. She normally watched her weight like a hawk, but not now. She was too hungry to care.

"Didn't they feed you guys today?" he asked with a friendly laugh.

"No time," she said between bites.

David gave her a sympathetic look, then stepped out into the living room. He picked up his tie from the floor and grabbed his sports coat from the couch. He was a handsome man with his rich, black hair, deep brown eyes and gentle face. He tucked in his shirt and attached his belt. His heart raced with anticipation. "You're still on for tonight, aren't you?" he asked.

"What?" Emily asked, quickly scanning through the mental organizer in her brain. She had just had a long day at work. All she wanted to do was take a break and chill out for a while. And he wanted to drag her back out?

"We were going to have dinner with Frank Klosterman, my boss. Remember?"

She slapped her forehead and rolled her eyes. "Oh. That was tonight?"

"Yeah."

Emily slipped off the table and brushed the crumbs off herself. "I'm sorry, honey. I'm really not up to it tonight."

" . . . Oh," her husband said, sounding hurt.

"Besides, it'll be cheaper if it's just you. I'll find something here for dinner."

"Cheaper? Frank's picking up the tab for us. And even if he wasn't, we have enough to go out to dinner."

Emily threw her hands on her hips and glared at him. "I didn't say that we didn't have enough."

"Not this time," David said, shooting back a dirty look.

"I just said that we have to be careful about how we spend. It's simply economics. We just can't go out on these extravagant dates of yours every weekend."

He knotted the tie around his neck and slipped on his coat. "They're not extravagant. A movie at the most."

"That alone is over twenty dollars!"

David gasped in disbelief. "We can spare twenty dollars a week. It's not that much."

"In one month, that's eighty dollars! Do you know how badly we need that? We can barely pay the rent, let alone for food! All I asked you was that we tone it down a bit on the spending sprees!"

"What are you talking about!" he exclaimed. "We should have a little recreation every once in a while."

"Not when we can't afford it!"

David walked off to the bathroom and combed his hair in the mirror. "No money to spend on us during the weekends, but waste all of it you want on your fancy dresses!"

Emily stepped forward and yelled, "I need those for my job! And without my job, we wouldn't be living here!"

"And what's my job?" David snarled back. "Licking toilets clean in the subways? I contribute just as much as you do, thank you very much!"

"If you're anything at work like you are at home, you just sit in a chair all day and have others do your tasks for you!"

David slammed the comb on the edge of the sink and stormed into the narrow hallway. "That's a bunch of crap and you know it! Perhaps if your job didn't come first all of the time, you'd realize that I am a very efficient worker! Which is why I have that meeting with Frank tonight! Which you, of course, don't want to attend. You have other, more important things to do—"

"You make it sound like I'm a work-a-holic."

"You are! You're just like how my parents were!"

Emily turned around, tightening her fists in anger. She didn't work any more religiously than he did. Sure, her schedule was a little more disorganized than his, but still! "Your parents wouldn't of had to work that hard if they had a son who did some chores around the house to help them out!"

"How the heck would you know anything about that!" David asked, offended at her blatancy.

"I live with you, don't I? You never do anything around here! Clothes all over the place, you never put the toilet seat down—"

"You just throw things where ever you feel like it! Who cleaned up your little feminine pad by the shower this morning?"

She starred at him in shock. " . . . Okay. You're just sick."

"You left it there! I didn't want to be the one to throw it away but—"

"Oh come on! It wasn't even used! You're always whining about the littlest—"

"And you're always fighting!"

"No more than you! I came home wanting to catch up on some badly needed sleep! I've had a terribly hard day. My back's hurting, I have a headache and feel like I'm almost ready to fall into a million pieces and you don't even give a lousy damn about it!"

"I do so!" he snapped back. "I'm tired, too! I've been up all day having customers shoveling their sissy complaints at me while my colleagues do nothing to help. You're in PR! You should know what it's like! And finally, after a year of this junk, my boss is finally talking about giving me a promotion, is offering my wife and I a lovely dinner, and she couldn't care less about the whole thing! She doesn't feel like offering the littlest support!"

She stared at him for a moment, her eyes full of anger and bitterness. "Fine," she agreed, walking toward the door. "I'll go. Don't mind if I fall over dead when my heart gives out from the stress, do you?"

"Don't go if you're going to be like this, Emily."

"Too late. I already have my shoes on," she announced. She grabbed her purse and flung the door open. She groaned as the hot, humid air enveloped her. "And what do you care?"

David locked the door behind him. They hurried down the stairs, grumbling and fighting. Sadly, it was nothing new. They had played out the same scene over and over again. The first year of their marriage had been great. They had just gotten out of college and were starting new, exciting careers. They had encouraged each other on in the face of adversity and were always comforting and consoling one another. Granted, there were a few concerning moments here and there, but nothing at all as disappointing as the fights they had fought with each other in their second year.

After the first twelve months, things became less adventurous and more routine. It seemed like nothing they did could edge them out of their financial situation. The apartment was a very nice deal, but it wasn't their dream-come-true to share a one-bedroom apartment that was falling apart with a hundred cockroaches and dozens of rats that came and went as they pleased. They loved each other dearly and, for the most part, got along splendidly. It was the money that was the problem. Any mention of finances brought the worst out of them.

"You didn't want to go, so don't!" David barked. Emily walked out of the building and down the front steps, ignoring him completely. "What's up with you?"

She whirled around at him. "What's up with me? Nothing! Nothing at all! Everything's down and boring! Everything sucks! You got that! It sucks!"

"Emily," David said, getting self-conscious as bystanders watched them.

"As I said before, what do you care! What does God even care!"

He gently grabbed her shoulders and looked her right in the eyes. "Honey, don't say that. I'm sorry. I—"

"was out of place and was acting like a total asshole again! Yes! I know! You say that every time! If you really meant it, you'd stop behaving like a jerk!" she hollered. She broke away from his hands and rushed out in the street. "Taxi!" she cried.

David felt his heart sink. She was right. It was the line he always used in trying to end these little squabbles. He used it as if he was typing some sort of command into a computer. Emily deserved better than that. "Honey, please—"

She turned around and shouted, "Just shut-up and let's go! I'm tired of this—"

It caught his eye long before he realized where it was hurtling towards. He felt his pulse freeze with terrifying awe. "Watch out!" he shrieked.

All she noticed was a luminescent glow showering her body. She hadn't even turned in time to see it.

The SUV slammed on its brakes, but it was too late. Emily's body was thrown like a little rag doll several feet before she crashed down on the pavement. There was a sickening crack when her head slammed onto the concrete.

Without thinking, David ran towards her, screaming out her name in horror. In an instant, he felt he had seen all his reason for living just vanish before his eyes. He rushed out into the street and over to her still body.

"Emily!" he wept, gently picking her up in his arms. He felt her warm blood generously bleed onto his hands. Her hair was soaked with it. He shook his head with utter disbelief and hugged her. "Oh God, no!" he begged. "Please, dear God!"

He stared in shock at the expression on her face. It was very peaceful and relaxed. She made no movement whatsoever. Her image quickly disappeared as his eyes became filled with tears. He sobbed bitterly, holding his wife's motionless body in his arms.

II

It was the feeling of the cold, wet, hard ground that awoke Emily from her slumber. She tiredly opened her eyes and lifted herself up. She looked ahead and gasped. A soft blue light was shining through the eerie mist from far ahead. Only inches above her head was a low ceiling made of heavy stones. There were no walls, but a surreal fog that gave way to total darkness. The floor was a giant slab of jagged, sharp rock, its slimy surface riddled with water puddles. Everything was reflecting the strange blue glow.

A faint breeze blew from behind and poor Emily shivered. She fearfully realized that she was naked. She worried at first, but unfortunately, it seemed that no one else was around. She looked behind her for her purse, but it wasn't there. She glanced down at her hand and saw that even her wedding band was missing. Her heart started to pump harder as the adrenaline rushed through her veins. *Where am I?* she wondered. *Where's my clothes?*

Then she remembered the accident. She looked down at her legs and felt the back of her head, but found no wounds. She leaned forward and looked at her reflection in one of the puddles. As dark as it was, she could barely make out her face, but oddly, there were no scrapes or cuts. She sat back, perplexed.

Another breeze blew in from behind. She lifted her knees to her chin and wrapped her arms around her legs. She trembled tensely, not knowing if it was for fear or from the cold, possibly a combination of both. She watched the bluish glow in the distance. It wasn't very bright, but filled the cavern with enough light for her to see.

Where am I? She thought again. She knew that she had been terribly hurt in the accident. The pain was indescribably excruciating, running from her calf to the back of her head. The last thing she remembered was David's arms around her. Then her mind went blank. Now it had to be several hours, if not even a day or two, since the accident. Her pain was gone and not a scratch was on her body. *Did I die?* she fearfully thought, on the verge of tears.

She sat there for a moment, pondering the dreaded thought. She shook her head with disbelief. She felt her nose start to run. A moment later, she was crying. She couldn't remember feeling more lost or afraid. Yet the question remained. Where was she? She remembered Father O'Neal at her church preaching about heaven and how God would give everyone perfect bodies. She looked down at her abdomen and stared in wonder. All her wounds had disappeared, but the scar from her appendicitis, fifteen years before, remained. *I'm just imagining that*, she told herself. Then she examined her leg, only to find another scar from when she fell off a bicycle in college. *Am I in Purgatory? Or Hell?* She looked up at the dreary ceiling, desperate for something to distract her from her thoughts. But the question did not go away.

"God?" she asked. "Can you hear me?" She waited. Nothing happened. "God? . . . I'm scared. Please help me." Still, nothing transpired.

She thought of her family. She hadn't seen them in months. Her mother and father last saw her during Christmas, when she and David went out to visit them in Chicago. She remembered giving them farewell hugs at the airport before boarding the plane back to New York. Would she ever see them again?

Then there was David. *How could I have said those things to him?* she wondered. *He knows I never meant them, doesn't he? Of course! He held me in his arms . . . Oh my God . . . I didn't tell him that I loved him!* She let the tears run off her cheeks and onto her knees. She had always made sure to say that she loved him before they parted ways, just in case it was the last time they ever spoke. That was the last thing she wanted him to hear. Instead, he had ended up hearing her tell him to shut-up. She missed him dearly. She longed to be in his arms once more.

She contemplated what to do next. She was curious about the light ahead, but was afraid of falling into some hole or trench if she tried to go near it. However, with darkness in all other directions, she decided to go for it. She started to crawl, but the coarse stone floor gouged her knees and scraped her feet. She stood on her legs and managed to walk with her back to the ceiling, occasionally making a painful encounter with a low rock. She kept her head up, intently staring at the light ahead. As she came closer, the air grew colder and the unwelcome breezes became constant.

What felt like a half hour had passed and she hadn't made much progress. The air felt like icy blades against her bare skin. Her feet were numb from the nearly-freezing water. Her back hurt from crouching over for so long and her legs were tired from being stretched. She still didn't want to rest. She would rather get out of strange cave she was in than to wait another minute doing nothing.

Without warning, she lost her footing on the slippery stones and fell forward with a scream.

She landed on the rugged rocks. She sat up and groaned. To her great displeasure, she saw that she was covered with pieces of dirt and decayed plant matter.

"Ugh! Gross!" she moaned, wiping the dirt off her arms. When she stretched them out, her right hand hit something hard. She turned and saw, at last, a wall. *The exit can't be far!* she thought hopefully.

She moved back and leaned against it. Despite the cold, wet stone, it felt good to rest her back. She closed her eyes and slowly exhaled. She tried not to think, knowing it would only lead to more questions and problems, but she simply couldn't. None of this made sense. It wasn't real, or was it? It had to be—

She wrinkled her nose at the sudden stench she smelled. She turned her head and saw a fat, wet, fury ball attached to the wall, just inches from her face. She watched it slowly expand, then deflate. A second later, it expanded again, as if it were breathing. She didn't know whether to be amused or to be afraid. She noticed that there was another one, identical to the first, just below it. They seemed harmless. But just in case, she decided to back away. Besides, they smelled like decaying animals.

She felt something hairy press into her exposed back. It was warm, moist, and definitely alive. With a shriek, she leapt forward and whirled around at the peculiar object. Then she saw that the whole wall was covered with them. She watched them for several moments, before gaining enough curiosity to venture towards one.

She stared at the object, carefully examining how it moved. She cautiously touched it with her index finger. It's fur was rough and bristly, quite unpleasant to feel. Feeling invincible, she reached for the ball with two hands, gently wrapped them around the thing, and gave it a gentle tug.

The thing stayed attached to the wall. She bit her lip and gave it another tug, determined to take if off. Still, the fury mass stuck to its place. She gripped it harder and yanked it.

It came free with a little pop. It was horrendously heavy, but she held it firmly. She felt victorious. *Woman defies nature!* she playfully thought. She carefully turned the object around. The other side was completely hairless with only a dark, brown skin that looked like rubber. The object appeared to be a simple fury balloon filled with some sort of substance. She stared at the large, gapping hole at the top.

She innocently moved her thumb towards the opening.

All of a sudden, several sharp teeth shot up around the hole and violently ground together. The little beast let out a high-pitched squeal and moved itself, trying to free itself from her grip.

Terrified, Emily threw it on top of another fury animal and jumped away. She watched in horror at what happened next.

The tiny monster she had thrown sank its teeth into the poor organism beneath it. In a series of vicious screams and shrieks, the two animals fell off the wall. The first devoured the second, sucking it into its body through its mouth with its hooked teeth. It took its time in eating its prey alive, since it was helpless to escape its vacuuming jaws.

The frightened woman stepped back, quaking with fear. She became nauseous when she saw the prey's body fluid seep out from underneath it as it screamed insanely with pain and struggled to get away. A few moments later, it ceased to exist.

Stepping away, Emily watched the wretched animal jolt forward. She froze, not believing what she had just seen. The creature had no legs. How could it possibly have moved like that?

Then, with a terrible scratching screech, the wild animal moved towards her, using its teeth to transport itself.

She tried to scream, but all that came out was a disoriented moan. She turned around and propelled herself forward as fast as she could. She kept her eyes on the light ahead, not wanting to see what was behind her. She was several times larger than the animal, but what if it latched onto her and she couldn't get it off? How much of her would it eat before it let go?

She slipped again, but jumped back up and frantically limped ahead with a scoured knee. She could feel her heart nearly exploding with every beat in her chest. She pressed forward, wanting to see anything but the vile creature behind her.

III

The hospital room was dark and quiet. David lovingly caressed his wife's swollen cheek as he leaned on the railing of her bed. He wanted to lay down beside her, but for obvious reasons, he wasn't allowed. He sadly looked at the thick bandage wrapped around her head and arm. The white cloth was dotted with red stains from where her blood had soaked through. The rest of her mangled body was hidden underneath the blankets.

She had several IV's running into her and an oxygen cord tucked under her nose. She was breathing and had a pulse, but just barely. A defibrillator and respirator were set beside the bed, the doctors certain that they'd have to use one or the other eventually. She didn't move a muscle or utter the slightest voluntary sound. All he could hear was her shallow breathing. She appeared to be in a deep, dreamless sleep. Or, as Dr. Maloney had said, a coma. He had warned him that she might not wake up.

"Oh my God," he said, "I'm so sorry, honey. I'm so very, very sorry." Not wanting to take his hands away from her, he let the tear trickle from his eye and down his face. "I love you, baby. I love you more than anything else in this whole world. Please hang in there, sweetheart." Then, with the salty drops of warm water streaming down his face, he leaned closer and whispered, "Don't leave me. Please, don't leave me. I could never—"

"Mr. Shanahan?" a soft, feminine voice asked. He looked up and saw a young nurse with an old, skinny priest standing in the doorway. "Father O'Neal is here to see you. And your in-laws just arrived at Kennedy and said that they'd be here as soon as they could," the nurse said, ushering the clergyman into the room.

"Thank you," David wearily said.

"David," the priest said with a reassuring smile. The old man walked up to him and patted him on the back. "Everything's going to be okay."

David could only nod in agreement, too afraid to even take his eyes away from her for a moment. "I've made a big mistake," he admitted.

"And what was that?" Father O'Neal asked. "You had an argument? It's nature to a perfectly healthy marriage. She knows that you love her. That's all that matters."

"If I wouldn't have pressed her on, none of this would've happened. I—"

"Shh. Shh. You can't go back and think about the what ifs. What has happened, has happened. All we can do now is hope to God and pray for her. It was an accident. If anyone is to blame, it's the intoxicated driver who hit her. Not you."

"But I—"

"Hush, my child," Father said, gently resting his frail hand on David's hair. "Just be here with her." He gently reached out and touched Emily's leg. Stroking it tenderly, he closed his eyes and whispered a small prayer. When he was finished, he gripped her husband's shoulders and suspired.

"She was a good woman," David said.

"Yes. I know. She and you were in church every Sunday. She was a wonderful lady. And she still is a wonderful lady. She loves you very much and no matter what, she will always be with you."

"I don't want to lose her, Father," David said, breaking down into tears. "She's too young! I'd do anything to end this all!"

The priest nodded. "Yes. You would. And she would do the same for you, too. But—"

"Emily!" someone cried out.

David looked up to see Emily's parents rush into the room. They tossed their coats on the floor and rushed to her bedside. Her mother, in tears, wrapped her arms around her little daughter, being careful not to hurt her. "Oh baby, no! I love you!" she sobbed uncontrollably.

Her husband gently rubbed her back and glanced up at David. He tried to show a straight face, but the emotion was peeking through. Trying to cover the pain he felt, he gruffly asked, "Are you okay?"

David sadly shook his head and looked back at him with his deep eyes filled with grief. *What kind of a question is that?* he thought. *Can't you see that I'm dying here?* Then, he saw the tears trickle down from his face. He had never seen Emily's father cry before. The sight broke his heart.

Father O'Neal gently introduced himself to everyone, then pulled out a little booklet from his pocket. He moved to the foot of the bed and motioned for everyone to join hands with one another. Everyone stared at Emily as he gave Anointing of the Sick to her. His words were said strongly and powerfully, yet they were soothing to the soul.

David kept his hand on his wife's shoulder, looking lovingly at her injured body. His voice quivered when he recited the Hail Mary and he broke down alltogether at the conclusion. Weeping, he fell to his knees and gently ran his fingers across Emily's face.

After a moment, Father touched him on the shoulder. He looked at her parent's, just on the other side. They watched him with worry and aching in their hearts.

David jumped to his feet and stared back at them, lost and terrified. Then he glanced at Father O'Neal, who didn't know quite what to say. He shook his head and sighed. "I'm sorry," he said.

"Perhaps a little fresh air will help you," his mother-in-law said. "It's almost three in the morning. There's no doubt that you've been with her all the time. We're here now. Why don't you go downstairs and get a cup of coffee?"

"No," he immediately said. "I'm not leaving her." He looked back at his wife. He didn't want to go. She needed him with her.

"You won't be leaving her," Father said, placing his hand on his shoulder. "She's right. You should go for a short walk. There's nothing else you can do right now."

With a reluctant heart, David gently leaned forward and softly kissed Emily's lips. He stood back and whispered, "I love you. I'll be right back." He let go of her shoulder and slowly walked around her bed and towards the door.

Her mother rushed up to him and hugged him tightly. "Don't you worry," she said, her face drenched with tears. "She's going to be okay. We're all in this together."

"Thank you," David said. "I'm so sorry."

"No. No. Don't be. It wasn't your fault. These things happen," she reassured, choking on her tears. "Now go get yourself a cup of coffee, dear."

David hesitantly let go from her embrace. He looked back once more at his beloved friend, then walked out into the hallway. He had to readjust to the bright, fluorescent lighting as he made his way down towards the waiting area. When he entered the small atrium, the only person around was an old woman, sleeping in a chair by a rack of magazines. She had a stressed look on her wrinkled face. Perhaps she was waiting for news on a spouse, too.

He walked up to the coffee machine and inserted a dollar bill through the slot. The machine took the money, made a few clicks, then signaled that it was done. He opened the small door at the bottom, only to find an empty cup with sugar sprinkled on the bottom. He threw the cup in a wastebasket and groaned.

Insulted, he turned around to go back. But, with a yawn, he realized how tired he was and how desperately in need he was of caffeine. He knew he had to stay awake for Emily. Remembering the vending machines in the Emergency waiting room, he decided to continue on down the hall.

Once he passed the Trauma Unit's doors, he could hear the familiar noise of printers and buzzing alarms. As he went further, he could see doctors rushing off to treat patients while ordinary people went about asking administrators where their loved ones were. By the time he got to the waiting room, he had expected it to be nearly full.

People silently sat in suffering and agony as they waited for help. He saw a boy clinging to his mother as she held a towel over his severed finger. An old man sat on the other side of the room, rocking in his chair and clutching his chest as his wife sat beside him, holding his arm. The staff at the front desk worked as fast as they could to treat the injured. It was just another night in the ER.

David walked over to another coffee machine and deposited another dollar. He rested his head against the contraption and shut his eyes as he waited for his drink.

"Help! My girlfriend needs help!" a man shouted. "She's been shot!"

Screams erupted and yelling ensued.

David whirled around to see a huge man drag a wounded woman half his size into the middle of the room. The victim was bleeding profusely and barely conscious. The people at the desk immediately scrambled to help her. They rushed a gurney over and carefully placed her on it.

"What's your name!" a doctor asked her. The woman only cried out in pain and clutched her hands over the massive hole that went into her abdomen. "Take her into the OR and get everyone ready!" he shouted.

They lifted the gurney up and wheeled her towards the emergency room. The woman's companion tried to follow, but the doctor pushed him away. "You have to stay out of our way!" he warned.

"That's my girl!" the man shouted, pressing forward with no intention of leaving.

The doctor cried out, "Security! Don't let this man into the ER!"

The boyfriend stepped away, an enraged look on his face. Without hesitation, he reached into his coat pocket and ripped out a revolver. "I said that's my girl!"

David watched in horror as the man pointed the gun at the doctor. The patients in the waiting room jumped up from their chairs and fled.

"There's no reason for this!" the doctor yelled. "Your friend's injured and we have to help her!"

"You're not helping her!" the man snarled. "If I can't be with her, then we're going back home. Nobody better get in my way!"

"No!" the woman cried. "Don't let him near me!"

Acting on impulse, David darted forward and nervously shouted, "Sir, stand back!"

The massive male turned around and glared at him. "What did you say, you piece of trash?"

"Stand back and let them take care of her," he said, trying to remain calm.

The man stepped towards him, unafraid and furious. He raised the revolver at him.

"Stop!" David begged, holding up his hands. "My wife's sick and I have to—"

"The hell with her!" the gunman barked. "The hell with you!"

Without warning, the gurney was wheeled into the emergency room and the doors were locked shut. The gunman turned around and gasped. He saw the doctor standing by the doors, glaring back at him with vengeful eyes. "I said that she's coming home with me!"

"Sir, put the gun down," the physician calmly asserted.

"Screw you!" he yelled, walking towards the defenseless doctor. "Get her back out here!"

David ran up behind the man and screamed, "Stand down!"

"Get out of here!" the doctor ordered. David ignored him and yelled at the gunman again, only to be ignored. The bystanders began to panic as the gunman closed in on the doctor. The cornered physician cried, "You don't want to do this!"

"You have no idea!" the gunman exclaimed. He raised his revolver at him and pulled the trigger.

David lunged at him and threw his hands around his neck. In an instant, he was thrown to the ground.

The gunman grabbed him by the throat and forced him up. He stared hatefully into his eyes and then, to his horror, he lifted his revolver up and brought it down on his forehead.

David let out a cry as he staggered backwards.

The gunman didn't give him a chance and pushed him to the floor.

David crashed onto the linoleum and winced in pain. Before he could even regain his orientation, a strong arm wrapped around his neck and dragged him back up. He felt the cold barrel of a gun press against his temple. "I'm sorry!" he desperately said. "Please don't hurt me! I have to take care of my wife!"

The doctor, bleeding profusely from his shoulder, managed to stand up. "Leave him alone! It's not too late to solve this!"

The gunman glanced back at him. "You want me to let this sorry ass go? Do you?"

Yes! Let him go! David thought, struggling to breathe. His whole body trembled with fear. Was this it? The man wasn't crazy enough to kill him, was he?

"I beg you," the doctor said.

The gunman studied the desperate look on his face, then nodded. "Okay. I'll let him go," he announced, releasing the hostage from his big arms.

David jumped back and stared at his attacker in shock. He rubbed his neck and tried to catch his breath. *That was close*, he realized.

"You're doing the right thing," the doctor praised him.

The gunman didn't take his beady little eyes off David. "I know I am," he whispered. He pointed his revolver at him and pulled back the hammer.

David shook his head with disbelief. Staring down the dark, hollow tube of metal sent a chill down his spine. The cold claws of fear sank deep into his heart, rendering him motionless. "No! Please! I—"

"No!" the doctor cried.

"Damn you!" the gunman screamed, pulling the trigger.

David let out a frantic cry and shielded himself. *This can't happen! This isn't real!* he thought, but it was too late.

The bullet smashed through his skull, jerking his head back as he collapsed to the floor.

The gunman stood over him, watching his still body on the floor. He ignored the horrified bystanders shuddering away in the corners of the room as they fearfully wept. When he saw the blood begin to ooze out of the wound in his victim's head, he sighed and turned to the front entrance. "Said that nobody better get in my way," he mumbled, casually walking away as if nothing had happened.

Once the coast was clear, the wounded doctor stumbled over to David. By the time he reached him, his breathing had stopped. He sadly looked away. The emergency room doors opened and several MD's rushed out, but he knew that it was too late to save him.

IV

Emily approached the glowing blue light with wonder. She had been rushing for quite some time to get away from the miniature monster that was after her. Now, with it nowhere in sight, she felt that the creature had given up on her. The ceiling, dripping with icy-cold water, was high enough for her to stand up all the way. Just ahead, she could see several tall, thin structures protruding from the rocky floor.

As she came closer, a smile appeared on her face. The sight was so beautiful that it took her mind off her fears and her aching body. Stalagmites of blue and white crystal towered above the ground in an array of shimmering gems and precious jewels. The cool air was fresh and moist. She was shivering from the cold.

She stepped past the first stalagmite and stopped. She gasped as she looked around at the intricate, glittering stones all around her. The cave sparkled like a massive geode. The actual light came from ahead, where the cave gave way to the outside world with an overcast sky and a sea of rolling green hills. She smiled at the sight.

She stepped onto a coarse bed of sapphire and cobalt, walking until she was in the middle of the strange chamber. She wondered again if she was in heaven, or at least near to it. The brilliant stones gave off a light that caressed her body with its soft, blue warmth against the chilling air. She couldn't help but smile in awe at the sight of what had to be the earth's finest collection of crystals all around her.

It was all enchantingly beautiful. The gently—

She hollered out in immense pain and tried to pull away, but the strange monster had her by the ankle and was held in place by two stalagmites between it and her leg. It sank its teeth deep into her skin and began to grind her tender flesh to pieces.

Emily pulled away, but the creature's grip was too great. She fell onto the sharp crystals, which raked her legs. She yanked, twisted, shook and fought, but to no avail. She watched in horror, screaming uncontrollably with tears gushing down her face, as the evil animal ate her blood and living flesh. The ball of fur had no intention of letting her free.

She tried to get back onto her feet, but stumbled and crashed onto the rough ground. Feeling her back scrape against the fine, precious stones and her head hitting a loose rock, she cried out in imploring defeat. The ravenous monster did not relent.

She rolled over and picked up the loose rock in her trembling hands before looking back at the evil creature. Without thought, she hurled the rock onto the animal's fury body.

A disgusting burst ensued as the little monster's body was crushed by the heavy crystal. A dark, pink ooze copiously flowed from the furry case it had been held in.

Emily jumped away, still screaming in terror. She stared at the dead creature in disgust, making sure that it didn't move and wasn't, by some impossible chance, alive. Then she saw her chest move with her violent heart palpitations. She felt the blood and adrenaline rushing through her veins as she tried to catch her breath. *It's over! Nothing to worry about!* she quickly assured to herself.

She knelt down and clutched the deep gash on her ankle. Her warm blood easily seeped through her fingers. She felt the edge of the deep wound shredded with tiny strips of bloodied skin. The pain was stabbing-sharp and burning hot. Then, she heard it.

She looked beyond the crystals and into the darkness. A faint chattering of screeching teeth echoed in the distance. She shook her head with disbelief. "Oh God have mercy," she begged in a quivering voice.

She jumped to her feet and limped towards the exit. The luscious green grass outside would be welcome to her bare feet. She climbed over a wall of cobalt and dodged a stalactite of diamond. She stumbled over to the edge of the cave and hopefully glanced at the ground below. Here, the fresh, breezy, moist air blew across her face. She felt like she had just walked out of the house and into a spring morning.

She jumped onto the ground and ran away as fast as she could. All that lay ahead was a gently rolling land of short grass. The sky above was ominous and dark with heavy clouds. She kept moving her legs, knowing that she had to get as far away from the cave as possible, even if everything in front of her was only a vast, endless world of nothing.

As her heart raced and lungs hungered for air, her legs became stiff and burned with pain. The wind tore tears from her eyes and made her ears deaf with its harsh scream, yet she didn't slow. She kept her eyes fixed on the gloomy horizon, desperately trying to get somewhere. Anywhere. Any place but here.

Finally, she gave in to exhaustion. She ran a few more yards before collapsing to the soggy ground. She buried her face in the wet grass, huffing and puffing as her lungs burned with pain. She scrunched herself into a ball and gripped the vegetation with her weak fingers. Her stomach was queasy as her head spun with disorientation. She wanted to vomit, but after a few dry heaves, she knew it was hopeless.

She stayed on the ground, too tired to move. Several minutes passed before she was relaxed enough to move again, but she choose not to. She wanted to fall asleep. Maybe when she woke up, she'd be back in bed, at home. David would be right there beside her with his arm around her, protecting her.

A cold, heavy drop of water hit her cheek. She ignored it. A second later, another water drop hit her shoulder. She turned on her back and looked up at the cloudy sky. From her left echoed a soft, gentle roar. Before she realized it, she was being showered with sheets of frigid rain.

She stood up and looked around, but there was nothing around. There were no houses, no cars, no gazebos, not even a tree under which to take shelter. She turned around and saw the entrance of the cave, over a mile away. She was surprised that she had run that far so quickly. *At least I know I'm in good shape*, she thought. *But in these conditions, for how long?* However, there was no way that she was going back near those evil little monsters.

She sadly stared up at the sky, shivering from the bitter cold. Alone, nothing around for miles except for a dark cave filled with devious creatures, standing naked in the cold rain. She never felt more miserable or vulnerable in her life.

V

David awoke from the sudden crash. He jolted his eyes open and looked at the hot, hazy clouds above him, glowing with the intense light of the sun. Trees, absent of any sign of life, sent their branches towards the sky, as if desperately trying to grab onto something that would uproot them from this forsaken land that held them. The warm, caked mud beneath him gave off a horrible odor of decay. He wearily pushed himself up, his hands sinking into the soggy ground.

He was in a lifeless bog. Dead leaves, dried and black, decorated the muddy floor along with rocks and sharp twigs. Thick, towering trees, stripped of their foliage and bark, surrounded the lifeless gap of land. A few of them had toppled over from the damp weak soil. All around, he saw nothing but disintegrating skeletons that used to hold life.

Taking in a sour gulp of the stale air, he cautiously stood on the moist ground. His mind raced through its memory, desperately searching to find out how he had come to this strange, lonely place. He ran his hand across his forehead, only to feel his oily sweat on his perfectly smooth skin. Nothing. Not even a scratch.

He nervously looked ahead. "Hello?" he softly asked. He waited for a few moments, simply standing in the murky, odorous air. With no response, he screamed out, "Hello! Can anyone hear me!"

A strong gust of fresh air blew against the side of his face, messing up his hair. With a grimace, he began walking toward the trees ahead. *Where am I?* he thought. *Where is everybody?* With every step he took, his foot broke into the soft ground, releasing a horrible stench. He tried his best to ignore it as he walked up to a fallen tree limb. He stepped over it, thinking nothing of the pile of dead leaves his foot landed on.

Without warning, an army of yellow hornets swarmed out around him. He had no time to think before several of the fierce insects had gouged their stingers into his flesh.

He let out a panicked scream and ran forward, waving and swatting violently at the angry wasps. They stung at him without mercy, crawling beneath his clothes to deliver their painful revenge. He desperately looked ahead, wondering how far he would have to run to lose the swarm. The adrenaline gushed through his veins as his heart beat explosively in his chest.

All of a sudden, his left foot hit a moist spot and sank in, holding him in place. He yanked his foot free from the shoe and propelled himself forward.

Only a few paces more, he tripped on a rock and was thrown into the mud. He jumped back up, yelling insanely as the hornets latched themselves to his body while a stream of blood flowed from his mouth. Every second, he felt his skin being pierced by a venomous stinger. His legs carried him as fast as they could, hurtling him towards the trees.

"Help! Someone!" he frantically cried, clawing at the ferocious insects. He dashed through the trees, looking far ahead with tired eyes. He had to get as far away as he could, or else he would be stung to death. Already, the back of his neck felt stiff and swollen from the several excruciating stings. The pain was—

His foot slipped under an uplifted root and he fell again, hitting his head against a massive boulder and ripping open the flesh above his left eyebrow. He waited for the swarm to catch up with him and inject his body with more of their burning poison.

A few moments later, when they didn't, he breathed a sigh of relief and rested his head on the ground, moaning in pain. He felt tired and weak, his body trembling like a terrified little puppy's. Then, a horrible screech broke the silence.

David looked up to see a large cuckoo bird perched on a skinny branch, staring down at him with its dark, beady red eye. With a hideous holler, it flapped its filthy wings and descended towards him.

He covered his face as the wretched bird attacked, sinking its claws into his arms and pecking at his head. He jumped back and threw his fist at the creature, hitting it square on its breast. The bird cried out and flew away.

He tried to catch his breath. He could feel the blood rush through his arteries with every pump of his heart. His head throbbed with searing pain. His hands were covered with bitter stings and hurt with every move they made. Blood generously dripped from where he had bitten his lip.

Unexpectedly, a sharp object penetrated his toe. He tore off his other shoe and knocked the huge wasp off his foot. With a vicious buzz, the angry insect fled, staggering through the air back to its nest, content at the cruel torment it had inflicted on its beaten enemy.

David stood back up, cursing under his breath. He looked ahead, only to see a wall of trees before him. With a heavy heart, he began his trek back to civilization, or at least to someone who would be able to help him. The trees were so densely packed together that he had to bend and twist his path to get past.

For the first quarter hour, he focused on simply getting through the forest, as well as trying to ignore the painful cuts and stings all over his body. But as time dragged on and his heart rate calmed, he began to worry more. He fearfully wondered how he had ended up in a forest.

After all, he had been shot in a hospital in Manhattan and not on some ranch in Colorado. Then it suddenly hit him.

Am I dead? he thought. *Is my life really over?* He shook his head, trying to dismiss the dreaded ponderance. But his emotions of fear flooded his head and forced him to reconsider. *A bullet to the brain can be fatal*, he surmised, *but not always. How do I know he actually shot me? I could've fainted and I'm only dreaming!* He tensed hopefully at the thought, but it didn't last long. *Then wake up! Wake up! For heaven's sake, open your eyes and get out of bed!* He felt lost, but he wasn't sure if he wanted to know exactly where he was.

He thought of Emily. She's going to be okay, he reassured himself, remembering that she was safe in bed at the hospital. Still, she was fighting for her life and was in grave condition. Would he be there for her if she needed him? He had always heard that people could hear their loved ones speak at their bedside, even when they were unconscious. He had to get back to her! He had to find a way out of here!

He called out for help several times, but never heard anything in return. Slowly, the sky was becoming gray with heavy clouds and shutting out the warm glow of the sun. The air was becoming cooler and breezy. He kept his eyes focused ahead of him, making sure not to lose his sense of direction in the labyrinth of trees as the light diminished.

He wondered what time of day it was. It had to be evening at the earliest. Once the sun set, there would be no way of continuing on. He would have to spend the night in the woods, alone. The thought made him move faster.

He gritted his teeth as he bore the pain of his sore feet stepping on the rough tree roots and sharp stones. His socks were in shreds and offered no comfort to him, but he didn't care. He had to escape this desolate land and find someone. Anyone.

Suddenly, he noticed a clearing ahead. He hurried through the forest, desperate to reach the clearing. There had to be a road, tower or even a house ahead of him. He smiled with expectation as he darted past the massive trees, longingly gazing at the sight ahead.

He rushed out of the woods and ran onto a gently rolling plain, covered modestly with short, green grass. The air was suddenly moist and refreshing. He ripped off what was left of his socks and let his bare feet feel the gentle vegetation. He stretched out his arms for joy and let the wind hit his body as he stared up at the overcast sky. *Thank you, God! Thank you!* he thought. Then he looked in front of him.

His jaw hung open at the sight of the desolate land. Nothing but emptiness lay ahead of him. No homes, cars, radio towers, power lines, or even the sound of a commercial airliner in the sky. There's someone around here, he reassured himself, collecting his thoughts. Just a little ways away, the land gently curved up and then suddenly dropped. It would be a perfect lookout point. Certainly he would spot something from there.

He ran towards it, his mind insisting more and more that there was another human being out there with each new step, while his heart sank deeper and deeper into despair and fear. *I'm not alone. I'm not alone!* he thought. *I'm not alone!*

"I'm not alone," he spoke, surprised to hear his own voice. He swallowed hard and got a hold of himself. There was no sense in getting panicked yet.

He came to the top of the hill and looked at the world ahead. The vast, rolling plain extended in all directions for as far as he could see. No sign of life other than the short grass. Not even a tree or a shrub. His mind admitted defeat, but his heart wasn't ready to.

David pulled his pager out from his jacket pocket. He nervously pressed the side indicator button to see the time. The clock had been replaced by four dashes. No problem. *The clock just died*, he thought, pressing another switch. He quickly wrote out a message, then, holding the device in the air, pressed the SEND button.

The little machine chirped several times before the acceptance message blinked on the tiny display. He read the words in horror. NO RECEPTION SIGNAL DETECTED.

"Oh God, no," he gasped. He tried it again, only to be hit with the same, agonizing results. He stared at it in shock and shook his head. "No . . ." he managed, letting his arm fall to his side.

He stared at the scene ahead in dismay. He was alone. He was all alone and no one, not a single human being, was in sight. He exhaled and looked around, frantic for signs of other life. His eyes welled up with tears, but he refused to let himself break down, as if clinging on to some hope of the impossible.

He made the Sign of the Cross and whispered a Glory Be, wondering if even God was around to hear him. "Please guide me," he said. "Don't let me be alone here. Oh please, don't let me be alone!"

The tears trickled down the side of his face. He was hopeless with worry. The fear pierced into him like a thousand knives slicing into a small citrus fruit, tearing out all of the sweet pulp and pleasant juices. He felt his throat tighten and mouth run dry. His head spun and his palms sweated.

Then he felt angry. Angry at all that had happened and angry at himself for allowing the fateful events to happen. Emily was sick and dying in the hospital and he was out on some wild odyssey of the mind when she needed him by her side. He gripped the pager in his fist.

He pulled back his arm and glared at the featureless landscape. With an angry cry, he hurled the useless piece of technology through the air with all his strength.

As his hurting eyes watched it descend to the ground, they spotted something unique. Far ahead, over a mile away, a faint, light figure stood out from the endless sea of green.

His desperate heart skipped a beat as his eyes fixed themselves on the object.

V I

Emily quivered and hugged herself as hard as she could to stay warm. The hot tears on her face mingled with the cold raindrops and rolled off her chin. She sobbed aloud, not caring because she knew that no one was around to hear her. She was abandoned in this cruel, empty world. She thought of how long she could go on living before hunger and lack of shelter would bring her to her demise.

She sadly watched the sheets of rain strike the earth. They fell like massive curtains onto a stage, striking the ground with a powerful splash of cool water. The sound was a constant roar, unrelenting and unchanging to any degree. The wind swept around her, pulling away any warm air her body radiated. She thought about turning back to the cave, but the pain in her ankle quickly changed her mind. She would stay here. Anyplace else was just as unforgiving and dangerous, if not worse.

She thought of David and how he had last held her in his arms. "Emily!" his plea echoed through her mind. "Emily!" How she wished she hadn't said those things. It was so stupid and because of it, she was torn away from him and—

"Emily!"

She thought for a moment, wondering if she was just remembering him crying out to her or going insane and hearing things.

She cautiously turned her head.

She gasped in splendid shock as she saw David rush towards her. Before she could even speak, he had his arms around her and his head resting against hers.

She embraced him, breaking down into joyful tears. She relaxed in his arms and cried, "Oh thank God! Thank you for finding me! I was so afraid! I thought I'd be trapped in there forever! And then the ball chased me and grabbed onto my leg! It wouldn't let go and I thought—"

"Shh. Shh," her husband soothed, affectionately caressing her face. He moved his head back and lovingly kissed her trembling lips. "Everything's going to be okay!" he reassured her, yelling over the sound of the rain. He stood back to tear off his jacket and unbutton what used to be a white shirt. He quickly placed it over her.

The cool rain felt good against his bare back, soothing the burning pain from the insect stings.

"Oh no," Emily cried, gently running her hands along his shoulders. "What happened to you?"

"Wasps. Big, ugly, yellow wasps," he said with great disgust, quickly buttoning the shirt. It was already soaked, but it would help keep her warm. He hugged her again, fondly massaging her back with his hands. "I love you! I thought that I would never see you again!"

"I have a question," she nervously announced.

"What?" he asked, not knowing if he wanted to hear it.

She took in a deep breath and asked, "Are we dead?"

David only hugged her harder.

"Are we dead?" she begged. "Please tell me!"

"I don't know," he said. "You were in the hospital. The doctor didn't know if you were in a coma or what, but you were technically still alive."

"Then how'd you get here?"

"I left your room when your parents came in and wandered into the ER where some idiot shot me in the head. At least that is what I think happened."

"Oh God!" she cried, embracing him harder. "You're still alive, aren't you? Please God! You have to be alive!"

"I'm not sure if I am or not," he said. "I care, but I don't. I'm with you and that's all that matters to me right now. God's watching over us, wherever it is we are. I know it!"

"Then are we in Purgatory or what? This can't be Heaven!"

David chuckled and said, "There's no massive white fire and it's not that cold out."

"As if someone who hasn't died and gone there knows for sure what it's like?" she demanded. The thought made her shiver even more. She rested her face on his shoulder and kept her arms locked around him, not wanting to ever let go.

He tenderly pushed back her wet hair and let his head fall on her. He felt her soft, warm neck pressing against his cheek. He cherished the feeling of being so close to her. He closed his eyes as he held her, so glad that he had thrown that stupid pager. He felt the tears swell up in his eyes before they released themselves on his cheek and onto her. He was so glad that he had found her. He was glad that he wasn't alone. He was ecstatic that he could be there for her. "I love you," he whispered. "I've always loved you."

"I know," she answered back, sleepily holding onto him. At last, she allowed herself to let the tiredness and weakness take over the adrenaline. She had been trapped in a cave, attacked by vicious monsters, cut numerous times by falling onto sharp rocks, out in the freezing rain and feeling worse than she could ever remember. Now he was here and God was watching over them, somehow, someway.

"Are you getting sleepy?" he asked. She managed to moan her answer. "There's a cave over there that we can—"

"No!" she adamantly announced. "There's something in there! It bit my leg and there's no way that I'm going back!"

"Fine. That's all right," he said. He glanced down at her leg and his eyes widened with shock. He let her go and knelt down to examine her wound.

Emily plopped herself on the ground and extended her leg. "It bit into me and wouldn't let go. I had to kill it to free myself."

David gently placed his hand over the injury, which was still bleeding. "What was it?" he asked, trying to think of what creature could possibly be so malicious.

"I don't know. It was some fat ball with fur and a very tiny mouth with sharp teeth. It moved with its mouth! At first I thought it was just some sort of a harmless plant. But then it came after me and I ran. I thought I had gotten away when it suddenly grabbed my leg! It hurt so much! The thing just wouldn't let me go! It was awful!" she exclaimed, choking on her tears. "I'm glad I killed it! I'd kill each one of those evil things if I could!"

"Nothing's going to happen now," he reassured her. "It's over now." He moved up beside her and placed his arm over her. It felt good to by laying down at last. His sore legs and back stopped aching. "I'm tired," he admitted.

She snuggled closer him so that their faces were touching. "Me too," she cooed, desirous of some rest.

David grabbed his sports jacket and pulled it over her to shield her bare legs from the rain. Then he subconsciously whispered a prayer to God as he closed his eyes. He felt her arm come to rest upon him. Her touch was soothing and reassuring to him. His smile told her again that he loved her.

Then, despite the cold rain, soggy ground and cruel wind, the two lovers fell asleep in each others' arms, as if oblivious to the elements set before them. At last, they were protected, safe, secure and cared for.

They were together.

VII

The fresh dew felt good against his face and he could feel his body being showered with the warmth of the sunrise. In the distance, he could hear a gentle, calming crashing of waves. He opened his eyes and smiled at the sight of her beautiful face next to him. She looked so peaceful and relaxed, stirring so subtly to gently breathe in and out. Her soft, red hair shone in the morning sunlight.

Emily inhaled the clean, rejuvenating air into her lungs. She smiled and opened her eyes to the new day. She stared at her lover, happily losing herself in his deep brown eyes. She gently moved her hand from his shoulder to his face, playfully feeling his whiskers.

He leaned forward and lovingly kissed her delicate lips. He asked, "Did you ever know that I loved you?"

"Was I not supposed to?" she inquired back, bringing her fingers over his lips.

He smiled and affectionately caressed her cheek as he gazed into her sparkling eyes. He cherished moments like these. They were so simple, yet so deep and intimate. She captivated him with enchantment like no one else ever could. It was a perfect start to any day.

A sudden breeze of fresh, warm air pushed his hair forward. Reluctantly, he sat up and turned around to look out at the desolate landscape.

His heart skipped a beat at the magnificent sight.

Beyond the grassy land, where the clouds had covered it the night before, was the glittering line of an ocean, standing below the rising sun and shimmering like liquid sapphire. Massive towers of purple crystal stood out of the water and against the sky that was dressed a virgin blue, with a gold crown along the horizon. Not a single cloud could be seen, only the fading stars from the night before.

"It's so beautiful," Emily gasped, climbing to her feet. The water drops beneath her feet were inviting and invigorating. The feeling made her remember her childhood, when she would run out of the house early in the morning in her bare feet, ready to start the summer day with the anticipation of playing vibrantly until the sun kissed the ground in the west. It was a wonderful emotion, something that she realized she had gone too long without feeling.

David let out a sigh. "It is. But still, we're lost. There's no one around." He glanced to the left, then to the right. The bitter feeling of isolation came back when he saw nothing but the abandoned land.

Emily suddenly walked past him, confidently strolling towards the sea. Grabbing the sports coat, he jumped to his feet and ran to catch up with her. "What do we do now?" he nervously asked.

"I don't know," she said, a hint of sadness in her voice. The world around them glimmered with light and color, but it was still an empty place. The air felt so splendid against her skin, and still, it seemed lifeless. She looked at the shore far in the distance, wondering and worrying. The giant crystals reminded her of the cave and its ferocious inhabitants. She shuddered at the remembrance, hoping never to see the creatures again.

David firmly grasped her hand, assuredly poised at their destination point. Inside, he felt an array of awful feelings and loneliness. As pleasant as it was to look at, the universe offered no security. He was with her, however, and had all of the security he ever needed.

"What day is it?" Emily asked.

David groaned as he tried to think. Everything had happened Friday night, but it had been early Saturday morning when he was shot, only to wake up what felt like moments later in a dank bog, just a few hours from nightfall. "Sunday, perhaps," he said at last.

"So we'd just be waking up and getting ready for church, wouldn't we?" she surmised. She glanced at him, then rethought with a giggle. "I would be in the shower and you'd still be sleeping."

"A man's gotta get his sleep," he defended, giving a weak chuckle, desperate for conversation.

" . . . I'd finally get you up and we'd rush out the door. If we were lucky, we'd get into mass ten minutes into the homily."

"Better late than never. It's the thought of being there that counts, not the fact that you're only there for twenty minutes."

" . . . I would be . . ." She gazed up at the sky, frantically searching for words. "Oh, I don't know," she said. "I can't think. I'm scared, David."

He slipped his arm around hers and tightly grasped her hand. "I know, honey. I know. Maybe we'll find something up ahead." He looked at the sun, shinning defiantly against the deserted land. He thought about the car accident and seeing Emily's body thrown across the street. Then he remembered being shot in the emergency waiting room by an enraged gunman. Oddly, it all led them to here, wherever here was.

They pressed on through the featureless plain, keeping their eyes fixed on the ocean before them. They tried to converse to pull their minds away from worry, but to no avail. After what felt like an hour, their feet began to tire, but they insistently continued without a moment to rest, determined that they had to reach the land's edge.

David thought about his family. He missed them terribly. It had been almost a year since he had gone back to visit them at their home in Richmond, Virginia. His mother had been in perfect shape, even though she was distraught over a few gray hairs. Mr. Shanahan was enjoying his career as a high school teacher with no plans of retirement, even though he was one of the older teachers where he taught. The thought of never seeing them again, which was a real possibility, broke his heart. Then he wondered about Emily's parents and how they must have felt when he never came back.

A faint squawk suddenly caught his wife's attention. She stopped and looked around, but saw nothing. "Did you hear that?" she asked. He only gave her a confused look and shrugged his shoulders. "I must be hearing things," she admitted, feeling stupid.

Before he could respond, a loud cry sounded. They looked up just in time to see a giant albatross skim over their heads, flapping its majestic, white wings as it hurtled towards the oceanfront.

They stared in shock as it flew away, not believing what they were seeing. Emily let out a laugh as David smiled in awe.

"After it!" he cried, gripping her hand and pulling her forward.

They chased after the bird, running with furious energy as they fervently watched to see where it would land. Their hearts leapt with joy at the sight of another being, moving, breathing, flying and alive. The animal led them for a half mile until the grass finally gave way to a beach of soft, silky sand.

They stopped and watched the albatross fly over the water to its nest on top of a crystal boulder. It carefully sat on its eggs and stared back at them with a curious expression, as if pleased to have their company.

Emily took in the sights around her. The ocean waves broke and crashed to the sandy shore with elegant prestige, splashing water in all directions. The sky was bright and blue against the sun. Then she looked back at her husband with a playful look. Entranced by the huge purple slabs, he didn't see her poised at him until it was too late.

She pounced on him and knocked him to the ground. But before she could grab his shoulders to pin him down, he had rolled forward and pushed her onto her back.

She lifted her knees up against his chest and forced him away. He stumbled backwards and fell. "No fair!" he cried, jumping up and lunging for her again.

Laughing hysterically and kicking up the sand around them, they frantically tried to force each other down. The hot sun and smooth sand felt so good against their skin. What they enjoyed even more was holding on to each other as they sportily wrestled one another to the ground.

David twisted his body and slipped away from her grip, leaving her defeated and lying on top of the sand. He darted over to the ocean's edge and kicked the water at her.

"Hey!" she cried, leaping up and rushing towards him. Without giving him a chance, she pushed him into the sea. He clutched her arm and pulled her in with him.

In an instant, they were submersed in the warm water. Emily squirmed free of his grip and lifted her head above the surface. A moment later, David jumped up with a splash and grabbed her by the shoulders.

"No! No!" she cried, laughing uncontrollably as she splashed at him. He retreated and prepared himself for the next advance. She nervously watched his contemplating eyes and devious smile as she waited for him to attack. *I'm dead,* she thought. "Tell you what," she said, trying to save herself. "I'll race you to that rock over there." She pointed at the purple tower of crystal several yards away.

He gave her a quirky look, thinking that she was cowardly trying to give up. "Fine!" he announced. He dove underwater and propelled himself towards the giant rock as fast as he could. The water was clear and clean, letting the sunbeams shine through it and onto the sandy floor that was decorated with ornate shells from muscles and periwinkle. The towering crystal ahead sparkled and shined with a bright purple glow.

Without warning, he was pushed down.

He lifted his arm up and grabbed her by the arm. Without mercy, he yanked her down into the water. She kicked her legs and flung her arms as she tried to free herself, but it was all in vain.

Sparkling effervescence floated up between them as they continued their match beneath the surface. They pushed and shoved each other until they had to come up for air.

Emily lucked out when David had to wait to catch his breath. He looked in awe at the massive rock before them. It was at least five stories high, if not more. It was dotted with gems and cracked geodes that sparkled in the sun like a million tiny mirrors.

She prepared herself to take him down the moment he got distracted.

"Wow!" he gasped. "This is just amazing! See how that—"

She pushed him down by the shoulders, only to be grabbed and thrown in herself.

Under the water, David stared his opponent face to face. She glared back at him with a poisonous look. He knew, however, that she was harmless.

She darted forward and wrapped her arms around him as she tried to pull him down with her. She was going to show him who was the stronger one even if she drowned in the process. Then, without warning, he kissed her.

She let their lips locked together as the sparkling bubbles drifted up around them. *Suck up*, she thought. *He just doesn't want me to beat him!*

He kissed her harder, thinking, *She loves this! Oh yeah! I win again!* Her delicate lips were gentle and warm, full of life and action. They felt so pleasant against his own.

They gently pulled back and shared a smile as they floated to the top again. They broke through the surface and shared another passionate kiss. They drifted in the water with their lips together and arms tightly around one another, never wanting to let go.

A sudden cawing made them look up at the albatross' nest. The perplexed bird watched them with curiosity.

David glanced back at the creature and waved. "Hello! We see you!" he laughed. He looked back at Emily. She, as always, looked fantastic. The clear water around her, the faultless beach and the massive natural towers made it all perfect. Without thinking, he asked. "Are you sure that we can't be in Heaven?"

Her smile slowly faded as she faced the bitter facts of reality. "If we are, then where's everybody else?"

He frowned. "I'm sorry, honey."

"It's okay," she said, giving him a reassuring smile. She turned and swam back to shore. Exhausted, she crawled onto the beach and plopped herself down in the warm sand. She let out a forlorn sigh and closed her eyes. David laid down next her and placed his hand on her shoulder. She looked up at him and with her deep blue eyes, asked, "Are we dead?"

He glanced away, not sure how to answer.

"David," she pleaded. "I have to know. Do you think that we're not alive anymore? Did we pass on?"

He sat up and sighed. "Honestly, I don't know for sure . . . But I know that I was shot in the head and that you probably weren't going to make it past the morning. Father O'Neal came in to give you the last sacrament . . . I'm sorry."

She sat up and stared at him, not wanting to believe his words. She felt the tears begin to well up in her eyes. "What if we're not dead?" she asked, clutching onto hope. "What if we're still alive?"

With a heavy heart, he embraced her. She rested her face on the base of his neck, letting the salty drops trickle from her eyes. "Is there any way that you and I are still alive?"

"There could be," he said, softly running his hand over her wet hair. "You were alive when I was shot. You could still be alive now."

"I was here for several hours before you found me. How long were you here before that?"

"No more than two hours," he realized.

She pulled her head back and rested her forehead against his. He lovingly reached up and wiped away her tears as she wept. Then she looked into his eyes, lost and afraid. "Then," she said, her voice quivering with fear, "if we're still living, are we going to survive?"

VIII

"I'm not quite sure," Doctor Maloney said. Frank Shanahan stood next to his distraught wife in the dark hospital room, listening to the doctor's words in horror. "We do know that for right now, the hemorrhaging is happening slowly. I regret that we can't guarantee that it will stop or even continue to progress as slowly as it is. Hopefully, his brain won't bleed any faster than it is. The unfortunate thing is that the swelling will continue and the pressure will increase."

The old man nodded and swallowed hard, holding onto his son's arm as he lay unconscious in the hospital bed. David's head was wrapped with thick gauze and tape as several IV lines disappeared beneath the skin of his arms. Dried blood was stuck to his face, which expressed great pain and discomfort. With great sadness, he started to ask, "H-h-h . . ." He felt his wife's hand rest on his shoulder. "How long?" he managed, fighting back the tears.

Dr. Maloney shook his head and sighed. "I can't set a time frame. Anything's possible, but it's a question of probability. I would say at least another twenty four hours. After that, anything beyond is on borrowed time and we'll probably need to use a respirator to keep him alive. Even with the technology, the hemorrhaging won't stop."

The words cut into their hearts like sharp knives, slicing through any thread of security they might have had left. Shocked and dizzy, Mrs. Shanahan grabbed onto her husband and began to weep. The man stared at the doctor in disbelief. "Is there nothing that you can do for my son?" he asked, fighting back tears.

The doctor sadly shook his head. "I'm afraid not. It's a miracle that he's alive now. By all the test readings we've received back, he shouldn't have made it this far . . ." He stopped. The painful sight of the couple, with their hearts torn and broken, clawed at his soul. He had tried the best he could to bring them the news as gently as he could, but the truth couldn't be averted. " . . . I'm sorry. I'm so very sorry," he said, placing a hand on Mr. Shanahan's trembling arm.

As his wife cried on his shoulder, he placed his hand over his eyes and looked down to hide his tears. "Thank you, doctor," he barely managed.

Dr. Maloney nodded and stepped back. "I'll be in later to check on him and give you an update," he said. With that, he let out a sad sigh and walked out of the room.

Breaking down in sobs, Mrs. Shanahan sat down in a chair and buried her face in her hands. Her husband knelt down next to her and hugged her. "It's going to be okay, Lisa," he reassured her. "Things will work out."

She didn't respond, too consumed by grief. The whole thing had been horrible. First they had received the phone call from David that their daughter-in-law was fighting for her life after a horrible accident. They rushed to New York as quickly as they could, only to be hindered by an hour delay at the airport and a morning traffic jam on the expressway. Each passing moment had been a miserable tribulation of dreading and worrying. By the time they finally made it to the hospital, their son was being brought out of the operating room with his head dressed in bloody cloths and his wife was barely clinging onto life.

Several minutes passed as they kept each other in an embrace and they watched their child. The room was dimly lit, with the only light coming in through the narrow window that faced an overcast sky and the gloomy Hudson, flowing eerily as if it were the River Styx. It was deafly quiet with the silence only broken by the occasional click of the IV pump. Mrs. Shanahan moved to hold her son's lifeless hand. She stared at his wounded body which was so strong, yet so little and ravaged by the elements of the cruel world.

Her husband patted her on the back and said, "I'll be right back." He touched his son's arm and then walked away. Once out in the hall, he headed for the little waiting room where the coffee machine was. Depressed and in disbelief, he needed something to wake him up and force him to face reality. When he got there, he saw Emily's father, Mr. Dennison, sitting in a chair, forlornly glaring at the blank wall in front of him.

Carefully, he approached the suffering man. "How is she doing?" he cautiously asked.

Dennison sadly looked up at him. "About the same. Perhaps a little worse than before. The bleeding won't subside and they can't do anything about it. The only thing they can do to help her is to give her the morphine and keep her comfortable. How's David?"

Shanahan sat down next to him. "Not good. There's not much hope that he's going to pull out of it." He frowned, disgusted at himself for being to pessimistically blunt. He nervously folded his hands and looked around. In a seat on the other side of the room, by a magazine stand, an old woman was quietly sleeping. Other than her, the room was empty. He felt that it was odd for such a place to be so quiet during the late afternoon, but he was glad that it was silent.

"Come down for the coffee?" Dennison asked.

"As a matter of fact, yes, I did," he said, getting up.

"It doesn't work," he informed. "It'll take your money, but forget about getting anything in return. The blasted thing's broken."

Shanahan rolled his eyes and sat back down with an angry sigh. “Figures.”

“How’s your wife taking everything?”

“As good as can be expected, I supposed,” he answered. “Mrs. Dennison?”

He shook his head. “She’s a wreck. But then again, I am too. I guess that we all are. I mean, none of this should’ve ever happened.”

“I know. It’s frustrating. I want to kill those security guards down there. How they could just let an armed man walk in and shoot two people is beyond me! I want to see every last one of those puny wretches fired from their jobs and fined so much that they’d have to spend the rest of their rotten lives working to pay it off! And that drunk who hit your daughter, damn him! Damn every single one of those bastards!”

“You can’t think like that,” Dennison said. “I know it’s easy to point blame. Some drunk guy hit my daughter. His license was suspended and the car wasn’t even his. No doubt I’m angry at him. But why be vengeful? Right now, my daughter’s dying. She wouldn’t want me wasting my feelings on plotting revenge. And David wouldn’t want that either.”

Shanahan nodded and unclenched his teeth. He tried to let the anger subside, but it was hard. He was going to lose his son who had just barely begun to live. Never in his life had he been more terrified and afraid. His son didn’t deserve this. It took him a few moments to realize, with a heavy heart, that this, like so many other things in life, wasn’t fair, but it had to be accepted. David needed him. That’s all that mattered now.

Dennison firmly grasped his hand and gave him a reassuring look. “It’s going to be tough, Frank, but we’ll get through it. We just have to hold together.”

He looked up at the ceiling in worry. "David's sister and brother are going to get in sometime this evening. When are Emily's siblings getting here?"

"Sarah and Michael are flying in from Seattle right now and Charise should be here within a few hours, depending on traffic. I'm afraid that they don't know how bad this is. It's going to be rough for them."

"I'm sorry," he said.

"They'll get here. Just as long as everyone's here for her, it'll be okay."

Shanahan looked away and let out a perplexed sigh. Then, with an almost desperate face, he glanced at him. "I was wondering," he said, nervous and tense. "if there would be any way that David and Emily could possibly share the same room." Dennison gave him a startled look. "Well, it was just a thought. I know that the rooms are crowded and cramped as they are, but I thought it would be nice for the two of them if we could somehow do that."

He smiled at the thought. The idea was odd and the doctors would probably advise against it, but he could see no harm in it. Besides, Emily would probably insist upon it if she could. "I'll talk to Nancy about it. Do you think Lisa would mind?"

"I don't know. I didn't ask her yet. I doubt that she would, though."

"Okay. It's a nice idea," he said.

"Thank you," Shanahan said. He glanced at his watch. He had left his wife alone for over ten minutes. "I have to get back there," he said.

"Sure," Dennison said, patting him on the back. "Take care. I'll come in to see how he's doing in a little while, if that's okay."

"Certainly," he replied, getting up. They shook hands and he walked back to the room, glancing again at the old woman sleeping in the chair. She looked so troubled and lost, yet calmed and certain of something. He turned away and walked back to see his son.

IX

Emily looked at the endless line of sand that lay in front of them with despair. Hand in hand, they tiredly trekked their way North, watching the sun rise to the top of the sky and the ocean waves fall against the shore. A soft haze had formed and glowed with the hot sun's noontime light, covering from view everything twenty miles around with a gleaming curtain. Besides the albatross, not a single animal had appeared. The endless green plain was to her left, inclined from the sandy dunes and out of view. With nothing on it, she knew that she wasn't missing much. The sights around them were magnificent, but they were still locked in a world of loneliness and emptiness.

"How much longer?" Emily asked, knowing that there was no answer.

"One hour, fourteen minutes and thirty three seconds, give or take a million years," he said with a depressed groan.

"Even if we did travel on for a million years, would we ever find a way out of here?"

David looked down at the sparkling sand and sighed. "I don't know. And I don't even think I want to."

"Well, it could be worse. Though I don't quite know how. I guess that we could be—" She squinted her eyes to see the strange object a few yards ahead. "Oh my God!" she yelped, stepping back.

"What?" David asked, looking around. He caught sight of the furry ball nestled in the sand. "That?"

Emily nodded, her eyes wide open with fear. "Please, let's go back!"

"That's the thing that attacked you?" he said, scratching his head in confusion. The thing looked so placid and innocent. He stepped towards it.

"Please! David! Don't!" she begged.

Without warning, a head with two shoots of fur sprang up. The rabbit turned around and looked at the strange wanderers with alarm.

David let out a friendly laugh. "Oh, it's so cute!" he mocked.

Emily forced a frown and proceeded forward. "That wasn't funny!"

"Yes it was!" he said with a teasing smirk.

Trying to keep from laughing and appear angry, she snapped, "You wouldn't have been laughing if it decided to chomp your leg off!"

"You hungry?"

She gasped in disgust. "You can't be serious!"

"Why not? It's a rabbit. They're high in protein," he innocently suggested.

The rabbit suddenly whirled around and darted up the incline. David rushed after it, dashing up the sandy slope and kicking up sand as he lunged at the fleeing animal. When he clawed his way to the top, he stopped and looked ahead in awe.

"What is it?" Emily asked, stepping up the incline.

He couldn't answer. He watched the rabbit scamper away into the luscious bushes underneath the fruitful trees. Delicate blue and purple moss hung down from their mighty branches like silk lace shades while the green leaves gently swayed in the sea breeze. Singing swallows and cooing mourning doves flew in all directions, picking off colorful berries from the flourishing bushes. Squirrels jumped from tree to tree as chipmunks raced in and out of their little burrows. All around, life was plentiful. He swallowed hard and forced himself up, wondering if he was just imagining where he was.

He turned around and helped Emily up. When she saw the beauty in front of her, she stood in shock. She cautiously ventured forward and under the trees. She looked up at the green ceiling of variously shaped leaves, glowing from the sun's bright light. "It's gorgeous!" she exclaimed. "It's like the Garden of Eden!"

David walked over to a shrub with vibrant leaves and yellow berries. He picked one of the fruits off and examined it. The thing was as large as his hand and made his taste buds desirous for food. He carefully bit into it to feel its sugary, crisp juice gush out onto his tongue. He chewed it wildly and took another bite.

"This is delicious!" he said with his mouth full.

Emily ran over to him and grabbed a fruit for herself. "I'm famished!" she declared. She sunk her teeth into the berry's soft skin and smiled at the wonderful taste. She ate it like she would never eat again, then took another. They were revitalizing and fresh. She tried to remember when she ever tasted something so pleasant, but realized that she never had.

"And these," David said, pulling a red seed, the size of a melon, from a tree branch. He peeled the skin and ripped apart the pink fibers inside. He greedily devoured the food without hesitation. The contents tasted mildly of tang and sour grain that teased his senses, all pleasing to his starving stomach.

Emily strolled over to a vine with flowers looking up at the sky. She gently dipped her finger between the petals and tasted the nectar. The sweet, sparkling liquid poured into the crevices of her gums, under her tongue and against her cheeks, tickling her mouth with delicious pleasure.

They feasted, enjoying every bite and every sip more than the one before. Time drifted past, but for once, they didn't care. The scrumptious food was all around them with enough to feed them forever. The big fruits, little berries, lanky stalks, fat bulbs and hanging clusters of juicy vegetables, warmed by the sun and refreshed by the misty haze, provided a fanciful meal for the weary travelers.

"Um! This is really good!" Emily declared, taking another bite out of a purple melon.

"Where?" David asked, rushing up beside her.

She held up the melon in her hands, the sticky juices glittering where she had bitten into it. She glanced at him with a smile and offered him a bite. Instead, he wrapped his arms around her and kissed her, trying to steal the food from her mouth. *Oh! Frisky!* she thought.

Dropping the melon, she laughed and tried to pull away, but he held her close to him.

"How about if I just bit your tongue off?" she chortled.

"Go ahead," he dared, kissing her again.

She wrapped her arms around his body and let herself fall against him.

David lost his balance and fell onto the soft ground with Emily's lips still locked around his. She lifted herself up and looked down at him, unable to stop giggling at the sight of the purple mess around his mouth. "You're such a klutz," she chuckled.

"I know," he said, entranced. "This is so great. You're wonderful."

"Of course I am," she admitted, reaching back for the melon. She grasped it in her two hands and bite into it again, looking back at him with a victorious grin.

"As strange as everything here is, I really find it adventurous," he said. "We used to go places and do things all the time when we were young."

"When we were young?" Emily asked. "We haven't even reached our prime yet! We're still young! You're not getting into the mid-life crisis thing now, are you?"

David laughed it off and stared back at her with a sad smile. "I know. Up until last night, we never seemed to be going off anywhere anymore. The weekends used to be ours. You know, taking trips up to Hartford and Newport, going down to Philadelphia or driving around in the Poconoes in a beat-up rental car. What happened?"

Her grin slowly disappeared. "Time. Work. Money. We just couldn't afford it if we were going to get somewhere with our lives."

"Where are we trying to go?"

She sat up and looked away in apathy. "I don't know. I'd like to live in a nice house for when we have children someday. I'd like to have a satisfying job, be able to come home without being tired out and be doing something productive. I want to make my mark on this world and have an important role in society. I want to be proud of the things in my life. I love going on adventures and seeing new places with you! But we can't afford it."

"It is in living that you become proud of what's in your life. How can we live when we rush off to work and spend the weekends without even being able to go see a movie or something like that."

"David!" she growled, slamming her hand on the ground. "Money does not grow on trees! There are bills to be paid and groceries to buy! The weekends in the past were fun, but we just can't afford it now! How can you be this dense!"

He turned away and sighed. Way to go, he sarcastically thought to himself. *Just had to go and open your big mouth again!* "I'm sorry," he acknowledged, placing a hand on her tensed shoulder.

She looked back at him, thinking, *Why do I always have to go off like that on him?* "No, honey. It's me. I'm just stressed, that's all," she said. *So what else is new? You're always stressed!* her mind scolded. *Oh shut-up!* she told her mind. So what if it was the same old excuse?

This time it was true! She gently laid back on top of him and stared into his eyes. "I love you. I shouldn't have snapped at you like that."

He gazed into her sparkling eyes with adoration. Her apology was said through them alone. He still felt guilty, though. Here he was, starting an argument about money when weekend spending sprees might never matter to them again. Of all places and of all times, he had brought it up here and now.

"Come on," she said. "Cheer up." She touched his lips with hers and seductively pressed herself against him. Rubbing her hands on his chest, she pulled back and said with an alluring smile, "Let's fool around! There's nobody else around and the birds won't mind."

"No, but that squirrel over there is watching us," he warned, glancing at a fury rodent with a sneer.

"Oh be quiet," she said with a quiet laugh. She gently turned his face back to her and kissed him again. She let him wrap his arms around her and roll her on her back. The warm ground felt comfortable against her back as the grass tickled her neck and legs.

He locked his lips around hers as he held her. She was feisty as well as beautiful. He loved the way she sexily moved her hands down his face and across his shoulders. He lost himself in her eyes as she romantically stared back at him. The way that she massaged his back was—

He jumped and looked behind him. A confused Emily stared back at him. He shot his head back around and saw her again.

"What?" she asked.

He leapt to his feet and stumbled back.

Emily gasped at the sight of the "what" who had been behind him. At first she wasn't sure if she was looking into a mirror or there was really another woman who looked exactly like her. She cautiously stood up and walked over to a nervous David.

The other woman glared at them. She had the same face, same shape, same red hair and same shirt. The only thing different was the cruel, empty look in her eyes. As she stood up, another woman appeared behind her.

"Oh no," Emily said in fear, clutching onto his arm. Who were they? What did they want? Why did they look like her? Were they even real? She felt him grasp her hand and slowly lead her away, not taking their eyes off the two mysterious strangers.

The two women walked towards them. They suddenly shifted apart to reveal two more identical women.

The lovers, scared and terrified, turned around to run away. Before they could even move their legs, they saw four other women approaching them.

"What's happening?" Emily cried.

"I don't know. Who are these people?"

She watched in terror as the eight closed in on them, all staring at David as if he was their long, lost lover, found after years of painful absence. She hugged him and pressed her head against his chest.

The first woman to touch him felt as real as the one he held. Before he knew it, he was being swamped by the look-a-likes.

"Don't let me go!" Emily begged.

At once, the other women, now numbering sixteen, cried out, "Don't let me go!"

Several strong arms suddenly wrapped themselves around her. She let out a scream as she desperately held onto her husband. His strong grip around her was torn apart by five of the imposters.

"Emily!" he screamed as she was pulled away. In an instant, she had disappeared into the crowd of fakes. He frantically searched for her teary eyes and crying voice among the sea of somber faces staring at him. Though they looked just like her, he could sense without effort that they weren't her at all.

"Emily!" he cried again, his eyes wide with panic and desperation.

"David!" Emily screamed, pushing through the group and grasping onto him again. He flung his arms around her and dropped to the ground.

At once, the other sixteen women lunged at him with eyes full of tears and puffy red cheeks.

"Honey!" one cried, grasping his arm. "I love you!"

"I'm Emily!" another declared, looking at him with hurting eyes.

"No she's not! Sweetheart! Listen to me! I'm her!" sobbed someone else, trying to wrap her arms around him as she pushed the real Emily out of the way.

David shoved her away and held his crying wife, ignoring the unwelcome kisses upon his cheeks from the strangers.

"I'm scared, David!" another voice wept.

Emily clung onto him. "Don't let me go. Please don't let me go," she begged, choking on bitter tears of horror.

"Please don't let me go!" an imposter cried, wrapping her arms around his neck and burying her face on his shoulder. Emily looked up at her with hateful eyes, only to receive a vicious stare back from the evil woman.

David tried to sit through the tugging, pulling and pushing, but it was too much. Any longer and they would suffocate them.

He rose to his feet, holding a terrified Emily in his arms, and pushed past the women.

They refused to let go, barraging him with hysteric pleas of their authenticity and love for him. Their cries were so real and touching. If she wasn't in his arms, she would've been lost from him.

Without warning, one of the women threw a punch at Emily, striking her across her delicate face.

David turned to shield her, only to have his feet kicked out from under him. He crashed onto the ground, but wouldn't let her go.

Emily covered her face against his chest and he tried to protect her from the cruel kicks and punches thrown at them from the wild imposters.

Then a bloodcurdling scream cried out.

The sixteen women stood back and looked at their two victims with immense worry.

He slowly opened his eyes to see a line of Emily look-a-likes staring back at him. They wore fear on their faces and terror in their eyes. Slowly, they began to retreat.

Emily glanced at them with vengeful eyes. *Get lost!* she thought, too afraid to scream it out.

Then she heard something more horrifying.

Clicking.

Thousand of chattering teeth among harsh growls and vicious barks.

They were approaching.

X

She nervously turned around and looked over David's shoulder. Through the eerie haze, now glowing a pale orange as the sun made its way through the western sky, hundreds of fury balls were coming towards them, darting past the trees and bushes. She shook at the sight, believing that she was literally seeing Hell invade Heaven, if it hadn't already.

Shaking like a terrified kitten, she grabbed his arm and forced him up. "We have to get out of here," she said.

The sixteen women stared at her with jealousy. Their bitter envy drove their attention away from the approaching danger and back towards their rival. Without hesitation, they rushed toward her.

Emily clung to her husband as they pressed through the hounding women. They were beaten mercilessly and spat upon, especially the envied wife.

"Hold on!" David shouted, frantically trying to push away the imposters.

Emily dug her fingers into his ribs, holding on for dear life. Fists hit her from all directions. Fingernails raked across her skin, tearing it so deeply that she even bled. She wanted to lash out at them with all her fury, but it would take them only a second to take her away from her lover.

David felt a pair of hands clasp around his ankle as sharp teeth sank into his calf. He let out a scream as he pressed forward, holding onto Emily with all his strength.

Another woman stepped right in front of him clawed at his face, frantically trying to hit his eyes. With four strong arms against his shoulders, he was forced back on the forest floor.

He was swarmed like an angel fish trapped in the middle of an army of piranha, being jerked left and right as his wife was helplessly assaulted. They screamed and spat at him, still trying to force him to believe that each one of them was actually Emily.

"I love you!" Emily screamed.

"I won't let you go!"

Then, to his horror, three arms slipped in between him and Emily. He clutched on to her with every ounce of energy that he had, unwilling to let her budge. The attackers only became more furious. The threw another series of punches and kicks while ripping at his hair and pulling—

"Mercy!" a voice screamed.

He looked down at Emily. She was nestled safely in his arms as the imposters suddenly fled.

"Help! Don't leave me!" the voice cried again.

Emily and David whirled around. One of the women was lying on the ground with four balls of fur attached to her body, grinding apart her flesh and bone as she frantically tried to force them off.

She looked back at David with eyes full of hopelessness. "Help me! My love! Rescue me!" she cried, the tears streaming down her face and mixing with the blood where one of the creatures had bit her cheek.

David's body trembled with fear. He couldn't believe that he was watching her being devoured alive.

Emily, in tears, grasped his shoulder and pulled him back as she saw the other vile animals coming for them. "David, it's not real!" she cried.

David shook his head in shock as another creature jumped on top of her and sank its fangs into the base of her neck. Blood generously poured from the wound as the animal ate the skin and muscle. She extended her arm at him, looking at him with begging eyes. "Please save me!" she implored.

He felt a collage of emotions sweep through him. She was the enemy, yet she needed his help. Her life depended on it.

"Come on!" Emily urged, shaking him as hard as she could. "It's a trap!"

David jumped up and rushed towards the stricken woman.

"No!" his wife screamed, dashing after him. She ignored the fact that she was running towards the sea of furry monsters. She had to get him away before it was too late.

David rushed up to the injured woman and grasped her arm. The moment he did, she let out a wicked chortle and held onto his wrist so tightly that his hand tingled.

"You will die with me because you love me!" she declared, yanking him towards her.

David let out a scream as he fell towards her.

Emily reached out and caught him just before he landed on top of the monstrous balls of fur that were eating the imposter. She now glared up at Emily with hateful eyes, wanting to hurt her more than anything else in the world. Desiring him and feeling that she deserved anything that she wanted, she was going to at least take her lover away from her. She was going to make sure he suffered her fate.

All of a sudden, another vicious monster leapt on top of her forehead, stabbing its teeth into her in a splash of warm blood.

She screamed and wailed as she violently shook her head to get the creature off, but to no avail.

David and Emily looked ahead at the predators, desperate for escape.

"Get out of here!" David hollered. She ignored him and pulled at the woman's solid grip around his hand. "Go!" he begged again.

"No!" she asserted, struggling as hard as she could to free him.

The woman screamed out in terror as the monster drilled through her skull. Nothing she could do would free her now.

She suddenly stopped moving. Her eyes, fixed so fervently on David, glazed over as her grip slowly loosened.

"Oh God," David whispered. "Oh dear God."

Emily peeled her distraught husband away and led him in the opposite direction as fast as she could. They raced ahead through the haze. The sun had been so overcome by the afternoon clouds that the world was left without a single ray of light. When they dared to glance back, the imposter's body was completely covered with the animals as they heartlessly ripped her to shreds.

David squeezed the tears out of his eyes as his wife pulled him along. She was safe. She was perfectly fine and alive. Yet the sheer image of seeing someone who looked so much like her gouged at his soul like the jaws of a hungry bear sinks into the soft sides of a defenseless salmon, all hope being lost and forever forsaken.

They ran past the trees with the fragrant flowers and the bushes that were blooming with ripe fruits. The birds had sought refuge in their nests and the small animals had fled to their burrows as the virgin land was scoured by the hideous monsters.

"Can we outrun them?" David asked, panting violently as he ran.

"I think so," she answered, gasping for air.

They ran for five minutes, darting among shrubs and barely missing tree trunks as they ran for safety. The adrenaline rushed through their arteries with screaming pain. Their hearts pumped wildly and violently. Their lungs burned with hunger for oxygen.

Suddenly, the clouds above broke and the sun reappeared, but it was much dimmer than before with the shadows of the trees stretching out for twice their length. The haze was torn with bright, orange strips of sunlight. But now, David sadly realized, sunset was only minutes away.

Several screams cried out from behind. Emily glanced back to see the balls of fur, safely off in the distance, being burned when they wandered into the sun's brilliant light. They scurried for cover under trees and beneath bushes. Once settled in the shade, the injured ones were quickly feasted upon by their colleagues. She turned back in disgust and kept running.

They ran for what felt like an hour before they stopped, though they knew that it had been less than ten minutes. Emily stopped and leaned over, clutching onto her legs for support. David stood next to her, looked back, decided that the coast was clear and collapsed to the grassy ground.

Trying to catch her breath, she said, "You're not just going to fall asleep here now, are you?" David mumbled a positive answer back. She sighed, looked down at him, and rolled her eyes. "Good idea," she said, letting herself fall on top of his chest.

He smiled at her touch and felt at peace. He closed his eyes and let his mind relax, thinking of absolutely nothing but Emily resting on him.

He felt her hand caress his face. "Are you okay?" she asked.

He looked at her loving face with his pained eyes. Raising his hand to feel her chin, he said, "I'll be okay. It was just very scary. I knew that she wasn't you. Heck, she wasn't even real. I could see the emptiness in her eyes. But it frightened me when I saw her like that . . . because it may have been you."

She placed her arms around his neck and tenderly kissed his forehead. She looked at his eyes, scared with a terror that would never leave him for as long as he lived. She kissed him again and hugged him tightly. "I love you," she reassured. "Everything's going to be okay. I know that everything here is so strange. The way the day passes by and then takes forever, these strange beings, people appearing out of nowhere. But we'll get through it. Somehow, someway. God's still watching over us. He wouldn't just abandon us here like this. We'll find our way out."

He tiredly mumbled back an answer, but she couldn't understand him. He was tired and worn-out. Now he wanted to sleep more than anything.

"Honey," Emily said, the fear returning to her voice. "I'm afraid to stay here. They might find us once the sun goes down."

David reluctantly let the idea of sleeping out of his mind. She was right and there was no sense risking the danger of life and death over catching a few winks. He stood back up and took his wife's hand.

Through the darkening twilight, they walked hurriedly, wishing that they knew where they were headed. The air was mildly cool as the chill of the night began to set in. Their feet ached from all of the walking and running. Their bodies were sweaty and sore from the natural elements placed against them. As they moved on, the sun finally fell behind the horizon, leaving before them only minutes to get out of the wooded land before total darkness enveloped them.

Their hearts began to beat with worry as they quickened their pace. *Would they come after us at night?* Emily fearfully wondered. She was certain that the answer was positive. The vicious beasts would take any advantage they had over them just to sink their tiny teeth into them. The sight of the ravaged woman who had looked just like her entered her mind. All of the blood, cuts, scrapes and the horrible gnawing sound that the teeth had made against her skull sent a chill down her spine. *It wasn't real!* she told herself. *It was all fake! Nothing actually happened!* She wanted so badly to immerse her mind with pleasant thoughts, but knew that she could just as easily be the animals' next meal as she was.

Then, to her great relief, the trees gave way to a clearing. No green plains that rolled on forever, but a landscape that appeared oddly Mediterranean. Ahead lay a majestic mountain, towering thousands of feet into the air and carpeted with thick trees and grass. Several smaller hills surrounded it, as if guarding it from invaders from the east. To the west was the ocean, sparkling with moonlight as it crashed against the sea-lined cliffs.

A perplexed feeling came over David when he remembered that at first the ocean had been on the east, but he shrugged it off. The massive purple crystals had since disappeared and been replaced with tiny wooden figures.

They walked out, feeling the refreshing water collected on the grass wash their dusty feet. The heavens above them sparkled, the massive belt of stars from the spiral of the galaxy stretching across the sky with vibrant colors. They shone against the blackness of the east to the light purple of the west. The sight was breathtaking. New York, with all its splendor, was the worst place in the world to try to find a star, let alone the trillions they saw before them. Then they noticed a strange light below the horizon.

"Oh my . . ." Emily gasped and stepped forward. In the distance she saw the light shining out from the window of a tiny house. It was a dilapidated building, the roof of red grooved tile and the stones on the side crumbling apart. But it had a cozy appearance.

"I take it that we're both seeing that," David said, rubbing his eyes and looking again.

She shook her head. "It isn't possible," she insisted. "It's out here in the middle of nowhere! Do you think anyone's in there?"

David bit his lip. It was confusing, but he didn't think that there was any danger associated with it. Unlike the imposter women and the hideous monsters, it hadn't just appeared in front of them. Perhaps it's just a part of the landscape, he thought. "I don't know. But there's only one way to find out," he said, gently grabbing hold of her hand.

Taking in a breath of the night air, they proceeded towards the building, clinging on to the desperate hope that a real person might be there and help them to get back.

XI

Their hearts pumped faster with anticipation as they came closer to the house. Beside the structure was a faint, wide path of stone leading off into the distance. *A road*, Emily realized. She wondered if she and David were simply imagining all of this. She had been so tired before as to actually see things in front of her that weren't really there. Oddly, however, she didn't feel tired at all. There was too much adrenaline still running through her veins to even consider falling asleep. But still, the sight ahead perplexed her senses. Something didn't seem right about it. It felt terribly wrong. A feeling was gnawing at her soul and warning her to turn back before it was too late. *It's only a house*, she told herself.

They smelled burning oil as they neared the building. The gentle glow from the window came from a lamp set on a wooden desk. Someone had to be inside, yet they didn't hear a sound.

David let out a little laugh. "It's so small," he said, coming to the front door. It was cracked open, allowing a view of the one-room interior. He gently knocked and waited for an answer, but no one responded. Cautiously, he pushed the door open, letting it squeak on its rusty hinges. He saw no one at the desk, so he proceeded in.

"Careful!" Emily warned. She watched him look behind the door, then back at her in despair. The look of fear and worry was all over his face. "What's wrong?"

"No one's here."

She shrugged her shoulders. "Maybe we should give it a few minutes and see if they come back?"

"That's the thing," he said, sounding lost. "I don't think that they will. I doubt that anyone even lives here."

She shot him a confused look. "What makes you think that?"

He only shrugged.

Frustrated, she walked inside and glanced around. The room was sparse and bare with only a desk and an oil lamp by the window. There wasn't even a pile of hay in a corner for a bed. It was simply empty, just like the other places they had come across. Still, someone was here and they would certainly return. "I don't understand," she said. "This is—"

Without warning, something furry ran across her foot.

She let out a holler of terror and bolted out the doorway as fast as she could. "Oh God! Oh God!" she screamed, crouching on the ground and shielding her fragile face with her shaking hands.

David casually walked out to her, his eyes full of confusion. "Honey?" he asked, reaching for her shoulder.

She glared up at him with horrified eyes. "Where is it!" she begged.

"Where's what?"

"The animal! The monster with the hair!"

Kneeling beside her, he took her in his arms. "There's nothing there," he gently reassured her. "Everything's okay. You're probably just getting tired."

An abrupt, yet innocent, *squeak!* sounded from the door.

Emily watched with furious eyes as a plump, little rat scampered out of the building and over to the edge of the road. It stopped and looked at her with its beady eyes and sniffling nose. "Why that little . . ." She jumped to her feet and lunged for the defenseless creature.

The tiny rat whirled around with an imploring cry and darted away.

"You stupid creep!" she screamed, picking up a rock and throwing it at the fleeing rodent. It missed it by only a few inches as it scurried out of sight.

David sat on the ground, laughing uncontrollably.

She turned back at him with a dirty look. "Do you think that was funny?" she demanded. Her chuckling husband, trying hard to hide his smile, nodded. She growled and stormed towards him with tight fists. Unable to stop snickering, he huddled down and braced himself for the blow.

She simply walked past him, not even bothering to look at him.

Uh oh, he thought, realizing that he had really ticked her off, *I'm in for it*. He leapt to his feet and ran over to her. "Sweetheart, I'm sorry—"

"Shut-up and live while you still can," she snapped.

He let out a defeated sigh, feeling guilty for hurting her feelings. She had been scared to death that something terrible was going to happen to her and here he was, making fun of it. But there was no danger, only a rat. In fact, the whole thing had been hilarious through his eyes. A moment later, he was snickering again.

She turned around and glared at him. "You're being very immature," she admonished.

He looked away and broke down into laughter. "I know," he admitted. "I know. But you should have seen yourself!"

She ignored him and stepped onto the road, the hard stone surface cold and rough against her sore feet.

"Don't you want to go back and wait?" David asked.

With a V on her forehead and arms akimbo, she shook her head. "You'll have to kill me first before I go back in there."

Knowing that he had edged her on too much, as all husbands realize they have done at one time or another, he decided to play it safe by keeping quiet. They traveled down the featureless road in the middle of the dark land with nothing bright to look at but the stars and planets in the sky. All that separated the road from the sea was a golden field of wheat that gently swayed in the night breeze.

After a while, he ventured for her hand. She grudgingly let him hold onto her, despite that she wanted him to think that she was still angry with him and he had to get on his knees and beg for her forgiveness. But it was a dark night and she liked his company, even though he was being an arrogant jerk.

As the hour wore on, her aching feet began to cramp with pain. She looked at the road ahead with uncertainty. For some reason, she felt that she was walking into a trap. *What's wrong with you?* she told herself. *This whole thing is a trap! You could be moving towards the only way out!* But it didn't help any. She was nervous and the dread was only growing.

"David?" she finally asked.

"I'm so sorry!" he cried out. "Please! I was out of place and—"

She groaned and rolled her eyes. "You're so pathetic!"

"Yes! I know I am! You're always right! I should be punished for—"

"That's very nice. Now be quiet," she growled, sensing his sarcasm starting to inch its way in. Staring down the road, she let out a suspire and asked, "How do you feel about all of this?"

"Very bad! I'm sorry! I had no right to—"

"I meant about the road, dummy!"

"Oh. Well, it's hard, cold and made of stone. Looks like a road to me."

"No. That's not what I meant either."

He stopped and looked at her. "Are you okay?"

"Of course I am!" she snapped. "Why wouldn't I be?" She angrily glared at his scrutinizing eyes. With a tired sigh, she admitted, "Well, maybe I'm a little tense. I have a strange feeling about all of this."

"You should. I'd be worried if you didn't." He saw her gaze down the road, lost and afraid. "Is it something ahead? Did you want to turn back?"

Thinking her thoughts over, she let out a laugh. "No," she said, shaking her head. "I'm just getting paranoid." She yawned and looked back at him with a warm grin. "Shall we proceed?"

He stumbled off the road and sat on the ground. The wheat wasn't soft, but tall and rough. Still, it felt more comfortable than being on his hurting feet. A wave of sleepiness washed over him as he felt his eyelids suddenly become heavy. He stared back at her with a weary face. "Not really. How about you?"

In need of a break herself, she languidly walked over to him and plopped herself down beside him. "Good point," she said, yawning again. She laid down, letting the tall wheat form a cushion for her back. It felt so good to rest that she wondered why she hadn't done it sooner.

David gently draped his arm over her as he nestled up behind her and buried his face in her hair. She smiled at the feel of his touch, even though she was still frustrated at him for making fun of her. She looked up at the starry sky and tried to ignore the troubling feeling of danger that was plaguing her mind. She wondered where God was, if He was really watching over them from the heavens above. How pointless everything would be if He wasn't.

After a while, her anguished thoughts settled down. She closed her eyes from the night air and fell asleep.

XII

Emily jumped from her peaceful slumber as the carriage roared past, kicking up a cloud of dust behind it. She shot her head up above the wheat in time to see a person, dressed in a brown robe, rush away on the back of a cisium, throwing a whip to lick the back of his horse. In only a moment, he had disappeared from view and the field fell into silence once more. *I must be dreaming!* she thought.

David sat up beside her. "What was that?" he asked.

"A guy on a carriage!" she exclaimed, refusing to accept what she had seen. She stood up and looked around. Just ahead, chirping birds were playfully chasing each other through the wheat as mice foraged for food. A refreshing breeze from the sea blew around her as the morning sun, already above the horizon, warmed the land with its hot light.

"Where are we?" David wearily climbed to his feet and staggered out into the road and rubbed his bristly face. He was in need of a nice, warm shower and a good shave. It had been two days now without the amenities of a modern life. But for some reason, it didn't seem to matter. He was too enveloped with curiosity to even care. He started to walk down the road.

"Wait," Emily said, rushing up to him. "Are you sure about this?"

"Of course," he said, quickening his pace.

She groaned and moved her legs faster to keep up with him. That strange, ominous feeling of danger was still with her and she despised it terribly.

Several trees lined the road ahead, shielding the stone path from the hot sun as it curved away from the sea. An anxious David broke out into a jog, desperate to see what lay ahead. Emily tagged along, regretting every moment of the journey. As he led her around the curve, he suddenly stopped and stared at the sight before them.

A quarter mile ahead, the road neatly cut its way underneath a stone arch that protruded from a massive wall, creating a place where several people milled about parked carts full of crops and whinnying horses as they pleasantly conversed with one another. Farmers dressed in dirty robes instructed their servants, who wore thick loin cloths around their waists as the sweat shined on their bare chests. Merchants wearing finer garments negotiated with the agriculturists the prices for their goods. At the center stood a tall man draped with a red cape and a sword at his side as he stood guard over the crowd.

"I'm not seeing this," David choked in disbelief. "Is this real?"

"Only one way to find out," Emily said, her voice quivering with uncertainty. She took her husband's hand and boldly stepped forward. Before she realized it, many people were staring at them. Looking so different from them, she knew that they were seen as foreigners. She wondered if they'd be hostile, or, as she was desperately wanted, could somehow help them to get back.

As they made their way towards the gate, they were received with curious, but friendly faces. The man with the sword reached out and gently touched Emily's arm as she passed him, his eyes full of admiration for her beauty. Flattered, she smiled at him adoringly as David jealously shot him a dirty look.

Once through the gate, they found themselves in a city of ancient buildings and busy people rushing to-and-fro about their daily tasks. The dusty street, with large stepping stones in the middle, was lined with tiny shops that were crowded by bartering customers and crafty merchants. The store fronts were elaborately decorated with paintings and moldings of ancient gods and legendary herces.

"Where are we?" David asked, a smile emerging on his perplexed face. "It's like we've gone back in time!" He started to run through the street, letting his eyes feast on the mysterious scenery before them. Emily didn't say anything. The feeling of doom was growing stronger in her chest. She felt like she had to get out. But why?

They passed a fruit stand and darted down a narrow alleyway. Strolling past a row of houses, they came across a magnificent garden, rich with flowers and palm trees. Humming birds swooped down to the lilies and drank their sweet nectar as bulky bumblebees flew around from flower to flower. Despite its heat, the luscious plants flourished in the summer sun. Life was everywhere.

Without warning, two small children rushed out from the bushes, playfully chasing each other in a euphoric frenzy. They rushed past the two travelers, nearly knocking them over as they continued their game out in the city street.

Emily gave a quiet laugh as she watched them wrestle each other to the ground, practically tripping the poor pedestrians who tried to get past them. Then she spotted a small theater ahead. Intrigued, she ran forward to get a closer look A semicircle of rock slabs descended to a stage where two actors rehearsed for a skit later that night. She hurried to a seat at the top and watched in wonder.

The actors, dressed in elaborate costumes as they pranced around, boisterously shouted out their lines. A few spectators suddenly laughed and cheered. The grinning actors took a bow, then returned to their positions.

David sat down beside her and studied the architecture. *An Odeon*, he realized, seeing how the front gave way to a massive wall. He intently listened to the actors below.

"Quid Agis, hodie!" one cried out.

"Nescio. Ego no hodie. Ego est meus, fatua!" said the other.

David jumped up from his seat and screamed out with great passion, "You didn't use the accusative form for meus!"

The two men, as well as the audience, glanced up at him with worry. Emily, swept with embarrassment, buried her face in her hands and groaned.

"A-a-acusi-i-it-t-t-tive?" one of the actors stammered.

An awkward silence fell on the theater. David worriedly glanced back at the displeased stares. Finally, he let out a nervous chuckle. "Ah . . . Bene! Bene!" he shouted, clapping his hands. The actors smiled and continued their lines. He felt Emily grab his arm and quickly pull him down.

"Don't attract attention," she warned. "We have no idea who these people are!"

"Sure we do!" he exclaimed, smiling blissfully.

She gave him a questioning grin. "We do?"

He confidently put an arm around her and said, "Romans. Who else? Just look at all of the buildings, the clothing and the way these people are living! They're speaking Latin all around us! Apparently they speak it correctly, without proper use of declensions and verb forms . . ." he said, his thoughts drifting back to his high school Latin classes where countless lists of endings were drilled into his head, all in the name of an authenticity that never existed.

The very thought made terrifying sense to her. "I'm afraid," she said, clinging to his arm. "This is all very nice, but you're saying that we're a million miles away from home with thousands of years separating us from our time?"

David reluctantly nodded. "Well, that is one way of looking at it, I suppose." It was hard to smile when he saw her so depressed. He nudged her with his elbow. "Hey, cheer up! We'll get out of this. I promise." His words were received with a pair of contingent eyes. "Come on," he said, grabbing her arm and lifting her up.

He excitedly led her out into the street. Immediately, they were surrounded by merchants shoving products in their faces. A beautician stepped in front of her and rubbed charcoal under her eyes while another salesman tempted him with a fresh fish. Once they knew that extracting money from the two was impossible, they abruptly moved on to their next customers.

The street curved and went down a hill. The two-story buildings, perfectly enforced with strong bricks and wood beams, protected them from the sun. The streets were filled with people: a city administrator accompanied by his mistress, a weary mother and her lively children, a group of musicians, two beggars, and a father carrying his daughter on his shoulders as he searched the markets. Smoke from stoves filled the air along with the scent of baking bread and roasting fowl. It was a different world entirely.

They came to a plaza, decorated with colorful tiles along the sides and with towering trees standing in the middle. Seeing an opened garment shop, they strolled over to look at the clothes. White robes with purple stripes, sheer silk drapes and fresh togas filled the shelves. A shallow pool in the back attracted their attention. They walked over and watched as two slaves scrubbed a couple of garments in the liquid and wrung them out.

"They have their own detergent," she said, astounded.

"Of course! What? You think that these people were slobs?"

Proudly lifting her chin into the air, she sat down alongside the edge and let her hands rest in the warm cleaner. It felt so soothing against her dry skin that she splashed some on her arms. "The study of barbaric cultures never appealed very much to me," she confidently admitted.

"Too bad," he said with a grin.

"Why do you say that?" she said, laughing back. With the exception of slipping into some sort of surreal dimension and traveling back in time, history was simply an unimportant thing of the past.

"Because if you knew how Romans washed their clothes, your hands wouldn't be soaking in urine right now."

Appalled, she glanced down and gasped. She ripped her hands out of the pool and violently shook them off. "Ugh! Gross! Why didn't you tell me that before!"

He innocently shrugged. "Why spoil a good moment?"

"A good moment for whom?" she snapped, desperately trying to dry her arms. "I'll teach you!" She chased him out into the plaza before she caught him. Wrapping her arms around him, she rubbed her wet hands against his chest. He frantically squirmed to get away from her grip, his eyes squinting with disgust. "There!" she laughed, sliding her hands down his cheek.

He jumped back and rubbed his face. "You're sick!" he cried.

"No I'm not! I'm just enjoying the culture around me!" she exclaimed with a cheery smirk. She saw the bewildered look on his face and felt guilty. She embraced him and stared at him with apologetic eyes. "I'm sorry, honey. Kiss and make up?" She leaned forward to touch her lips with his.

He coughed in her face and stepped back. "Wow! That stuff smells terrible!" he said, then laughing at her.

She tried to hide her smile as she playfully punched him in the ribs. "Jerk!" she shouted.

"Oh! I'm the jerk? Who was the one who put her hands in—"

"Pater!" a meek voice cried out. They turned to see a little girl on the side of the plaza, desperately trying to free her bleeding foot from the crack between the stones. "Adiuva me!" she begged, her eyes filled with tears as she looked ahead with terror.

The rumbling of chariots grew louder as they approached from up the street.

XIII

Without thinking, David ran towards the girl. He put his arm around her frail body and slipped his hand under her foot. She clung onto him and buried her face on his shoulder. He could feel her warm tears against his skin. With care, he gently wiggled her foot. To his disappointment, it wouldn't budge. He had only caused the poor child to yell out in pain.

Emily darted to his side and grabbed her tiny ankle. "Hurry!" she cried, pulling her as hard as she could.

The child screamed again as her foot remained locked between the stones.

David looked up to see three chariots careening towards them with the drivers completely oblivious to them. In the background, he heard someone yelling, "Sexta! Sexta!"

"Slip it back!" Emily cried.

They pulled her foot back, grinding her flesh against the stone even more. With one swift move, they yanked her foot free.

They rolled to the left as the chariots flew past, throwing up a cloud of dust behind them. A concerned soldier looked back, but continued on when he saw that the three people had moved just in time.

A middle aged man rushed over to them and scooped the crying girl into his arms. "Sexta," he soothed, holding her dearly as he wept.

Emily choked on the dust as David helped her off the ground. He looked up at her two rescuers and happily cried, "Gratias! Gratias vobis ago!"

"What's he saying?" Emily asked, worried that he was angry with them.

"He's saying 'thank you'," he explained.

The man went on with a string of words that he couldn't interpret, but he remained pleasant none-the-less. The girl, her face streaked with salty tears and holding her wounded foot, stared at him with thankful eyes. She pushed back her shiny black hair and turned to rest on her father's chest.

They watched with tender smiles as the father turned around and left with his daughter to his storefront. His child was safe and sound. Then they fearfully realized that the eyes of many people were on them, having seen their heroic deed. Not wanting to attract any more attention, they tried their best to appear casual.

"Well," Emily said, trying to comprehend the fact that she was almost run over by a trio of chariots. "That was interesting."

"I'll say," David agreed, brushing the dirt off his hands.

The father suddenly turned around and shouted, "Venitis hic!"

"I think that he wants us to follow him," David said. He held her hand as they walked across the plaza to meet the father once more.

The man sat his daughter down on a table and picked up a white tunic and a red palla from beside her. With a generous grin, he placed a pair of sandals on top and handed the bundle to Emily.

Not knowing what to do, she could only look back with a confused face. The merchant stepped forward and lifted them up to her face. "I don't have money to pay for that," she quickly said.

"Nonne habitis pecunam," David quickly interceded.

"Sciro!" the man exclaimed, still grinning. "Gratias vobis ago!"

Emily worriedly glanced at him, not sure whether to run away or take the clothes. To her relief, David said, "Apparently they're a gift." She looked back at the shopkeeper and gently accepted the garments before suddenly rushing into the store.

"Et te," he said, grabbing David's arm as he picked up another tunic from the table. He turned him around and slipped the tunic over his head. The cloth felt rough against his sunburned shoulders, but it blocked them from the broiling sun. It was a relief to wear something that helped him blend in with the crowd rather than to be walking around and receiving curious stares as an outsider.

Emily emerged from the shop dressed in her new clothes and with a big grin across her face. "Look at this!" she cried to David, whirling around in front of him to show them off. "It feels great!"

"Beautiful!" he declared. The merchant shot him a confused look. "Pulcher," he cooly explained with delight.

"Ita vero!" he agreed. He turned to his daughter and pointed to her two rescuers as he asked her how they looked. Even though the tears were still fresh on her face, she managed a weak smile of approval.

Emily admired her gorgeous clothes. The fabric was barely coarse with each stitch being perfectly sewn. She looked back at their benefactor with a grateful heart. *How kind*, she thought. Despite its dark troubles, human nature had its up sides too. Compassion for one another existed, even though they were so different in culture, so separated by time, and so apart in thought.

"Vale, amici," he said with a farewell gesture.

They waved good-bye and walked away, leaving the generous merchant to take care of his daughter and to attend to his other customers. The sandals were an amazing relief for their tired feet, freeing them from the painfully rough road. They made their way down another alley and out to a residential road. Oddly, large houses, elaborate and demonstrative of their owner's wealth, towered right next door to tiny shacks. Children happily played in the streets as a tax collector passed from door to door to collect city payments.

After a while, they began to feel sleepy again. The sun was growing hotter and the city streets were beginning to swelter with its heat. They traveled on, becoming more thirsty with each step. As they came onto the main road, they saw several people surrounding a public fountain, eagerly scooping out buckets of water to take back to their homes.

They ran up to the pool of refreshing water, eager to quench their dry throats. Emily cupped the water in her hands and politely drank it, wanting to appear proper and dignified. David, standing across from her, couldn't care less what people thought as he sank his lips into the water and sucked it in as quickly as he could. The liquid felt wonderfully pleasant in his mouth. He enjoyed every single drop like it was the only one he would ever have.

"You're like a hippopotamus!" Emily exclaimed.

David looked up, the water dripping from his face and hair. "And so what does that make you?" he asked with a witty smirk. She smiled deviously and covered her mouth with her hands as she sipped some more water. "Oh! No comeback! How weak!" he proclaimed.

She lifted her head back up and said, "I believe it is the custom in this society that lowly plebes, like yourself, are to be seen and not spoken to."

He ignored her as he drank more of the satisfying liquid. Then he innocently lifted his face up and squeezed his cheeks together.

Without warning, Emily was hit on the neck with a stream of water. She let out a scream and jumped back with an offended look. The bystanders laughed out loud, one man patting David on the back for his cunning move.

She glanced at a woman drawing water beside her. She gently took the bucket from her and filled it to the brim. David, looking away as he chuckled with the people around him, never saw it coming.

Drenched, he turned around and looked at her with surprised eyes, desperately trying to ignore the cheers and laughter of her victory. "Why you little scoundrel," he said, slipping his hands underneath the water. He splashed the water back at her, hitting her along with the woman beside her.

Infuriated, the woman seized her pail from Emily's hands and filled it. Looking bitterly at the foolish man, she threw the water at him.

He dodged.

The wall of water hit a slave, who quickly retaliated by splashing water back at her with the help of his two partners.

Emily assisted her in fighting back, showering them as they hurled buckets of water at them. She saw the street, wet with all the spilled water, glisten as the liquid sparkled in the sun. It amazed her that mature adults, seen by the eyes of her generation as only mundane characters of history, could be so playful. Then she felt someone tap her shoulder. She turned around without thinking.

The warm water showered her face.

She stumbled back and lost her balance, falling halfway into the fountain.

With an embarrassed shout, she leapt back to her feet and glared back at her snickering husband. The water felt good, but it was the principle of not being taken advantage of that compelled her revenge. "You'll pay for that," she declared.

Turning around, she sucked in a mouthful of water and looked back at him.

He cautiously backed away, still chuckling.

Trying not to laugh herself, she ran after him.

He ran down the city street, dodging pedestrians, stepping stones, and a cart full of wheat. After a short while, thinking he was safe ahead, he stopped and turned around.

Too soon.

She spat half the water out on his face before he could duck for cover.

She gripped his arm, but he wrenched free and rushed away with mocking laughter.

He squeezed through a tiny crack between two buildings and slipped out on another road. Knowing that she was right behind, he didn't look back. As soon as he did, she would squirt him with the rest and the battle, as petty as it was, would be lost. He hated losing to her and he wasn't going to let it happen at any cost. She would have to—

"Hey!" he shouted as she yanked him back by his tunic.

She pulled him around and sprayed him in the face again.

"Salve, meus optimam feminam et viram!" a voice bellowed out.

Emily spun around to see a fully decorated Roman Soldier with a friendly smile. Regardless of his cordiality, he seemed unimpressed at their childish behavior. Suddenly feeling stupid, she let go of David and swallowed the rest of the water in her mouth.

"Quid estne tuus hodie?" the Roman asked. David only grinned as his wife anxiously squirmed beside him. An uneasy silence fell as both sides waited for the other to speak.

Emily punched her husband in the ribs. "Say something!"

"Something," he smartly replied, entirely relaxed and unconcerned.

She nervously glanced back at the soldier. He crossed his arms and gave them a scrutinizing look. He was becoming irritated. *Fine!* she thought. *No help from him!*

Remembering some of the words she had heard, she stepped up to him and said, "Adiuva me!"

The alarmed soldier pushed her aside and lunged at David.

Before he knew it, her husband was pinned against a wall with a knife drawn at his throat. "Oh God! What did you say!" he screamed, trying to keep the knife from cutting his neck.

Emily panicked. "I don't know!"

The soldier shouted out several sentences that were too fast for him to comprehend. He struggled to breathe, but the man's weight against his chest was too heavy. The blade felt cold against his skin. With any more pressure, it would sink right through his skin. "Quick! Say something!"

"What!" Emily implored, covering her face with her hands in disbelief.

"Anything!" he ordered, barely managing to squeeze the word through his throat.

She looked around for help. All she received were the curious stares of spectators as they watched the drama unfold. She desperately looked back at her husband. "Anything!"

David pressed his knee into the soldier's shiny breastplate, frantically trying to force him away. But it seemed that the more he struggled, the harder he pressed. "That's not funny right now!" he choked.

In tears of despair, Emily threw her arms up in hopelessness. "I'm sorry!"

"That's okay," he said through clenched teeth as he stared his attacker in the eyes. The burly man held him in place without mercy. His breath smelled like rotten fish and his face was as dirty as an occupied flower pot. "Say 'non'!"

"Non?" she said. "Non! Non!"

The soldier turned and gave her a bewildered look. Without thinking, she ran up and pulled him back from David. Her exhausted husband breathed a sigh of relief as he stumbled away from the wall, grasping at the indented blade mark on his neck.

"Non!" Emily scolded, angrily staring into the soldier's confused eyes as she wagged her finger at him. "Bad! Very bad! Non! Now get lost!" She waved her hands at him to leave. "Shoo!"

Not wanting any more trouble, the perplexed soldier slipped his knife back into its scabbard and walked away. Halfway out of view, he stopped and turned around.

"Scram! Beat it!" she commanded.

Like a guilt ridden puppy that was caught digging up flowers, he turned his head and took an intersecting road.

"What was that all about!" David exclaimed. "What on earth did you say to him?"

"Don't look at me! You're the one who started all of this!"

"I did not!"

"Who started that fiasco at the fountain?"

"You! . . . Oh wait," he realized with great pain in his voice. "You're right. That was me." He hung his head down in embarrassment. There was no way around it. She had won this one by a long shot.

With a victorious smile, Emily embraced him and planted a kiss on his cheek. "You win some, you lose some."

Normally he would've pouted. But after being saved by her from an enraged guy with a deadly weapon, he felt inclined to be a fair sport. "I didn't mean for any trouble," he said.

"Yes you did!" she admonished. She laughed at him and sat down against the wall. She was tired, out of breath and hungry. She needed a moment to recharge.

He sat down beside her and rested his head against hers. For what felt like the first time since he woke up that morning, he let his body relax and heart rate slow to under one hundred and twenty beats a minute. The heat was unbearable, yet he snuggled close to her anyway. "I love you," he admitted, suddenly feeling soft.

Emily giggled and shook her head. "You're hopeless," she said as she watched the busy street. The bystanders, now bored, started back to their chores and left the two foreigners alone. Among the noise of clamoring hammers from inside the shops and the squeaking of wheels from the passing carts, shouting could be heard. An argument from just behind the wall ensued, hot-tempered and more passion than she had ever heard before.

"Do you hear that?" she asked.

David perked up. Listening carefully, a smile came to his face. "I can't believe it," he said, standing up.

"What?"

He grabbed her hand and pulled her to her feet. "I know where we are! Quick! This way!" he exclaimed, excitedly leading her up the road.

XIV

They rushed down the side street and turned into the city's forum. They stopped and stared at the sight in awe. Ahead of them were several detailed statues of famous politicians and military leaders that stood proudly against the hot sun. Behind them was an open plaza that stretched for several hundred feet. It was tightly bordered by six temples, a basilica, baths, and government offices. Civic leaders mingled with merchants and other important citizens, making sure that their popularity remained intact.

The yelling they had heard came from the side of the forum, where a man and a woman argued with each other in front of a judge who sat on a tall platform. A massive crowd surrounded them, eagerly taking in the words of their heated fight.

"The birth of public relations!" David said with a smile.

"A debate!" Emily cried. "A real, live debate!" She ran forward, taking him with her as she pushed her way through the crowd to get a closer look.

The woman was quiet as the man, apparently the plaintiff, scolded her and belittled her in front of everyone. She politely let him take his turn, even though her anger was growing at his outlandish remarks.

"What's he saying?" Emily asked.

"He's accusing her of cheating him out of his money. She apparently sold him an expensive piece of pottery and he says that it was poor quality."

The judge granted the merchant her turn. With a firm voice, she stated the facts she knew of and the man's actions as she witnessed them. She had barely said a few sentences before her opponent interjected, rudely denying her accounts. She waited patiently for him to settle down before talking again. She ignored the occasional jeers from some of the men in the crowd as she explained her case.

David scratched his head. “I think that she’s saying that she used a certain clay and the reason that it broke is because the customer dropped it.”

Amongst the taunting from much of the crowd, the woman spoke as loudly as she could without being disrespectful to the judge. Emily was impressed with her strength, wondering if she would ever be able to stand such humiliation and still appear so elegant.

Finally, the judge raised his hand and, nearly laughing, gave his ruling. Looking at the defendant with gleeful eyes, he said, “Tu rem non probias!”

David groaned. “He says that she has nothing to prove herself with.” He watched in disappointment as she dropped her shoulders and looked at the ground in embarrassment.

“Sed,” the judge continued, now glaring at the plaintiff. “Tu quamquam rem non probias et tu est mendax!”

Several cries of displeasure sounded among the plaintiff’s supporters. The accuser stared back at the judge with enraged eyes, insulted at being called a liar.

The merchant was quickly acquitted, despite the unfair effort against her.

“And she won,” David said.

Emily, with a smile across her face, shook her head in disbelief and wonder. Justice, though rare from what she knew, managed to exist in a world thousands of years apart from theirs, where the courts were still severely corrupted.

The sound of music played from the other end of the forum. With the trial over, they walked over to the group of travelling musicians, playing cheerful music with their shiny lyres, wooden flutes, and decorative tambourines. While not deviating from their musical accords, they exchanged friendly glances with their audience.

"How do you like it?" David asked. He seemed perplexed by the sounds the instruments made. They didn't play the way they looked.

Emily tilted her head. "I've never heard anything like it before," she admitted, mesmerized. From the films that she had seen, Hollywood had always portrayed ancient Rome as having an eerie, setback type of music. But this music was lively and exciting with a romantic edge. The style was entirely different from anything she could've ever imagined. "It's rhythmic," she said at last. "It has sort of a dancing feel to it."

"I think so too," he said, reaching for her hand.

She fearfully glanced back at him as he gently set his other hand on her side. "What are you doing?"

"Care for a little waltz in an ancient world?"

She let out a nervous laugh. "These people think that we're strange enough. If we start—"

Without a care, he led her into a gentle whirl, ignoring her protest. She grudgingly went along. The musicians only added to her worry when they played their melody more intensely with their notes sweeping up the scale and then trickling back down against contrasting percussion.

As the spectators around them grew larger in number, he shifted back and twirled her around. He brought her back to him as he lifted her arms into the air. She stared into his enraptured eyes, still trying to distance herself from his audacity. But a reprise later she had fallen for him as she gazed lovingly at him.

"You're insane," she finally said.

"I know," he acknowledged, quickening his moves. He let go of her hand and twisted around, lifting her arm into the air as she twirled about.

She let out a laugh as she collapsed back into his arms. People were watching them, but she could care less about their curious glances and offending stares. She was having fun and for the first time since she woke up that morning, she didn't feel worried. She wondered what had made her feel so anxious in the first place.

David spun her around once more. Then, leaning against her, he let himself fall to his knees as he gazed into her warm eyes. Following the ambient melody, she slipped her hand under his chin and guided him back up to take her in his arms once more. He brought her into a convoluting pattern, lightly skipping over the ground as they moved.

The glowing sun beat their skin with its hot rays. The sweat trickled down David's face as he held on to her sticky hand and moist side. Her face was red with the hot fervor of energy as the perspiration made her body feel wet and icky, but she was too enraptured to even notice. They only realized that they were together, their only obligation for the moment.

They danced a few minutes longer before the music finally stopped. Laughing like children, they let go of each other and stood back, letting the faint breeze cool their steaming bodies. The spectators around them cheered and chuckled at their artistic feat, though the musicians appeared somewhat perturbed about having the focus of attention taken away from them.

She smiled as she took his hand once more. "What else is here?" she said, eager to explore the ancient city. There was so much to see and do! She couldn't bear the idea of missing any of it.

With a happy grin, he led her down towards the road, passing busy people, running around with scrolls of paper that held records, and the tremendous Temple of Jupiter, standing tall and looming over the opened plaza, on their way out.

They started down another street, lined on both sides with modest houses and cozy apartments. The sun was slowly sinking over the ocean, letting the blue sky fade into an evening curtain of faint yellow and soothing orange. Puffy clouds, darkening with moisture as they grew from the humid afternoon winds, drifted in from the sea, occasionally covering the land with a cooling shade.

Emily watched as people returned to their homes from their jobs. After a long day, a man wearily stumbled towards his door, looking as if he were in bad need of peace and quiet so he could rest, only to be bombarded by his wife and three children, all joyful to see him. Then, seeing another man in the middle of the street beat his own son with a rod as his wife begged him to stop, she cringed. "That's terrible," she said, the sadness cracking her voice.

David froze and watched with a solemn face. The child wiggled free from his father's grip and retreated to his mother. The father, irate, threw his stick down and scolded the two of them before storming back into his dwelling. He heard Emily suspire forlornly. "It could be worse. He has the right to kill either one of them for any reason."

"What?"

"Patria potestas. This world isn't always as civilized as history makes it out to be," he said grimly. He started walking again, but took a left at the next intersection, not wanting to go past the abusive father's apartment. The road was quiet and the houses were more upscale, yet an occasional shack still stood between two rich homes and kept diversity alive in the neighborhood.

As they strolled past one home where the door was open, curiosity urged them to stop to peek in. Thinking that an innocent look wouldn't harm anyone, they did.

David pushed the door open a little more and poked his head inside. He gasped at the sight of the elaborate atrium. The ceiling met the brightly painted wall with a flamboyant border of carved stone. A shrine set up in the corner, with a roof held up by miniature columns, paid homage to the household god. In the center of the room was a marble-sided impluvium that collected the rainwater that fell through the opening in the ceiling. "This is amazing," he said, entranced as he stepped in.

"David!" Emily said, appalled. Who were they to just walk inside someone else's home? *This is none of my business*, she stubbornly thought as she watched him walk inside. Then she saw the intricate interior and her wonder made her second guess. *But it wouldn't hurt as long as no one found out. Why not?* Ignoring the little pinch from her conscience, she decided to explore.

She was mesmerized by the complex designs of the tiled floor. A line of light blue tile rested where the wall met the ground. She followed him as he quietly slipped down a hallway and out into a peristylium. She instantly found herself back outside in a flowering garden with a pond nestled in the middle. A colonnade of white pillars surrounded the beautiful place with great finesse. The ceiling was opened to the cobalt sky, the drifting clouds flaming with orange and red as the sun's last light was disappearing from over the sea. "Unbelievable," she said, watching a bird land on a tree branch beside her.

"Check this out." He pulled off a bundle of ripened grapes from a vine that climbed up one of the columns.

"Food!" she exclaimed, darting over to him. They sat on the ground and shared the cluster, savoring every grape for its delicate flesh and sugary juice. After a few minutes, each and every single one of the tiny fruits had been devoured.

David crawled over to the pond and looked at his reflection, barely seeing it as the sky above him darkened with the onset of night. He could barely make out the shadow on his face from the whiskers he hadn't shaved in over—

"Hey!" he cried, shielding himself.

It was too late. Emily had splashed him and once again, leaving the top of his tunic soaked. She sat back and laughed at her little victory as he glared at her. He wasn't quite in the mood for another game that would likely end up in total disaster.

"I should throw you in for that," he said.

"You wouldn't have the guts to," she confidently asserted.

He shook his head in surrender. "Now I have to wear wet clothes again. And I didn't even do anything to deserve it!"

"Well," she said with a playful grin. "You don't actually have to wear anything you don't want to." He raised an eyebrow at her. "Hmm?" she asked, crouching up to him as she began to pull down her tunic from her shoulder.

Are you serious? he wondered. *Or is this another cruel setup? You're just dying to push me into that pond, aren't you*? Not wanting to take any chances, he boldly dared her, " . . . You first."

With an alluring smile, she slowly slipped her arms around him and let him stare into her sensuous eyes. "But of course! However, I was hoping that you might want to help me."

XV

"Make sure that you unplug that," a nurse ordered her colleague. He slipped back the lock on the IV cord, letting the healing medicine flow from the bag.

Mrs. Shanahan watched over her son, ignoring the chaos as the hospital staff tried to settle him into the new room. His wife rested in the next bed over, unconscious and unresponsive. How she longed for everything to be a bad dream. They were too young for this to happen to them. It wasn't fair. It wasn't right. It wasn't supposed to be.

Her husband watched Mrs. Dennison with worry as she sat next to Emily, lovingly holding her hand and staring at her as if she were in a trance. She didn't seem pleased with the idea of David sharing the same room with her daughter and all of the unfortunate commotion that came with it. He could hear the rain pattering the window behind him as the afternoon thunderstorm roared outside. *At least the weather fits the occasion*, he sadly thought.

Sarah Dennison stood next to her boyfriend, holding onto his arm as she gazed at her dying sister with tears rolling down her puffy cheeks. She was a pretty woman with dark hair and blue eyes that looked liked her sibling's, only they were tired and bloodshot. The long flight from Seattle had been horrible. While there were no delays, it was the constant worrying that nagged her. The man whom she was traveling with hadn't helped out much either when he simply left her alone with her feelings. To make matters worse, her brother-in-law had been brought into the room, destroying the privacy that she needed. She wanted to be with her family and spend some private moments alone with her sister, not with her brother-in-law lying in the next bed with his emotional family crooning over him.

"The brakes!" the nurse yelled to her associate.

He quickly slammed his foot on the lever attached to the wheel. "Check," he said.

David's sister stood next to his mother, gently caressing his face. "Oh David," she cried, her voice cracking with forlornness.

Mrs. Shanahan put her arm around her. "It's going to be okay, sweetie. It's going to be okay."

Doctor Maloney briskly strode through the doorway armed with his stethoscope and clipboard. The troubling news that he was about to bring was written all over his face. He came to Emily's bedside and checked her pulse. With great tenderness, he rested his hand on her arm and stared at her swollen face. "Mr. and Mrs. Dennison," he managed to say. "I have the results from the scan we took at six." He turned and looked at them with sympathetic eyes. "They aren't what we had hoped for."

Mr. Dennison felt his heart sink into his stomach. His wife grabbed onto him with a fearful grip, not wanting to hear what was about to be said but knowing that she had too.

"Oh God!" a voice cried out.

A young woman ran into the room and collapsed at David's side, bitterly weeping as she clutched his arm and stared at him with despair. "Why!" she demanded. "Why!"

All eyes watched her hug her dear brother. She seemed so lost and afraid, yet innocent and undeserving of such painful torment, as they all were.

With a bitter scowl, Sarah suddenly stormed out of the room, ignoring the worried looks from her family as she rushed past them. Her boyfriend shrugged and followed her out.

Once out in the hall, she placed her hand over her eyes and felt more tears starting to build up within her eyes. She wanted to leave. She simply wanted to leave and go home where everything would be fine and secure. But, with a heavy heart, she knew that things wouldn't be that way, no matter where she went. Her big sister, the woman who had nearly raised her, was slowly drifting away before her eyes and no one else seemed to even care.

"Honey," her boyfriend said, gently placing his hand on her shoulder. "It's tough. I know." She turned around and glared at him with hurting eyes.

What would you know! her mind screamed, almost forcing the words onto her tongue. Here he was, prancing around and the least concerned, letting her fall apart as she watched her sister die, and the arrogant jerk thought he was qualified enough to tell her that he knew exactly how she felt?

She crossed her arms and turned away. "Do you even care?" she snapped.

"Of course I care!" he exclaimed.

She wanted to roll her eyes and laugh at him, but it was the last thing that she felt like doing. She longed to be held in his arms and rest her head on his chest as she cried. She needed to be comforted and she had to hear that things, one way or another, would be okay. At the same time, she felt selfish for wanting the pleasure of love and company while everyone was suffering so horribly, especially her sister.

Her boyfriend threw his hands up in the air. "I'm sorry!" he cried. "What do you want me to do? I'm not God! I can't make her better!"

She took in a deep breath and held her tears, not wanting to cry in front of him. He didn't seem to realize what was happening, let alone be warned. This was just an inconvenient field trip for him and he couldn't possibly be less sympathetic towards her. She wondered why he had even decided to come with her in the first place.

"Fine," he declared. "If you need to be alone, I understand that." With that, he lifted his head and walked away.

She fell against the wall and watched him disappear down the corridor. *Please don't go. Please don't leave me*, she thought, suddenly feeling very alone. A moment later, he was gone. "Shoot," she said with a sigh of defeat.

"Sarah?" a timid voice asked.

She slowly turned to see her younger brother staring back at her, the hope all but vanished from his eyes. He was a tall man with thin, brown hair and a modest mustache. Despite their long history of sibling rivalry, he was always the one she could depend on at times like these. She wished that he would've been the one sitting next to her on the flight instead of her fair-weather friend, but he had been stuck in the back of the plane due to over booking. Sadly, however, she sensed that what he had to tell her would be anything but comforting.

"What's wrong?" she asked.

He gently put his arm around her and led her away from the wall. "How about if we find a place to sit down? Its rather—"

She twisted away and shot a stubborn look at him. "Tell me what's happening to Emily," she insisted.

He sighed and let his shoulders drop, realizing that there would be no way of making the truth easier for her to hear. "The bleeding hasn't slowed and the pressure is getting worse. She has only a few hours before she won't . . ." He glanced down at the floor, searching for the words and courage that he so desperately needed. ". . . she won't be able to breath on her own."

Sarah felt absolutely nothing. His words had hit her with total apathy, defying all the logical senses of despair that she knew she should be feeling. Instead, it was as if nothing was wrong. His words hadn't registered. "She won't be able to breath?" she calmly asked.

Michael nodded. "Mom and dad want to let her go—"

"What!" she screamed.

Now it slammed her. She felt as if she were being crushed to death under a pile of bricks, unable to move as the air was forced out of her lungs.

"But they—"

She pushed him aside and rushed back down the hall. She blasted into the room with clenched teeth and eyes full of fury. She glared at her two parents and shouted, "You will not allow her to die!"

"Sarah—" Mrs. Dennison started.

The tears flowed from her eyes and her voice quivered with fear as she pointed at her and said, "She's my sister and you have no right to take her from me! Do you understand?"

Her father rushed to embrace her. He flung his arms around her and held her as tightly as he could. "We're going to use the respirator, honey. We're not letting her go without a fight. It's okay. We're not giving up." She rested her face against his shoulder and cried. "There's still time yet," he insisted.

She pushed herself away from him. "Yet?" she innocently asked, the pain trembling in her voice.

"Sweetheart," her mother soothed, placing a hand on her shoulder. "We're here for her and we're going to try to do everything that we can. We have to be understanding, though, and we can't make her suffer. Eventually, we're going to have to do what's best for her. But for right now, let's—"

"No!" Sarah snapped, angrily glaring at her mother with furious eyes. How could she even propose such an idea? Emily would want everyone to do everything they could to keep her alive, no matter how long or painful it would be. Hearing the words from her mother sounded like a cry of surrender. Would she give up that easily? She wanted to scream at her with every molecule of air that she could manage with her lungs, but she forced herself to be placid and calm instead. "How can you think about that? What's best for her is to keep her alive until she wakes up."

Michael said, "There is a very good chance that she might not—"

She whirled around at him and shouted, "We do not know that for certain!"

"Do you realize what is happening here?" her mother asked.

"Yes! And if she needs to use a respirator, we're putting her on one and you're not taking it off! Think about someone else for once in your life rather than yourself!"

Mrs. Dennison gently let go of her as she moved to cover her face. Hiding the tears, she stumbled back onto a chair and wept silently.

Sarah could feel herself breaking down inside. She knew that her mother loved Emily more than any other mother ever could. She realized that she had been cruel to say that to her, but she wasn't going to let Emily just disappear.

She glanced at the Shanahan family, watching her family drama unfold before their eyes. They were very concerned, but were quiet out of respect. They knew it wasn't their place to get involved.

In Mr. Shanahan's eyes, it had been a miracle that Mrs. Dennison had allowed them to move David into the room and he wasn't going to jeopardize it unless he had to. Everyone was tense and ready to pounce on each other, if they hadn't already. He had no doubt that his family would get the same way as time went on.

Sarah sat down at her sister's bedside and held her lifeless arm. *He's not right!* she thought. *How would Michael know anything! She's going to wake up!* She stared at Emily's face. The images from several years ago of being carried by her through the hallway of their house on Saturday mornings flashed by in her mind. She remembered how she would play board games with her when she was a child and the advice she gave her about the boy she had a crush on in the fourth grade. Then there was the deep sadness she had felt when she moved off to college, only coming in to visit for the holidays and a few weeks in the summer. Other than her faint pulse and shallow breathing, her sister remained motionless. She suddenly found herself wondering if Michael was right. *She'll come out of this . . . Won't she?*

"Pardon me," someone asked. She looked up to see a young man in the doorway, his face full of uncertainty and sympathy. The stranger, dressed in a sopping, black trench coat and with his hair matted from the rain, looked more like a drowned rat than a visitor. "Ah . . . I'm terribly sorry. I can see that I've come at a bad time. I'll be back later." With a shy nod, he excused himself and dashed out of sight.

XVI

Emily snuggled closer to him, shivering from the cold. The tunic could hold in only so much warmth from the cool night that hovered above them in the garden. The streets outside the walls of the peristylium were silent with only an occasional traveler passing by. Far in the distance, she could hear a dog howling. She looked up at the dark sky with awe. The misty clouds occasionally broke to reveal a thin sliver of the yellow moon, but kept the light of the stars hidden. "It's so dark," she sleepily said.

David, too tired to speak, only groaned.

"I wonder what time it is. Maybe it's already morning and—"

A sudden rustling in the bushes caught her attention. She felt her heart skip a beat as she heard a coarse voice whispering along with the sound of approaching footsteps.

"David," she warned, rousing him from his sleep. "David. Someone's coming."

"Hmm?" he replied.

Without warning, a bright light flashed on from ahead, showering the garden with a fiery glow. Two slaves darted through the bushes towards their unwelcome guests.

David jumped up from his slumber and grabbed her hand as he scrambled to his feet.

"Pestis!" one of the slaves cried, swiping a rake at them.

They dodged to the left and ran through a patch of bushes.

"How do we get out!" Emily shouted.

"I don't know!" He desperately looked ahead. He saw their only hope at escape. It was a was a narrow gate that lead out to the street.

Unexpectedly, another slave, brandishing a flaming torch, jumped out from a bush in front of them. "Vos sunt moriturunt!" he screamed.

David slammed his foot against his shin, knocking the man to the ground.

"Watch out!" Emily hollered.

Too late.

The other slave had his arms around David's neck as he tried to strangle him.

David gouged his elbow into the man's stomach, throwing him off his back. Grasping Emily's arm, he ran to the gate. He lifted the latch and pushed, but the door wouldn't budge. "Oh crap," he growled.

The shouting slaves were closing in. They had trapped their prey like a cat fixes a mouse into a corner. Without mercy, they hurled themselves at the two intruders.

The force was just enough to push the door out. David and Emily fell out onto the hard, cold road. The bitter slaves stood their ground as they snarled insults and brutal words at them.

Emily stood back up and brushed the dust off her tunic. Her weary husband, bleeding at the knee, climbed to his feet and started to stumble away. She shot the slaves a dirty look before turning around and running after him. They turned down a side street and stopped to catch their breath.

"For heaven's sake!" she exclaimed. "We were just looking around! . . . And perhaps doing a few other things, but still!"

"That one guy said that he was going to kill us!" David said with an indignant scowl. "How dare that lousy knave even thought of that! We could've been guests for all he knew!"

They let a moment pass before they started walking. As they strolled down the quiet street, he looked down at his bare feet and let out a sad sigh. "I never put my sandals back on."

With a chuckle, she said, "Poor baby. Did you want me to go back and get them for you? Of course I might be killed in some horrible way, but at least I could try."

"Would you mind?"

She didn't answer. The sight of such a large city at sleep had stolen her attention away from him. No carts, horses, arguing merchants, or children playing in the streets. Everyone was asleep in their dwellings. Despite the eerie clouds looming overhead and the cold air, things felt very peaceful. *This would never happen in New York*, she realized.

They turned onto a narrow road tucked between two tall buildings. They could hear laughter from the intersecting street ahead, accompanied by angry voices. A white dog, walking away from all of the excitement, languidly made its way towards them. Emily knelt down and held her hand out to the small canine. It sniffed her fingers, then licked them hungrily. "Oh, how cute," she said.

"I think it's trying to eat you."

"Do you have to spoil everything?" she asked, giving him a spiteful look.

"Well," he quickly said, trying to defend himself. "I was merely pointing out the very fact that it was—"

His words were cut short by a sharp, piercing scream.

The dog scampered past Emily with a forlorn whimper. She stood up and watched him disappear into the darkness, then looked back at the crossing road.

David cautiously moved forward, not knowing whether or not he wanted to find out what the trouble was. She stayed behind him, feeling the sudden sting of her old fear she had when she first entered the city. Now the feeling was as fresh and strong as ever.

He walked out into the intersection and glanced over at a brothel that was a few buildings down. A woman held her torn stollam in her hands as two soldiers harassed her. Her face was covered with sticky sweat and hot tears. "Parce!" she begged, staggering away from them.

One of the soldiers grabbed her by the strap of her tunic and pulled her towards him.

"Minime!" David cried, stepping forward.

Emily grabbed him by the shoulder, but he slipped away. "Don't!" she implored, watching him storm towards the soldiers.

"Vos missimus eam!" he commanded. He marched towards them like an invincible robot. The two men only glared at him as one drew his knife from its holder. He paid no attention. "Iam! Ex ite huc!"

Emily desperately cried, "What are you saying to them!"

"Stay back. Everything's going to be okay," he assured without looking back. He stared at the two soldiers with a bitter face. "Vos missimus eam!" he repeated, pointing to the distraught woman.

The soldiers broke out into laughter. The one with the knife seized the woman's arm.

He jumped in front of her and tried to wedge his hand underneath the soldiers.

With furious eyes, the other soldier poised a fist at him.

"No!" Emily cried, throwing herself in front of him. The soldier kept his fist in position, ready to punch her if he had to. "Non! Non!"

"Tu estne non Caledoniicus?" the first soldier demanded to know.

"Don't say anything!" David warned.

"Tu estne non Caledoniicus?" he ordered again.

Worried and scared, she asked, "What's he asking! What should I say!"

"Ah . . . Ita vero."

"Ita vero!" she cried.

"Mendax!" the soldier shouted, grabbing her red hair and pulling her back.

"Stop!" David hollered. He helplessly watched his wife as she was thrown to the ground.

She jumped back to her feet, only to be slammed in the side of the face by the soldier's fist. She collapsed onto the road again, moaning in pain.

David kicked at the soldier as his partner held him back. "Tu est furcifer!" he shouted.

"Minime," said the soldier, stepping up to him. He looked intently into his eyes like an angry wolf staring down a defenseless rabbit. Then he briskly shot his knee up into his groin.

David screamed out as the pain surged through his abdomen and into his chest. He felt the air rush out of his lungs and his nerves tingle. He glanced back at the soldier just in time to see the fist rushing towards his nose.

Emily felt a gentle hand on her shoulder and looked up to see a fuzzy image the woman with the torn stollam. With her head throbbing with pain, it took a moment for her eyes to focus. "Who are you?" she asked.

She heard a sudden grunt and saw David fall to the ground, the blood pouring from his nostrils and lips. The woman turned around and ran away into the dark night.

"Get out of here!" her husband shouted.

"No!" she instinctively shot back. She carefully stood back up.

The two soldiers picked him up and forced his hands behind his back. One bound them together with a thick rope as the other pressed the tip of the knife against his spine.

Emily ran up to him and clasped her hands around his face. “Honey! Where are they taking you to? What’s going—”

She never saw it coming.

The soldier plowed his elbow into her stomach and shoved her back onto the road. Her head hit the stones with brutal force, nearly knocking her out. Dazed and in pain, she remained motionless as her husband was forced off.

“Barbarus!” the soldier shouted to her.

“I love you!” David exclaimed as the soldiers led him away.

She let the tears flow from her beautiful blue eyes as she listened to the voices grow distant. After a few moments, they were gone. She shivered in the chilly air and felt the blood running from the side of her head become cold against her skin. “I love you too,” she barely managed to whisper. Tired, afraid, and disoriented, she closed her eyes and wept.

Without warning, she heard a soft rumble. The ground beneath her softly trembled, causing a few mere pebbles around her to roll out of their place. A short while passed before the shaking stopped. She fearfully wondered if it was a prelude to what might come next, but then figured that it was just a harmless tremor.

She forced herself up, wincing as she felt the aching pain all over her body. She looked around at the dark buildings around her. The only sounds she could hear came from the harlots and their clients inside brothel. Their sultry, libidinous cries made her stomach turn with disgust. She limped away without hesitation.

She went down any street she came to, frantically searching for her husband. Before long, she found herself in an open square. Not a single light shone from the windows of the surrounding buildings. She frowned as she felt a tiny raindrop hit her shoulder. A fine drizzle floated down from the sky all around her. Tired, she walked over to a fountain and could hear her footsteps echo off the walls of the plaza.

Exhausted and weary, she sat down on the edge and covered her face from the cold with her hands. She moaned from all of the aching and closed her eyes, wanting to go to sleep. *Are you crazy?* her mind admonished. *You can't go off to dreamland now! You've got to find him! He's in danger and so are you! You have to get out of here!* She shook the thoughts out of her head, then groaned from the pain of it. *Why do we have to run away?* she wondered.

She took in a deep breath and made herself stand back up. She turned around and looked at the flamboyant statue of a woman spilling water from a heavy jar. Beneath her was an elaborate mosaic with Pompeiian borders of brown boxed insignias of—

Pomeii, she fearfully realized. She had studied about it in an art class during her senior year of college. For weeks on end she had heard about the city that had an artistic world of wonder within itself, only to be completely hidden from the rest of the world until only a few centuries before her time.

She looked up at the gigantic mountain that towered over the town. She shivered at the sight of it. Its magnificent prestige meant nothing to her now. She knew that she had to find David and leave the city as soon as she could.

She turned away and started to walk towards the next street. Slowly, her pace quickened to a light jog, then to frantic running.

There was little time left.

XVII

Emily rushed down the street as fast as she could. By the time she had made it back to the forum, which was dark and deserted, the gentle precipitation had changed to pouring rain. The streets turned into mini viaducts as they filled with water. The heavy drops pelted the buildings with a deafening roar.

A sudden clap of thunder made her shriek and duck underneath the stone arch that stood as a gateway into the other part of the city. She shivered as the cold water flowed over her feet and the howling wind swept around her body. She took a moment to catch her breath, then trudged through the raising water a little more before reaching the temple.

She cut through the forum and to the adjacent road. Her heart raced with terror. She had to get David back before it was too late. *Where could he be!* she thought. She kicked up small waves of muddy water as she ran, figuring that she was going eastward, away from the coast.

All at once, a crushing pain ran up her calf as her foot slammed into a stepping stone. She fell face-first into the water. It was so deep that she was certain that she would have drowned if her head had hit the road hard enough. She forced herself back up and continued down the street, now limping painfully and unaware of her bleeding toes.

Another flash of lighting lit up the street as a beggar man threw himself out in front of her. "Babae!" he shouted in rough voice. His hair was sloppy and his face was dirty and in need of a shave. She felt that she probably appeared just as wretched. He shot out his hand and yelled at her again.

She screamed and cowered away.

The man only laughed, watching her move around him with tears of frustration in her eyes. Shivering, she hurried on, thinking only of her husband.

She staggered on for nearly a half mile, each step sending a searing pinch through the nerves in her leg. She didn't care. She wouldn't let herself be concerned with any lesser matter than rescuing him. The buildings on the right suddenly gave way to a small garden.

Without warning, she heard a haughty chuckle. She glanced over to a gloomy structure without any windows that stood in painful contrast against the luscious vegetation around it. Three soldiers stood at the entrance, conversing lightly to pass the time. They were protected from drenching rain and brutal wind by a long overhang. The guard held a lantern and a strap of keys at his side, smiling pleasantly at his two companions.

A soldier suddenly looked over at her direction.

She hid herself behind a pedestal. *Shoot! He saw me! What's he going to do? I'm just minding my own business, right?* She closed her eyes and tried to forget her thoughts and just let the time pass, but the fear chilled her blood and made her tremble.

Then, to her horror, she heard footsteps. They were coming towards her, cruelly slow and leisurely. She could hear his sword clanging against its holder, the noise growing louder as he approached.

He walked right past the pedestal, then stopped and whirled around.

This is it! she fearfully thought.

"Vale!" the man called out, waving back at the soldier with the lantern. Laughing, he turned back and walked past Emily, ignoring her completely as he shielded himself from the rain with his cape.

She felt the relief wash against her like an ocean wave crashing over a sand castle. She moved her head out just enough to see. She stared at the building, sensing in her gut that David had to be inside. The other soldier shook hands with the guard and left in another direction. With nothing else to do, the man set his lantern on the ground and sat down in his chair. He watched the rain for a few minutes before he closed his eyes and let his head down. He never noticed the red-haired woman in the tunic sneak out from behind the pedestal and tiptoe towards him.

Emily cautiously moved closer to the guard, her eyes fixed on the keys strapped to his waist. She knelt beside him, watching him closely. He seemed to struggle for every breath he took, but kept his eyes closed. Could he be still be awake? No. He had to be sleeping. She glanced down at the keys again. She gave in to her impulse and gently wrapped her fingers around them and lifted them up. There was only a thin, leather strap connecting them to his belt. *Would he wake up if I yanked them off quick enough?* she wondered.

Knowing that she had nothing to lose, she pulled them.

They stuck.

The man jumped awake and glared at her, his eyes full of alarm.

"Oh no." She looked back at him with terror. "Me sorry! My bad!" she cried.

The man lunged at her with a ferocious growl. He squeezed his hands around her neck and pushed her to the ground.

She let out an uncivilized scream, clutching his hair in her hands and forcing his head down onto the stone floor. He groaned sleepily and loosened his grip. She pushed him off of her and ripped the keys free from his belt. She jumped up to the door and slammed the largest key into the slot. She pushed as hard as she could to open the door, allowing her entrance into a dank corridor filled with the miserable groans and agonizing cries of the prisoners who were locked behind heavy gates inside their tiny cells.

She carefully stepped inside and choked on the dank, foul air. "David," she said, inching forward. She slid her hand against the wall for direction, looking ahead into the pitch blackness. "David? Where are—"

She screamed out as the grimy hand wrapped around her ankle.

The prisoner with his arm through the little food door pulled her injured foot out from under her. She fell to the floor and frantically clawed at the hand like a terrified cat.

"Tu iam liberavis eam!" David's voice bellowed from ahead.

The prisoner forced her against the door, crushing her toes against the slimy wood.

"He's got me by the leg!" she cried out. "What should I do?"

"Bite him!"

"I'm not biting that hand! It probably hasn't been washed in a year and who knows where it's been!" she shouted with disgust. "Plus I can't even reach . . . Wait a minute here . . ." She contorted herself towards her ankle and snapped at the hand, but missed only by a few centimeters.

She heard the prisoner grumble discontentedly before he unexpectedly released her. "Oh! He let go of me!" she announced, jumping back to her feet. She moved further down the corridor. "Where are you? I'm about three doors in and—"

Another prisoner's hand latched onto her ankle and knocked her to the ground.

"Oww," she groaned, getting annoyed.

"You're kidding me!" David exclaimed.

"Shut-up! I'm trying to rescue you!" she snarled, gouging her fingernails between the bones of the man's hand.

With a sudden cry of defeat, the prisoner freed her.

She stood back up and pushed her hair back with an angry growl. She hesitantly continued on, hoping that the next guy would keep his hands to himself. "Okay. I'm all right. Do you know where they—"

She felt the fingers slip between her heels.

She kicked them back against the door.

David let out a holler and retreated back into his cell. "For heaven's sake! Why'd you do that for!" he asked, rubbing his injured hand. He leaned against the wall, sitting on the thin layer of straw that was crawling with bugs and a hideous rat.

Trying not to laugh, she forced a key into the hole. It didn't fit, so she tried the next. When the second didn't work, she moved onto the third, then the fourth. "None of these are the right ones."

"Keep trying. You'll find it."

"Well, maybe." She grabbed onto the next key. As she moved it towards the slot, the keys suddenly slipped. "Son of a . . . Er. I won't say it," she said, getting down on her knees to find them.

"It's okay," he happily assured, sounding as if he was off in a world of his own, like he often did. "No one here understands what you're saying besides me."

" . . . Bitch!" she cried, grasping onto the strap of keys.

"Ibi!" a voice screamed from the entrance.

She glanced at the entrance and saw the two soldiers marching towards her. She nervously grabbed a key and tried to find the hole. *This could be the same key as before!* her mind said. *Be quiet!* she thought back. She started to put the key into the slot.

Two strong arms wrapped around her waist and pulled her back.

"Non!" she cried, kicking at her attacker's shins. "Tu est . . . You're a jerk!" She forced her elbows back into the soldier's breastplate. He only laughed as he leaned back and lifted her off the ground. "David! Help!"

"I'm doing everything I can," he said, looking out of his food door. He could barely see the people outside; too far away for him to reach out and trip.

Emily blindly kicked her foot out to the door, pushing the key into the slot with the tip of her sandal. "Ugh! Let go!" she demanded, struggling to wiggle herself free. "Do something David!"

He froze solid for a moment with confusion. Then he did the only thing he could think of. "Uh . . . Everybody cheer! Go Emily! Come on! You can do it! Win the game! Yeah!"

Being held above the floor by a crushing grip, she groaned and rolled her eyes. *If they don't kill him, I will!* she thought.

"Tu est bestia!" the soldier exclaimed. His arms were getting tired and she wasn't letting up. She twisted, kicked, punched and screamed like a stubborn animal unwilling to be tamed.

She threw her head back, hitting the man in the nose.

He screamed out in pain and dropped her.

She scrambled back to the door and wrapped her hand around the key.

Without warning, the other soldier pinned her against the door and shouted into her ear. He punched her in the side and forced her onto her feet by her tunic.

She lifted her knee into his abdomen and turned the key towards her, producing an unlatching clank that was music to her ears.

The soldier doubled over and stumbled away as his partner rushed at her with a dagger.

She didn't have a chance before he forced her against the door with his arm. She fearfully watched him raise the dagger above her.

All at once, the door behind her flung open, throwing her away from the murderous man as he tripped forward. David greeted him with an uppercut to the jaw and pushed him onto the ground.

He leaped out of his cell and forced the other soldier away from her. "Come on!" he shouted, holding her hand. He turned around and sprinted for the exit.

The soldier with the dagger darted out of the cell and chased after them with his colleague at his side. Neither of them saw the outstretched hands reaching for them from the tiny food doors.

The first soldier crashed to the floor with his partner landing on top of him. They struggled to free themselves, but the prisoners held them in place. They screamed insanely for assistance as they watched their two fugitives run out of sight.

Hand in hand, the two lovers hurried out into the rain, running away from the jail as fast as they could. They feared that someone was already after them.

XVIII

Emily led him down the flooded street as the raindrops pelted them. He fell behind and she had to pull him. "Hurry!"

"Where are we going?"

"We have to get out of the city!" she yelled over the loud gusts of wind.

David suddenly stopped and looked at her. "They're gone. They'll leave us alone."

A tall man in a red cape shouted from ahead, "Ventis celerrime! Sunt est hic!"

Emily took him by the arm and glared into his eyes. "You're the historian here and you can't even figure out where we are!"

The soldier was joined by two others. With their swords drawn, they ran towards them, ready to kill if they had to.

"Oh shoot!" David gasped.

"Come on!" She darted off to the right. Just ahead was a massive arch, possibly their only chance out of the town.

"We're in the Mediterranean somewhere!" David said, running with her. He ignored the soldiers shouting at them as they trudged through the water towards the opening.

"Does Naples 1944 ring a bell in your numb skull by any chance?" she yelled. "Mount Vesuvius? The volcano that everyone thought was dormant until it erupted over an ancient city in the first century?"

He remembered reading about such a town, but never gave it much thought. He suddenly felt queasy and sick inside. Everything had been there in front of him all along and he never stopped to notice!

They ran under the arch and then stopped. They looked at the wall that surrounded them and the seats of the amphitheater that rose above it. They had brought themselves into a fatal trap.

"We're in Pompeii," she sadly explained. She sighed as the soldiers surrounded them, pointing the tips of their swords at their throats. She could see the desire for vengeance scribbled all over their faces. She gripped her husband's hand tighter. "Good morning," she wryly said, "It's August twenty fourth, seventy-nine in the year of our Lord, and we're about to die."

"I'll get us out of this," he reassured, giving a sheepish grin to the soldier in front of him. The man only moved his sword closer to his neck. "Vous sunt noustrimus optissimus amici! Nous—"

"Silentium!" the soldier barked.

"I'm guessing that he just told you to shut-up?"

"Pretty much," he said, gently raising his hands up.

"Now what?"

"I'll go for the guy on the left and you take the one to the right?"

"What about the guy in back?" she asked, trying to look at him without moving her head. He was nuts if he thought they could survive pulling another stupid stunt against three armed men. However, even if they were only locked back up in the jail, they'd still be killed.

"We'll get to him when we come to it."

"You're crazy."

"I know," he said, reaching back down for her wrist. The soldiers glanced at each other with confusion as their captives chatted away, but he didn't let it bother him. "Ready?"

"Ready as I'll ever be," she nervously said.

David let himself fall to the ground, pulling her down with him. He kicked the soldier to the left in the ankle, knocking him over. But before he could get back on his feet, the man rolled on top of him and fought desperately to keep him on the ground.

Emily forced her foot into the other soldier's groin. He screamed as the pain enveloped his body and dropped his sword. She swiped it up and turned around just as the man behind her flung his weapon at her, catching her sword with a bright spark.

The soldier sneered at her as he ripped his weapon back and briskly shot it towards her again.

She dodged aside, barely missing the sharp blade.

There was no time to think before he rushed at her with several quick, deadly thrusts from his sword. She blocked his blade with hers, each clash sending out a spray of shimmering sparks.

She found herself being forced back towards the wall, desperately fighting to keep herself in one piece.

Suddenly, he sprang back and jabbed the sword forward, puncturing her leg with its tip.

David heard the wrenching scream. He looked up at the soldier who was pressing his shoulders into the ground. He grabbed him by the sides of his face and jammed his thumbs into his eyes.

The man hollered out in pain and jumped back.

David leaped to his feet and punched him in the face. The soldier fell back, hitting his head against the wall. He groaned and dropped to his knees, holding his bleeding nose. He was harmless, for the moment.

David wiped the water off his face and whirled around to help Emily, only to meet the third soldier with his knife tightly gripped in his hand and the murder beaming in his eyes. *Oh no*, he thought.

The man started toward him, poised to strike at any moment. He glanced quickly at Emily, on the other side of the amphitheater, who valiantly struggled to fend off her attacker. He looked back at the soldier before him.

"Tu est pestis!" he cried.

"Liberamus nous!" David cried, ordering the man to let them go.

The man suddenly charged at him, screaming like a barbaric warrior.

David grasped his wrist and elbowed him in the ribs, leaving the knife to dangle over his head. The soldier spat in his face and gouged his fist into his stomach. He gasped for air and stumbled back, not letting go of the man's arm.

Several yards away, Emily lifted her sword in front of her just in time to block the side-swiping blow. She swallowed hard, knowing that she would've been done for had she missed.

She dropped to the ground and rolled away from the wall before jumping back up with her weapon poised at the ruthless soldier. He cruelly smiled at her, as if he was certain of a victory.

"Come on!" she dared, gripping the sword with both hands. She noticed now that it was getting lighter out and that she could better see him. A distant rumble of thunder echoed over the city as the rain drops began to lessen. She kept her eyes on the man, just waiting for him to try and strike.

All at once, he lunged at her, wildly flinging his sword in the air and then bringing it down over her.

She caught the blade just inches above her head and pushed it back up. She wasn't giving up without a good fight.

On the other end of the arena, David struggled to breathe as the soldier clutched his throat with one hand and tried to grip his knife with the other. He threw blind punches and didn't even manage to scathe the man. The water on his face was mixed with the blood that seeped from his wounds. Then he saw the knife being raised into the air.

He let go of the hand around his neck and grabbed the soldier's hand. He dug his fingers underneath his grip and tried to get a hold of the knife's handle.

The man growled and brought the knife down on him.

David yanked the knife to the side, flinging it out of the soldier's grasp.

The soldier let go of his neck and frantically tried to reclaim his weapon, but he wasn't fast enough.

David grabbed the knife and twisted it up under his protection plate, slicing the blade into his tender stomach.

The soldier cried out in pain and rolled off him.

David turned him on his side and ripped his sword out of its holder.

He suddenly stopped, his hand resting on the soldier's arm as he gripped his wound with his bloodied hands. *I've killed him!* he fearfully realized. The man could bleed to death before anyone could bring him to a hospital. And even if he did make it to a facility, there was no telling if he would get the treatment he needed and what kind of infection he might get. *Oh dear God, have mercy on us.*

"Tu lerociter!" the soldier screamed at Emily.

She desperately swung her sword back at him, her arms weakening with every move. The weapon felt extremely heavy in her sore hands. She couldn't remember feeling so—

She darted to the left, scrapping her shoulder against the wall.

The soldier's sword slammed onto the ground.

She took her chance.

She hurled her sword at him with all her strength.

He jumped away with a mocking laugh, easily pointing his sword back at her. "Tu est stultissimus femina veniebam!"

"Back at you!" she cried, mightily thrusting her weapon towards him.

He shifted to the right and stabbed his sword forward, cutting into her upper arm.

Emily's mouth dropped open, but no sound came out. She slowly let go of her sword and fell onto her knees, unable to scream from the shock of the stinging pain. She clutched her arm, watching the blood flow out from between her fingers. With eyes filled with forlorn defeat, she looked back up at the soldier.

To her horror, his sword was raised and poised at her neck. "Non! Non!" she begged. Was this it? Was it all supposed to end like this? "Please! I implore! I beg! Non!"

The heartless man plunged the deadly weapon towards her.

David shot his sword over her neck and blocked the descending blade. The soldier glanced at him with eyes full of confusion. "Neccabam tibi virum et iam necco te!" he growled through clenched teeth. "So help me God, I'll kill you!"

The soldier sneered at him as he readied himself for another offensive.

David didn't give him the honor, slashing at him first with wild fury. He fanned his sword at him. His opponent stepped away, confused.

David swiped the sword down and nicked the soldier in the knee. The man shouted out in surprise and fell. He spun around and forced the sword towards his neck, suddenly stopping just before it hit his skin.

The soldier gently released his weapon and looked at him with imploring eyes. He asked for mercy, his honor diminished at his own will in turn for his life. David stared at him with angry eyes. He felt like he could kill him, or anyone who tried to hurt Emily, and walk away perfectly justified. But in his heart, he knew he would be wrong.

"David," Emily meekly said, standing up.

He stood where he was, holding his enemy's life in his hands. The soldier looked down, fearing that he had no way out. The sword shook in his angry conqueror's hands.

"Honey," Emily softly said, placing a hand on his shoulder. The rain had stopped now and the sun's pink glow was shinning through the thin clouds, coating everything in a serene glow of morning, a new day and a new beginning. "Let him go." She leaned her head against his back. "Come on. You can let him alone."

David suddenly threw the sword aside and stood back, covering his mouth as he stood where he was in disbelief of what he had just contemplated and why. There was little guilt, only hurt and shame as he tried to suppress the anger. His breath trembled and a tear trickled down from each eye.

The shocked soldier let out a sigh of relief, but stayed where he was. He looked back up at the merciful foreigner with sad eyes.

"Shh, shh," his wife soothed.

David suddenly stepped towards the man. "Ferte auxilium eius!" he screamed at the top of his lungs, pointing to the wounded man across the arena floor.

The soldier obeyed, climbing to his feet and limping over to help his partners. He and the first man David had wrestled carried the other back out of the gate, leaving the two alone.

"Oh thank God," Emily gasped, collapsing into his arms. He embraced her, careful not to press on her wound. They were bleeding in several places. Old wounds had been reopened or torn off as their entire bodies ached all over from the new ones. They were tired, hungry, and weak. But yet, they still had all they needed as they looked into each other's eyes. "I love you."

"I the same," he said, trying to calm his emotions. They stood together in the amphitheater as the fog from the rain drifted off the wet sand. The clouds ahead were broken and the sun's rays were streaming through, showering the land with its brilliant light. "Thank you for everything."

She lifted her head up and frowned. "We have to get out of here, David. There'll be more soldiers here any moment and if we get caught, we're done for. When Mount Vesuvius erupts and thousands of people die, we'll be trapped inside this city with them. We have to escape!"

XIX

Sarah walked into the waiting room. It was unusually full with three whole families, a few people by themselves, and an old woman sleeping by a magazine stand. She spotted the man in the trench coat by the coffee machine, looking curiously at a cigarette in his hand. He seemed to be trying to divert his attention away from something. But what was it? And how did he know her sister?

She cautiously approached him, wondering if it was her place to even ask him his business. "You said that you were here for Emily?" she asked.

The startled man looked up, and nervously fumbled to put away the cigarette. "Uh, yeah," he said, standing and shaking her hand. "She's my boss and I really care about her. I've just never felt as . . . appreciated as I do now, and it's with thanks to her. I'm very sorry that all of this has happened."

"Thank you," she said, extending her hand to him. "Sarah Dennison. I'm her sister."

He gladly welcomed her tender hand in his. "Nathan Alden. It's a pleasure to meet you, though not under the circumstances," he said, his voice tender and kind.

She plopped herself down in the seat next to him and folded her hands. "So you're into public relations, I take it?"

"Yes. I never went to college, which I'll always regret, and it was incredibly hard to get a decent job in the field. It was your sister who gave me the boost I needed. She strikes me as someone who's confident and not afraid, qualities which are hard to come by without the arrogance she lacks."

"That would be her. I'm not too sure on the lacking of arrogance, but I'd agree with you for the most part," she said with a light chuckle. She sighed and forced a smile, letting her thoughts take her away into her worries as she stared relentlessly at the blank wall ahead. She anxiously gripped the armrest and tried to divert her attention to the other people in the room, but she couldn't After a few moments, she felt brave enough to tell him, "I'm really afraid that something's going to happen to her."

Not knowing how to respond, he only looked at her with eyes that bled sympathy. "I'm sorry. I know it sounds simple to say, but it's all I really know how to." He noticed her hand and her knuckles that were turning white. He gently placed his hand over hers.

"I'm okay," she said, quickly retreating. She didn't want to, but wasn't about to unload everything onto a total stranger either. She knew that human touch could be addicting and to multiply it by the situation wouldn't be the greatest idea. *I can deal with this myself*, she told herself. "But thank you. I noticed that you—"

Michael stormed into the waiting room with his face broken out into a cold sweat. He glanced at his sister with eyes full of fear and hoarsely said, "We need you in there right away."

Sarah leaped from her seat and rushed down the corridor as her heart raced with fright. A nurse standing at the door suddenly stepped in front of her. "We need you to wait out here," she bluntly snapped.

"I'm her sister!" Sarah growled.

"Ma'am," said the nurse while holding up her hand, "it's too crowded in here and we can't—"

Sarah pushed her out of the way and stormed over to Emily's bedside. She grabbed her hand as she watched in horror as Dr. Maloney inserted a thick tube into her mouth. Her mother held her Rosary against her bandaged head and whispered a short prayer.

"Ma'am," Maloney growled, "please get out of the way." He knew that her family wanted to be around her, but if there was any chance in making her live longer, he needed the space to make it happen. He shoved the tube deeper into her throat.

She quickly retreated with a hurt look.

David's sister watched the tragedy unfold with tears in her eyes. Everything had been fine just a few short minutes ago. Then Emily's respiration rate suddenly plummeted, sending Mr. Dennison running off to the nurses in a fit of panic. It was so tragic and—

"Oh God," her mother suddenly gasped. Her son's hand had suddenly moved. The feel of life in his fingers sent a rush of excitement through her. "He's waking up!" she cried.

Without warning, his feet started to quiver. A moment later, his arms were shaking violently as his head shifted back and forth.

She found herself struggling with her husband to keep him from flying out of bed. His body contorted to the left, then back to the right as his limbs moved in all directions.

Maloney tried to ignore the commotion. It only took one wrong move to ruin the procedure and he needed to concentrate. As he slowly fitted the tube in place, a loud scream tore his patience. He whirled around and screamed out, "What is going on!" Then, seeing David's body in a spasm, he choked with fear.

"He's having a seizure!" one of the nurses cried.

"Hold him down and get him—" He felt something warm running down his hands. He glanced back at his patient in utter horror as her blood dribbled out of her mouth. "Oh shit!" he snarled.

"Emily!" Mrs. Dennison shouted.

"Stay back!" Maloney ordered, trying to grip the tube with the slippery blood on his hands. He desperately looked over at a nurse. "Get Johnson in here now!" he shouted.

"What's happening!" Sarah demanded. She lunged forward and touched her swollen face, feeling her feverish heat radiating from her.

"Get away!" he cried, grasping her arm and pushing her back.

"No!" she shouted.

"Sarah!" her father ordered.

She was about to rush forward again when she suddenly felt a firm hand rest on her shoulder. "It's going to be okay," Nathan soothed, so terrified himself that he felt like a hypocrite for saying it.

"He's not breathing!" David's brother shouted.

"Damn it!" Maloney swore. *Stay calm*, he told himself. *You can work this all out. For God's sake, stay calm!* It wasn't working. He could feel the panic rushing through his veins quicker than the adrenaline.

Without warning, Emily started to tremble, her body gently quivering like a shivering child without a blanket in the dead of winter. Everyone watched in terror as she began to gag on the tube and the light shaking grew into massive convulsions.

"Oh God. Oh God. Oh God," Sarah whimpered. The tears welled up in her eyes and distorted the image of her beautiful sibling to a blur of colors. She glanced over at David, his body still shuddering out of control. *Please don't let this happen! Oh God, where are You!* she thought, wanting to scream it out from the top of a mountain.

Maloney couldn't believe his eyes. The tube in Emily's throat was slowly sliding out and back into his hands. And of all times for the husband to need crucial assistance, it had to be now. His patients were fading out right before him. "We need help in here! Where the heck is Johnson!" he screamed.

XX

They ran out into the street, dodging the eager vendors as the began their daily assault of soliciting on the public. Wagons rolled down the road, kicking up trails of dust behind them. All around, the new day was starting as normal as any other. Twenty thousand people were completely oblivious to the massive danger that lurked in the east.

Emily clutched her chest, feeling the impending sense of doom pounding inside of her with every heartbeat. "How do we get out of here?" she asked.

Before he could answer, a voice rang out from behind. "Caesus barbari!" the soldier yelled, ripping out his sword from its holder. Five other armed men stood behind him, their faces filled with murderous intentions. Shouts of surprise cried out as the panicked crowd around them suddenly scattered.

The two lovers didn't take the time to see what would happen next. They darted forward and turned down the next street. The soldiers rushed after them, screaming furiously at them to stop.

They hurried down a tight passageway, skipping over the heaps of trash that had been tossed out from the windows above. As they ran past an old woman, David's foot caught her ankle and sent her tumbling to the ground with a painful wail. Despite his better judgement, he stopped and helped her up to her feet.

Just as she was standing again, the lead soldier pushed her back down and stabbed his sword at him.

He jumped back with a shout of surprise and dashed after his wife.

They dashed out of the alley and found themselves in a small ghetto with two soldiers guarding the only other road leading out. They were trapped, again.

"This is unbelievable!" Emily exclaimed, throwing her arms up in anger.

The five soldiers swarmed out of the alleyway with their weapons poised to strike.

Emily and David slowly moved back towards the wall as the soldiers glared at them with odious eyes. Blissful civilians watched them from the windows above, guffawing and wickedly taunting them as the soldiers closed in.

David stepped back again. This time he felt the wall scrape his heel. There was nowhere else to go. He grasped his wife's hand and watched in horror as the armed men approach. He felt a cold sweat break out on his forehead and his stomach churned with nausea. *Is this it?* he wondered. *Is this really it?* "I love you," he said.

With her mouth hanging open in incredulity and tears the welling beneath her eyes, she sadly whispered, "I love you too."

The lead soldier was now close enough for them to smell his breath, stinking of rancid fish and spoiled pig meat. He brought his sword back, staring intently at David. "Tu est pestis!" he cried.

"No!" Emily screamed.

She tried to jump in front of him, only to be pushed back as he shot his arms out to block her and screamed out, "Our Father, Who art in Heaven, hallowed be Thy sacred name . . ."

His voice was drowned out by a sudden, deafening roar.

The ground trembled under his feet. The shingles from the building overhead tumbled off their holdings and fell to the ground, almost dealing the two fugitives a fatal blow. The soldiers nervously looked around, the terror written on their faces.

The lead soldier dropped his weapon and shouted, "Currere!"

The soldiers dispersed in a frantic retreat. The people at the windows cried out with worry as the shaking didn't cease.

"What's happening!" David yelled.

Emily, fighting hard to stay on her feet, looked up at the sky in dismay. "We have to get to the sea. It's our only way out!" she shouted, grabbing his hand and leading him down the road.

The shaking stopped just as quickly as it had begun. A hot breeze blew from the east, blowing up clouds of sand from the street that stung their eyes. They ran past a line of stores were terrified merchants were closing up their shops. Children looking for their mothers wandered the streets while husbands desperately called out for their wives. People grasped as many items as they could from their homes and tried to carry them through the congested streets.

Once they came to an intersection, they could see Mount Vesuvius. The majestic mountain had transformed itself into a burning volcano, sending up plumes of smoke that were miles high into the sky. Bright orange lava copiously flowed from the massive cavern with deadly speed down the mountain's slope.

"Oh dear Lord," he gasped.

Emily swallowed hard and took him further down the street. There had to be a gate ahead, some way to get out. They tried to move through as the streets were flooded with terrified citizens trying to escape.

The murky clouds, gloomy with ash, quickly blocked out the hot sun and enveloped the city in darkness. Another earthquake rumbled the town, crumbling the walls of buildings and exposing the rooms inside.

Emily clung to her husband to keep her balance.

All of a sudden, the three story apartment building ahead collapsed, sending a wave of heavy debris onto the defenseless people in the street. They could hear the chilling shrieks of terror and pain erupting from underneath the rubble.

As they ran, they suddenly spotted a man whose head was barely sticking out from under part of a wall and moved to save him. He wailed in distress as his two rescuers lifted the wreckage off his back. Once he had enough space, he climbed to his feet and ran off without even thanking them.

Emily wiped the warm ashes from her face. She looked up to see millions of tiny gray flakes descending from the black clouds like vile snow. A few more moments was all it would be before they started to suffocate from poisonous gasses. "Are we going the right way?" she asked.

"Only one way to find out!" David yelled over the clamor. He carefully stepped on the debris, being sure that no poor soul was underneath him. He peered ahead, but could only see a few feet through the falling embers.

A burning pebble struck the back of his head. He let out a cry and darted forward. The adrenaline made his heart beat explosively as he wildly ran down the street with Emily's hand being crushed in his.

Partially cooled pellets of lava streaked from the clouds, crashing onto buildings and defenseless people with their intense heat. Flames ripped open the roofs of the disintegrating edifices around them.

The putrid air smelled of rotten eggs and stung their nostrils, but they kept moving, squeezing through the people and climbing over a wide wagon that was sitting in the middle of the road. A few yards later, they saw the forum on the left. Politicians scrambled out of the government buildings carrying scrolls and tablets. The

Temple of Jupiter was lit up in flames and set an eerie orange glow upon the ash-covered plaza.

The terrified mob of people swarmed towards an enormous stone arch that stood ahead. They squirmed through the crowd, as desperate to reach the exit as everyone else. They anxiously waited to move through, watching the gate like terrified captives, begging their conquerors not to kill them. The terror sank deep into their hearts like a wild cat's claws into tender flesh as they realized that there was already a foot of ash on the ground being kicked about between their ankles as more fell from the clouds. Once through, they scurried alongside the wall and away from the road. The water met the land only half a mile ahead.

They ran through the field of grass, dodging the hot stones and shielding their mouths from the ashes drifting around them. The water in the cove ahead glistened with the hellish glow from the fire that spewed out of Vesuvius. A tiny rowboat sat unattended on the water, gently bobbing up and down in the gentle waves.

David rushed into the water and grabbed hold of the boat, the cool water feeling refreshing against his aching legs. A burning rock suddenly hit his back. Gritting his teeth in pain, he quickly helped Emily into the boat and jumped in with her. He grabbed the rotting oar and paddled the boat out of the cove.

He looked ahead to the island of Capri, which lay several miles ahead. Its two massive mountains of rocks, with a green valley resting in between, were speckled with sheltering trees. It would be a safe haven from the volcano's wrath.

Emily stared back at the shore, watching as several boats from the seaport set sail into the choppy water towards the north. A crowd of people anxiously waited at the water's edge, hoping for a place on the next boat out. The tragic sight slowly drifted out of view as the tiny rowboat fled into the Mediterranean.

With the fear driving him, it was nearly an hour later before David laid down the oar. They had made an impressive distance and not surprisingly, his arms had grown too tired and cramped to go any farther. He looked at Emily. She was still shaking with fright, watching the massive clouds loom over the ancient city as it was swallowed up in ashes. "Is this real?" he asked. "Do you think that we've really gone back in time and those people were all real?"

With misty eyes, she sadly nodded. "It very well could be." She shifted herself around and put her back towards him, not wanting to see anymore. She stared at the island, trying to forget the sorrow in her heart.

He rested a hand on her shoulder. "We're getting out of here," he said. "We're not—"

"Damn it, David!" she shouted. "We've almost died several times! It's been by sheer luck that we're alive! We were probably supposed to have died long before we even reached Pompeii!" He only stared at her, too lost to reply. "We're trapped in a dimension, or whatever this place is, and it's only a matter of time before something finally kills us off! We're going to die!" she exclaimed, the anger burning in her voice. She looked away, her eyes scanning over the featureless ocean. The sky ahead was crystal clear, yet the sun was blocked from the clouds behind. Then she turned and glanced back into his warm brown eyes. "I don't want to lose my life, David," she said. "I'm not ready to go yet. I'm not ready to say good-bye to each other."

He grasped her shoulder harder. "We are never saying good-bye, Emily. Do you hear me? God does not separate what He puts together. Neither anything you could ever do nor death can pull me away from you. Is that understood?" he asked, the severity in his voice making her slightly afraid.

" . . . Yes," she said at last.

"I love you. Here, now, and forever," he admitted, releasing her and raising his hand to feel her face. She felt the last of the threads that fixated her to her worries break away as she felt his gentle fingers drift over her forehead, eyes, nose, and mouth. "You look exhausted."

"I am." She let herself recline into his arms. They laid themselves on the floor. The wood was rough and uncomfortable, but at least it was stable and flat. The moment his head touched the planks, he felt a wave of sleepiness gush over him.

He brushed her hair back and looked at her beautiful face. "I love you," he said again, before resting his arm on her and closing his eyes. A moment later, he found himself helplessly drifting off into a deep slumber.

"Go to sleep," she said, touching his dirty cheek. She kissed his lips and nestled her head underneath his chin. She exhaled and let her eyelids shut. The beating of his heart and the calm splash of the water against the sides of the boat gently pulled her away from consciousness and into a peaceful sleep. The last thing she felt before she dozed off was his heartbeat against her forehead. *Here, now, and forever*, his voice echoed in her mind. *Here, now, and forever*.

XXI

David opened his eyes to a misty sky that glowed with gentle radiance from the sun. The boat delicately bobbed as it floated among the peaceful waves. A mild breeze softly scraped the sea as the sounds of several squawking birds cried out from ahead. He thought about lifting his head up to get a look, but was too tired to stir. Emily was pressed against him, all warm and cozy as she rested. He shut his eyes, ready to drift back into a world of sleep with her.

All of a sudden, the tiny boat was forced to a halt as its bow grated into wet sand. David and Emily groaned simultaneously, but didn't bother to move. They couldn't care less about what was happening in the world around them, just as long as they were left alone.

A beautiful tern, however, perched itself on the edge of the boat's starboard side and peered at the live cargo inside. It cocked its head as it looked at Emily, then at David. As if to play a cruel prank, it lifted its head and cawed out as loudly as it could.

Emily lifted herself up and stared at the obnoxious avian with a cold sneer. The stupid animal only looked back at her, as if it was trying to see how annoyed it could get her before she swatted at him. The thought of it entered her mind, but when she saw the palm trees ahead, faintly covered with a veil of fog, her mind drifted back to worry.

She carefully climbed out of the boat and trudged through the water onto the warm, sun-baked sand. She turned around and glanced back at Mount Vesuvius, only it wasn't there. Instead, she could barely make out three islands rising from the ocean water in the distance, holding massive mountains and towering cliffs that were sheltered by luscious palm trees. "David?" she wearily asked.

Her husband staggered out of the boat and onto the beach. He was in awe at the sights around him. The white sand felt soft and delightful against his sore feet. "Are you okay?" he inquired.

She shook her head. "Where are we?" she asked, looking out at the other islands. She appeared to be on the verge of tears. If she did cry, he figured that she had plenty of reason to do so. They had fallen into another world with new problems and troubles.

For the moment, however, things were peaceful and serene except for a few birds that playfully chased each other over the ocean as its waves gently splashed against the shore. He sat down and sighed. His eyelids still felt heavy and his body was begging him for more rest.

Emily turned away from the sea, clutching her stomach as she stumbled towards him. She laid down on the smooth sand and let out a dispirited sigh. She didn't want to accept the fact that they were lost. Her fears scoured her mind with the fact that they might never see their home or families again, sending a harrowing chill down her spine. She turned on her side and watched David sleep. He seemed so relaxed and unconcerned, yet would be locked back into a world of consternation the moment he awoke.

She closed her eyes and tried to let her body repose. She ignored her worries the best she could, but still found herself jittery. At this rate, it would take hours for sleep to come. *What's the point!* she angrily wondered. *Things couldn't possibly get any worse!* She felt more like running a marathon than taking a nap. At least then she would be getting somewhere.

Suddenly, a low, savage growl sounded from behind her.

Emily remained still, her eyes wide open in fright.

Without warning, she felt a heavy paw rest on her face. She dared not move, even when she felt the retracted claws press against her cheek. She could hear the animal breathing heavily as its hot breath, moist with stench, enveloped the air around her.

"David," she whimpered. The animal let out a disgruntled groan and started to sniff her. "David," she begged again.

He opened his eyes and froze with fear. "Don't move," he whispered.

"What is it?" she asked, feeling a raspy tongue lick her neck, drenching her with sticky saliva.

David cautiously climbed to his feet and nervously backed away. "Hey!" he suddenly shouted, waving his arms.

The jaguar looked up from her with hungry eyes. It licked its chops and stepped over her, easing towards him and preparing to pounce.

Emily saw the beast and let out a scream of horror.

The giant cat looked back at her.

"Here kitty, kitty, kitty!" David called.

The animal glanced at him again, as if trying to decide which one of them would make a better meal. Even though the woman was in easy lunging distance, the man who looked like he was attempting to fly seemed more appealing.

All at once, the beast let out a wild shriek and ran towards him.

He whirled around and dashed down the beach as fast as he could.

"David!" Emily cried.

The massive feline was gaining on him with every step. With razor sharp claws and pointy teeth, the animal would rip him up in only a few seconds once it got a hold of him.

David dashed into the sea, frantically splashing water in all directions. After a moment, he turned and looked at the dumbfounded animal trapped on the shore staring back at him. His wife stared at him too, unsure of what to do.

"Emily!" he shouted. "Jump in the water!"

She looked at him, then glanced at the cat. *Jaguars can swim, can't they?* she wondered. She swallowed hard and timidly stared at her husband, bobbing in the water before the voracious cat like a sitting duck.

The jaguar delicately dipped its paw in the salty water. Then he looked at his floating prey and leaped in the ocean after him.

"Shoot!" he screamed.

He desperately struggled through the water, feeling the sand beneath his feet slip away as he scrambled away.

Emily picked up a rock and hurled it at the jaguar. She rushed forward and threw another one at it, this time striking its head.

David moved past the beast and rushed back onto shore. He collapsed on the warm sand, coughing as he tried to catch his breath. Emily put her arm around him and helped him up. She yelled, "Run!"

The irritated jaguar was through with playing games. It wanted a freshly killed meal and it was going to have it, no matter what it took. It swam back to shore and bounded after its prey.

The two lovers dashed through the trees and thick underbrush. Tiny birds of all colors flew out of their path as they chirped in alarm. The forest was dark with only thin streams of sunlight beaming through from the canopy.

The jaguar growled and jumped over the bushes and shrubs. It hungrily eyed its fleeing targets, knowing that it was only a mater of time before they became its feast for the day.

They ran past a few more trees before they saw a wall of rock in front of them. They looked up and saw the top of the cliff towering hundreds of feet above them. They fearfully realized that there was no where else to go. The jaguar roared once more.

Emily turned just in time to see the large cat leap into the air with its claws extended at her. Before she could even scream, a narrow stick flew out of the bushes and impaled the animal in midair.

The beast let out a cry of pain and dropped to the ground, its head hitting a rock next to her feet. It made a soft whimper, then became still.

David gasped at the sight of the wound. The stick, which was actually a spear, had been driven through the animal's abdomen, letting blood flow from both sides.

Emily let out an ear-piercing scream as a shadowy figure grabbed her by the throat and pressed a knife against her side. The cold blade, nearly slicing through the tunic, sent an icy chill through her chest as her heart was gripped by fear.

"Kaketali!" the man shouted, crushing her neck with his grip. He was dressed only in a tiny, tan cloth that hung from his waist. He had a mysteriously dark complexion and black hair. His face and chest were streaked with white and red paints and his dark eyes, emitting the look of cold brutality, were outlined in black.

She glanced at David. The poor man, surrounded by hunters, was being held hostage as well, the sharp stone pressing against his neck making his whole body freeze with terror. They placed a pole behind him and bounded him to it with a thick rope. A moment later, they were binding her to a pole as well, despite her struggling.

"Stop it!" she screamed, kicking her feet at them. It was no use. They wrapped the line around her as tight as they could. She could feel her blood barely squeezing into her limbs with the forceful gushes of her heartbeat.

"Let go!" David cried. She looked up just in time to see one of the hunters bring a heavy rock down on his head. The blow knocked him out. He slumped forward as the blood poured from his new wound.

"David!" she shrieked. "No! No—" She felt something hard hit her skull and her body felt sleepy as she sank against the pole. Her vision blurred into fuzzy colors. Unable to speak or move, she watched the world around her fade out into total darkness.

XXII

It was the ear-piercing scream that jolted Emily awake. *Where am I?* she thought, trying to remember what had happened last. She felt like she had been asleep for hours and her head throbbed with pain worse than any hangover she had ever experienced. She found herself still bound to the pole and sitting on a dirt floor inside a grass hut. David sat across from her, still unconscious with a dried stream of blood caked to his face.

The scream sounded again. This time it was more chilling than the first. It was followed by angry words that she couldn't understand. She leaned forward to see out of the tiny door. A crowd of people stood around a man that was tied to a post anchored in the ground. The sweat trickled down his trembling face as an old hunter, decorated with war paint and elaborate feathers, held a bloodied knife to the hostage.

"Teteliku calawi vegresco!" the hunter shouted. He lifted the knife up to his victim's face and carefully sank the blade into his flesh.

The man rapidly begged, "Hibbertut kilodre—" His words were cut short by his scream as the hunter sank his thumb into the incision and tore off a strip of skin from his face.

"David!" Emily gasped. "Wake up! Wake up!" When he didn't move she kicked him in the calf. He jumped awake with a surprised yell. "We have to get out of here!"

"What? Why—" Another scream from the suffering man outside made him glance through the doorway. He gasped in horror as he watched the blood generously pour from the massive wounds. The man would be dead in only a few minutes. The hunter callously made another incision, ready to pull of a second strip of live flesh. "Oh my God," he said in disbelief.

"Come on!" She wiggled herself from side to side, but the rope held her in place. David nervously picked at the knot tied around his hands, but it wouldn't budge. After five minutes of straining his muscles while hearing the painful cries from outside, he exhaled and looked at Emily. Her face was red with urgency as she helplessly struggled to get free. Finally, she looked up at the ceiling and screamed. "Help! Help us! Let us go!"

"Emily! Shh! Be quiet!" he harshly whispered.

"Someone untie us! Please!"

"Emily, calm down!" he barked. Panicking wasn't an option. They had to think clearly and find a way out before they became the next ones up for the sacrifice.

"I don't want to die like this!"

"You're not!" he yelled. He yanked his arms as hard as he could, ignoring the searing pain flaring up his arm, but it was no use. The ropes were too tight.

In a fit of despair, she threw herself against the back of the pole and violently fought to free herself. After a few moments, she relented from exhaustion and looked back at him with her warm tears streaming down her frightened face.

The man outside let out one, last, despairing scream before his body hung limp in the ropes pressed around his bloodied body. The sight sent a harrowing chill down her spine. Her stomach grew nauseous as she watched the gathering around him break out into a ritual dance, happily cheering loudly as if to celebrate the man's demise. "Oh God," she moaned.

"Emily. It's going to be okay," he reassured, staring deeply into her eyes. She was shaking like a terrified kitten, all scared and alone. He wanted so desperately to hug her. He couldn't remember ever wanting to hold her so much.

She hung her head down and suspired. "No. It's not. There's nothing that—"

Without warning, a hand grasped her shoulder.

She shouted out in alarm.

"Kalise," a soft voice said. Emily felt the hand move to caress her cheek. The touch was warm and gentle. She suddenly felt less afraid. "Kalise. Quele latuto viscarla."

She looked up to see the face of a little girl, no more than eleven, looking back at her with pity. She was a beautiful child, clothed in a modest attire. She had long, black hair and skin that was coconut husk brown. She only saw her for a brief moment before she darted behind her and picked up a stone blade from the ground. A minute later, she could feel the stone cutting through the rope behind her.

A feeling of stupidity swept over her. She had lost control and it could've been deadly. But she had little time to dwell on it before the ropes loosened enough to slip free. She dashed over to David and yanked wildly at his restraints.

"I'll be damned," he said, gazing at the girl with admiration.

"I think you already are." She untied the knot behind him and threw the ropes off. "Come on," she ordered, grasping him by the arm. He staggered to his feet, moaning in pain as he gripped the lump on his head. The little girl darted to the other side of the hut and lifted a cloth from another doorway. They rushed out into the dirt street, lined with huts and shacks made of twigs and grass sheltered underneath a blanket of tropical branches topped by an overcast sky. When they turned back to thank the girl, she had disappeared.

"Criskeri!" a high-pitched voice exclaimed. They turned around to see a large, pudgy woman pointing at them with a stick. Her face was mean and spiteful like an irritated cat's, glowering with hatred and savageness. She trudged toward them, screaming psychotically for the hunters. A huge clamor of shouting erupted from behind the hut.

"Oh shit," Emily growled through clenched teeth, her voice trembling.

David rushed forward, dragging her with him. They ran past the woman, taking a few stinging swats from her stick as they fled. A clap of thunder boomed from the sky and the forest was engulfed in a deafening roar as heavy raindrops pelted the earth.

All of a sudden, a rakish spear shot past David's head and into the ground in front of them. They ran past it without looking back. They didn't want to see how many spears the army of shouting barbarians had aimed at them.

The road suddenly disappeared into a massive grove of towering trees. Two more spears lodged in the trunks of the trees ahead of them, missing them by only a few inches.

"I love you!" David yelled.

"Don't say that!" she screamed back. *We're not saying good bye! We're not going to die here!* she thought, ducking under a branch. She stood back up just as another spear crashed into the wood behind her. She grasped her husband's hand as tight as she could, feeling her heart sink inside of her. "I love you!"

They slipped through the tangled vines and intricately weaved themselves through the thick vegetation as they were drenched by the cool rain. The furious hunters, decorated finely in paint and feathers, hurled more spears at them, but missed.

Suddenly, David tripped over a tree root, sending him crashing into a puddle of mud. He frantically scrambled to get back on his feet, only to slip on the muck. Emily grabbed him and lifted him off the ground, but it was too late.

"Kaeliscera chouvister macadella caki!" the leader of the hunters shouted, brandishing his weapon at the two lovers. David, gasping for air, stared back at him with his eyes glowering with abhorrence. "Telleva misco listera pascou . . ." He stopped and glanced at the tree root.

It was moving.

Emily and David cautiously stepped away. A hunter boldly moved towards them, but his comrades held him back. Everyone watched in wonder as the tree root slowly rose into the air.

All at once, the hunters raised their spears at it. The giant bushmaster snake, its skin shimmering with the raindrops, stared back at them, waiting for the one moment in which it could sink its venomous fangs into one of them.

The two lovers whirled around and hurried away into the dense jungle.

"Scit! Kiterit!" the leader screamed at them. Then he heard the ominous snake move. He looked into its eyes with trepidation. All it would take was one swift bite from the reptile and he would be at his demise. The creature simply watched him and his men with cruel amusement. It seemed to be welcoming the challenge of their twenty spears as if it were invincible. For all the hunters knew, it was.

Emily and David didn't wait to see what would happen. They dashed through the sultry puzzle of thick vines and fallen trees with their hearts beating violently with every step. The humid air didn't relinquish any heat from their hot skin as they ran or offer a single, satisfying breath. Their sweat and blood mixed with the rain that streamed down their faces. They kept moving, too terrified to look behind. Even after the hunters' voices fainted away in the distance, they furiously struggled through the forest. They didn't stop until they came upon a small clearing that gave way to a river.

"This is crazy," Emily said, trying to catch her breath.

A loud screech sounded out from above. She shouted out in alarm and shot her head up to see a tiny black monkey with a white chest staring back at her from a scrawny branch overhead. It cheerfully shrieked again and jumped onto another tree, sending a dozen resting spectacled parrotlets flying off their branch and into the sky, chirping wildly in anger.

David rested against the trunk of a tree and felt his head. The wound ached terribly, but it was numb to the touch. He sat down between the roots of the massive tree and closed his eyes. The rainwater hit him as it dropped from the leaves above. He longed to be back home. If he could, he would take a quick shower to wash all the dirt and blood off of him, and then stumble into bed, snuggling up to Emily and pulling the soft sheets over themselves. But home seemed so distant now. He thought about how wonderful it would be to make it back to New York. Then, as he looked at the foreign world around him, he wondered if it was even worth the effort to think of such hopeless things.

XXIII

The rainforest was alive with life as it received its daily shower. In a clearing, by the edge of the river that cut through the island, birds of all kinds huddled together in the surrounding tree branches, fending off their perches from the frolicsome monkeys and a zealous tree porcupine. A basilisk lizard, glowing with an emerald green color and with fins along its back, scampered underneath a rotting log while just a few yards away, a pair of crocodiles laid out in the rain beside the steep banks of the gushing river.

Emily knelt beside her husband and rested her hands on his shoulder. "You okay?" she asked. She knew it was a silly question and she would have to be blind not to know the answer. But she wanted to do something, say something, just to let him know that she was there.

"I've been better," he tiredly admitted.

She squeezed his shoulder lightly, gazing at his weary face. He was weak from fatigue, in pain, and haggard. Yet, he still looked powerful and robust. She knew that he could run for miles on end through the dense jungle without dawdling if he had to. The whiskers on his face, his handsome brown eyes, and his strong chin showed off a sexy stamina about him. She smiled and picked a cluster of fruit off from a vine behind him.

"Here," she said sweetly, plucking a ripe red berry from the bunch. She gently slipped it into his mouth, then took one for herself.

He swallowed it and laughed. "I'm not an invalid."

"Mentally or physically?" she inquired.

He playfully glared back at her. "If I had the energy, I'd throw you in the river."

"And then I'd kill you," she said, grinning as she stuffed another delicious berry into his mouth.

"Even so, you'd still get wet. Besides, you wouldn't have the guts to kill me."

"What would you know about guts?"

"I at least know that I have them and that they're hungry. I need to find something more nourishing."

She sat back in shock. Here she was, feeding him so that he didn't have to lift a finger, and he wanted something else. "What would his highness desire?" she teased.

He sighed and looked around. "Something quick, easy, and preferably crunchy," he said, his eyes stopping on a pair of colorful scarabs resting on the exposed root next to him. He snatched one up and popped it in his mouth. "Like that," he explained.

"Ugh! Gross!" she gasped. She trembled at the vile sound of the beetle's exoskeleton being crushed between his teeth. Worse yet, he was enjoying it. She winced as she watched him swallow it and looked back at her with an innocent smile. "I don't want you talking to me ever again until you brush those teeth of yours."

"They're not that bad," he said, picking up the other scarab. "Try one . . . I *dare* you."

She looked at the insect with disgust as its legs desperately kicked at the air, trying everything within its power to free itself. She cautiously put her fingers around the defenseless bug and took it away from him. She watched the innocent creature squirm and wiggle, but to no avail. She glanced back at David's smiling face. *He has to be kidding*, she thought. Whether he was joking or not, she wasn't about to lose a dare to a little bug.

The scarab tasted terrible and clawed at her tongue as she tried to chew it. With every bite, she felt the beetle's sour juices spill out into her mouth. *At least it's crunchy*, she thought to herself as she gulped it down. It left an acetous taste in her mouth that was grossly nauseating. She lunged for the puddle of muddy water that had collected by a bundle of flowering reeds in front of them and sucked in the dirty liquid. Oddly, the water tasted fresh and cool, despite the gritty texture of the dirt.

"You actually ate it!" David exclaimed. Not in a million years would he have ever expected for her to stoop to such disgusting levels for a simple dare. "I can't believe you did that! Wow! I would have . . ."

Emily lifted her lips from the water for just enough time to say, "Shut up before I really hurt you." Then she drank more of the water, desperately trying to rid her mouth of the scarab's foul taste.

All of a sudden, she felt a tiny splash of water hit her face. She looked up and froze solid. A brown fury animal stared back at her with big brown eyes above a tiny snout. It was about the size of a cat with a tail that was longer that its body and sharp claws on its feet, one of which was raised in the air with water dripping from it. It timidly watched her as if it knew it was in trouble.

"Oh my gosh," she said, unable to help smiling. The nervous creature slowly backed away, squeaking softly as it trudged back under cover. She moved towards the animal on her hands and knees, eager to get a better look. "David! Check this out."

He wearily crawled beside her and peered into the reeds. "Ha! He's a cute little guy, isn't he?"

The helpless little animal kept its distance from the humans, now regretting that it had ever ventured out into the open. Suddenly, it backed into something hard. It easily moved aside and waddled away from the object.

The lovers froze with fear. A giant pair of black boots stood firmly on the ground. They slowly looked up to see sleek pants with a silver buckle, then a black shirt, and finally a face so white with coldness that the sun could never penetrate it. The eerie man was decked in a black trench coat that matched the color of his mangled hair and the stubble on his grungy face.

Emily jumped to her feet with a bright smile and ready to burst into tears of joy. "Oh thank God you're here! Where are we? What is this place? What . . ." Her voice trailed off as she noticed the man's dead expression. He stared back at her with icy eyes that injected coldness into her like the sight of a bitter blizzard in the middle of February. " . . . Who are you?"

David clutched onto her arm and barely managed to pull himself up. His eyes fixated on the man, too afraid to look anywhere else. *This can't be him*, he told himself. *For the love of God, this can't be happening!* He only gripped his wife's arm tighter.

Emily composed her uncertainty and cheerfully explained, "I'm Emily Shanahan and this is my husband, David. We're from New York and . . ." David tentatively stepped back, pulling Emily with him. "Honey, please!" she scolded. She glanced back at the man in black, trying to ignore the chilly feeling seeping down through her body. He wasn't responding to anything that she was saying. He simply stood there with his frigid eyes locked on them. "We don't know what happened and we don't know where we are . . ."

David pulled Emily against him and forced her around. He harshly pushed her out of the reeds by her arm and started to drag her with him.

She wrestled free of his grip and glared at him in anger. "What's wrong with you!" she shouted. Then she saw the panic in his eyes. "David. Calm down. This isn't—"

He frantically lunged at her and threw her to the ground.

She looked back up to see the man in the trench coat standing over her with a glimmering knife tightly clasped in his hand as he watched her with his bitterly cold stare. She opened her mouth to scream, but the sound never came. Her body was petrified with fear and her thinking was frozen solid.

David ripped her off the ground and gathered her in his arms.

The man lurched forward, swinging the blade at them.

David dodged, missing the knife by mere centimeters, and sprinted away. The adrenaline seemed to take the place of his blood as he dashed past the trees and leaped over the logs with furious speed. The rain began to let up and a break in the clouds let a ray of sunshine penetrate the steamy forest, but he couldn't possibly care less as he ran.

Emily clung to his neck as he carried her through the underbrush, still too afraid to utter a sound. It wasn't so much the man that terrified her as it was David's fright. She glanced at the ground ahead and gasped. "No!" she shouted.

Too late.

They plunged into the quicksand like lead weights into water, splashing the sandy mixture in all directions. David found himself submerged up to his shoulders with Emily lying in front of him, her back halfway indented in the quicksand. He frantically turned around to see where the man in the trench coat was, but saw nothing except for the narrow path they had made through the vegetation.

Emily groaned and opened her eyes. The sticky sand felt miserably cold and gooey against her back. She glanced at the uplifted tree root hanging overhead. With a groan, she reached up and grabbed onto it with the tips of her fingers.

"Oh God," David whispered, his voice quivering. He had to get out. There was no way he could just let themselves remain stuck when there was a mad man after them with a butcher knife. But every time he moved, he sank a little more.

"Keep it together and stay still," she warned, intently focusing on the branch. She pulled herself up just enough to get a better grip. "We're going to be okay." *Yeah, right*, she thought to herself, feeling like a hypocrite.

David closed his eyes and tried to concentrate on the thick quicksand imprisoning him. He didn't care what it was he was thinking about, just as long as it wasn't the man in the trench coat. He glanced back at his wife and watched her lift herself out of the muck. She rolled onto her stomach and clung onto the tree root with both arms as she tried to catch her breath. She stared back at her husband's forlorn eyes and stretched out her hand to him.

He carefully lifted his arm out of the quicksand, feeling himself sink as his arm broke the surface, and slipped his hand into hers. She pulled him over to the root where he climbed out beside her and jumped back onto solid ground. He helped her off the root and managed to thank her with his trembling voice.

She held his hand as they walked through the dark forest, afraid for him. In just one moment he had transformed from a brave, confident man to a meek child. Under normal circumstances, she couldn't blame him. But after everything they had been through and how well he had held up, everything had suddenly crashed down upon him.

They walked into a thicket full of thorny bushes that hid lizards with its leaves and snakes beneath its branches. The chirping of birds and howling of monkeys sounded from all directions. Faint beams of sunlight shot through the canopy once again, this time with its rays glowing in the humid air.

"Who was that man?" she asked. "No! Let me rephrase; *What* was that!"

David, still trying to catch his breath, looked down and shook his head, searching for a way to explain. He stopped and fearfully looked back at her. "Richard Akron."

She stared at him in shock. She hadn't meant for him to answer, especially with the name of the man who had tortured her husband's younger years with so much malice. The whole event with his neighbor had lasted for only a few days, but the fear of what almost happened had lived on in him, even after Akron had died during his incarceration. He simply never got over the fact that he had been kidnapped; always afraid to lay his full trust in anyone but her, despite his exuberance in making friends with strangers. Though it felt odd at first, she came to admire his honesty with her, though sometimes she heard more than she wanted, such as now. "What? David!" she exclaimed. "You're flipping out here! Richard Akron's dead. He can't do anything to you, me, or anyone else for that matter. He's dead! He died in prison! Remember?"

"And are we not dead!" he shouted back. She forced herself to hear his words, wanting to scream at him for being so inane and, at the same time, hide him in her arms from his fears. He continued, almost on the verge of tears. "He came after me before and he'll do it again now that there's nothing to hold him back!"

"We're not dead!"

He held his arms out in the air and looked up at the sky. "Look around us! Is this all just some bad dream? Why can't we wake up! For God's sake Emily! Where are we!" He let his arms fall to his side in despair. Why didn't she understand? Then he saw the tears welling up beneath her eyes and he could feel his heart breaking to pieces inside of him. "Oh honey, no." He gently moved to hug her, but she shifted away.

"You really think that this is over, don't you?" she asked. She remembered thinking the same thing herself a short while ago, but it was his confidence that restored her faith. Now that confidence was fading away.

"I don't know," he admitted. She sat down and spitefully crossed her arms. He took a seat beside her and gazed back at her. "I'm sorry." He rubbed his face and groaned. "I'm just . . . I'm . . . I can't explain."

She didn't say anything at first. She just let his words filter through her mind along with the collage of nightmares they had lived. An awkward silence fell between them that was as ungraceful as the reticence experienced on a failing first date. Finally, she cleared her throat and said, "Here, now, and forever."

He looked at her, his eyes bleeding with the pain imbedded inside of him. Despite the anguish he felt, however, a faint smile began to stretch across his face. She held onto his hand and smiled back. They savored the moment, letting the seconds turn into minutes as they sat facing each other.

Without warning, a palmy plant ahead of them began to rustle. A juvenile bear rolled out into the open and stopped to watch them. It had a beautiful brown pelt with white fur around its beaming eyes.

"Ah," Emily cooed, reaching out to the cute animal. The cub stood on its hind legs for a few moments and sniffed her hand. Then, with a soft gurgle, it dropped back on its front paws and walked over to her. She gently ran her fingers over its fuzzy fur as David scratched its head.

All at once, a loud growl bellowed out from behind. They froze in terror as they heard twigs being crushed and plants being broken as something heavy and large approached. They nervously stood up and turned around.

A giant bear poked its head out from the bushes and glared at Emily and David with hateful eyes. They carefully stepped back, only to hear another husky snarl behind them. Emily looked just in time to see the second adult bear let out a ferocious growl and bare its teeth. It looked similar to the cub, only uglier and terribly hostile.

Surrounded, they held onto each other and looked in opposite directions at their opponents. The tiny cub, oblivious to its protective parents, innocently stood up at Emily's leg, holding onto her for support. She stayed still as her heart raced with fear, gripping David's hand even tighter. Then the bear looked up at her and gave a soft cry for attention.

The adult bears charged.

XXIV

Sarah shivered as the cold wind blew across her face. She didn't know if it was the chilly breeze that was making her tremble or if it was the fact that her sister, barely clinging on to life with the help of a respirator, might not be there when she came back to see her the next morning. Emily and David had almost died right in front of her. Dr. Maloney later admitted that he was certain he shouldn't have been able to save them and that it was only by luck, or perhaps a miracle, that they had survived.

She had wanted to stay at the hospital, just in case something should happen. She wanted to be there if something did. It was only after her parents had nagged her for hours on end that she finally agreed to go to the hotel and get some rest.

The sidewalks were very lonely with only a few prostitutes on the street corners and the other strange night life characters that passed by her with evil glares. She hated the city. What Emily had seen in it was beyond her.

Quietly, she heard a friendly voice behind her say, "Kind of late to be out by yourself, isn't it?"

Sarah turned her head and saw Nathan behind her, a cordial smile across his face despite his sad eyes. "Ah, Mr. Alden, I see we meet again," she said, half-heartedly trying to imitate a Russian accent.

He chuckled lightly. "Why yes, we do. How are you holding up?"

"I appreciate your concern, Mr. Alden—"

"Nathan, please."

"Nathan. I'm sorry. I'm okay. I appreciate it, but you really don't have to check on me."

"I know," he quickly replied. "I just saw you walking out as I was leaving and thought that maybe I should just stop by and . . ." He sighed and looked away. "check on you," he admitted with a forced smile.

She nodded and grinned back. "Thank you."

"You're shivering."

"That generally happens to me when it gets very cold," she said wryly. "I have to get back to the hotel. It was nice meeting you again."

"Is there anything at all that I can do for you?" he persisted.

Starting to walk away without taking her eyes off him, she shook her head and said, "Not unless you want to stay out here in the cold with me."

He proceeded to walk with her. "A little wind never hurt anyone," he said. "What part of the country are you from?"

"Seattle. And yes, it is usually colder there than this. I'm just being a wimp."

He shrugged his eyebrows. "No you're not. You're just going through a rough time. It's to be expected. But, if you're so cold, did you want to warm up a bit?" he asked, pointing to St. Patrick's Cathedral, just across the street. The steeples were lit up with flood lights as the lights from inside shown through the stain-glass windows. It was one of the nicer sites in the city. Or at least he thought so.

"All right," she reluctantly agreed. She followed him past the cars stopped at the intersection, wondering if she should ditch the guy and let him be, or embrace him and let him help her. *Help me?* she though. *I'm perfectly fine!*

She looked up at the massive church doors and suddenly felt very weak. Nathan opened the door for her and she hesitantly entered. It had been well over a year since she had last been to church. With all her time devoted to college and her friends, it had simply disappeared from her life.

It was warm inside, but she felt a tinge of guilt abrading her conscience as she walked down the aisle. The scent of faded incense drifting by in the musty air quickly pulled her thoughts back to the memories of the chapel in the town where she had grown up. There, in that tiny building with chipping paint and drafty windows, she had made her first reconciliation and received her first communion. It was Emily who had helped prepare her for it, using crunchy Neco Wafers as the blessed sacrament.

The church, with its bordered arches of white and elaborate stained-glass windows, was empty and dark with only a few lights shinning from the vaulted ceiling near the altar. She slid into a pew a few rows from the front and let out a sad suspire. Nathan sat down beside her and leaned back as if he were about to go to sleep, but he was too awake and alert to even think of rest. His boss was nearing death and, even though he was never on a personal level with her, he felt terrible for her. His heart ached for her younger sister as well.

Sarah carefully reached down to pull out the kneeler, only it slipped from her hands and crashed to the floor with a loud bang that echoed off the church walls. She swallowed hard as she knelt and folded her hands, her eyes transfixed on the massive crucifix before her. *Why God? Why are you letting this happen?* she prayed. *Please don't take her away from us. She's too young! We still need her! She's . . .* She suddenly found herself lost in thought as hundreds of precious images of her sister flashed through her mind. From the family vacations to the mountains to the regular schooldays, from the moment she was born to the moment in which she lived, her sister had been a part of her life. The realization, growing ever so definite, that her sister was going to die, was like a stake gouging its blunt tip through her heart.

Feeling the burning tears welling beneath her eyes, she buried her face in her hands and wept. *Why did this have to happen to her? Of all people!* she sadly wondered. *Is there something I could have done to help?*

She felt Nathan's hand on her shoulder, squeezing her gently. Of what little contact it was, it helped. She resisted the sudden urge to embrace him and cry on his shoulder, though she desperately felt she needed to. She longed for protection, for security, for love. Perhaps it was because of everything that was in her life. Or, maybe it was something that she was lacking in it. Whatever it was, despite her entire family being just a few blocks away, a supposed boyfriend lingering about, a friendly stranger right beside her, and God all around, she felt utterly lost and alone.

"I'm sorry," she said, trying to compose herself.

"There's nothing to be sorry about," he softly whispered. "It's all right. Everything's going to be all right. You'll get through this."

She looked up and stared at the crucifix. The image of Christ suffering in agony upon the wooden beams only made her feel worse. The whole world seemed to be caving in and even God Himself, the protector of all hearts, was hurting. What did it all mean? What was the point of anything anymore?

She closed her eyes as tight as she could as an eerie coolness seeped through her veins, making her tremble. "Oh God," she whimpered, hiding her face once more. "I just can't take this right now."

Nathan leaned forward and, not wanting to be intrusive, cautiously put his arm around her. He thought about asking her if there was anything he could do, but decided against it. How could he possibly help her? All he could do was hold onto her as her entire world disintegrated around her.

XXV

The female bear vaulted out of the shrubs with its gritty teeth bared at the two lovers as its mate bounded at them from behind. The little cub scampered away with a cry just as its parents crashed into the humans, throwing them to the ground with ferocious force.

Emily lifted herself up, only to be batted back down as the female rolled on top of her, gouging her claws into her sides. She desperately tried to push the bear away, but was helpless as the pain surged through her arm from her punctured shoulder.

David grasped the female by the neck and tore her away from his wife. She forgot about the woman and turned on him, swiping her sharp claws at his face. At the same time, the male threw himself against David, trapping him between two vicious walls of fur and sharp claws. All he could do was cover his face and scream as he took the painful lacerations across his back and arms.

Emily, dazed and in wicked anguish, forced herself up. An explosion of adrenaline shot through her system at the sight of her defenseless husband. She picked a heavy branch off the ground and struck it on the female's head.

The bear let out a shriek and turned around. With a vengeful fury, it lunged at her.

Emily dodged, but was too slow. The female sank her teeth into her calf and maliciously shook it.

Emily screamed out as the searing pain flashed through her leg and she found herself unable to move.

David scrambled away from the male's claws and slammed his fist into the female's side. Before he could react any further, she spun around and struck him across the face with her heavy paw, knocking him over onto his back with fierce might, nearly knocking him unconscious.

The two bears looked back at Emily. She nervously climbed to her feet, picking up the branch, and glared back at them. They slowly lurched towards her, gnashing their teeth and hideously growling.

"Stay!" she hollered, holding out her arms. The bears only took offense and snarled even more. "Stay!" she cried again, a hint of fear seeping into her commanding voice. She kept her distance, staggering away as she glanced at David motionless body lying by a line of shrubs, then back at the wild bears.

David opened his eyes, aching all over and feeling his warm blood trickling down his arm from a shoulder wound. He wearily looked through the scrawny bushes beside him. To his surprise, there was nothing but the edge of a steep bluff.

Only a few yards away, Emily shoved the branch at the male's face. He caught it with his teeth and tore it out of her grip, leaving her defenseless. "Back!" she ordered.

The bears moved even closer and she began to panic.

The female suddenly stood on her hind legs and gave a victorious roar as she swiped her paw at her.

Emily cowered back, trembling with fright. "Oh God!" she whispered, on the verge of tears. "Oh God! Oh God! Oh God!"

She felt a hand grasp her ankle and yank her off her feet.

In an instant, she found herself rushing down an incline on a slide of mud behind her husband, dashing out of the bear's malevolent reach. The leafy plants by her side appeared as a green blur as she rushed down the slippery slope. The cold mud covered her wounded calf and sprayed against her face, but, for the moment, she didn't seem to mind. *This feels good!* she thought.

Then David let out a worried cry. It was then that she saw the thick bushes ahead. With their arms out stretched, bracing for the imminent impact, they screamed.

They crashed into the shrubs with the sound of breaking branches and rustling leaves. A moment later, they found themselves on their backs, looking up at the lively canopy.

David stayed where he was, exhausted and out of breath. He gently rested his hand on her arm. "You okay?" he choked.

"Um-hmm," she murmured back. She wiped the glob of mud off her forehead and looked up the incline. The two bears stood at the top, looking down at them with penetrating gazes as they savored their victory. After a moment, they went to take care of their cub and disappeared from sight.

She rested her head against the ground and let out a sigh of relief, grateful that she was still alive to do so. She could hear the birds chirping in the trees above her. The gentle croaking of some frogs in the distance—

Without warning, a loud voice shouted, "No se mueva!"

The two lovers turned around to see the end of a blunderbuss pointed at them. The man with the fancy mustache and in the shiny helmet who held it glared at them with uncertain eyes. He wore a red uniform underneath a metallic breastplate that glimmered in the sunlight. *A Conquistador!* Emily realized in amazement.

"Help us!" David exclaimed, raising his hands in surrender. "Do you speak any English?"

The man sneered at them, grossly disgusted. "Usted tontos ingleses estupidos!" he barked, shoving the blunderbuss even closer to them.

"That couldn't have been good," Emily uneasily said.

He watched them intently, the pupils of his eyes lined with crimson-red bloodshots as they fixated themselves on the terrified couple cowering before him. He glowered at them and yelled, "Mueva!"

Emily and David exchanged a worry glance.

"Mueva!" the man ordered again, gesturing with his weapon for them to rise.

They slowly stood up, being careful not to make any false moves. They stepped out of the bushes and found themselves in a vast clearing. Across the grassy plain, another line of trees began. And to the north was a river that stemmed from a towering waterfall that was hugged by rugged rocks of a steep cliff.

Several tents stood out in the middle of the field with nearly a hundred men standing around outside, either repairing weapons or sharing a meal by an evening fire. Some were dressed in fully armored uniforms with shiny breastplates and muskets at their sides while others strutted around in only a pair of pants. Everyone seemed to be relaxed and enjoying each other's company as twilight began to set in; the sky above them lit up with a brilliant orange contrasting against the darkening hues of the oncoming night.

"Mueva!" the man shouted again, gouging the tip of his blunderbuss into David's back. He quickened his pace towards the camp. He wondered if they could survive trying to flee, but quickly realized that they were no match for the loaded weapon behind them.

Emily grudgingly stepped through the long grass, her bare legs being scrapped by their coarse blades. As they came closer to the tents, she saw several posts imbedded in the ground. A native man sat against one with a blindfold over his eyes and a look of doom upon his face. She squinted to see him better. He was one of the hunters from the indigenous village they had escaped from, trapped in the same predicament that his tribe had placed them in. Then she noticed the huge gash in his chest.

The man was dead. A fatal gunshot wound to the heart.

Oh no! she thought. *No! Please, not us!* As the man with the mustache forced them towards the post, where another soldier awaited with a musket in hand, he cruelly began to chuckle.

With her eyes transfixed on the dead man, Emily softly begged, "Please—"

"Sea reservado!" he shouted.

She stopped and whirled around with a look of desperation on her face. "Please, don't!—"

The man screamed out something unrecognizable and aimed his weapon at her head.

She screamed and shielded her face. "No! No!" she implored.

"Emily!" David cried, throwing himself in front of her and gathering her in an embrace.

The conquistador butted him on the back of the head with the blunderbuss' handle.

David's head throbbed with pain, but he didn't let go.

The other soldier ran up to help the first. They wedged their arms between the lovers and pulled them apart. David frantically struggled to reach his wife, only to be elbowed in the face and knocked to the ground. Emily stared at him with scared eyes, longing to be beside him. Instead, she was sitting in the grass with the tip of a musket only a foot from her face.

"Aqui estan dos mas!" the first soldier shouted. He jumped back and brushed himself off. "Mateles en cuando usted es listo."

The other soldier nodded, then glared back at Emily with a devilish grin. "Tontos ingleses," he snickered, stepping even closer.

Emily winced, dreading what would happen next.

David jumped to her side and the weapon was shifted at him. He froze in place, not sure of what to expect.

Nothing happened.

A warm breeze blew across the clearing as the bugs nestled in the long grass hummed and chirped above the relaxing drone of the waterfall. Nature abounded all around them, even as their lives hung in the balance.

The man suddenly broke out into laughter as his victims helplessly watched on, wondering what would happen to them. “Ingleses non—”

The sound of something hitting the ground startled him. He glanced down and saw an arrow shaft sticking out of the soil. He looked at the shaft with a puzzled expression on his face as he tried to figure out where it came from.

To their relief, he lowered the weapon to bend over and pick up the arrow. Before he stood back up, they could hear the faint sound of something slicing the air.

Suddenly, the man let out a tremendous scream and dropped the blunderbuss, clawing at his back with savage fury.

“Estan viniendo para arriba de detras!” a voice screamed out.

Emily and David looked up just in time to see blanket of arrows shooting out from the trees. The cold grip of fear seized their minds as they stared in awe at their impending demise.

They dived face-first into the grass and covered their necks as the pointed shafts rained down upon the field. They heard the frantic screams of the man as he was struck with more arrows.

David lifted his head and saw five shafts sticking out of the ground beside him. *A little more to the left and I would've been a goner*, he fearfully realized. He turned around and saw the man on the ground, madly trying to pull an arrow out of his ribcage.

"Parelos!" a voice from the tents commanded. "Ataque!"

The two lovers watched the camp as men rushed to slip on their armor and gather their weapons. Then, in the other direction, a massive clamor of yelling and screaming erupted. They looked back to the forest and saw a line of native hunters careening out from behind the trees with spears in their hands. They screamed wildly as they rushed towards their foes with murderous intent.

Emily and David turned around and saw the conquistadors running to meet them with their swords in the air. The terror gripped their hearts as they realized they were surrounded.

"The waterfall!" David exclaimed, grabbing his wife's hand and darting through the grass.

Another round of arrows showered upon the field, narrowly missing Emily's neck and striking down two of the conquistadors.

The assault was answered with several bullets streaking across the clearing. The two friends dodged the projectiles and flying swords.

Without warning, a native crashed into David, throwing him to the ground.

He looked up just in time to see the frenzied man thrusting a spear at him. There was no time to scream, yet the moment seemed like an eternity.

Emily threw herself forward and clutched the spear with both hands, stopping it an inch above her husband's abdomen. The native glared at her in shock, appalled and terrified that it was a woman who had stopped him.

David kicked out his foot and tripped the man. He leaped back to his feet and darted through the grass with Emily right beside him, desperate to escape the ferocious battle taking place behind them.

A minute later, they came to the edge of the side of the waterfall. They cautiously stepped onto a slippery ledge of rock. They slowly inched their way towards the gap between the cliff and the massive sheets of water that dropped from several hundred feet above.

Once shielded by the wall of water, they could see an opening to a small cave, a sight that made Emily only shiver with fear. "I'm not going in there!" she asserted.

"You want to wait it out here?" he yelled over the noise of the crashing water.

"Yes!"

"Parelos! Parelos!" David turned to see the conquistador with the mustache rushing after them. There was a hatred burning in his eyes as he fired his blunderbuss at them. The bullet hit the rocks with explosive force, sending a shower of pebbles upon them.

With nowhere else to go, he grasped her hand and darted into the cave, barely missing another bullet.

They were instantly enveloped in an eerie darkness, but ran as fast as they could, ignoring the painfully sharp stones beneath their feet.

The conquistador stopped at the mouth of the cave and stared into the darkness with dismay. "En el nombre de Espana, le ordeno salir alli inmediatamente!" he screamed. When nothing happened, he angrily lifted his blunderbuss and fired one last bullet.

The shot echoed off the stone walls inside. Emily ducked her head and gritted her teeth. *How much more of this!* her mind screamed. The ricochet slowly died away into a soft whine, as if the projectile was flying off into the distance forever.

All of a sudden, a blinding flash of orange light appeared before them. They froze in terror as their eyes saw the unbelievable. Where the empty darkness had been was a tall, lanky man in glasses pushing open a door.

XXVI

Newark International Airport was in its usual morning chaos as hordes of anxious people rushed through its concourses. The noise of jets landing and taking off clashed with the yelling and shouting passengers to create a massive, nerve-shattering clamor that, at only a few hours into the day, had already been responsible for many irritated tempers and aching headaches. In terminal D, where the brilliant sunlight streamed in from the eastern windows that gave view to New York's shimmering skyline, Eve sat in a chair at gate area seventy one and watched the hurried people go by.

She was a pretty girl of seventeen with short, bleached hair that had a hint of orange and a slender frame in need of a few healthy pounds, something she adamantly denied to herself. Aside from a few blemishes she had caked over with make-up, she seemed very confident in her appearance. But she wasn't there to be observed. She couldn't care less about what people thought of her at the moment. It was her turn to make judgements.

Quiet, relaxed, but secretly terrified, she thought of the man next to her. For the past fifteen minutes he had sat perfectly still, moving only to turn the pages of the novel he was reading. She glanced over at a couple passionately kissing as they embraced. *Get a room!* she thought. Then, seeing a woman across from her trembling with fear as she stared at the plane, she thought, *Get a grip!*

She glanced at her watch and groaned. It was already getting on towards eight o'clock and her parents' plane still hadn't landed. It made her angry to think that she should already be enjoying a fancy breakfast at the Hotel Gerard in Midtown Manhattan. Instead, she was stuck inside a noisy airport terminal. She wondered what airliner they were traveling on, but then figured that it didn't matter. Whatever company it was, it certainly wasn't a punctual one. She was content, however, being able to see the world around her, even if it was only an airport.

She loved the people. Sitting back and watching them was an adventure all in itself, though it could be disheartening at times. Even with all of the beauty just outside of the airport windows, from the glimmering waters alongside the towers of Manhattan to the glorious colors of the sunrise, most of the passengers moved about without a care for anything but their own agenda. They passed each other without greetings, let alone smiles, and made the few that did appear as jovial spirits walking among doomed souls. Doomed because they would never see the beauty life had to offer them.

Business travelers typed endlessly into their laptops as they waited to board their flights while families huddled through the crowds. Everyone had some place to go and something to get done. They would let nothing, not even a moment for relaxation, get in their way. It was no surprise, therefore, when no one seemed to notice the two people in dirtied garments walk out of a storeroom. No one, that is, but Eve Chardon.

She watched the two strangers, with the confusion and worry written all over their faces, with an intrigued smile. With the dirty and torn cloths over their bruised and ravaged bodies, they looked like they had just come out of a war. The man was bleeding at the arm and head while the woman with him clutched her shoulder where blood seeped from a massive puncture wound. And yet, despite whatever ordeal they had gone through, they looked at each other and grinned.

"They're speaking English!" the man shouted, suddenly unable to stop smiling. He looked down the terminal, then back up. His eyes filled with joy like a child's on Christmas morning at their first peek at all the presents under the tree. He threw his arms up and bellowed out a victorious scream. "Yes! Thank You God! I love you New York!"

Where's security when you need them? she sarcastically wondered. Anyone who would be happy to be stuck in an airport while they were bleeding to death was in desperate need of psychiatric help.

His companion gently took him by the arm and drew him towards her, gazing lovingly into his eyes as he calmed at her touch. They shared a kiss in each other's embrace, completely unaware of the hundreds of bustling people moving around them, or anything else for that matter. It was as if they were in a world of their own, impenetrable by the everyday coldness of their reality.

Eve jumped up from her seat and boldly strolled over to them with a perky smile stretched across her face. "I'm waiting for my parents to arrive. You wouldn't happen to know if a flight from Detroit has come in yet, would you?"

The couple glanced at her with beaming smiles. A peaceful light seemed to radiate from their eyes, as if they had just discovered the solutions to all of the problems in the world. "I'm sorry," the woman said, shaking her head. "All I know is that I'm here."

The girl's smile faded as she raised an eyebrow. "You mean *here*? An airport?" Emily nodded with a big happy grin. "I guess that there are worse places to be," she admitted, letting out a sigh and scanning the terminal once more for her parents. They were nowhere in sight. "You guys look like a friendly bunch. I'm thirsty.

Perhaps a drink would keep us in good spirits. Do you have time to sit down for a bit? My treat."

The two lovers exchanged uneasy glances. No one was that amiable unless there was something in it for them, especially in a city like this. But then again, perhaps she was just a lonely girl looking for some attention. Not seeing any harm in it, they awkwardly agreed.

"Great then!" she said with a big smirk. "There's a bar right over here." She didn't give them a chance to protest before she darted off towards O'Gladdy's Pub, an elaborate airport lounge with green booths and a massive counter trimmed in gold. They followed her to the bar and sat down.

"What can I do for you today?" the tender asked, wiping dry a shot glass. He seemed to be pretending not to be appalled at their filthy appearance. They were, after all, business.

Eve took a stool beside Emily and curiously watched the bartender, analyzing him like everyone else she had seen. She came to the conclusion that the complacent man, dressed in the traditional black vest and crisp white shirt, was nostalgic for some sense of formality in an insecure world. She shrugged and glanced at David. "Go on. Don't be shy. Whatever you want. It's on me."

"If you say so," he said, looking at the menu, "A Glenmorangie Scotch, please."

"I'll take a Long Island Ice Tea," Emily sheepishly ordered.

"Good then!" she declared, slamming her fists on the counter. "You heard it! A Long Island Ice Tea and a Glenmorangie Scotch!"

The tender set down his rag and leaned towards her with a playful smile. "Sorry. All we have today is water. But I'll give it to you on the house."

"Excuse me?" she asked, aghast. "This is a bar and I ordered—"

"Water's fine," Emily quickly said, not wanting any trouble.

"Yep," David agreed, rubbing the back of his neck hard and lamenting at the fact he had just given up a free drink. *This is a good thing*, his mind told him. *The last thing you need right now is alcohol in your system*. He told his mind, *But I want some!*

Eve thought for a moment, impatiently tapping her fingers against the wood, then indignantly lifted her chin at him. "Fine then. Three waters it is," she ordered with a wave of her hand.

The tender shook his head and rolled his eyes as he grabbed three glasses from the rack. "Ice?" he asked. He was answered with a brisk nod from the spunky teenager. He said a short prayer for his three little ones at home not to turn out like this teenybopper and set the drinks in front of the customers.

David and Emily hungrily grabbed a glass, suddenly surprised how thirsty they were. Eve watched them consume their drinks as if they had just been rescued from a desert.

"So, where'd you guys come from?" she asked as they set their empty glasses down.

David shook his head, still smiling as he stared out at the massive terminal built around them. "I'm not quite sure, but I'm so glad to be back!" he said, tenderly holding Emily's hand. "Let's just say that we had a very long trip."

"How long?"

"Days," Emily answered. "How about you? Where are you from?"

"Oh," the seventeen year old said, waving her hand like an old lady talking to her friends over a coffee break. "I'm from all over. I make every place my home. And right now, I'm in New York. So, I'm from New York!"

"Do you have family that lives here?"

"Yep. My mother's brother lives in Yonkers and my cousin Julie lives in Brooklyn. Then my grandfather lives in . . ."

It was the sight of the man in the black trench coat standing by a magazine rack that tore David's attention away from the conversation. His pulse rate quickened and his mouth ran dry as the adrenaline seeped into his system. He wanted to run. He wanted to runaway now more than ever before.

Stay calm! his mind scolded. He glanced back at the girl, who was mentioning that her Uncle's cat lived with him in Jersey City but was found on Staten Island after the last hurricane. "Um, I-I-I think that perhaps we should start moving," he stammered.

"Yes," she agreed, jumping off her stool to lead the way. "You seem very anxious to get home."

Emily shot her husband a nervous look as they started out of the pub. He didn't want to look back and quickened his pace down the terminal. But a few yards later, the curiosity was too much and he clenched his teeth and quickly turned to watch the man in the trench coat. The man glanced up with a rather disgusted look on his bearded face. David instantly looked away from him and dodged Emily's dirty look, feeling embarrassed, but grateful the man wasn't Akron.

". . . My other cousin, Mathew I think is his name, lives out on Long Island. And I can't think of anyone else," Eve finished.

Emily asked, "Is most of your family from New York?"

"No. Mainly everyone's from Chicago. Let's see. There's Uncle Roy and his wife; she's a real witch, by the way. Then there's . . . Well, everyone else. How about you?" She realized that she had talked enough and didn't want to become a nuisance.

"My family's spread apart. I'm the only one who lives here."

"You live here?" she asked, perplexed.

"Why yes," she said with a laugh. "Of course!"

"Honestly," she stopped and waited for them to turn around to her. "Where do we really live? Perception is more important than reality, mind you. But where do we live in reality and where do we live in our perception?"

David thought for a moment, but her words didn't affect him. His perception was his reality. They were together and back in the world where they belonged. "We live here," he said at last, and otherwise at a loss for words.

She only smiled and stared. An unexpected kindness, a sweet peacefulness, beamed out from her adoringly beautiful eyes. It was comforting, warming, and even a little scary as she simply gazed at them, seemingly trapped inside her own perception of things. After a long moment of silence, "It's good to get back, isn't it?" she asked.

". . . Yes," Emily answered. "It is."

A married couple rushed down the terminal towards the teenager. "Eve!" the woman happily exclaimed, waving her hand high into the air as she rushed towards her daughter.

The girl kept her eyes transfixed on her two new friends, not even bothering to look at her parents behind her. "It's going to be okay," she assured.

"It is okay," David said, suddenly feeling very self-conscious.

She grinned even more.

"Eve!" her mother beckoned.

She gracefully twirled around and dashed away, running towards her parents with open arms and eyes full of joy. A moment later, she and her family had disappeared into the bustling crowd.

"Wow," David said, trying to make logical sense of what she had said.

Emily cocked her head. "She was cute. I wouldn't mind having a kid like her."

"Hey, I wouldn't mind you having anyone who was willing to buy me a good scotch."

"That's horrible!" she snickered, tapping his shoulder. She put her arm around him and they started towards the ticketing terminal. They passed the gift stores and food shops with lusting eyes, but wanted to get home too much to stop and look. They saw a line of busses and taxis waiting outside the front doors of the ticketing terminal and fought their way towards them through the enormous crowd, dodging people and their heavy luggage.

They burst through the doors and spotted a taxi with its back door hanging wide open, welcoming any stranded traveler to a seat inside. They dashed in the car without hesitation. "Hi!" Emily greeted with a nervous smile. "Can you take us to Greenwich Village? All of our money's at home, so we'll pay you when we get back." After a minute of complete reticence, she felt her heart sink. The driver paid no attention to them, giving them his answer without words.

"I'll pay you double the tab once you get us there," David assured him.

"Nah, come on," the driver grumbled,

"Sir," Emily begged, leaning forward. "We really need to get—"

A man in a black business suit suddenly jumped in, practically hitting David in the face with his briefcase. The callous person, with his black hair slicked back and his tin-framed glasses clinging tightly to his narrow face, didn't even bother to glance at the cab's other two occupants. "The Brenckle Center on West Third Street," he demanded, slamming the door shut.

"Manhattan?" the driver asked.

"Where else?" the man snarled.

"Sorry," the driver said, shrugging his shoulders as he started the engine.

Emily and David did everything they could to restrain themselves. Their apartment was near the business man's destination, so there was little point in complaining other than for the principle of being the first customers.

They leaned against each other and watched the vehicles and people outside as the car began to roll down the crowded parkway. Their frowns transpired into radiant smiles. There was no reason to be angry. They were happy. They were going home at last.

XXVII

The taxicab rolled to a halt just before West Third Street on the Avenue of the Americas. The man in the expensive suit shoved a twenty dollar bill in the driver's hand before dashing out of the door and onto the busy sidewalks. The driver rolled down his window and leaned back into his seat. He happily gazed at the pedestrians passing by as his two other passengers impatiently waited in the back seat.

"Can you please take us to the Village?" David finally asked. The driver simply ignored him. "Look, buddy. I'll pay you as soon as you get us home. We're desperate!"

The driver only grabbed a Kleenex from his pocket and rudely blew his nose before tossing the dirty tissue out the window. He yawned loudly and scratched his nose, as if trying to see how annoyed he could make his wayfarers before they exploded into shouts of threats and vulgarities, which David felt ready to do at any moment.

"We're getting nowhere fast," his wife said, slipping out of the car. "Let's just go."

He reluctantly followed, feeling somewhat guilty for leaving the driver without compensation. The sights and sounds of the city around them, however, quickly took his mind off his conscience. The humid breeze blew softly, gently caressing their skin as they walked down Third Street. The pedestrians around them passed by without any cruel stares, too busy to pay any attention to a couple wearing muddy clothes. The cars in the street slowly inched along and blared their horns at one another without mercy, as usual for rush hour in Manhattan. Just above them they could see a low-flying commercial jet roaring across the sky as it made its way towards one of the airports.

"We're in New York!" Emily shouted, throwing up her arms in joy. She ran ahead, twirled around, and looked back at David with a joyous grin. "We made it! We're home!"

They hurried down a few more blocks before reaching their apartment building, which seemed cozier than ever before, despite the summer heat. They ran up the steps and punched in the security code by the doors. A moment later, they opened with a loud clank.

An uncontrollable smile came to her face as she rushed up the stairway. Normally the cumbersome steps were a miserable drudgery, but now they were welcomed as their home awaited their return at the top. The humid, musty air felt alive with wonderful familiarity. She dashed up to the door and grasped the crude knob, but it wouldn't turn.

"The keys!" she realized.

David gently led her aside and slammed his shoulder into the door. The brittle, wooden frame creaked and shifted, but stayed intact. He threw himself against it again. This time, the door flew open as an explosive shower of wood chips rained on their living room floor and a wave of cool air gushed out at them.

They darted inside, taking the sights in around them with awe. The pictures on the wall, the dirty clothes strewn about the hallway, the kitchen table cluttered with junk, and the books sitting on the chairs. It was all there, just as they had left it. They were home at last.

David walked over to the telephone and activated the voice mail. "You have fifty one unheard messages," an electronic voice said in monotone. "First message, sent July 19, at ten fifteen p.m. 'Hey there Dave. Klosterman here. I'm still waiting at the restaurant . . .' "

"Fifty one messages?" he asked. "How long were we gone?" He waited for her to answer, but she never did. Instead, he heard the water running in the shower.

He languidly made his way to the bathroom, admiring the dirty walls of the tiny apartment as if they were the world's greatest artwork. After everything they had gone through, they were, for all he knew.

He stepped into the bathroom where Emily's tunic was lying on the floor and the mirror had already been fogged by the steam from the shower. He wiped the condensation away and froze in shock at the sight of the man staring back at him. He saw a dirtied face covered with bristly whiskers and dried streams of blood. His hair, which had once been neatly combed and slicked back, was now a matted ball of hair with clumps of dried sand and mud stuck to it. He frowned at the image as he turned on the faucet and splashed the water against his face. Fresh, pure, New York City water with all of its splendid impurities. It was so good to be back!

"I love this!" Emily cried from the shower. "The dirt's starting to clog the drain, but hey! I can see my skin again!"

David carefully dragged the razor across his cheek, cutting a smooth path through the field of bristly whiskers on his face. He couldn't help himself but to smile at what was usually a normal drudgery. *Hygiene*, he thought. *It's a beautiful thing!*

The phone out in the living room suddenly rang. He dropped the razor and dashed out of the bathroom. The phone had rung once more before he snatched it up. "Hello?" he asked.

"Ah, David, this is Frank from the office . . ."

"Frank!" he exclaimed. "It's great to—"

"Sorry, but I gotta go. I'll talk to you later tonight. Take care." His bosses' voice terminated at a sharp click.

David sighed and set the phone down. *We're gone for who knows how long and the first friend I talk to hangs up on me*, he wondered. *Go figure*. At least he'd have something to tease him about when he got back to the office.

Emily, barely clad in a skimpy towel and with bandages over her injured shoulder and her bitten calf, waddled into the room, leaving a trail of wet footprints behind her. "Who was that?" she asked.

"Just one of my office buddies," he said, scratching his head. "He hung up on me. I wonder if he was told that we were gone."

"Were we?" she asked. He glanced up at her and saw the sudden worry in her eyes. "I mean, for all we know, this could be Saturday."

"It can't be. We've been gone too long. It has to be at least Wednesday, if not Thursday."

"For us, David. For us," she said, gently raising her hands as if to calm him down. "We've gone through what had to be days. Maybe even a week or more. But how long has it been for everyone here? Our hours may have gone by faster than seconds here. Whatever happened to us, no one probably suspects. There's no reason to."

"But there were at least fifty messages on the voice mail. We had to be . . ." He looked around, lost and confused. It didn't make any sense. Something wasn't adding up. "I don't know," he admitted, glancing back at her.

"There's nothing to worry about," she reassured. "We're back and everything's okay." She smiled and stared into his deep eyes. He grinned back, but seemed entangled in some sort of a trance. "What are you thinking?"

Indeed, he was in a trance with his attention focused on her. She looked so pleasing and alluring in the tiny towel that scarcely managed to cover her. With the tinge of amorous desire running through his veins, he skillfully plotted his next move of seduction. "I'm thinking about how wonderful it would be to strip that little cloth off you."

She quietly laughed and turned away towards the bedroom. For a brief second, his hormones flared with excitement. Then, to his disappointment, she crushed his anticipation with a sharp set of words. "You'd be best off taking a shower."

He knew it was true. He shrugged his shoulders and headed off for the lavatory. Fifteen minutes later, he emerged into the living room, fully cleansed and perfumed with his favorite cologne. He felt fresh and revitalized, though quite surprised at all of the large abrasions and bruises across his back and chest. He wandered around the room, looking for some clothes to wear, with his hair dripping and a tooth brush dangling from his mouth.

Emily already had a slip on and was moving about the room, collecting papers she needed for work from various places and stashing them under her arm. Her eyes were filled with terrified concern as she listened to the television set, which was tuned to a local station where a journalist stood outside of the Manhattan Courthouse, shoving a microphone into a balding man's face as he ascended the stairs towards the building's front doors.

"Why did the paper lie about Wallace Steel's working conditions?" the reporter asked.

"The Battery Park Courier told the truth when it said that Wallace Steel, based out of Newark, New Jersey, was compromising the safety of its workers!" the man avowed. "Five deaths in the past eight months is not a coincidence! Had the factory director spent the money to pay for the restraints on the lifting cranes instead of embezzling it, perhaps those five people would still be alive."

"But sir," the reporter persisted. "The Battery Park Courier has no proof to . . ."

Emily threw up her arms in exasperation. "Have you seen my briefcase?" she asked, looking frantically around the room.

"On the couch," he said, nearly growling. "Why?"

"That," she groaned, gesturing to the television. "I have to get down to the office as soon as I can."

"Now?" he asked. He breathed deeply to keep himself from bombarding her with questions. She had to have a reasonable explanation for wanting to rush off to work all of a sudden, though he doubted she did.

She glared back at him. "Yes! And, more importantly, I want to find out just how long we've been gone and what people know about Friday." She rushed past him and darted back into the bedroom.

He followed her and stopped at the doorway, resting on the frame with his arms folded and a mean scowl across his face. "You can't be serious."

"Well, I am," she said, flipping through the garments on the hangers in the closet. She pulled out her red velvet dress and held it against her. "How does this look? It's all I have that's clean."

"Emily!"

She angrily grumbled something under her breath as she tore the hanger away and slipped the dress over her. The fit was comfortable and fresh, especially considering that it hadn't been worn in over two years. The dress delicately clung to her shoulders by two spaghetti straps that crossed near the center of her exposed back. The velvet overlaid her silky legs from the ankles on up, except for a rather libidinous slit that ran up her left thigh. After a quick glance in the mirror, she turned back to see her husband's frown.

"Here," she said, reaching back in the closet and ripping out one of his cream-colored dress shirts. "Wear this." She tossed the shirt to him, which he caught with aversion.

"Should I put anything else on?"

She tossed him a pair of pants without saying a word. She felt the tension building up between them and didn't want to escalate it. She had to get back to the office with her papers as soon as she could. Deep down, she knew David was right. There were more important things to be worried about at the moment than a stupid libel case. *But they've already got a guy at the courthouse! That's supposed to be me!* She was miserably tired and in pain, but she had to make an appearance. This was the one chance to really take her profession off the ground. It was her job. It was her career. It was her life.

David strolled over to the closet and picked out a nut brown sports coat. It was a shabby item, having been worn to the point where he could see his left elbow through the fabric and one of the buttons was missing. Emily shot him a look of disapproval, but that didn't stop him from putting on his favorite jacket. He sat down on the edge of the bed and waited for her.

"Okay. Are we ready?" she asked, watching herself carefully in the mirror as she applied her lipstick. She snapped the cover back on her cosmetic case and bolted for the door. David grabbed her around the waist and pulled her back onto the bed. She glared at him with flaring eyes. "What's the matter with you!" she cried.

He put his arm around her and held her hand. "Emily, darling, calm down. You're moving too fast. We just got back here a few hours ago. There's no need to go rushing out. You're tired. You need to lay down and rest, preferably after eating something healthy. Please," he soothed, gently brushing her wet hair back from her forehead. "just take a moment to figure out what's happened. It's okay." Without further ado, he gently started to kiss the side of her neck.

She stayed still for a moment, then let herself sink back against him as he slowly moved his kisses up upon her. A rush of passion suddenly burst through her veins as she found her pulse rate quickening as she had to breathe deeper for air. She let her hand slide up his arm and onto his face, drawing him closer. At last, she gave in and brought her lips against his.

He slowly began to bring her down upon the bed as his hands started to pull her shoulder straps aside. She moaned softly and closed her eyes. He kissed her harder as he tenderly brought his hand beneath her dress and up her thigh.

"No," she suddenly said, slipping out from underneath him and sitting back up. She pulled her straps back over her shoulders as she breathed in deeply, then slowly exhaled, feeling each second passing by like an eternity of frustration that would lead to no productivity. A tragedy in her eyes. "No," she declared, slapping her hands down on her knees. "I have to go."

With that, she sat up and marched out of the room. He rushed after her, wanting to yell at her to stop and stay. Instead, he calmly said, "And so I guess I'm not deserving of a little rest myself?"

"Just stay here then. I'll be right back."

"Too late. I'm ready," he snapped, putting on his shoes and rushing out of the doorway and into the muggy hallway.

"You honestly don't have to come." She tried to shut the door behind them, but to no avail. She left the door ajar half an inch and figured it was better than nothing. She briskly turned around and started down the stairs, ignoring the pain in her calf and descending each step with professional elegance, as if she were in front of a line of cameras. She hoped that she would be greeting a mass of journalists outside of the office when she got there, and smiled at the thought. Each exposed piece of film would catch her prestige as she beautifully executed her task of defending the truth against barbaric lawyers and a steel factory that—

"I can't believe you," he complained, shooting her another dirty look.

Drawn out of her little fantasy world, she frowned and pushed open the front doors. "I'm sorry, but I have to do this! They need these papers!" she cried, rushing out between the parked cars in the street to hail a taxi.

David ran up to her and gently seized her arm. "Wait! Honey, I—"

She whirled around and glowered at him. "Just give me five minutes and I promise that we'll be out."

He was taken aback. He thought for a moment, the hurt etched into his eyes as she stared at them, trying to make sense of it all. "You're crazy!" he finally admitted. "There's more important things to life than a bunch of papers!"

"Exactly! It's what's on those papers! Listen, David, this is the biggest thing that has ever happened and I have to take it!" She saw a taxi coming down the street and jumped out, waving her arms frantically at the driver as she continued, "Please understand! I—"

"Get back!" he screamed, grabbing her by her wounded shoulder and yanking her back.

She was ready to turn around and give him a harsh lashing with her tongue when she saw the blue Caravan careen past her. She stood there for a moment, trying to make sense of the fact that she had almost lost her life, again. She nervously turned back to her husband, who looked back with shocked eyes.

She suddenly felt ashamed and ready to go back inside. Her heart was racing like it would never be able to stop. Her throat felt hot and dry, despite the humid weather.

She glanced at the ground and saw that she had dropped her briefcase which had unlatched, spewing tiny mounds of papers out around it. She also realized that she couldn't care less about what happened to the *Battery Park Courier*.

David bent down and gathered the papers back into the briefcase and relatched it. With an indignant grimace, he started down the sidewalk for the subway station. He felt wronged, betrayed and even violated. But it was her career and if she deemed it so important as to rush to tend to it and disregard everything that had happened prior, than it was a choice she made on her own. Wanting to be only who she needed him to be, even if all she cared about was her career, then it was his job to make sure she got to where she needed to go.

She sadly followed him with drooping shoulders, not uttering a single word. She felt that she had crossed the line, and indeed she had in his eyes. She watched the cars pass by in the street, the pedestrians stroll by on the sidewalks, and the occasional vendors at the street corners. She felt guilty. It was all beautiful and she had blatantly neglected to soak it in, even after almost losing the opportunity to see any of it again.

They came to the next subway station, a basic hole dug into the concrete that led to a dingy tunnel below, and went down the steps without delay. After stopping to fish out a few subway tokens from her briefcase, they stepped through the shoddy turnstile and out onto a platform that was dimly lit with flickering fluorescent lights.

"Battery Park City, right?" he uneasily asked, suddenly desperate to make conversation. She stared at the dirty wall beyond the tracks with a dead expression. Inside she felt an array of emotions that were thrown together in a sad, sorrowful peace. *I almost let it happen again*, she realized. *Oh God, what's the matter with me?* She abruptly turned to him and said, "I'm sorry. I'm making a mistake and . . ."

Her voice was drowned out by a loud rumble. She looked behind her and saw a set of lights shinning brightly from the dark tunnel. A moment later, the train rolled into the station and came to a stop before the doors flung open, letting the hordes of passengers inside swarm out onto the platform.

Once they could get through the crowd, they boarded the train and took a pair of seats in the back. As she watched the other passengers find places to sit, she felt her eyelids grow immensely heavy. She gently turned her head and rested against him with a quiet sigh. Forcing away his anger, he affectionately caressed her face and kissed her on the head, feeling her soft hair pleasantly tickle his face. He could never stay angry at her for long.

The doors slammed shut and the lights flickered as the train jolted forward into the dark tunnel. Once there was nothing to be seen out of the windows but darkness, he found himself lost in thought. Emily felt so wonderful against him. It was splendid to be back in New York, even if they were on a crappy train car that was falling apart. He was thirsty, hungry, but most of all, tired.

They were safe and sound at last. Back at home, in their own time, mingling about their fellow New Yorkers, in good health and, most of all, together. He smiled as he watched a group of passengers happily converse at the front of the car. But he couldn't sleep.

Something didn't seem right.

XXVIII

The wheels squealed against the tracks as the train came to a stop inside the brightly lit subway station. The doors flung open and the eager passengers began to file out. David nudged Emily awake and grabbed her briefcase.

"This is our stop," he declared, standing up. Emily moaned as she turned and let her face fall against the headrest, wanting to fall asleep for another twelve hours.

"Come on," her husband urged. "You have to deliver your papers."

Groaning, she forced herself up and walked out with him, pushing back her disheveled hair, which was still damp. They hurried up the steps and onto the city sidewalk above. With the first breath of fresh air, she felt awake and alert. By the time they had made it to her office building, she was grinning with expectation and ready to take on the world.

She briskly strode through the doorway and politely greeted the clerk at the elevators with a big smile. She glanced up at the vaulted ceiling, intricately decorated with painted imprints of flowers and plants, astonished as if she had never seen anything like it in her life before.

Several reporters were congregating near the elevators, ready to snap pictures and take video recordings at the first sight of any Battery Park Courier employee who decided to come down to the foyer. Emily tried to stay out of sight, using David as a shield. She couldn't help but to smile as she delicately sneaked past them. She wanted to dance right over to them and give them all the information about the corrupt steel company that was suing the innocent newspaper, but she knew it would be suicide without first consulting her boss. "They don't know who I am yet," she whispered as they darted into an elevator.

David said nothing. There was only a blank look on his usually happy face. Once the doors closed, he fell against the wall and looked up at the ceiling, pretending to be sad instead of angry. Emily felt guilty again, but knew that only good things could come from this. Handing in those papers would be like cashing a winning lottery ticket. "I'm sorry," she apologized.

He glared at her. "Sure," he growled, though with a hint of sarcasm.

She smiled and stepped up to him. "I'll make it up to you as soon as we leave."

"How?" he demanded.

She turned around, scratching at her side. "This dress is so itchy! I could just—"

"Wait! You think that you can just drag me out of my home after we've been gone for days, have me save you from getting run over, take me to your office and have me wait while you go about your job, and then erase all of that with a simple moment of physical pleasure?"

"Well," she said, seductively playing with her shoulder straps, "I was hoping to."

He thought for a moment, then shrugged. ". . . Okay."

She let out a laugh and the elevator doors opened to the thirtieth floor. She bolted into the busy office like a puppy dog getting the run of the house for the first time. The workplace was busy, as usual. The opened room, flooded with tiny cubicles and desks overflowing with papers, was as noisy as ever. "Hi, everyone!" she happily cried, rushing past her colleagues to throw her briefcase on her desk near the center of the room. "What did I miss?"

Her fellow co-workers ran about the office like little children playing a game of tag, performing task after task. They completely ignored her, as if she had never been gone. She let her shoulders drop in disappointment. With a depressed suspire, she opened up her briefcase and tore out the files on the Wallace Steel factory while she quickly thought of what excuse for the papers' absence she would tell her boss.

"Anything I can do?" David meekly asked. He already knew the answer. Emily never let him get involved with her affairs at work, even when she was in dire need of assistance, such as now.

"Do you see my boss?" she asked, carefully scanning the faces of all the people walking past her desk. She spotted the tall blonde in the red mini-skirt standing by the receptionist's desk, sharing a cup of coffee with the managers from the human resources department and chatting up a storm, as if completely unaware of the chaos that ensued all around her. Perhaps she needed the break. Being at the center of all the media attention while trying to defend the newspaper had to be draining. "Susan!" she called, waving her arms. "I got the papers!"

Susan didn't even bother to glance in her direction. She was too enraptured in her conversation. She didn't even notice when her disgruntled employee was marching toward her.

"Susan!" Emily cried, standing right in front of her, holding out the vital papers. "These are the Wallace Steel files and they need to be . . ." Her jaw dropped in disgust as her boss blatantly ignored her.

"It's just one thing after another!" Susan exclaimed to her friends. "When I told Roger that the vasectomy is better birth-control than getting the pills, he just gets upset. So last night, I told him to get out. Then I went over to Greg's. Now there's a man who knows what to do in bed! The guy . . ." Emily took a step back, not knowing whether she felt like laughing or rushing off to the restroom and throwing up. “And then there’s this girl, Shanahan. You know her, right?” The other two nodded. “Well, she’s been a real problem too. She stormed out of here Friday night and was all pissed off because she had to do a little extra work. Monday, the day we need certain files back for a court appearance, the bitch doesn’t even show up!”

Emily stepped forward, the fury boiling in her arteries. “Excuse me?” she asked, trying to remain calm. “Whatever you’re doing, I don’t see this as being funny. I have these papers that need to—”

“She’s usually a good worker,” Susan continued, trying not to smile. “but I’ve never seen a more pitiful creature on the face of this earth. I know that I shouldn’t say this, but I wonder how her husband puts up with her. He probably stays for the sex. I doubt she’s good for anything else. She’s . . .”

She can’t see me! Emily fearfully realized. *I’m invisible to all of them!* She sank away from her boss, who was now laughing along with the other managers. She was surprised to find herself fighting back tears. She suddenly felt very alone. Though she couldn’t care less about what she was saying, Susan, her supervisor who had always been pleasant to her, was stabbing her right in the back before her eyes as she stood right beside them, trapped from their sights. It hurt. It really hurt.

She turned around, not even noticing that she had dropped her papers all over the floor. She didn’t want to look at her anymore. She felt too sick to even think of her at the moment. She wanted to go home and crawl in bed with David’s arms around her, holding her safe from all of this nonsense.

Across the room, David strode over to Phil’s desk, one of Emily’s subordinates who had become a good acquaintance of his, though it had been well over a month since they had last talked. He was eager to catch up on the latest in city politics, something Phil always hated. "Hey buddy! What's happening?" he cheerfully asked.

The man didn't look up from his paper work. He continued on, inserting numbers into his expense report as if no one was around, looking up only once to check the clock on the wall.

"Phil?" he asked, suddenly worried.

Still, no answer.

He leaned over, practically laying on the desk, and stared deeply into the man's eyes. He could see the life and vibrancy in them, but they did not see him. He waved his hand in front of his face.

Nothing at all.

He stood back, rubbing his chin. *Oh God, not this. Anything but this!* he prayed. It couldn't be! It was impossible! He was standing right there in front of the guy! How could he not see him? He held his stomach, feeling sick and tired. They had come this far, and for what?

"Love?" a meek voice emerged from the office noise. He turned around and saw Emily standing there. She was lost, frightened, and trembling with fear. She shook her head in disbelief as a tiny tear trickled down her red cheek. "I'm sorry," she said.

He rushed up and hugged her. "You have nothing to be sorry about," he said, gently rubbing her back. "It's okay. Everything's going to work out. We just have to figure out what's wrong first."

"Everything. Everything's here but us. We're what's wrong."

Holding her dearly, he soothed, "No." He felt like a hypocrite, seriously wondering himself if such a horrible thing could be true.

"I want to go back home now," she lamented, still quivering in his embrace. She watched her friends and colleagues walk right past her, unable to be seen or heard by them. Kregan, who had been a close friend since her first day at work, sat at her desk, blowing a gum bubble as she sadly glanced over a set of inventory reports. Franklin typed away at his computer, probably networking with the other departments. All around her, life went on without her presence. Her heart felt like it was about to be torn apart and there was nothing she could do to stop it.

Without warning, the telephone on the desk beside them rang. Nathan Alden picked it up without taking his eyes off his paper work. "Alden here," he glumly announced. "Sarah! How's Emily doing?"

She turned around and watched him intently. He stood up, suddenly worried. His face fell as the hysteric voice on the other line cried out to him in desperation. "Stay calm, Sarah. You're speaking too fast . . . Wait! What do you mean she's failing?"

"Oh no," David gasped.

Emily squeezed him, as if holding onto him for dear life.

"I'll be there as soon as I can," Nathan said. With that, he slammed the phone on the hook and scrambled to put his papers away.

"What's the hurry?" Susan asked from across the room, amazingly broken away from her socializing.

"Emily's not well," he explained, picking up his laptop case. "I have to get to the hospital right away."

"Why?" the inured woman asked. "We have work that has to be done! Wallace Steel's going after our asses right now and there's a convention in the Bronx that has to be covered! You can't just waltz out of here . . ."

Nathan, along with five other employees, ignored her as they packed away their work and locked their desk drawers. They had a friend in trouble and nothing was going to keep them from being there for her. Susan threw her hands up in the air and groaned in defeat.

"Come on," David said, rushing off to follow Nathan. Emily only moved because he had her by the hand. She didn't want to go. She was too afraid.

They followed them out into the street and back down into the subway station. Once through the turnstiles, they waited by the tracks in each other's arms for the train as Emily's five co-workers milled about, worried sick and terrified.

"Why can't they see me?" Emily whimpered. "I'm right here!"

A thousand thoughts ran through David's mind. Everything from the girl they met at the airport to the taxi driver that ignored them to Phil at the office. What was going on? It didn't make any sense.

Their train came through the tunnel and slowed to a stop. As the passengers deboarded, the two lovers watched them with morose expressions. This time they had gone into a real world, where everything was alive and living. There was a spirit of life in the beings and objects around them. They sadly realized that it was they who held the emptiness, the lack of vigor.

They watched as the train cars were filled with new passengers, including Emily's co-workers. Once everyone else was on, they boarded with heavy hearts and sat down on the floor, leaning against the support poles. They didn't have the energy to stand.

The cabin quieted as the train started forward.

"I'm afraid," Emily whispered, clutching onto his arm. Her strength had all but disappeared, leaving her as defenseless as a sparrow in a thunderstorm. "I'm afraid."

XXIX

Emily had never seen the particular hospital corridor before, which made things all the more frightening. She wanted to scream out at the people around her and make them see her, but it was useless. There was absolutely nothing she could do. It was as if she were a lost ghost wandering about a world to which she no longer belonged.

They passed a crowded waiting room filled with downhearted people. Not a single ray of hope shined through for anyone. Not for the children crying in their mother's arms. Not for the husbands holding their wives. Not even for an old lady, sleeping by a magazine rack, whose wrinkles showed signs of distress.

"Nathan!" a voice cried out. Everyone looked up to see Sarah somberly walking down the hall, wiping a tear from her eye. She met him with an embrace, suppressing the need to break down and cry in his arms. "She's my sister and I can't believe this is happening!"

"Sarah!" Emily cried, rushing forward. As Nathan let go of her, she slipped in between them, staring her sister directly in the face. She saw a beautiful, grown woman, tormented by a sense of abandonment. She could feel her sweet, gentle breath against her face as she gazed into her deep blue eyes. "Sarah," she whispered, watching another tear trickle down her soft face. "It's me. Can you hear me?" Her sister couldn't hear her to respond.

"Everything's going to be okay," Nathan was saying.

Shivering out of sad disbelief, Emily gently raised her hand and lightly touched her sibling's reddened cheek. She felt her warm skin and her wet tears against the palm of her trembling hand, but her sister didn't feel her. She only heard Nathan. She stared on, not looking at her, but at him. "I love you," Emily said, shaking her head in sorrow.

Sarah stepped back and regained her composure. She thanked everyone for coming and quietly led them down another hallway where the only sounds to be heard were those of mechanical machines and monitors as the patients they served dwindled away.

Emily and David followed from behind, holding onto each other tighter as they approached the room toward which Sarah was leading them. They watched as everyone filed through the doorway of a small hospital room. Everyone except themselves.

"I don't want to go in," Emily said, swallowing hard.

"Why not?"

"Because I know it's us in there." She found herself trying to catch her breath. She felt like she couldn't get enough air. Worse, she couldn't bear just to stand here and do nothing. She glanced at the doorway, fearing with all her heart at what she would see if she went though it. "I just don't want to go in . . . But why do I feel I have to?"

"I'm right here with you," her husband reminded. "I'm never going to leave you."

She gripped his arm and tried to calm herself. " . . . Let's go," she barely managed to say, her voice trembling with fear. She nervously moved towards the door. Each step felt like suicide, but she pressed on.

The room inside was quiet as twenty people crammed around the two beds. As they moved past the people, they saw the patients wrapped in bandages, restraints, and tubes as the several machines around them gave them air to breath, water to replenish, and food to nourish.

Father O'Neal stood beside Emily with his hand resting gently on her shoulder. He hung his head low, having said the prayers needed. Dr. Maloney sadly entered the room with two nurses behind him. Regulations prohibited so many people from being in a room at once, but he figured there was no point in ordering everyone out at a time like this.

"Is this it?" someone asked.

Maloney didn't answer. He brushed past Mrs. Dennison, patting her on the back and reassuring, "You're doing the best thing for her."

Mrs. Dennison didn't respond. She could only hold her daughter's hand and weep. *Who am I to make this choice!* she bitterly thought. There was no point in trying to fool herself. Emily was young and strong, but she was also suffering and her condition was only worsening. Deep down, she knew that it was the loving thing to do, though she couldn't help but to think otherwise. *I can't make this decision!*

Her husband knelt beside her, holding her close to him as he gazed lovingly at his daughter's pained face. Already on the verge of panic, he pretended not to see the doctor preparing to shut down the life support systems.

Emily stood across from her father, looking at herself in the hospital bed. She was breathing faster than a runner after winning a race, desperate for oxygen. She felt her muscles tremble and her mind locked in a terror that would not let her think.

One of the nurses kindly put her hand on Sarah's shoulder and said, "It's time."

"Oh God, no!" Sarah cried, covering her face in despair. She rushed to her brother's side and held onto her sister's arm. "Don't go! Please! Don't . . ."

"Shh," Michael soothed. His arm around her shoulder calmed her, but didn't make her feel any better as she watched her sister's chest mechanically rise and fall with each burst of air from the ventilator.

"It's time," Emily whispered. "It's time." David pulled her close to him and sheltered her head against his chest. "It's time?" she asked, the tears starting to stream down her face.

The nurse glanced up at Dr. Maloney and gave a nod.

The doctor gently put his hand over the power lever for the equipment sustaining Emily's injured body. He looked at all of the people in the room. Emily's family, friends, co-workers, even her husband, were all around her. Over the humming of the all the mechanisms, he could hear the sniffles and murmured prayers of everyone in the room. With a flip of a switch, all optimism was about to be lost. Hope would soon cease to exist. Life was going to be no more.

"Please, God," Emily implored. She felt nothing inside but a burst of energy that was dying quickly inside of her. She felt dizzy from breathing so hard, but she still couldn't get enough air. With eyes filled with terror, she watched the doctor's face grow eerily relaxed.

Maloney closed his eyes and pulled the lever down.

The whirring of the motors died with a sinking whine and the beeping of the monitors were silenced.

For a second, nothing happened as absolute stillness filled the air.

Emily saw herself exhaling for the last time. Her heart was gripped by mortal fear. She was too dizzy to stand any longer. She suddenly found herself falling to the floor. A moment later, she lost consciousness.

She woke up only a second later in David's arms, but felt like she had slept through something. "No!" she screamed. She broke free from his embrace and jumped to her feet. "I'm here! I'm right here! I'm not ready to go! For the love of God, don't let me die!"

"Emily!" David cried, desperately holding onto her. He wasn't going to let her slip away.

Sarah broke down into tears, crying uncontrollably. She tried to scream out a plea of mercy, but all her words were jammed together and didn't make any sense. Her brother sobbed, covering his face with his hands. Mrs. Dennison turned to her husband and cried against his chest. He delicately held her, trying his best to fight back his tears, but to no avail.

Father O'Neal slowly pulled a black prayer book out of his pocket to say one, last prayer. The other people in the room backed away to give the family some space. One man was so overcome that he had to leave.

Emily didn't dare to let go of David, crying, "Please don't let me go! Oh God! Here, now, and forever! Right?"

"Here, now, and forever," he reassured with a quivering voice. *Please! Dear God! Have mercy! Don't let this happen! Don't take her away!*

"Turn it back on!" Sarah shrieked, jumping to her feet. "Turn it back on now!"

"I can't do that," Maloney explained.

"The hell you can't!" she swore.

Mrs. Dennison looked up at him. She felt her heart being gnawed away inside of her. She couldn't stand the pain. There still had to be a chance! And if there was, she had to take it! "Please, doctor, turn it on," she pleaded.

"I can't . . ." Maloney hesitated. If he did this, he would be going against everything he had ever learned as a doctor and he would violate the crucial ethics that every physician had to abide by. His patient would be forced to suffer through more—

He whirled around and turned the machines back on. In an instant, Emily's chest rose as the ventilator pumped fresh air into her lungs. A moment later, her weak pulse rate strengthened back to what it was before.

"Oh God," he gasped. He couldn't believe what he had done. He felt selfish, yet heroic. He looked up to see the two nurses glaring back at him with looks of disapproval. He swallowed hard and turned away, knowing that there would probably be a letter of inquiry on his desk the next morning.

Then he saw the smile on Sarah's face as she watched her sister breathe. It was a smile not of satisfaction, but of hope. A strange feeling swept over him, making him think that perhaps, just perhaps, he had done the right thing.

Emily looked up from her husband's chest and looked at herself in the bed. Still bandaged up and bleeding, but alive. She carefully stood up and walked over. She felt sick just looking at herself. Even if she could wake up, she would still have a long road to travel.

She felt David's hand upon her shoulder. She felt alive. The life was still in her. She turned and rested her head against his chest, letting the tears stream from her delicate eyes. She wanted to tell him how much she loved him, but didn't have the energy. He already knew, which was all she needed him to know.

David looked over at the bed where his body rested. His whole family sat beside him. His sister's face was a mess of tears and mascara, while his brothers tried everything they could to keep themselves composed. His father was holding his hand, a deep expression of sorrow veiled across his face.

"Dad?" his sister asked him in a frightened whisper. "We can't let him go."

He watched in horror as his father placed his hand on her shoulder and softly said, "We have to think of what's best for him. We'll give it another day. Maybe he'll improve."

"Dad," she said, more sternly. She was now visibly shaking with fear. "We can't—"

"Shh," he soothed. "Shh, honey."

David turned away and closed his eyes as tight as he could, not wanting to hear any more. "I love you," he said, his voice barely able to speak.

"I love you, too," Emily answered back, clutching onto him even tighter.

"And so do I," a new, deep voice said, its low octave chords sending a sudden chill down their backs.

Emily and David felt a hand on their shoulders. They slowly looked up to see a bristly face with messy, black hair and two eyes as icy as a winter storm. The man in the black trench coat gave them a crooked smile as he stood up.

David gasped in dismay. The terror clutched at the inner workings of his chest and squeezed them to a halt. He felt the blood freeze inside his veins as his muscles were paralyzed with fear. As he watched Richard Akron slowly pulled a knife from his pocket, he found himself unable to move.

Emily leaped to her feet, pulling David up with her. "Get away from us!" she screamed, backing away with her fists poised to hit him if he came any closer.

Akron only grinned some more. He stepped forward with the knife clutched in his gloved hand. The murder in his eyes evilly shimmered like the knife's blade as he approached.

Emily grasped her husband's hand and darted towards the door. Akron rushed after them, taking his time as he knew they had no place to hide and no way to stop him.

With her heart racing wildly, she ran down the hallway with her husband's hand clasped to hers. They didn't know how far behind Akron was. And they didn't want to find out.

XXX

David and Emily ran through the crowded hallways, dodging the several patients and nurses. As they ran through an intersection, a nurse with a cart rushed by from the other corridor and hit David in the side, harshly throwing him to the ground. She continued on, oblivious to the man she had just knocked over.

Emily quickly helped him up. Out of the corner of her eye, she could see Akron approaching with the knife down at his side and tried not to panic. “Come on!” she cried.

They rushed down the next corridor, following the exit signs to a set of glass doors. Through a lobby and out the doors, they hurried onto the city street.

“Where are we!” Emily cried. She turned around and saw Akron briskly striding toward them with merciless eyes. “Where do we go!”

David spotted a subway entrance down the street. He seized her hand and ran down the sidewalk, his heart rate ever increasing as more adrenaline gushed through his bloodstream. They darted down the steps and to the platform below just in time to see the last few passengers getting onto a train. They hurried on board without even bothering to see where the train was headed. They didn’t care. Just as long as they got away.

David turned around and looked out at the platform, knowing Akron would appear there at any second. When the doors didn’t close right away, he began to fret. “Hurry!” he exclaimed, waiting for the doors to shut. A second later, they closed with a loud clangor. A wave of relief swept over him as he still saw no sign of Akron outside. Perhaps he had given up on them again.

He turned and grabbed onto the nearest pole as the train started down the track. He let out a happy chortle, smiling in disbelief.

"Are you okay?" Emily asked, perplexed.

He only laughed harder, unable to stop. He soon found himself unable to breathe, desirous for a break to breathe. But all he could do was smile and chuckle some more.

"Honey?" she asked, putting her hand on his shoulder.

With his laughter at a roar, teardrops were streaming out of his eyes. Then his giant grin transformed into a sad frown, his body jerking no longer with laughter, but with forlorn sobs. He sank to his knees, covering his face in embarrassment as he wept.

Emily knelt down beside him and put her hand on his back. He turned and retreated into her arms, hugging her dearly as he cried. She held his head against her breasts, gently stroking the side of his tear-strewn face. "It's okay," she cooed, not sure if she could keep from crying herself.

"I'm sorry," he choked. "I'm so sorry." The emotions were stabbing his heart and tearing him up inside. Everything, from being back in New York while only to be unseen by its inhabitants, to Akron's persistent pursuit for him, to nearly loosing the woman who was holding him at the very moment, was hitting him all at once. He felt that he had used up every ounce of strength he had. He was hot, tired, sweaty, hungry and ready to simply fall apart. "I'm sorry."

"Shh. It's all right. I'm right here," she softly reminded. He sniffled and moved to wipe his tears, but her tender hand was already there, brushing them away for him. "I love you and I'm not going to let you go. Here, now, and forever."

He closed his eyes, letting her calmness flow into him and settle his frightened soul. "I love you, too," he said back. He rested in her embrace. New York or not, there was no place that he wanted to be but here, with his best friend's loving touch surrounding him.

She held onto him as the train hurtled through the tunnel. His sobs eventually died away as he came to rest, leaving her ears with only the sounds of the wheels clicking against the tracks and a few distant conversations transpiring between the other passengers. She let her face fall against the top of his head, her nose taking in the clean scent of his soft hair. "I love you," she said again.

After several minutes, when David had composed himself enough to stand up, they quietly moved to the back of the car. They took a seat in the hard, plastic chairs and rested their heads against the window.

David rubbed his eyes, then let his hand fall on his lap as he stared blankly at the empty seats across from him. He didn't seem to notice when Emily reached to hold his hand. To his right was a window that gave view to the car behind them. Through the window, he could see the car's occupants appearing just as ordinary as the passengers he was with and didn't divert his attention from his sorrow.

The train slid through a shallow dip and the lights flickered.

All of a sudden, he saw a face watching him from the other car. His body tensed with fear and he felt the sweat on his forehead grow cold as he began to shiver.

"What's—" Emily's sentence was lodged in her throat as she saw Richard Akron glaring at them, his face and hands pressed against the window of the other car, his eyes monitoring them as he skillfully planned his next move.

They watched in horror as a sly smile came to his face.

Without warning, he suddenly jolted from his seat and towards the door.

Emily and David jumped up and leaped back, their terrified eyes locked on the set of connecting doors as the man in the black trench coat on the other side tried to open them.

"We have to get out of here," Emily gasped.

David was too sick to speak. He tried to surmise, but the fear had gripped his mind away from logical thinking. *Oh my God!* he thought. *He's going to kill me! He's going to kill me!* Akron flung open the first door and bolted for the second. He felt Emily pull him back by the arm.

She brought him to the center of the car. She nervously watched the side doors, wanting to just pry them open and jump out. But they were secured in place until they reached the next station.

A loud crash came from behind.

The door flung open as Akron stormed inside. He glared at the two lovers like a vulture staring at its prey. His cheerful face slowly faded to a bloodthirsty glower as he stepped closer.

Emily and David stayed where they were. They stared back at him with fearful faces, but stood their ground, clinging onto hope that the train would arrive at the next station at any moment.

The man was now only a few feet away. He reached into his pocket and pulled out his knife, the razor-sharp edge glimmering against the light from the fluorescent bulbs above. He said nothing as he advanced, but the look from his dead eyes, absent of any kindness, said it all.

He raised the knife into the air.

The two lovers now found it appropriate to jump away, screaming insanely with fright.

Akron lunged at David, descending the blade toward his chest.

David caught his arms and held them up with all his strength as the knife, poised to kill, remained grasped in his attacker's hands.

Emily forced her elbow into Akron's stomach. The man let out a painful cough and stumbled back, crouching over in pain. She rushed forward to knee him in the face, but he caught her thigh and twisted her to the side, slamming her head against one of the poles with a loud peal.

Powerless from the throbbing pain, she slid against the pole until she hit the floor. She gasped for air and found herself struggling to stay conscious as Akron went back for her husband.

"Emily!" David cried. He glanced back at Akron. There was no time to think. He met Akron's moving forward with a fist to the face, but his efforts yielded nothing more than a groan and a pair of retaliating arms pinning him against the connecting door. Akron threw his knuckles into his nose and repeatedly slammed his foot against his shins as hard as he could, then let him go.

David screamed out in pain as he crashed to the floor, wondering if his leg had been fractured. But his opponent wasn't about to give him time to contemplate the thought as he lunged at him again. This time his knife was pointed at his throat.

Emily wearily forced herself onto her feet. Her head spun with dizziness and she felt like throwing up, but knew there was nothing in her stomach to regurgitate.

She suddenly felt the car slowing down and saw bright lights fill the cabin as the train hurtled into the next subway station. She glanced back down at David, struggling for his life as the madman loomed over him.

She rushed forward and grasped Akron by the neck.

He threw himself backwards, throwing her off his back and against another pole.

She hit her head a second time and dropped to the ground with a whimper. She could see the doors open now, letting the people aboard walk out while new ones came on. She wanted to jump up and leave, but not without David.

She rushed forward again with a barbaric scream.

David was holding Akron back with all his power, but the knife was sinking closer to his neck as he became weaker with each passing second.

He saw Emily jump onto his opponent's back again, this time digging her fingernails into his throat with vicious fury.

Akron snarled out in pain, letting go of the knife and grasping her head above him.

She cried out in pain as he twisted her head to the left, then sharply to the right.

David grasped the knife that had fallen on his chest and thrusted it into Akron's stomach.

The light inside the cabin dimmed back to what the interior lights could offer as the train traveled back into another dark tunnel.

Akron glared back at the man who had stabbed him with shocked eyes. Then he glanced down at the handle sticking out of his abdomen. He moaned in disbelief. He had been gravely wounded.

Emily wrenched herself free from his grip and slammed the heel of her foot against his spine. David pushed Akron off him and stood up. The man lay on the floor, curled up in a fetal position as a thin stream of blood flowed onto the floor.

Emily retreated to her husband's side. "Are you okay?" she asked, her voice trembling.

Still unable to speak, he nodded. His whole body shivered as he stared at the body of the man who had almost killed his wife and himself. He wiped the blood dripping from his nose and stared back at his bloodied hand in disgust, but feeling no guilt. When Akron suddenly tried to stand up, he quickly kicked him in the side, letting the man holler out in pain as he dropped against the cold floor again. He couldn't care less if the man died, no matter how slow or painful.

Emily turned around and staggered back to the middle of the car, clutching her head and gritting her teeth as her headache only worsened. She looked around at all the other passengers in the car. If they had been able to see the fight, they would surely be in a panic and just as desperate to get off the train as she.

David came to her side and slipped his arm around her. They glanced back at Akron once more, only to see him lying motionless at the back. They turned away simultaneously.

"I want to feel sorry for him, but I can't," David said.

"I know," she sadly replied. "I know."

XXXI

The train arrived at its next stop a minute later. They were the first ones off the car and onto the wide platform crowded with people carrying suitcases and purses. They trudged their way through the crowd and onto the escalator against the wall.

On the level above, they found themselves in a wide atrium. A family with a cart full of luggage, a pilot and her first officer walking beside her, a business woman chatting away into her cellular phone, and a man carrying two bags, briskly strode underneath a sign that read: Welcome to La Gaurdia International Airport.

Emily walked out into the middle of the foyer and gazed around. There was no Akron in sight, but hundreds of people were passing right by her without a single look accredited to her. She held up her arms in consternation, then looked back at David. His face was as confused as hers. She let her shoulders drop in disappointment and walked back.

"What do we do from here?" he glumly asked.

She let out a sad sigh. "I don't know. But if you'll excuse me for just a moment, I have to use the restroom," she said. "I'll be right back." She glanced at him with a forced smile and then darted across the atrium to the women's' restroom.

David leaned against the wall and watched her disappear into the crowd. Once she was gone from sight, he closed his eyes and tried to let all the thoughts jammed in his brain organize themselves out into something logical. They were fears, mostly. Fears of what would happen to them next. And, if they survived, what would happen after that.

He suddenly realized how wonderful things had been before. True, there was a lot of tension between Emily and him, but still, they were alive and in their own world, able to be seen and heard and felt by others. And that tension would have eventually gone away. Or at least he had hoped it would have. He had been living in a real world, sharing life with his best friend, and had taken every single moment of it for granted. The revelation was disheartening. He had wasted too much by being careless.

He exhaled and looked back at the restroom entrance. Emily had been in there for a while. She was usually a dawdler when it came to making lavatory visits. He wondered how anyone could spend so much time in a restroom as she sometimes did. Other than taking a half-hour long shower in the mornings, which he did every day, there was no excuse!

In the women's' restroom, Emily walked over to the sink and slipped her hands under the faucet. A cool stream of water automatically shot out. She quickly scrubbed her hands clean and then splashed some of the water on her face. The wave of fresh liquid felt good against her skin, relieving the strain on her face.

She heard the door open as another person walked in. Tired to the point where almost anything would be amusing, she smiled at the fact that they would see only the water running from the faucet and perhaps think that the place was haunted. She splashed some more water against her face. She looked in the mirror and watched the droplets trickle down her wet face and to—

She suddenly stopped in fear at the sight of the dark figure behind her.

She whirled around.

Akron grabbed her shoulders and threw her back against the mirror. Before she could scream, he had lifted up a long pipe and swung it at her.

She dodged.

The pipe hit the mirror with tremendous force, showering poor Emily with a blanket of broken glass.

She scrambled to get away, but tripped and crashed on the floor. She turned around just in time to see him standing over her and throwing the pipe at her again.

She rolled to the right.

The tip of the pipe crashed against the floor with a deafening clang, missing her only by a few inches.

He flung it at her again.

She rolled to the left.

Missed a second time.

In a rage of fury, he lifted the pipe above his head and stared down at her with glowering eyes, ready to kill her with a mortal blow to the head.

Helpless and paralyzed with fear, she held her hands in front of her and let out an ear-piercing scream.

Akron hurtled the pipe at her.

She closed her eyes, not want to see it coming.

"Get out!" David's voice screamed.

She opened her eyes and saw David fighting for the pipe. Akron growled like a wild animal as he yanked to free his weapon, but he wouldn't let go.

A lady suddenly walked into the restroom and over to a sink. She blissfully opened her purse and pulled out a lipstick. She gazed into the mirror, admiring herself as she applied her make-up, totally unconscious of what was happening behind her as two men fought for the deadly weapon.

Emily jumped forward and grabbed Akron's ankle. She pulled his foot out from under him, sending him tumbling to the hard floor.

David grasped the pipe in both hands, not sure whether to run away and leave him or finish him off. The later of the two sounded the best, but there was no question in his mind that he wouldn't be able to live with himself if he took it. "Come on!" he shouted.

They rushed out of the restroom and back into the atrium. He dropped the pipe on the floor and ran with Emily into the ticketing terminal. They looked around, desperate for an exit. There were taxis lined up outside on the parkway, but where they would take them was anyone's guess.

"Oh God!" Emily gasped. She pointed far back down the corridor where Akron, his face as vengeful as ever, was marching towards them, holding his abdomen with one hand and the pipe in the other.

"Shit!" David growled. *Why can't he just go away!* his mind screamed. He grabbed Emily's hand and darted into the nearest terminal. They rushed through the metal detectors and passed the security guards without a care, knowing that they could do nothing to help them.

They found themselves in a small, narrow concourse with relatively few passengers. The carpeted floors were darkened from all the dirt scrubbed into them and the ceilings were yellow and murky from bad lighting. The sunlight beamed in from the windows as the sun began to set in the west.

At the next gate area, where the departing sign above the check-in counter displayed Denver, Colorado as the destination, they saw a group of passengers filing through the jet-way door to board an MD-11. The wide-body jet, painted a brilliant white with a red tail that held an Ambridge Airlines logo, brought a glimmer of hope to their eyes.

They jumped behind the line, picking up two meal bags as they passed the large cooler near the doorway. They realized that it had been well over a day since they had last eaten. Their stomachs had been growling for food for quite some time, but they never noticed until now. But they were still too nervous to eat.

David watched the terminal behind him, fearing that Akron would catch up at any moment. The line filed onto the jet-way, moving ever so languidly. *Will you people move!* he thought, wanting to scream it out loud.

Suddenly, Akron appeared. He shot a devilish look at him and he was holding the pipe up as he approached. David felt his mouth run dry and his pulse quicken. He looked back and saw that the line wasn't going anywhere.

"Damn it!" Emily swore. She turned back to the old man in front of her who was almost through the doorway. "Move it!" she hollered. She tried to push him forward, but she had no affect on him. She could punch him and he'd never feel it.

"Let's go, let's go, let's go," David quickly urged, beginning to panic and his heart pumping explosively.

He turned around.

Akron was only a yard away, his pipe already poised above his head and ready to strike with deadly force.

David felt his blood freeze inside of him. He was trapped. There was no escape—

The gate attendant slammed the jet-way door shut an inch from his face.

Akron ran up to the wire-mesh window, dropping his weapon as he pressed his hands against the glass and watched in bafflement as his prey walked simply away from him.

Two exhausted people boarded the MD-11 unnoticed by the flight crew. The cool cabin air was fresh and clean. The first class seats were filled by passengers settling in for the long flight. One man was already leaning back in his chair with a blindfold across his eyes, unaware of the complimentary glass of champagne that was already being poured out on his tray table by a stewardess.

They moved through the portside aisle, toward the back, passing by the agitated passengers trying to stuff all of their luggage in the tiny overhead bins and the flight attendants running a drink service. A pair of seats remained empty near a window in the middle of the cabin. They quickly took it and hoped that there would be no one who would want to claim it.

"Oh God," Emily exclaimed, pressing her hand against her forehead as she tried to make sense of everything. "That was too close. It's getting closer all the time."

David didn't know what to say. She was right. Survival was getting harder. It was only a matter of time, a mathematical certainty, before they'd lose a struggle. He opened his meal back and pulled out a tuna fish sandwich. He tore off the plastic wrap and hungrily tore his teeth into the delicious food.

Emily was less enthusiastic, critically sniffing her sandwich before venturing to bite into it. *Needs pickles*, she thought as she chewed. She had never liked airline food. There was always something wrong with it. Either the meals were too cold, too hot, over cooked, still alive, and so on.

They moved onto the potato chips and candy bars as the plane taxied out to the runway. They watched with boredom as the flight attendants stood in the aisles, giving their passengers the mandatory safety instructions that coincided with a pre-flight video. They had heard it all before and were too tired to really care.

" . . . Please make sure your tray tables are up and your seats are in the full, up-right position for take-off," the pilot's voice said over the speakers.

David crinkled his empty bag into a ball and tossed it in the aisle. He was surprised to see when a flight attendant walking by stopped to pick it up. He sighed. "If only she saw us," he said.

Emily, finished with her meal too, crushed her bag into the pocket of the seat in front of her. She let out a sigh and looked out of the window. She could see the bridges that led into Manhattan and the tops of the taller buildings glow with the light of the setting sun as New York was slowly being devoured by the darkness of night. "Think we'll ever get back?" she asked.

He didn't have time to answer before the engines suddenly revved up. The jet started down the runway, hurtling through the air at a tremendous speed. The cabin trembled violently as the roaring engines propelled the plane up the bumpy runway. After a moment, seeing the world outside their windows flash by, the nose of the aircraft lifted up and the ride smoothed.

The two lovers watched the ground below sink away as they traveled into the sky. After a few minutes, the plane banked to the right, flying over Harlem at several thousand feet. They could see the rivers lit up with the fiery reflection of the sun, but they were too high to see anything else clearly through the thick haze. With heavy hearts and sober minds, they watched their home disappear from view.

As the MD-11 climbed higher into the air, the cabin grew more stuffy. Emily felt her ears pop once, then again, and then for third time. She stared ahead, watching the video screen that displayed a map of the eastern portion of the United States and the plane's current position.

She felt her eyelids growing heavy with sleep. She closed her eyes for a brief second, relishing the relief of a dark shield over her tired pupils. She thought of nothing. The only thing that registered in her mind was the drone of the engines, the cool cabin air, David next to her, and how comfortable she felt for the first time in days.

You can't fall asleep! she told herself, fluttering her eyelids back open. She knew that if she drowsed off that she could end up awaking somewhere else than where she was. The thought terrified her, but not enough to keep her from fantasizing about falling asleep.

She gazed out of the window and stared at the beautiful sky. Dark purple clouds with wispy tops, outlined with the bright red sunlight, contrasted against the fluorescent-pink sky that transpired to a bright orange in the west and darkened to a caliginous hue in the east. She couldn't remember seeing a more spectacular sunset before. Still, she wanted to sleep. "It's so beautiful," she said, her words slow and exhausted.

"Yes. It is," David agreed, weary himself.

She curled herself up into a ball and leaned against David's shoulder, still fighting to keep awake. "Whatever you do," she warned, "don't let us fall asleep. We can't close our eyes. It's dangerous . . ." She stopped to yawn, then forgot what she was about to say and remained quiet.

A few more quiet minutes passed. She closed her eyes once more, just for a short rest. She listened to the jet engines, determined to be alert and not fall into a slumber. But slowly, the engines faded away from her mind. A moment later, her body was limp and her breathing shallow as she peacefully rested against her husband's shoulder.

Don't let us fall asleep, her words repeated in his mind. He watched the passengers around him, desperate for something on which to focus his attention. The thought of just being able to close his eyes and fall asleep played through his mind, taunting him with what was forbidden.

Everything felt so calm and relaxed. Only a few passengers were talking, their voices barely audible over the purring of the engines and the sound of the slipstream. The air was comfortably cool and, best of all, Emily was right beside him with her arm resting against his.

He suddenly realized Emily was asleep. *Don't let us fall asleep*, he remembered again. He turned his head to her. *Emily, wake up*, he said, or so he thought he did. *Emily, honey, we have to stay awake!* But he was too tired to utter the words. He closed his eyes just for a short moment. He pictured turning to her and gently shaking her awake and telling her to stay alert. A moment later, his dream faded away and he drifted off into sleep.

XXXII

It was the sudden roar that jolted Emily awake. She looked around, her eyes full of trepidation. David stirred right beside her in a tiny co-pilot's seat that was more like a chair cushion. A cockpit console with missing dials and a broken control wheel sat in front of her. The ceiling and walls around them were charred and covered with a grimy, black soot. Outside of a giant hole where a windscreen had once been, she could see a field of tall, brown grass stretching out for miles ahead.

At first she wondered how long they had been out. It had to have been twelve hours or more. She felt fully rested and—

The roar sounded out again, this time it was much closer.

She opened the flimsy door beside her and hopped out. She already found herself sweating from the scorching heat as she turned around to see a family of elephants, ever so majestic, walking in the distance. The baby stayed at its mother's side as the father traveled behind, keeping a keen eye out for predators.

Emily watched in awe at the sight. She had never seen live elephants in the wild before. She turned and looked off to the west, rubbing her aching shoulder, which was more sore than ever. A cluster of towering trees around a lake loomed over the Serengeti, providing a cooling shade for the land beneath them. A herd of gazelles grazed together, only a few yards away from a pride of relaxing lions. With their stomachs full from an earlier meal, the giant cats were no threat to the graceful bovids.

She squinted as a hot wind scoured the grassland with a low howl and blew her hair back. The breeze provided no relief from the hot sun, which hung high in the noon sky. She shook her head in revulsion. "I can't believe this," she said to herself, looking up at the sky. The white clouds that drifted overhead were too thin to give any protection from the blazing sunlight.

She looked back at the plane, or what was left of it. The twin-engine Cessna lay imbedded in the ground with grass reeds growing up around it. The wings, blackened from fire, were broken off the sides of the ravished plane and the tail was completely torn off. Its rakish appearance had been diminished to the likeness of a crumpled ball of foil.

They saw an odd, white rock sitting just beside the cowling. She lissomely walked over to it and picked it up. The object was surprisingly light in her hands as she turned to see—

She dropped the human skull and let out an ear-piercing scream.

David bolted out of the plane and rushed to her side. "What is it!" he demanded.

Screaming hysterically, she pointed down at the skull. "That!"

"Calm down!"

She turned to him with a look of fury on her pained face. "How can I calm down! I was just holding someone's head in my hands! We're . . ." She spun around and gestured at the endless grassland around them. ". . . as far away from any civilization as we can possibly be! It's a hundred degrees out here! No food! No drink! And you want me to calm down? How!"

David looked around the endless landscape of tall grass, with only an occasional tree here and there in the distance. He let out a frustrated sigh and bit his bottom lip. "This isn't good."

Emily crossed her arms and turned away from him. She was thirsty enough to wrestle a lion just to get a drink. Without a word, she started through the grass towards the grove of trees, eagerly staring at the small lake with a watering mouth. The tall blades were abrasive against her delicate arms as she moved through them, ever becoming more annoyed at the world around her.

"Guess I should've asked for a cup of coffee on the plane," David said with a forced chuckle, trying to sound upbeat as he trudged through the grass behind her. "At the very least, I could've gone back into the galleys myself and taken one. It would've been nice to wander into the cockpit too. I could imagine you just—"

She whirled around at him and snarled, "Shut up!" He stopped dead in his tracks, his face falling into a look of hurt. "Just shut the hell up!"

"What's wrong?" he innocently asked.

"What do you think is wrong! How dense do you have to be!"

"I'm sorry," he quickly apologized, realizing the answer was obvious.

She turned her back on him and continued through the grass. "I mean, do you have shit for brains, or what?"

David lingered behind, emotionally injured and not knowing what to think. Then he decided to take the offensive. "You're not the only one here with problems, you know," he growled, marching after her.

She spun around again. "This isn't a joke! You're going about this as if everything's going to be okay and that—"

"It is!" he reassured.

"David, look!" she hollered, throwing her hands up in the air. "This is it! After everything we've gone through, after how close we came to getting back home, and this is where we end up! Right in the middle of a forsaken wasteland!"

"We'll get back!"

"I doubt it. Even if we did, things would never be the same."

"I would hope so."

"Why?" she sneered. "You definitely lost that promotion and I, well, who knows if I even have a job anymore!"

"You do so! Emily," he said, stepping near. She shifted away from him, not wanting to be touched. "Things will work out. We'll get any problems sorted out and everything will be fine."

"That's just it! Wake up! They won't be! We're dead! It's a one-way ticket! This is it! Everything I've done, the career I've built, the friends I've made, the things I've learned, is all pointless now!"

"It is not! Will you be quiet and just listen to what you're saying!" he exclaimed.

"And what was life to you? Huh? You just sat around the office all day, did as little as possible, came home and complained about how much more exciting things would be if we did this or that instead of working with what we did have and make something useful of ourselves!"

"We did!"

"I'm not ready to die out here! I wanted more out of life than this! All I did was spend my time at the office!"

"That's for sure!"

"What are you saying? You spent just as much time obsessed with your work as I did!"

"At least I had time to—"

"Time for what? Complaining about money—"

His face was glowering with anger and red with contention as he tried to hold back his tongue, but the heat of the moment was too pressured to contain him. "I wasn't the one who was bitching about the money!" he roared. "That's all you cared about! It was to hell with me and whatever else we needed! And your only focus on your career was working your way up the ladder and throwing off whoever got in your way!"

"My primary concern was always with doing my job! Nothing else!" she hollered.

"All you want is the money. Then what? Perhaps more power in a company as you manipulate and control the minds of its employees and the public? Big deal! Where's it going to get you in the end?"

Her mouth dropped open in abhorrence. "Try taking some of your own advice! You represent a bunch of money-grubbers who tear homes away from widows and orphans! Of course, the people you talk with never know that because you lie straight to their faces that they're getting the best possible—"

"That's not true! And another issue! You have this thing where you have to control everyone and everything! And if something falters, it's the end of the world!"

"You're exaggerating!"

"Am I?" he shouted back. "A missing electric bill last month sent you on a rampage through the house, as if it was the essence to all life on earth!"

"That bill was three months behind!" she defended.

"It was a stupid bill! It doesn't constitute screaming and yelling, tearing the house apart and wasting a whole Saturday trying to find the damned thing! There's more to life than that! I know I certainly want more from life than a stupid bill payment!"

"Don't you think that I want more from life?" she cried through clenched teeth. "I just said that! Are you deaf or what!"

"I want more from life than you!" he bellowed back.

She made two fists with her hands, trying her best to ignore his cruel words cutting into her heart like a blade made of ice. "You have no life!"

"I would without you!"

She pulled her arms back. She could feel the slippery sweat in the palms of her clenched hands. "You couldn't . . ." She stopped. *What am I doing?* she thought. *Oh God, I'm about to hit him. I'm ready to hit him right across his rotten face!* Her eyes wide with fear, she stepped back and let her hands fall to her side. She shivered at the realization of how terrifyingly close she had come in anger to striking the man she loved. She watched him stare back at her with glowering eyes. *If he says another word, I'm going to die*, she thought.

David's face softened. His mind was just now processing the callous words he had thrown out at her without thinking. A wave of guilt gushed through him as his heart sank in his chest. *Oh no. What have I done?* he thought. He saw her frown across her pretty face that was red with disconsolation. *Oh God, Emily, I'm sorry!*

He swallowed hard and stepped forward, his eyes full of remorse as he tried to comprehend everything that had just happened. "Oh God," he whispered to her. "I didn't mean it. I didn't mean any of it! You know that, don't you?" He gazed into her eyes and saw a tear drip from her bottom eyelash.

They stood there, watching each other with bruised hearts. Another gust of wind swept the Serengeti, rustling the grass around them. Another elephant roared in the distance and a bird squawked as it flew overhead. The blistering weather had brought several beads of sweat to their skin.

They felt none of it. All they could think about was the damage they had caused to each other. In just a few minutes, they had maliciously torn away the trust and support that they had thrived on. The destruction left in their hearts was immeasurable.

Emily blinked her eyes, forcing more tears down her cheek. "I'm sorry," she whimpered.

David gently moved to hug her. This time she didn't resist. She rested her head against his shoulder and mournfully whispered, "I was going to hit you." It stung her conscience to say it, but she had to tell him. He had to know how close she had come to striking him.

He gently stroked her hair, taking in her words and fully digesting them in his mind. The idea of being hit in anger by her was painful to the thought. But he found himself to blame. He had lost control and said the most incisive things he could possibly come up with. "I would have deserved it," he admitted.

She squeezed him closer to her. "No. No. You'd never deserve it."

"I could shoot myself for what I just did."

"Please, David. It wasn't your fault. I—"

He slipped his finger under her chin and raised her face up to his. "No," he said, shaking his head, trying to constrain the tears welling up beneath his eyes. "I lost my temper. We both did . . . But I had no right to say those things to you. They weren't true . . . I only said them to hurt you . . . And I'm sorry."

She sniffled and tried to smile, but couldn't. She hurt too much inside.

He gently kissed her delicate lips and then her forehead. They leaned against each other with their foreheads touching and their arms around each other. Their mouths were mute. There were no words to be said. Only hearts to mend.

XXXIII

The cool water felt refreshing against the back of her parched throat. She drank savoringly as the sun beat down on her back, already reddening her skin with its heat. She lifted her head up from the lake and splashed some water on her face, then glanced to her right. A lion sat twenty feet away, watching her with curious eyes. He looked ferocious, but his intentions were harmless for the time being. She looked away and sat back, wiping the dripping water off her mouth.

"That was good," David gasped in between deep breaths of air. He felt as if he had taken in enough water to last him a month. He gave Emily a satisfied smile, then laid back on the ground, sprawling out his arms and legs.

Emily tried not to laugh. She lifted her knee to her chin and undid her shoe buckle to relieve her sore and blistered heels. "Have enough?" she asked, throwing the shoe aside and reaching for the other.

"Too much," he said, wondering if he was going to throw it all back up. Water or not, the sun was still brutally hot. He unbuttoned the first few buttons on his shirt and kicked off his shoes. He laid down and rested his arm over his eyes and tried to relax like the other animals lying around the lake.

"God," she said, tossing the other shoe away. She looked up at the brilliant sky and could see a wall of black clouds approaching from the west. She fell back against the soft earth. The loose dirt pleasantly tickled her back like soft silk. "Do you wonder if this sort of thing happens to other people?" she asked.

He thought for a moment, then said, "I don't know. On one hand, I would hope so. On the other, I'd pray to God that it doesn't."

"Hmm. I think I see what you mean. It's all—"

A high-pitched screech asounded in front of her. She looked up to see a little brown monkey, it's long tail swaying happily back and forth, holding one of her shoes with admiring eyes. It glanced at her and became fearful. With a tiny holler, it jumped away.

"Hey!" she cried.

David leaped to his feet and saw the monkey scampering away on its hind legs, carrying its prized possession in its tiny arms. He darted after it, racing alongside the pebbled shore of the lake. He was gaining on him quickly. A few more seconds and he'd have him.

Too late.

The monkey climbed up the tree to rejoin its family. David stood back, defeated as he peered up into the branches. The monkeys playfully shrieked out and sprung from limb to limb. The little monkey with the shoe climbed out on a branch right over him. The thief watched him, screeching wildly to taunt him as it let the shoe dangle above him on its furry paw.

Without warning, another gust of wind blew and swayed the branches. The monkey let out a desperate holler as the shoe suddenly fell. It watched in despair as the object hit the ground and the human leaned over to pick it up.

"Here you go," David said. He turned around and handed Emily, now standing next to him, her shoe back.

"Thank you," she replied, taking it and then glaring at the annoying mammal. She sat down and put her shoe back on, figuring it wasn't worth the risk to go without them. "You better get yours back on before someone decides to take them," she suggested.

David thought the better of it and quickly dashed after his shoes, leaving Emily alone as she fought with the stubborn buckle on her shoe strap. “Come on,” she growled. “Why won’t you—”

“Eee!” the monkey screamed, jumping on her lap.

Emily almost punched the animal off her before she saw the large flower bud in its hand. With a friendly look, the monkey extended his paw. She cautiously lifted the bud from its hand, keeping a keen eye on the fury animal. It stayed on her lap, looking back at her with its big brown eyes.

“Don’t move,” David’s voice instructed.

Emily turned to see him standing behind her, ready to fling one of his shoes at the monkey. “No!” she cried. “Leave him alone!”

The startled monkey jumped off her and moved back a few feet.

David let the shoe drop to the ground and walked over to her side. “What’s that?”

“I don’t know?” she said, ripping the bud open. She brought it to her nose and sniffed the sweet petals inside. She looked up and saw the other monkeys in the trees feasting away at similar buds. “Hmm. I wonder.” She slipped the bud in her mouth. The texture was soft, but the taste bitter. She swallowed it anyway and stared back at the monkey who was eyeing her shoe once more. When it realized it was being watched, it instantly looked up at her, as if to ask how she liked its gift.

Emily groaned as she moved to unbuckle her shoe. She took it off and placed it in front of the monkey with a grimace. Her ankles were aching from them anyway.

The monkey grabbed the shoe with both arms, hugging it closely to its chest like a mother holds her baby. With grateful eyes, it darted off behind the tree trunk.

“What do you think he’s going to do with it?” David asked.

"Who knows," she said. Her stomach growled with a craving for food. The tiny bud had made her realize how hungry she was again.

The monkey jumped back into view, this time carrying a green fruit the size of a grapefruit. It ran to Emily once more and plopped the fruit on her lap. She looked up at David. "Give him my other shoe."

He rolled his eyes as he knelt down and handed the animal her second shoe. The monkey shot him an untrusting look as he approached. It snatched the shoe from his hands and ran off again.

"Now this is . . ." Emily struggled to pry her fingers through the skin. "Got it!" a piece of the skin peeled off, exposing the juicy pulp inside. She sank her teeth into it, relishing it with delight. "You have to try this!" she declared, handing it to him.

David had barely tasted it before the monkey appeared for a third time. Now it held a large stick. It ran over to David and rudely threw the stick down. Then it grabbed both of his shoes and scampered away.

Emily let out a laugh. "He really doesn't like you!"

David tossed the fruit back to her and picked up the stick, unimpressed. "This is all I get for a pair of forty-dollar shoes?"

"At least you got something for them." She took another bite of the succulent food and looked at the sky. The line of storm clouds, still miles away, was approaching quickly, throwing the land beneath them into darkness. She could hear the distant rumble of thunder and faintly see a flash of lightening.

David dropped the stick on the ground and let out a sigh. He hated the idea of being underscored by a wild animal. "I should break his neck and put him over a fire. He'd make a good meal. Wouldn't you think?"

"You leave him alone," she said with her mouth full. "I wouldn't mind taking him back home with us. That is, if we ever get home."

The monkey appeared from the tree trunk and lissomely walked over to them. Once it had their attention, it jumped on its hind legs and let out a frolicsome squeal.

"Now what does he want?" David growled.

The monkey, hopping up and down like a little kid on caffeine pills, frantically pointed toward another tree that lay across an arid field. He dropped to his front legs, ran over to them, stared at them for a moment, then ran back and pointed at the tree again.

"Who's in the well, Lassie?" David grumbled, standing up. Emily followed, took one last bite of the fruit, and tossed the peel on the ground. She jumped to her feet and followed him.

At once, the monkey scampered off, occasionally stopping to make sure the two humans were behind it. He led them across a dusty field, where the earth had grown too dry for anything to grow, and over to the tree. Not a single leaf protruded from its branches. The dry limbs hung dead in the air, swaying forbiddingly in the breeze. A massive hole in the trunk, carved out by various animals, clearly showed how the tree had met its demise.

The monkey happily darted over to a pile of loose dirt beside the trunk. The two lovers scowled in disgust as they came nearer and saw hundreds of fat termites patrolling the mound. The monkey picked a few termites off the top and popped them in its mouth. It chewed them for a few moments, then swallowed and looked back at its two new friends, waiting for them to dig in.

Emily reluctantly stepped closer. "I've tried beetles. I can do this," she said to herself. She reached towards a tinier bug. With trembling fingers, she picked it up and forced it in her mouth. She quickly chewed it until it stopped moving. Then, with hesitation, she swallowed it. The taste, surprisingly, didn't bother her. She reached for another.

David was more averse towards eating the insects. He looked past the soldier termites and spotted a defenseless, fat bug sitting alone in the dirt. He glanced at Emily, who was blissfully chewing away, and then back at the lone bug. After gathering the courage, he snatched up the insect and ate it. "Not bad," he later admitted.

They devoured the insects without a care. After a while, more termites appeared on the mound, being wary of their disappearing colleagues. The monkey shamelessly picked off one insect after another. It didn't even bother to finish chewing the insects in its mouth before it reached for more. After she had eaten about thirty of the bugs, Emily was no longer hungry enough to eat any more. She sat and waited, watching in amusement as her husband and the furry mammal finished off as many bugs as they could.

Without warning, the sunlight vanished and a dark shadow was cast over them. She looked up to see the dark clouds floating overhead.

The monkey, its mouth still full, looked up at her in alarm. As if to say good-bye, it shot a glance at David, then back at her before darting off with a friendly holler toward its family in the other trees. They watched as it climbed up the trunk and disappeared behind the globe of leaves. Another breeze, cooler and harsher than the previous ones, blew forcefully.

David stood up and turned to the west. Ahead, rushing toward them with rapid speed, were blankets of heavy rain. "Oh, my," he said in awe.

Emily came to his side, gazing out at the plains as the watery veils drenched down upon them with magnificent prestige. They turned around to see the animals by the lake retreating to cover and the birds in the sky landing in the trees.

An instant later, a cold blast of rain hit them. Their sun-burnt bodies were welcoming to the chilly drops of precipitation. They laughed out loud over the roar of the rain, feeling every drop hit their body with a refreshing splash of water.

A bolt of lightening flashed across the sky with a tremendous rumble that made them cower, but not forcing away their smiles.

They shivered as the rain pounded more harshly against the ground. David clung onto his wife's arm and led her towards the tree. They ducked inside the large hole and found enough room to sit down. A pair of yellow-winged bats hung upside-down on the decaying ceiling as a family of mice huddled together in a corner without taking any threat of them. They nestled close together and peered out at the rainy world.

The couple watched the rain pelt the ground outside with smiles on their faces, grateful that the heat had been broken. Emily leaned on him, wrapping her arms around his neck. She kissed his cheek and then snuggled against him with her head against his chest. In a low whisper, she prayed a short prayer of thanks to God. Then she listened to the falling rain, the white noise soothing to her sense of hearing. A moment later, she let her tired arms unclasp and fall to her side as her eyelids closed and breathing shallowed.

XXXIV

The cool, misty air felt vitalizing in David's lungs as he peacefully rested inside the hallowed-out tree trunk. It was when Emily shifted her head with a sleepy moan that he awoke. The scenery outside existed no more as a thick fog enshrouded the land. He could hear the gentle breeze hitting the tree and the noise of crashing waves in the distance.

"Mmm," Emily groaned, lifting her head up. She squinted, peering out at the misty world with drowsy eyes.

"Now where are we?" David asked, mystified and perplexed.

She forced herself up and stepped over him. "There's just one way to find out," she said, walking outside. She stepped onto soft grass that was drenched in dewdrops and green with life.

A sudden gust of wind blew her hair back and the cloud around her. In an instant, she found herself looking upon gently rolling hills of green, dotted with dogwood trees, that gave way to a forest just a half mile north. To her left was the edge of a massive cliff that bordered the choppy ocean waters below.

David came to her side and gazed out at the beautiful land around them. Far ahead, as the heavy mist cleared away, they could see the ocean bluff going on for miles alongside the green meadow. He looked over the waters and saw the image of the sun trying to shine through the gray clouds, but to no victory. "Where are we?" he asked again.

Emily knelt down and picked up a small plant. She studied it peculiarly before standing back up and placing it in his hands. "Ireland," he heard her say as he glanced down at the shamrock.

"Huh. Fancy that," he chuckled. He stepped forward and took in the sights around him, wondering if he was still asleep and dreaming or actually awake. Everything here seemed so much more peaceful than the other places they had been. "I always wanted to see this place."

Emily felt her dress heavy enough to be a lead suit. She squeezed the side of her dress, releasing the water trapped in the fabric. With his back turned to her, she quickly slipped it off and wrung it out, being careful not to damage it. She hung it on the flimsy tree branch of a nearby dogwood, letting the rest of the water drip off.

With a brisk smile, she strode past David and over to the edge of the ocean bluff. Gazing out at the endless Atlantic before her, she put her arms together in the air and stretched as another burst of wind hit her face.

"Aren't you cold in that?" he asked.

"Just a little bit," she said, turning around.

He started to take off his jacket. "Did you want my—"

"Nope," she asserted, holding up her hands. "I'm fine. Besides, this goes so much better with the green, don't you think?" she asked with a little curtsy.

He lifted his eyebrows as he placed his jacket back on. The white slip did seem more ambient. "I suppose so."

She grinned and walked up to him, placing her hands on his shoulders. "You *suppose* so? You mean that you don't know?" He suddenly looked guilty. "I *do* look better in white. Of course, I look better in anything!"

"You're a goddess," he sarcastically taunted.

Her smile dropped to a scowl. "Okay. Shut-up now," she growled. She hated it when he gave in like that. He was always too easy to agree and took all the fun out of her expressing self praise. She moved closer and slid her hands together behind his neck.

"Your hair shimmers in the sun like the sparkling ocean waters," he said as his hands came to rest on her waist. "Your lips are the color of a field of roses. Your skin is as soft as the finest Egyptian silk. And your eyes shoot out laser photons that kill anyone who gets in your way."

"Hey," she grinned, gently shuffling to the right. "I only kill the people I don't like."

"How much money do I have to keep paying you to let me live?"

"I let you live for my own amusement," she stated with a diabolical laugh.

"Humph!" he exclaimed, raising his chin into the air. Then he glanced back down at her. She could tell by the look in his lively eyes that he was in his playful mode again. "Dearest sweetheart, may I ask what it is that we are doing?"

She only smiled as she led him in a small circle. "Dancing," she admitted. "I suppose."

"You *suppose*? You mean that you don't know?" He suddenly looked guilty. "I, for one, *do* happen to know that we are dancing!"

"Shut-up, you freak," she said, smiling uncontrollably. "You're just standing there, waddling back and forth."

"I need the music!" he dramatically declared, raising his hand in the air as if to omnipotently grasp the sky.

"No, you don't," she said, forcing his hand back down to her side. "You just need me." She suddenly swung him around, leading him into an intricate dance pattern. Without singing, without music, without even words, they danced. Among the grass laden with refreshing dew and sheltered by the wispy clouds that floated overhead, close together and lost in each other's eyes and the world around them, they waltzed about without a single care but to live life.

He let her go into a lithe twirl. She fell back into his arms, bringing her hands to touch his back and her face just centimeters from his. They gently swayed back and forth as they moved in a simplistic circle. So plain, yet so complex.

She suddenly stood on her toes to kiss him off guard.

Before he could respond, she freed herself from him and whirled around again with her arm high in the air. She turned to—

She tripped over her feet and stumbled to the ground. Dizzy and laughing helplessly, she laid back in the grass and felt the cool water drops soak through her slip and onto her back.

David laid down beside her, propping his head up in his hand with his elbow on the ground. "What was that!" he asked with a chuckle.

She shot him a look that told him she was only embarrassed for messing up, not for the fool she appeared to be when she did. "I'd like to see you spin around like that!"

"Sure thing. Next dance we're at, I'll do all the ballerina stuff and you can just stand there like a board and occasionally hold my hand."

"If you do that in public, I'm not even going to be there! Let alone hold your hand!"

"Ha!" he shouted. He watched her lovely hair sprawled out on the grass. A cluster of shamrocks lay between them. He gently picked one of the clovers and carefully slipped the stem into the front of her hair.

She gazed back at him with her kittenish eyes sparkling, even though the sky above her was sunless with gray clouds. "How do I look?" she inquired.

"Indescribable," he answered.

"Good! Now tell me. Should I say how you look?"

He didn't answer, lost in the depth of her eyes as he placed another shamrock on her head. He picked a third one and started to put it in her hair, but stopped. He let his hand touch her forehead, then slowly drift down the side of her face until his arm was over her.

She suddenly found herself smiling with sudden anticipation.

He stroked the side of her face while his other hand lay gently upon her breast as he stared into her eyes, taking in her beauty. He benevolently said, as if in a trance, "Let me make love to you."

She brought her arms around him without saying another word, letting their bodies passionately come together without further ado as they shared a long, intimate kiss.

XXXV

The tiny room was alive with the whirring of motors and buzzing electronics. The putrid smell of developing fluid filled the dark room. There was only a fluorescent bulb and a lighting board for light to see by.

"Bring him in a little more," Maloney instructed.

The physician in the other room typed a few buttons into the computer beside the massive CAT-Scan machine. He quickly abandoned his station and hurried back into the other room with Maloney as David's lifeless body was slowly pulled into the giant tube. He shut the door and sat down at the monitoring data processor. "Same ones as the woman?" he bluntly asked.

"Yes," the doctor ordered. The other physician began the scans as he read over Emily's results for a sixth time. He was baffled. Nothing in medical school could have prepared him for what he was seeing. There had to be a mistake!

The side door suddenly opened as a nurse ushered in Mr. Dennison. The weary man's face was pained with frustration and grief. As strong as he was trying to be, Maloney seriously wondered if he could take what he had to tell him.

"Something wrong, doctor?" Dennison asked.

Maloney nervously set Emily's results back down on the counter. "Ah, yes. I'm afraid so. We can go out into the waiting room and—"

"No," he declared. "You know something. I want to know what that is. Tell me what's wrong with my daughter."

Maloney bit his bottom lip and sighed. "Okay. Let's just go out to the waiting—"

"Doctor," Dennison said, standing his ground and with his chin up high. "My daughter?"

" . . . Your daughter is not showing any sign of brain activity. The term for that is brain dead. She's no longer able to run any thought processes. She's not even dreaming."

Emily's father stood there, trying to make sense of the dialog. He wasn't ready to believe it just yet. Something was being left out. "What aren't you telling me?" he asked dryly, his body already trembling with shock.

"Well," the doctor said, grabbing her results, "She's not showing any sign of brain activity."

"I know that. You've just repeated yourself."

"No. I mean that she's not showing *any* sign at all. And yet her heart continues to pump and while on the respirator, her body is making an effort to breathe. The twitching, the fluctuating body temperatures, the simple physical happenings inside of her are impossible without some sort of activity in the brain!"

Dennison took a step back, unsure of what to make of all this, as any distraught father would be. "I'm not following."

"She's alive, somehow, someway. We know that simply by observing her. You've been in there with her for the past couple days and yet you have no question that she's still alive. Do you?"

"Not at all," he said, trying to hold back his tears. *Keep it together!* he thought to himself. *You're a man! You can take it!* He turned away as he wiped the tear from his face so that the doctor wouldn't see. "Could it be something with the machine?" he asked.

"No. Another lady was in here after your daughter and everything was operational." He noticed him rubbing at his face. "Is there something wrong?"

"Nah," Dennison said, looking back at him with a straight face. "Just a loose eyelash."

"Oh," he said, not believing him for a second. "The machines here are the most up-to-date state-of-the art devices that hold capabilities unfathomable until just last year. That's what scares me the most. Something very strange has happened to your daughter. Right now, I can't explain it."

"Is there any chance of recovery?" Dennison demanded, knowing that he was far from ready to hear the answer.

" . . . Anything's possible," Maloney reminded. "But by everything I and the other doctors here at the hospital know, she's still brain dead . . . I'm sorry." It was heart-wrenching to see the man's shoulders drop as he turned away to let the tears gush out. "There are some decisions that are going to have to be made," he reluctantly continued. "If your daughter had any wishes for organ donations—"

"Maloney!" the other physician cried, rushing up to him with David's results.

He ripped them from his hand and glared at them. He felt his heart skip a beat. Shanahan's results were identical to his wife's. "God in heaven," he gasped. He glanced out of the window and looked at David's body lying on the CAT-Scan board.

He heard the door open and looked back in time to see Mr. Dennison huddling out into the hallway. He set the results on the counter and hurried after him. "Mister Dennison?" he called, rushing up to him.

The father of his patient kept walking, ignoring him completely. He tried his best not to make contact with anyone he passed, embarrassed that his face was a mess of tears that streamed from his eyes, tears that were too painful to hold in any longer.

"When I break the news to the rest of your family—"

"You're not going to," Dennison announced. "I'll take care of it."

"Sir—"

Dennison whirled around and shook his finger at him. "Don't! Not now! I don't need this!" he shouted. He stood back, trying to catch his breath and regain his composure. "I'm sorry, doctor. You've done everything you possibly could and I thank you for that. Please let us be for a while." With that, he turned around and stormed away.

Maloney hung his head low, feeling like the whole world was ganging up on him. He slowly turned around, wondering if things could possibly get any worse. It was then that he saw the hospital president and the chief of surgery walking towards him. *Darn it!* he thought. *I'm really in for it now!*

"Doctor Maloney?" the president asked, coming to a halt just inches from his face. "We have a few questions about an incident that occurred the other day involving one of your patients, Mrs. Emily Shanahan. Do you know what incident we are referring to?"

"I believe so," he admitted, his throat becoming tight as a cold sweat broke out across his forehead. "I did what was in the best interest of the patient and her family, but not without the consent of her family. What seems to be the problem?"

"The policies of this hospital, the rules that you were supposed to obey but deviated from, and your ethics as a doctor. I think we need to have a talk."

"I would love nothing more than to get this all straightened out," he admitted. "But right now I'm trying to go over a patient's scans and see what—"

"By tomorrow. I have my kid's birthday party at five, so I'm leaving at four thirty. I'll be in my office until then. If I don't see your ass in there by the time I leave, don't plan on coming back here the next day until after the hospital inquiry's been completed. That is, if you're allowed to ever set foot in this place again after yesterday's happenings!" the president snapped, her face mean and sour.

Maloney let out another sigh and watched the president and the chief surgeon walk away with scowls on their faces. He turned back into the viewing room. Seeing David's and Emily's scan results lying side by side, he realized that it was only the middle of the afternoon and he was already wanting to go home. He wanted to go anywhere, just as long as he got away from here and the sorrowful madness that plagued it.

XXXVI

As the evening twilight began to set in over the Irish coast, Emily shivered and nestled closer to her lover. She had put her dress back on long ago, as well as David's jacket. Still, she was freezing. The temperature seemed to be dropping and the dew droplets on the grass blades now felt like beads of ice.

Freezing or not, she loved being where she was, in her lover's arms, safe from everything the world could throw against her. She wondered how she could go on without him. Then she decided that she couldn't. Physically, perhaps. Emotionally, she'd rather be dead. She tried not to think of what it would be like. Things were already painful enough and he was the only thing in the world that God had given her that could save her from all the suffering.

"Still cold?" David asked, rubbing his hand up and down her arm.

Seeing the moisture of his breath turn into an icy vapor, she trembled even more and nodded. "I haven't been this cold since the heater broke last January," she barely managed to say.

"I think that you're right. Its . . ." He watched as a snowflake tumbled onto her eyelash. She quickly wiped it away with a flick of her finger. But no sooner had she removed it when two more fell upon her face. She sat up and brushed the cold snow off her and looked up at the sky filled with millions of descending snowflakes.

The wintry shower silently enveloped the land. In just a few short moments, a fine layer of the white precipitation was coated upon the hillsides.

"It's so beautiful," Emily said, shivering even more.

"I think we should find cover," he said, standing up and brushing off the snow. He helped her to her feet, gazing out at the ocean once more as it was inundated with snowflakes.

They started for the trees, regretting that they had given up their shoes as their feet became numb from the cold. Once in the forest, they found the tree limbs coated with the white snow. It was like walking through a winter wonderland.

Emily was disturbed by the quiet. She could almost hear her heart beating, let alone breathing. All throughout college she had hunted relentlessly for places to study that would give her peace. Even David spent several weeknights studying alone just to give her the silence she wanted. Now, with it all around her, it seemed scary.

As they traveled down a small incline, they saw a pole sticking out of the ground with a rotating green light beaming above it. "That's very peculiar," she commented, moving on.

A few minutes later, they found themselves in a small clearing. A deer trying to pick a few blades of grass through the icy snow looked up at them in alarm.

"Wow!" David exclaimed, slowly stepping forward.

The deer watched him with fear. It let him come a few feet closer before it bounded away, headed for cover in the shelter of the woods.

Emily picked up a handful of snow and packed it into a ball. She aimed it at David's back, then flung it at him with all her strength.

He felt the snow hit his back with explosive force. With a devious smile stretched across his face, he whirled around, scooping up some snow and tossing it back.

Emily dodged to the side and threw another snowball, hitting him in the shoulder.

"Ugh! That does it!" he exclaimed. He squeezed the snow in his hand and ran towards her.

"No!" she playfully screamed, turning away.

He threw the snow against her bare back.

She jumped away with a surprised holler, even though she had known it was coming.

She grabbed some more of the white stuff and turned around to grab his collar. "I'll show you!" she cried, trying to stuff the snow down his shirt.

He was one step ahead of her. He pulled his jacket off her shoulders and slipped a large, cold, ball of ice down the front of her dress.

She shrieked out and jumped back, desperately clawing at herself as the ball came to rest beneath her dress and against her bare stomach. "Oww! That's cold! You idiot!"

"Oh, but it's okay for you to do that to me!" he defended with a laugh.

"You're not wearing a dress!"

"No, I'm not. But you would still be trying to do the same thing if I had a dress on or not."

She sank away, miserably feeling the ice melting against her numb skin. "If you had a dress on," she growled. "I wouldn't be talking to you right now." She turned around and sucked her stomach in, frantically trying to rid herself of the pesky snow trapped beneath her clothes.

Then she felt a cold blast of snow hit her back.

She stood where she was and endured the pain of defeat, emitting a high-pitched growl without opening her mouth.

"And another ten points for the stupid male!" David happily cried.

"You're in for it!" she roared, whirling around and charging at him. She pounced on him and knocked him to the snowy ground.

Before she could pin him down, he slipped out from her grip and forced her on her back. He held her down by the shoulders, refusing to let her go free.

"Cold!" she screamed as the wet snow pressed against her bare back. "You win! You win! You win!"

" . . . I haven't counted to three yet," he said with a diabolical smile.

"What!"

"One . . . Hmm. Honey? What comes after one?"

"Two! Damn it! The number's two!"

"Oh yes! One . . . Two . . . Now what?"

"I warn you that my knee is strategically poised at a very sensitive area of your body and if you don't get off me this instant . . ."

David quickly retreated. "No hard feelings!" he said, holding up his hands in surrender. "You win!"

She stood up, gasping as the painful cold sucked the breath out of her. "You're a dead man!" she exclaimed, glaring at her husband.

He handed her his jacket to put on with an innocent smile. She snatched it away from him without showing any gratitude. "I hope that I have six kids just like you and then die in some horrendous accident so that you have to take care of them!"

"That one was below the belt," he criticized.

"That shouldn't matter to you!" she teased.

"What? Are you implying that I lack certain masculine traits?" He tried not to laugh as she adamantly nodded her head. "Not too long ago you were going on and on about how I could make you feel like a *real* woman—"

"Stop," she said with an embarrassed smile. "Someone will hear us."

"What?" he asked with a playful sneer. "No one else is around." He cupped his hands together and shouted out, "How I could make you feel like a—"

"You're perverted! And you're going to make the animals sick," she protested.

"They won't mind! They're—"

"Halt!"

"What?"

"I didn't say anything," she said with a shrug of her shoulders. Then she froze in place, hearing the sound of an approaching vehicle. "Uh-oh."

They turned to see a jeep burst out from between the trees. Three soldiers immediately jumped off carrying steel rods in their hands.

"Stay where you are!" a voice boomed over a loud-speaker. "You are on the premises of the World-One Military Training facility of Ireland!" Then the message repeated in German and French.

"Oh God!" Emily exclaimed, not knowing whether they should run or surrender. The soldiers dashed towards them with furious speed.

David stood in front of his wife with his hands high in the air. "We surrender!" he cried, watching the guards approach. "Please! We—"

The first guard reached him and jammed the rod into his thigh. A burst of electricity shot through his leg with searing pain. He collapsed to the snowy ground, unable to move and powerless to help Emily. He heard her scream before feeling her fall on top of him.

I'm paralyzed! he realized. He watched in horror as one of the soldiers pulled out two syringes from her waist-pouch. She ripped the caps off with her teeth before jamming one into his arm. He instantly found his eyelids heavy with sleepiness. *No! Stay awake!* he told himself.

He heard Emily suspire and her body fall limp over him. *Leave her alone!* he wanted to scream. But he didn't have the strength. He was too tired.

A moment later, he was unconscious.

XXXVII

When Emily opened her eyes, she found herself lying on a flimsy cot with her husband beside her. A bright fluorescent light shined in her eyes from above and she could hear several footsteps around her.

"Hello!" a happy voice said.

She glanced up and saw a man dressed in a blue hat and uniform looking down at her with a cheery face. He looked harmless, except for a gun that was stuck in a large holster on his belt. On his badge, below his name and picture, she noticed the bold script: WORLD-ONE JUSTICE DIVISION.

"Hi?" She pushed her hair back and tried to sit up. "Where are we?"

"Under arrest, I'm afraid," he answered with a frown.

It took her a few moments to digest all of the information. *Arrested? For what! You have to be playing some kind of joke! And it isn't funny!* But the look on his face told her that he was far from joshing her. "Why?"

"Well, you and your friend," he said, pointing to David who was coming out of his sleep, "trespassed on the grounds of a military training facility in Ireland yesterday evening. But the two of you apparently were just in the wrong place at the wrong time and not some terrorist spies. So, they brought you here to see the Arbiter."

David rubbed his eyes, not wanting to believe what he was hearing. He was partially still too asleep to even care. "Who's that? We didn't mean to trespass! It was a mistake! We weren't doing anything!"

"She's going to determine if you're guilty or not," he politely said, holding up his hand to calm him. "We want to assume that you are, based on the evidence. Or lack of, I should say. And trust me, she'll understand. This kind of thing happens all the time. So, if you'll come with me, I can take you down to see her now."

David groaned as he stood up, the worries rushing through his mind faster than he could realize they were even there. He held Emily's hand as they followed the man in blue. He took them out into a busy corridor filled with hurried people rushing about their daily tasks. Military personnel, wearing dark clothing as they carried their weapons at their sides, walked among white-collar workers dressed in the usual business apparel.

The two lovers saw morning sunlight streaming in through the windows as they turned down the hall. They loathed the feeling of being trapped inside when the fresh outside was beckoning them to rush to it, especially in the situation they were in. They glanced back down at the end of the hall where two large doors stood, separating them from whomever was on the other side.

"Now the Arbiter," the man explained to them, "is very busy, so you will have to be quick and concise about the reasons for your trespassing. Good luck and best wishes."

He opened the doors to a large office and gestured them inside. Their mouths hung open in awe at the sight of the massive room, paneled with cherry wood and the vaulted ceiling coated with elaborate paints. Down a row of bookshelves stacked with encyclopedias was a desk. The young woman who sat at it worked busily at the piles of papers before her.

"Arbiter Feldstrasse?" the man asked.

The woman looked up. "Yes Victor?" she asked.

"I have the two trespassers you requested to see."

She thought for a moment, then set her pen down. "Ah, yes. Thank you, Victor. That will be all for now. Leave us please."

The guard nodded and gave the lovers a friendly wink as he walked out, closing the doors behind him.

Emily and David worriedly watched the woman as she stood up and came around to them. She seemed friendly in appearance with her long, black hair nicely combed and her pretty face fresh and awake. "It's nice to meet you. Could I interest either of you two in a cup of tea?" she kindly said, easily crossing her arms and sitting on the front edge of her desk. She gave them a warm smile for reassurance.

Emily grinned back and shyly shook her head. Her stomach was too full of butterflies at the moment to even think of putting anything in it.

"Very well," the woman said. "I hope that you feel welcomed here. If there's anything I can do to assist you in any way, as far as treatment goes, please let me know."

"Thank you," David said, bowing his head slightly. "We're far from any complaints. It's an honor to be here. Though, I think that we're in a heap of trouble."

"Originally, yes. You intruded on our military training grounds in the province of Ireland. With all the trouble this new government's had with the Old World Resistance, the penalty for such a violation is execution."

Emily felt her throat run dry and the air exit her lungs. A wave of dizziness swept over her as she tried to understand what she were hearing. *Old World Resistance? What is she talking about! What year is it?*

"But—" David, equally nervous, started to say.

She held up her hand and cut him off. "Now, of course, the radicals working against us usually carry sophisticated weapons and work in massive groups. Anyone can figure out that two people, barely wearing enough clothes to survive, are not going to smuggle a nuclear weapon onto military grounds, let alone shoot someone. That's why you're here right now instead of the military court in Dublin."

"Where is this place?" Emily asked.

"The Alien Inference Authority in Baghdad," the woman said, shrugging her eyebrows. "I understand that you were asleep when they took you off the jet and you haven't been outside since. Obviously, you wouldn't know. So don't feel bad."

You brought us to Iraq! Emily thought with alarm. *You couldn't have picked Dublin, London, Glasgow or some other place that wasn't on the other side of the world?* She decided to let the thought go, realizing that by now she had to have been farther from home than this. Or had she?

"I do question, however, how you managed to wonder into a marked military training zone," the Arbiter continued.

"Well," David began, stepping forward. "We were traveling in Ireland, having that sense of wanderlust, and were unfamiliar with the area. We were by the cliffs when it suddenly became very cold and started to snow, which was very odd. We were simply looking for shelter when we came upon wherever it was that we were captured. Before, we passed a pole with a light on it, but we had never seen anything like it before and just went on. We meant no harm."

He gave her a confident smile, trying to show their faultless intentions. *Please don't ask where we came from!* he thought, knowing such a question would plunge them into trouble. No one in their right mind would believe their story. He could picture her laughing at them now as he explained to her everything from the crystal pillars in the ocean to the Roman town of Pompeii. They would label them as psychotics.

She studied him for a moment, then nodded amiably. "Very well, my fellow friends of the World-One Commonwealth. I don't have a lot of time on my hands, so I will pardon you under one condition."

David and Emily nervously held their breath, wondering what possible task they would have to accomplish to clear their names.

"Each of you must have a WOCAM Chips implanted as soon as possible. By law, I'm allowed to have you thrown in prison for not already having them inside of you. But, for some odd reason, I get the impression that you simply made a mistake and were registered without one."

"Registered?" David asked.

Emily cleared her throat and turned to him. "Yes," she said, trying to play along before the judge's suspicions arose. "Registered. We must have slipped through the cracks. That's all."

"I'm sorry," David quickly apologized. "I'm not feeling like myself after being knocked out like that."

Feldstrasse smiled pleasantly. "It's okay. The government will take care of all the expenses. I'll have you leave for the medical center in Babylon at once with an escort."

XXXVIII

Twenty minutes had passed between their meeting with the Arbiter and boarding a rakishly built train at Baghdad's newly built World-One Station. The law enforcer quickly ushered them through the aisles and onto the second deck, where he led them into a second-class cabin and shut the door behind them.

"Wow!" Emily gasped, looking at the elaborate chairs. The cabin was small, but held five leather seats, each equipped with its own mini-television set attached to the armrests. Outside the massive window, she could see the towering steel beams and endless sheets of glass that sheltered the train tracks. Hundreds of people crammed the docks below, rushing to and from various rail cars.

"Just take a seat," the law enforcer cordially instructed.

Emily sat by the window with her husband next to her. "This is unbelievable!" she exclaimed. Her eyes sparkled with the excitement of discovery as she tried to soak in all the sights around her.

David was less impressed. He replayed the Arbiter's last words in his mind over and over again. The idea of a populated city called Babylon, existing in the Middle East, made him cautious. With everything he had learned about the coming End Times, it just didn't feel right. For years, the resurrection of the ancient city had been watched with severe scrutiny. Now it was an apparent reality. And yet, most confusingly of all, everyone was very nice and pleasant.

The law enforcer lifted up a magazine and began flipping through the pages as the train started out of the station. Emily kept her eyes transfixed on the scenery outside, watching the train hurtle her out of the glass dome and out onto a desert. She could see the city of Baghdad basking in the hot sun just a few miles away. The images of the larger buildings of downtown seemed to swivel as the heat rose from the ground in front of her. *I can't believe it!* she thought. *All my life I wanted to see this place! And there's peace, technology and civility!*

"So," David began as the urban images outside faded away into a deserted landscape. "Where is this medical facility located?"

"In the heart of Babylon," the law enforcer casually said, not even bothering to look up. "Its construction was just finished last year. You'll find it a very amiable place. They take good care of their patients. Even for the short surgeries, like yours."

"What are they going to do, exactly?" Emily asked.

"They just stick the chip in," he said, pointing to the base of his skull. "You'll be out of there within an hour. Then you can take a look at the city. I take it that you haven't been there before, have you?"

"No," David said, not meaning for the apprehensiveness to seep through in his voice.

"Well," the law enforcer said, setting down his magazine with a cheerful smile. "You have to stop and take a look at our leader's palace. It's just amazing! For a nominal fee, you can go in and visit the first floor. And, if you're lucky, you may even get to meet him! But try not to expect it. Though he's in town, he's a very busy man. Especially with trying to protect us from the Resistance."

"What is that?" Emily asked, suddenly intrigued.

"Oh, a bunch of silly, whiny people. Some want things to return to normal, where the world was split up into hundreds of different countries. Others are caught up with beliefs of the old order and think that our leader represents some sort of evil."

"Why?" David bluntly asked.

"Many follow this ancient story about a guy named Jesus who could supposedly perform miracles and bring people back from the dead. Some even think that he's God." He looked back at the magazine, shaking his head in disgust. "It's ridiculous. You'd think with the way things have improved that they would realize that he simply doesn't exist."

"You mean that God doesn't exist?" Emily asked, suddenly getting worried herself. *Where are we? What time are we in? We were moving towards the future. But this can't be! I'm not hearing this!* She nervously held her hands together, expectantly waiting for an answer.

"The one who can truly give this world what it needs, delivering us from all of our suffering, is our beloved leader, himself. Haven't you heard all of the great things he's done? The man has performed miracles in front of billions!"

More like he's deceived billions, David thought, resisting the urge to say it. He felt very sick inside. He wanted to rush out of the cabin and find a lavatory where he could throw-up. He tried to keep the frown off his face, appearing as casual as he could as he fought with the bitter consternation inside of him.

"All four billion people on this earth know what a gift it is to be living in this age! Finally, we're all united! United in peace, religion, hope, and a strive for advancement into the future!" the law enforcer exclaimed.

"How many people?" David asked.

"Four billion. Three point nine if you want to get technical."

Emily shot a worried glance to her husband. *What happened to the billions of other people who were here before?* she fearfully wondered. She surmised that she didn't want to know. Instead of pushing him further on the issue, terrified that he would get suspicious, she delicately asked, “How do you like the religion?”

He shrugged his shoulders. “It’s okay, I guess. I go to the temples whenever I feel I need to. We listen to the instructor and try to find ourselves in the things we do each day.”

“All without thought of the Creator?” David asked with a forced smile, as to hide his true feelings. God was God. He existed and he knew it in his heart. Against all lack of evidence and every advancement in technology and the biological sciences, he knew, without a doubt, that the Lord existed, watching over them at the very moment.

The guard chuckled lightly. “Yeah. None of that junk. Just the truth of discovering who we really are and how we fit into this world. It’s so much easier to look at building up the god that we are rather than trying to pretend there’s this big figure out there, watching over us and doing nothing to save us. I used to be a Christian. What a waste of time. I never got anywhere with it. All of this energy being directed towards . . .”

Hold the tongue, Emily warned herself, wanting to lash out at him for taunting the knowledge she knew in her heart. She suddenly felt very alone again, but found strength inside. Perhaps it was just a defense mechanism. Or maybe, instead, it was a confirmation of the faith she had.

She glanced back out of the window, watching the desert whip by as the train sped down the track at tremendous speed. She estimated that they were moving at two hundred miles an hour; speed of which she had only experienced in a jetliner until now. The land looked so hot and dry, yet the climate inside couldn’t be more perfect. She turned away, knowing that landscape was the last thing she was caring about at the moment.

The law enforcer babbled on happily about the new government and its religious politics, not taking a single hint as the two lovers squirmed uncomfortably in their seats. "So I rest my case!" he finished. "If there's a god, then it's our cherished leader."

"He's a very remarkable man from all the things I've heard," David said. *Remarkable in the fact that he's being allowed to control virtually every mind in his grasp and no one seems to notice!* his mind finished.

"He is," the law enforcer said with a happy grin. "I'm proud to be serving the position I do for him and his world. He's . . ." His voice trailed off at the sight of the massive buildings in the distance. "And there it is!" he declared, standing up and pointing to them.

David and Emily stood up beside him. Several buildings were bound together around a lofty structure in the shape of an obelisk reaching a half mile into the sky. Domes of gold and silver sitting upon modern structures sparkled in the sunlight as the glass-paneled buildings around them soaked the light into the rooms inside. Helicopters flew in circles above the city center as various aircraft rushed in from the west towards the international airport. Like a glittering gem appearing out from an endless wall of featureless rock, Babylon stood out of the dry desert.

"The greatest city in the world!" the law enforcer proclaimed. "The center of the economy, culture, and politics for a global community!" He looked at them, his smile suddenly vanishing as he cleared his throat. "Sorry," he said. "I just really love this place."

"I understand," Emily said, sitting back down. "I used to have the same feeling about New York City."

"Hmm," the law enforcer said, taking his seat as well. "It's a pity that it doesn't exist any more. I miss it dearly. But hey, if it weren't for the Old World Resistance, our leader would have never lost it in the war."

"The war?" David asked.

"The Third World War. Not the American Campaign that came before. Los Angeles and Washington DC were lost in that one. Those poor people. I was lucky enough to be here, already beginning training for the job I have now, when the City of Angels was hit. Which is also another reason why I love my leader."

David clutched onto his armrests as the train started to slow upon entering the station. The city outside disappeared from view as the front of the train turned towards it. A moment later, the scenery outside disappeared behind a massive wall and the train came to a stop alongside a platform lined with shops and filled with busy people.

A feminine voice charmingly announced on an overhead speaker, "Welcome to the city of Babylon where the local time is ten fifty-four and the current temperature: thirty five. Thank you for using World-One Railways as your source of transportation. Have a nice day."

"Let's go," the law enforcer said, standing up and stretching his arms. He opened up the door and walked out. Emily and David reluctantly followed, letting him lead them down the stairs at the end of the corridor and off the train.

They stopped and looked around them, enraptured with awe. The docks were alive with vibrant people. The smell of cooking hotdogs and spinning cotton candy contrasted with cigarette smoke and other unpleasant odors. The sun beamed through the skylights on the ceiling, hundreds of feet above them. Birds flew from rafter to rafter, building their nests out of harm's way or simply to observe all the action below.

"This way!" the law enforcer called.

They quickly rushed to his side. Past the hordes of people and through a large gateway, he brought them out onto a city street. Modern apartment buildings and office facilities stood around them, bordered by clean streets and sidewalks. A food vendor was perched at every street corner, offering various food items to crave the needs of anyone. The cars, of designs and models they had never seen before, rolled past at a moderate rate, but without the fumes of exhaust or the noise of broken mufflers.

"This place is huge!" Emily gasped. "It's gotta be ten times the size of our city!" She suddenly stopped, remembering that their city no longer existed. If the members of the clergy at their church were correct, the few that did talk about the Apocalypse, then New York was probably nothing more than a wasteland of rubble and twisted metal.

The law enforcer said, "There's the facility," and pointed to the brown building with tinted windows across the street.

A frown came to David's face. He suddenly felt very fearful. The idea of having a microchip implanted anywhere, let alone in his head, made his stomach even more sick. He glanced at Emily. She wasn't smiling either as she stared in dread at the building.

Once the traffic was clear, their escort rushed across the street and held open the door for them. They reluctantly supervened and walked inside, wanting to get the procedure done and over with so they could hurry up and leave.

XXXIX

The nurse in the white lab coat quickly wrote out her signature on the bottom of her patient report and slipped it in the tray sitting on the cluttered counter. Of the hundreds of other staff and patients running around, no one seemed to have any time to notice that there was a terrified look on the woman's face. She glanced down at her watch, then went over to a medical cart and started to roll it down the hallway.

"Amanda! I need those papers notarized!" a voice shouted. "Now!"

She turned around to see her boss standing behind the counter, his arms akimbo and the darkness glaring out at her from his beady eyes. *Why can't you just leave me alone?* she thought. "They're in the folder," she meekly replied. She turned back around and continued walking, feeling her ears begin to burn as they turned red with embarrassment.

She walked down the corridor and turned left at the intersection, into the operating sector. She passed the rows of doorways until she came to room 252. As she wheeled the cart into the tiny examining room, she could hear the doctor explaining a procedure to her two patients sitting abreast each other on a bed, trembling like terrified birds.

" . . . I'll prescribe a few medications to keep the pain and swelling down, but you'll probably find that you don't even need them," the doctor said with confidence.

"How long is the procedure going to last?" Emily asked her.

"You're looking at about five minutes. That's after all the preparation, though. We can hopefully start . . . Oh! Now! Here she is!" she happily exclaimed, gesturing to the weary nurse next to the medical cart.

The nurse grabbed David's arm and pulled it towards her, washing the under-part of his wrist with an alcohol swab. Any live organisms on his skin needed to be killed before she inserted the IV needle. "This will just take a second," she said.

"Needle?" he asked with a wince, already knowing the inevitable.

"Just a tiny one," she reassured him, looking up into his eyes. She noticed how deep and brown they were, warmly absorbing all of the images around him. Absorbing the image of her. " . . . You probably won't even feel it."

The doctor cleared her throat and said, "I have to get dressed for the surgery. I'll meet the two of you back here in a few minutes." With a pleasant smirk, she turned away and walked out of the room.

The nurse threw the alcohol swab away, then reached for the plastic IV lines, which were sloppily hanging out of a drawer on the cart.

Without warning, she jumped up and rushed over to the door, closing it quickly before anyone else walked by. "There!" she exclaimed.

David and Emily looked at her with shocked expressions. "What's wrong?" they asked in unison.

The nurse hurried over and knelt before them. "Nothing yet," she explained. "But I need the two of you to get underneath the bed."

"What's this about?" Emily asked.

"I'll tell you once we get out of here," she said, her voice starting to quiver with uncertainty. "Please just trust me and get under the bed before she comes back to get you."

"Why?" David demanded.

"Please! Just do it! I don't have time to explain!" she cried, holding her hands up in desperation. If there was any way that this was going to work, it would have to be done now. There was no time to stall.

"This doesn't make sense!" Emily shouted. "Who are you!"

The nurse stood up and looked her directly in the face. "You know who I am. The question is if you remember."

"Remember what? We never saw you before!"

"You have so."

"Where?"

"Where did you come from?"

"Baghdad," David uneasily answered.

"And before that?" she asked.

"We were in Ireland," Emily admitted. "But we didn't see—"

"Okay. Before that then," she said, crossing her arms. She smiled as she watched their faces suddenly fill with consternation. "Does New York ring a bell? If not, perhaps being tied up to a pole in a hut on a tropical island?"

David suddenly felt dizzy. A surreal fear gripped at his organs beneath his ribcage and squeezed them to a momentary halt.

" . . . How do you know that?" Emily worriedly asked.

"I'll explain later. Just please, trust me. I know what I'm doing. Get under the bed."

Emily exchanged a skeptical glance with her husband before deciding to follow her instructions. They slipped off the mattress and crawled onto the shelf below.

"Stay quiet and hold on," the nurse warned, spreading out a blanket over the bed. She unlocked the wheels, opened the door, and pulled the bed out into the hallway.

Emily and David clutched onto the wheel posts. They could see the shoes of the hospital staff and the patients as they traveled down the corridor. They watched the tiles on the floor whiz past at an alarming rate and the unpleasant thought of falling out into view came to mind. They moved over a small bump, a turn to the right, through a doorway, and then down another long stretch of hallway.

Suddenly, the cart stopped.

They waited for the silence to pass, but it didn't. Each second, seeming like an eternity, was enough time to think of a thousand new questions. Why did they stop? Was someone else there? Were they going to be found?

"Where are you taking this to?" a low-octave voice finally asked.

The nurse replied, "Over to pediatrics. They said that they needed another bed right away."

"Go down the hall, take a left, then follow the signs."

"Thank you," she replied, pushing the cart forward again.

The two fugitives breathed a sigh of relief. The ride lasted a few more minutes as they were pushed through corridor after corridor. At last, bright light shined upon them as the sound of moving cars reached their ears.

"Get out!" the nurse urgently whispered.

Emily and David crawled out onto the cement sidewalk. Before they could ask her any questions, she took off across the street towards a city park. They hurried after her, catching up to her once they were past the entrance.

"This is all very nice and adventurous!" Emily stated sarcastically. "But if we were caught back in there, who knows what would have happened to us! Do you mind telling us what this is all about?"

Still walking with her back against them, she bluntly said, "Saving you from the Antichrist himself before he gouges a maze of wires into your heads. Look around you. This is Babylon! The city's been rebuilt and is now the headquarters of a global government that is responsible for the deaths of billions! Welcome! You've just arrived at the final years of the Tribulation."

"Good," an agitated David snapped. "We have one thing out of the way. Now tell us who you are."

She turned around and stared him straight in the eyes. Her face calmed as a smile emerged at her lips. "I told you that you already know. I'm Sexta, Krelisco, Eve Chardon, and, as I'm called now, Amanda Warner. I much prefer Eve, however. It's doesn't sound as abrasive, I think. It's nice to meet you again, Shanahans. Through Pompeii to the early Americas to New York and then to here! It's been a long trip. Has it not?"

The two lovers were left speechless. They stared at the woman with their mouths hanging open in shock. She had beautiful blonde hair and a slender frame that was slightly taller than Emily's. Her brown eyes seemed so familiar. They knew that they had seen them before, somewhere as they watched them from a terrified face dripping with tears.

"Eve? You were the little girl who got her foot stuck between the stones in the middle of the street?" David asked, still in awe.

She nodded with a grin. "I can never thank you enough for that. Even after I helped you escape the natives on that island, I felt an immeasurable debt of gratitude. In Newark, well, you two seemed pretty much at ease. I wasn't going to spoil anything for you there."

"So you know all about this!" David exclaimed. "You know how we can get out of this mess!"

"Of course!" she cheerfully said. "I know how you can get home."

"How?" Emily asked, a hopeful glimmer in her eyes.

"It's simple. You had the power to go back all along. Just click your heels three times and say, 'there's no place like—' "

"Very funny," David growled, stuffing his hands in his pockets and turning away.

"I'm lost," Eve admitted. "This whole thing is just as complex to me as it is to you. I know one thing, however."

"What?" the husband and wife asked together.

Eve's face lost some of its light. She didn't know if she really wanted to tell them. To them it could either be a terrible tragedy or a great blessing, but she wasn't even sure what it was for herself.

"What?" David persisted.

"This is it," she said slowly. "This may sound far-fetched, but we've been traveling forward through time all along. And for right now, we've made it up to the twilight of the Second Coming. Now to think how wonderful it would be to witness that is unimaginably exciting! No soul will be able to know what exactly will take place after Christ comes back for us. So, unfortunately, this is the farthest into the future we can possibly go. But, even from here, it's a year, if not more, away from happening. Most of the leaps we've taken have spanned several centuries. After we pass this dimension, warp, or whatever you want to call it, we're done."

David hesitated before asking what would happen next.

"I don't know. Maybe you'll get back home to see your families and live in your time. Perhaps you'll go elsewhere, surpassing life as we know it now as we mature into something more."

Emily stepped back and rubbed her neck, trying to relieve the pressure and stress building up in her muscles. "Shit," she murmured.

David put his arm around her, staring with sad eyes at Eve Chardon. "So we have to try to stay in this world as long as we can?"

"Even if you did manage to stay here, you would still vanish before the Second Coming. And the chances of you surviving until then are impossible."

"Nothing's impossible," David said, his voice saddened with the thought of living in a world full of life, but desolate of love. "We've come through so much already."

"Yeah, but look at yourselves," she said, somewhat coldly. She could see from the wounds on their bodies that every step caused them pain. They had barely made it to where they were. "I hate to say it, but I'm not expecting either of you two to survive past this evening."

David let out a frustrated sigh, not knowing if he should laugh at her or take her words for the truth. He felt dizzy again, even more so than before. He had received too much information too fast and it was having an adverse effect.

"I'm sorry," she sympathized.

David looked up to her, the hurt bleeding from his eyes. "I thought that you said that everything was going to be okay."

"I did," she asserted, her smile gone from her face. "And it will be. I promise from the bottom of my heart. Trust me. There are magnificent powers that abound all around. There is love. Here, now, and forever. With that, everything's going to be okay in the end." She started to reach for his shoulder. *Stop!* her conscience ordered. *What are you doing?* She brought her arm back down. "It's going to be okay."

The three adults stood together in uncertainty. The birds in the trees around them chirped vibrantly, as if the world couldn't be in better shape. It was an irritating irony.

Suddenly, something caught Emily's eye. "Who are those guys?" she asked, pointing to a pair of uniformed men strolling towards them.

Eve quickly turned her back on them. “This way,” she nervously instructed, leading them further down the path. “They’re World-One Law Enforcers. They can kill anyone on the spot who they deem as an enemy of the government.”

She glanced behind her and saw the two men following them. They didn’t appear to be suspicious of them, yet. She looked back and moved a little faster. Once around a curve and out of their view, the trio made a run for it.

They ran down the pathway as fast as their legs would carry them. Pigeons flew out of their way in alarm as concerned pedestrians stepped aside. A moment later, they were looking out at a city boulevard filled with speeding vehicles.

They ran across the street, instantly sending off an echo of horn blasts and tire squeals as several cars and two busses slammed on their brakes to avoid hitting them.

“Over here!” Eve cried, running over to the entrance of another massive building. She grabbed David by the arm and forced him down behind a trashcan. Emily ducked in beside him, shivering with fear.

“Stay here and don’t come out!” she ordered. “I promise that I’ll find you! Just stay out of trouble and don’t come looking for me.”

Emily started to say, “What—”

“Stay!” She nervously looked behind her and saw the two law enforcers walking out of the park. *This just isn’t my day!* she thought, quickly walking away.

“Hey!” one of the law enforcers shouted.

She broke out into a frantic run. She kept her eyes focused on the sidewalk ahead, zipping through the pedestrians as agily as she could. She heard a whistle blowing at her from behind.

She moved her legs even faster, ripping her arms back and forth wildly as if to grab onto the air to pull her forward. She felt the wind hit her face with magnificent fury as, for a brief moment, she thought, *I'm flying away!* She could picture the law enforcers drifting farther and farther behind in her mind as she—

A businessman purposely threw his foot out to trip her.

She fell to the ground with a cry, hitting her chin on the pavement.

"Eve!" Emily cried, starting to get up. David grabbed her and held her down, covering his hand over her mouth. They watched in despair as their friend took a brutal blow from one of the law enforcer's baton. The heard her chilling scream ring out across the boulevard, but no one else seemed to care. David pressed his wife's head against his chest and shielded her ears as she wept.

Eve clutched at the cement underneath her as her body throbbed with pain. She looked up at the people casually walking by, unaffected by seeing her lying defenseless on a sidewalk while being beaten by two law enforcers.

Her back flared up with searing pain as the baton struck her again. "Please!" she begged. "I give up!" She turned herself on her back with her hands up in surrender. "Please! I give—"

She felt something hard hit her head. Her vision blurred. Hear ears went deaf.

Then, nothing.

XL

"Stay calm!" her husband ordered her, pushing her in through the doorway.

"How can I stay calm!" she screamed back.

"Breathe in, breathe out, hold it, and then you should start to get very light-headed and begin to pass out. That always works for me." He wanted to kick himself for being so trivial in such a serious situation, but he needed something to pull his mind away from what just happened.

The collection of his thoughts no longer made any sense as they were distorted and out of order. Eve had been there all along. She had traveled with them, always in the background. He remembered her the best in Pompeii, as a little girl. He thought of how he had held her little foot in his hand as he tried to free her from the grip of the cobblestone before they were crushed underneath a soldier's chariot. On the tropical island, she was the reason for their escape. In Newark, she was the only a welcoming face they saw, untelling of the separation they would later face from everyone else there. And now she was rescuing them again. But from what?

They found themselves walking down an avenue of shops, sheltered by a glass roof that let the sunlight in. The white floors, spotless of any debris, shined brilliantly. The clean walls and artistic storefront designs gave a fresh, contemporary feel that was perfect for any shopper. Huge banners hung from the ceiling; every other one showed a picture of a young, dashing, smiling man. Emily glared at his image, knowing who he really was. They quickly mingled in with the hundreds of people roaming the concourse.

They stopped to watch a television display at the entrance of a music store, but quickly moved on when the pictures switched from a rock band to explicit images of a copulating couple. Emily rolled her eyes and said, "That was gross."

"I'll agree!" her husband said with a perky smile. "We look so much better than that."

"Please, *honey*," she groaned. "I'm really not in the mood right now." She didn't like to be bitter, but she saw herself trapped in another world of emptiness. This time the emptiness was worse. It was an emptiness of love and truth.

As they came upon a bookstore entrance, they spotted a newspaper stand. Emily snatched up a copy of the World-One Messenger and held it out to read.

A grainy picture of an older man dressed in white took up half of the front page. The article directly below read: And the Pontifix Maximus of the Roman Catholic Church, based out of Rome, has avowed to our World-One Leader that he will not ask the people he leads to join the World-One Unionized Religion. In a meeting with the World-One Messenger, the religious leader was quoted as saying, "I will do everything within my power to keep this church and the sacred beliefs it holds from falling to paganistic ideals. All people of faith know that there is a God. He is our creator, redeemer and hope." Our beloved One-World Leader was disappointed with the Roman Catholic's decision and called the move arrogant and selfish. Meanwhile, legal battles are still ensuing in the European Union Court over whether or not the Roman Catholic Church represents a threat to the World-One Government and should be banned . . .

"I don't like the sound of that," she uneasily said, setting the newspaper back down. "It seems as though God's no longer welcome in this world."

"I wonder if that can be said for every time." David felt like a cynic, but he felt it to be true. The church had been in crisis since the beginning of its existence. One way or another, it had to survive.

They walked further down the lines of stores. The windows were filled with everything imaginable. One store held precious rock collections consisting of the finest diamonds and gems on earth. Another displayed bottles of drinking water and fall-out detectors, as well as other emergency supplies. Others showed off camping equipment, government books and insignias, and even World-One Soldier action-figures.

They came to a rakish escalator with steps plated in gold. They silently boarded and descended to the next level, watching intently as the demonic clues of the world they were trapped in made themselves known. More disturbingly, no one else around them seemed to be worried. Everyone appeared jovial, or at least content.

Once on the other floor, they walked past a row of magazine stands. It was sad to notice that the bottoms of every magazine held a World-One Government-Approved emblem. "There's no freedom of speech," Emily said.

"Look at this!" David gasped, stopping and pointing at the picture on a World-One Geographic magazine. A picture of a vast plain covered by a dark sky and filled with heavy boulders and unidentifiable objects was on the front cover. Underneath it was a caption explaining how the city of Berlin was trying to rebuild after loosing seven-eighths of its population in a nuclear terrorist attack.

"No," she whispered in disbelief. She grabbed the magazine from him and flipped through the pages. The pictures inside were just as depressing as the one on the cover as they showed images of collapsed buildings, burnt bodies, and even a severed leg lying in the middle of a sidewalk as it was still bleeding. She could only view so much of it before her stomach tensed up with revulsion and she had to set it back down.

They moved on to the windows of a candy store. Hundreds of different chocolates were lain out in display, each one looking delicious enough to make even the most difficult connoisseur salivate.

All of a sudden, the man next to them let out a horrendous sneeze.

"God bless you," Emily chirped.

The man glared at her. "Excuse me?" he growled.

"God bless you," she said again. She looked back at him and felt uneasy about his dark, mournful eyes setting their sights upon her.

The man shook his head in disgust, mumbling, "I still can't get away from you people." He folded his arms and looked back at the chocolates, trying his best to ignore the people beside him.

"What!" Emily exclaimed. "All I said was—"

"I know what you said," he snapped. "You should keep your petty religion to yourself and quit trying to force it on others!" With that, he turned his back on her and stormed away.

"Gesh!" she said to David. "What's up with him?"

"Who knows," she said with a groan, turning to walk away.

David let his shoulders drop. Nothing seemed to be working out. He followed her down the concourse and into another atrium. In the middle was a huge opening that gave way to the floor below. It was surrounded by a decorative banister and glass elevator shafts that delivered people from level to level.

Emily leaned against the railing and looked down at the people walking about in the atrium below. A massive fountain sat in the middle, shooting a stream of water two stories high into the air. The people seemed to be having fun. Armed with wallets and shopping bags, they marched from one store to another, spending shamelessly as they bought nearly everything their greedy eyes fell upon.

She let out a soft sigh. "What's happened to this world?" she asked.

David leaned on her from behind, peering over her shoulder to see the atrium floor. "Money. These are the world's elite consumers who don't have to worry about the oppression and starvation facing the rest of the globe." He knew something was wrong. Something was very wrong. The people moving about them acted without concern for the world around them that was being devoured by war and famine. They had simply buried their heads in the sand and were reaping the fruits that bribery had offered them.

Emily listened closely to the faint sound of music that was hidden under a clamor of talking and shouting. It was very lively and fast, traveling to a splendidly fast beat. Then she grabbed his hand and said, "We need something to cheer us up. And I think that I know just the thing that will do it."

XLI

The dark hall was booming with a heavy bass as loud dance music was blasted from several speakers. A ball with several tiny mirrors rotated above the middle of floor, shooting out beams of tiny lights upon the people below. White, blinding strobe-lights fired out in contrast against the blue glow emitting from the bulbs strewn along the edges of the tiled floor.

Short dresses without sleeves seemed to be the most popular among the women while the males sloppily wore tuxedos or black suits. Emily and David automatically felt over-dressed as they walked in.

They came to a small bar where several, tiny, glass plates lined the counter. Each plate contained a different colored liquid that glowed under the black lights above them. The man in the blue shirt behind the bar, laughing as he sold the beverages, seemed amiable and jovial enough to risk talking to.

"Hello!" Emily exclaimed, forcing herself to be a little cheery.

He looked at her with glimmering eyes, as if he had just been reunited with a lost friend. "Greetings! I've never seen you folk here before. Want to try something that will really give you a ride? This is the place to be!"

They looked nervously at the substance in the plates. The bar seemed more like a chemistry experiment gone bad rather than a beverage stand.

"This stuff's the real shit! You wanna get cranked up? Well, try this baby!" the man happily continued. He grabbed another dish and poured some of the blue liquid in it before adding a few crystals. "Sir, I make this one just for you. Since, you know, you're new here." With a gleeful smile, he pushed the dish across the counter and eagerly waited for him to pick it up.

"How much is it?" David asked with a skeptical look.

"Nah, man! It's free! Try some! Give your pretty woman here a shot too!" He slipped another dish over to her. "You'll love it! If you don't, I'll give you ten woeacs."

David forced a smile as he picked the dish up. He cautiously brought it to his lips, sniffing it first. He carefully let the liquid flow into his mouth. At once his taste-buds danced with tingling excitement. He finished what was left and set the dish back down.

"Well?" the man asked.

Emily set her empty dish down as well. "Good!" she exclaimed, impressed. "How much for another?"

"They're a woeac a piece."

"Woeac?"

"World-One electronic allocated currency?"

"Oh yes! Of course! Hmm. I think I'll order up three more of them. But we're going to go out and dance for a little bit first," she said, taking her husbands arm.

"We are?" he asked as she led him through the crowd.

"Yeah! Why not!" she yelled over the music.

"Well, the song isn't quite my style," he complained, just to be difficult. She gave him a playful sneer and pulled him to the middle of the floor.

"I know I'm being a grouch—"

"I can't blame you."

"Well, I can. But hey! We're here and it's cool! Let's have a little fun!" she cried. She listed to the ambient tune, sultry in the wordless vocals and intense with percussion, and found the alluringly sexy music to be in rhythm and style. It was an opportunity she wasn't about to let slip by as she took his hands and pressed herself against him.

"I can already see that you're blushing," she grinned.

"Just a little," he admitted. "Being in public and all of that."

"Trust me," she said, gesturing to the couple next to them who were suffocating each other with passionate kisses. "They won't mind!"

As the beat picked up, growing more exotic and stealthily cooler, she placed his hands on her hips and began to sway back and forth, so close to him that she could feel his breath against her face. Her smile faded as her eyes suddenly longed for deeper sensuality. She turned her back to him, guiding his hands a little farther down her sides as she leaned against him.

A dark figure watched the dance scene from a metal walkway above the floor. His sights were focused in on the couple in the center. He slipped his hand in his pocket and pulled out his gun. He popped the empty rack out and forced in a new rack. The bullets were designed to explode on impact, damaging their victim irreparably if fired correctly. He slipped the gun back in his pocket and kept his attention focused on the dancers.

Emily gave into the temptation to pull his hands even lower and in. *He's got to be turned on by now*, she excitedly thought.

He suddenly spun her around and forced her against himself while savoring her arousing moves. She slipped her hands under his jacket and peeled it off in one slick move. Draping it across his shoulder, she reached for the buttons on his shirt, libidinously smiling as she unbuttoned it.

To take revenge, he brought his hands to her shoulders and slowly pulled her delicate spaghetti straps to the edges of her shoulders. He gazed into her lusting eyes and found himself enraptured.

All of a sudden, the straps slipped off her shoulders.

"Hey!" she cried, letting go of him to grab her dress before it fell off her.

"Opps. Sorry," he meekly apologized, standing back and rubbing his neck in embarrassment.

She pulled the straps back on, trying to look offended, but her smile failing the attempt. "Sure you are!" she exclaimed, pulling him to her again and relishing the feel of his body rubbing against hers. "How about if we . . ." She suddenly stopped, seeming lost and dazed.

"What's wrong?" he asked.

"Oh," she said, turning away with her hand to her head. "Nothing." She stumbled away, looking as if she was going to faint.

David caught her by the arm. "Emily?"

She turned back to him, smiling and half-heartedly laughing. "I realized that I want another one of those drinks. I need it."

"Not really," he said, giving her a studying look. She was already visibly intoxicated. The last thing she needed was one of those drinks.

"Ah, come on," she said, dragging him back towards the bar. "Let's see how many you can down."

"Well!" the man in the blue shirt exclaimed. "It's great to see you guys back so early!"

"I want another drink," Emily said, hungrily looking at the dishes as if nothing else mattered. She picked one up and downed it in a single gulp.

The man chuckled modestly. "I guess she really likes the stuff."

"Here," she said, handing David two. "I dare you."

He shrugged and sipped them down as she reached for a second.

"Ma'am?" the man asked, a little concerned. "People usually just take one of those in a four hour period. Two maximum."

She swallowed a third portion, letting a little dribble down the side of her cheek. Laughing hysterically, she reached for a fourth dish.

"No you don't!" David declared, quickly downing two more.

"Guys?" the man asked, now getting worried.

Emily set down another empty dish and snatched up a full one. "Ha!" she cried, taking it in one draught.

"I don't think that this is a good idea," the man said, watching as they took more of the dishes. "These are highly hallucinogenic drugs!"

"What?" Emily asked, setting the glass down with a cheerful laugh. "You're shirt's blue! Fancy that!"

The man only rolled his eyes. "You people are going to have a really bad hangover once that stuff's through your systems."

David blissfully reached for another dish.

"No!" the man shouted, blocking his hand.

David only laughed and stumbled back. He suddenly lost his footing and crashed to the floor, taking a few of the dishes down with him.

Emily found herself laughing uncontrollably. She reached over to help him up, only to lose her balance and fall on top of him.

"Oh!" David happily cried out. "I want some more!"

"Me too!" she cooed, resting on his chest as she felt the whiskers on his chin. She suddenly pulled herself up and kissed him. She leaned up and stared at him, gently running her fingers through his hair.

"Are you okay?" he wearily asked.

"I'm sleepy," she purred, then kissing him again. This time she was bolder, kissing him as hard as she could. When she stopped, she grinning from ear to ear. "Wow. I've never felt so horny! Let's just do it here," she said, her speech almost slurred beyond recognition. She untucked his shirt, slipping her hands underneath and feeling his chest. "You're my big, sexy . . . poodle."

He was too intoxicated to understand what she was saying as he reached for her shoulder straps again.

"Say, 'arf arf!' " she playfully ordered.

" . . . Meow," he managed with a laugh.

"No! Say, 'arf!' " she demanded, then kissing him before he had a chance. She closed her eyes, feeling him against her and aching with desire. When she brought her head back, she saw him staring blindly at her with a sleepy grin on his face. "No 'arf'?" she innocently asked.

"Arf!" he cried, then closed his eyes.

She giggled and rested her head against him, tangling her arms in her shoulder straps as she tried to remove them. She struggled for a brief moment, then let out a sigh and rested her head against his chest. Shortly after, she was unconscious.

The man in the blue shirt walked out from behind his beverage stand. With his arms akimbo and eyes wide with astoundment, he stood over the two lovers. "Damn! Where'd you people come from?"

Then, out of the corner of his eye, he saw a dark figure approaching. He turned to see a man storming towards him and holding up a card. "My name's Rich Akron and I'm with the World-One Law Enforcement Agency!" the man called out. "I have to ask you a few questions about your two customers!"

The man glanced back down at the two people, intoxicated into unconsciousness. "Oh man. This isn't good," he groaned.

XLII

David wearily opened his eyes. It took a moment for the sights around him to come into focus. The tiny room, windowless and dim, had beige walls without any pictures or charts. He found himself strapped down on a gurney without his shirt on. The air in the room felt cold against his bare chest, making him shiver as he wished he had a blanket over him.

"Oh!" a feminine voice said. David looked to the right. A doctor in a white coat stood up from her chair. She walked up to him with a cautious look. "How are you feeling?"

"Not good," he admitted. "Where's my wife?"

She stood there for a moment, staring him down with a cold pair of eyes. Then she briskly turned around and walked out of the room. "He's awake!" he heard her say.

He threw his head back against the pillow and let out a worried sigh. *What's happening?* he fearfully wondered. *Oh God. Please don't let anything happen to Emily. Please be with her and—*

"Mr. David Shanahan!" a deep voice shouted out.

David turned just in time to see Akron shut the door behind him. His heart froze in terror along with the rest of his body. "What do you want?" he meekly asked.

Akron only smiled as he moved closer. He studied his victim closely, first looking almost admiringly at his delicate eyebrows. Then he glanced down at his firm chin and chest. The man wasn't very muscular, but he looked capable with the meat that he did have on his bones.

David shivered in horror as the man in the trench coat reached down to his side.

All at once, he heard a distinct *pop.*

Akron pulled one of the straps off. "Stay where you are," he warned, unlatching another restraint. Within a minute, David was free from the gurney. But not from Akron. "Sit up!" he commanded.

David reluctantly did so. "What do you want?" he asked again, staring him directly in the eyes.

Akron only grinned. "Just you, David. Of course!"

"I have my rights here and I—"

"You have no rights!" he screamed, his face instantly transpiring into an evil glare. "Right now I own you! You and that scurvy little sidekick of yours!"

"Where is she!" David demanded.

Akron, not used to such insubordination, grabbed him by the arm as hard as he could. Before David could protest, he slammed his other fist into his face, knocking him off the gurney and onto the floor.

David sat back up and leaned against the wall as he tried to catch his breath. It took him a moment to regain his senses. His nose and lips stung with bitter pain. He pressed his hand against his face, then brought it back to see his palm drenched with blood. "Oh no," he gasped, looking back up.

Akron took his time walking around the gurney. Once facing his opponent again, he lifted his foot back and kicked him in the stomach.

David let out a scream as he crouched over in agony.

Akron kicked him again, throwing him against the wall like a rag doll.

"Please!" David implored.

The evil man stood back for a moment as he watched his victim trying to recover enough strength to stand up. Then he lurched forward, grabbed him by the hair, and forced him on his feet and back against the wall. "Do you know who I am?" he growled. His foul breath made David's nose twitch as he moaned in pain.

"You're Richard Akron," he managed to reply.

"That's right. So why don't you give me the respect that I deserve?"

Glaring back at him with pained eyes, he said, "Why should I give you respect?"

Akron shot his knee up into the man's groin.

David let out an excruciating roar as he felt his stomach rush up to his chest. He started to cringe again, but Akron pinned him back up.

"I deserve respect!" he declared.

"Fine," David admitted. "Whatever you want."

"I want to know why you didn't have that chip implanted," he said, cutting right to the chase.

"Why?"

"Because you're not a citizen of the World-One Commonwealth until you have that chip inside of you!"

"Maybe I don't want to have a chip surgically pounded into my brain!" he shot back.

"There's a reason why you and that woman of yours ran out from the facility without undergoing the surgery and I want to know why that is!"

"We just didn't want the chip!"

"Why not!"

"I don't give a damn about your unionization!" he screamed.

Akron didn't say anything for a moment, studying him relentlessly with his scouring eyes. Then his grip on his shoulders tightened. "You're one of them, aren't you? What is it? Are you still one of those *I believe in God* people? Oh yes! Go to church every Sunday, worship a guy who's been dead for centuries . . ."

"He lives!" David insisted. His words momentarily surprised him, making him feel like a crazy preacher standing at a podium to a crowd full of fanatics on television.

Akron stood back, not knowing whether to hit him or to laugh out loud. Then he asked, "Who told you that? Who convinced you not to get it?"

"No one! Screw you!"

Akron slugged him again. "I warned you to treat me with respect, you little shit!"

David's head swayed back and forth from the harsh blow. He felt dizzy and nauseous. He wondered what would happen if he threw up all over Akron, but quickly came to the conclusion that he'd probably be killed, or worse. "Sorry," he apologized, wiping the blood from his nose onto his hand again.

"Now," Akron continued, more calmed and relaxed. "Who was talking to you about the chip? If you don't tell me, I'll get the answer from that courtesan of yours." He smiled as he watched the fear envelope his victim's eyes. "Yes. I can tear that little whore apart limb by limb. Of course, the weakling would probably give me names at the bend of a finger. But it would be so much fun to make her bleed. To cry out in pain as her flesh is torn apart—"

David spat on his face.

Taken aback, Akron staggered away, wiping the sticky saliva off his face in disgust. He glowered at him with an evil scowl. "You stupid wretch!"

David closed his eyes and braced himself for the incoming strike. He waited, but it never came. Hearing withdrawing footsteps, he cautiously opened his eyelids.

Akron hurtled the metal chair at him from across the room, hitting him in the side of the head with incredible force.

David collapsed to the ground, clutching the bleeding bump from where he had been hit. Akron rushed over, picked up the chair, and brought it down on him again.

The defenseless man screamed out as the chair's legs crashed against his ribs with crushing force. He crawled into a ball and covered his neck.

Akron threw the chair down and kicked him with his boot. Hearing him scream out in pain entertained him enough to do it again, and again, and again.

David's vision began to blur as the pain paralyzed his body. He felt himself drifting out of consciousness as the heavy blows to his back emptied the air from his lungs.

But Akron wasn't finished. He rolled David's mangled body over and stomped on his stomach. Then he stood back and watched him squirm as the blood flowed from the several cuts on his skin. His teeth were clenched as he tried to endure the anguishing pain. He hurt all over with no part of his body left unscathed.

Akron leaned over and spat on him, hitting his bloodied face with his vile spittle. "I had you before and I have you now," he said with a sneer. He stood back. "We'll meet again. And when we do, I'll make sure that it will be the last you time your heart ever beats again."

David felt a wave of relief wash over him as the man in the trench coat turned around and walked out of the room. He looked up at the ceiling in despair, trying to catch enough air in his lungs before he fainted from lack of oxygen.

He thought about Emily again and hoped that she was safe from harm. He started to wonder if he would see her again, but quickly forced the thought out of his mind. "Oh God," he said aloud. "Don't leave us. Please don't leave us."

Then he heard the door open again. His body tensed with fear as he heard approaching footsteps. Too weak to stand up and see who it was, he cried out, "Who's there!"

No sooner had he said that when he felt a hand firmly grab his shoulder.

He let out a frantic yell.

XLIII

She felt that she had been asleep for several hours when she finally awoke. Maybe even a whole day. She found herself lying on a cold, wet, cement floor. Three brick walls surrounded her and with the forth wall being made up of a row of steel bars. The floor was covered with paint chips that had flaked off the walls and plaster that had fallen from the crumbling ceiling. Her nose wrinkled at the putrid scent of urine all around her.

She turned around and saw several other women sleeping against the back wall. A tiny toilet in the corner served as the only furniture piece in the room. *David!* she realized. The man was nowhere in sight. *Oh shit! Where is he!* she thought, jumping to her feet. She stumbled over to the bars and peered down the corridor of cells. Her heart sank as she didn't even see a guard to ask for help.

"Hello!" she cried, her voice echoing off the walls.

"Shut-up, bitch!" another woman growled.

"Beg your pardon?" she innocently asked, turning to see one of the inmates glaring back at her. The little punk had her hair mangled in a mat above her head, which was pierced in several different places.

"I said, 'shut-up, bitch!' You got a problem with that? Because if you do, I'm going to come over there and bust that little shit-hole face of yours into the ground!"

Emily resisted the urge to fire back with insults. "I'm sorry," she calmly apologized.

"You better be! Stupid bitch!"

Emily tensed up. *Just relax!* her mind instructed. *She's an uneducated harlot who wants attention. Let her be.*

She crossed her arms and stared out of the cell, desperately wondering where David was placed.

"Yo, bitch," the woman said again, snapping her fingers.

Emily pretended not to hear her.

"Hey! Bitch! I said—"

She whirled around with two fists raised and shouted, "If you want to fight, fine! I'll take that puny neck of yours and twist it around until it sticks up your ass! Then your mother will cry when she finds out how the limbs of your body were ripped off and you bled to death!"

The woman stared at her with shocked eyes. At any moment, she could rush forward and pulverize her into a bloody pulp with ease, perhaps even finesse. *I just had to open up that big mouth!* she thought, wanting to kick herself.

The woman shrugged her eyebrows and held up her hands in surrender. "Sorry. I was just going to ask you for a cigarette."

Emily forced on a tough sneer, trying to look like she had more testosterone in her than estrogen. She turned around and gazed back down the corridor. After a few minutes, she sat back down on the wet floor and tried to remember the events of the night before. "Oh God," she said aloud, as she remembered telling David that he was a poodle. *I shouldn't use the Lord's name in vain*, she suddenly thought, and realized that she hadn't prayed yet.

Glancing at the women against the wall to make sure she wasn't being watched, she folded her hands and started to whisper a series of prayers. " . . . bread and forgive us our trespasses as we—"

"Mrs. Shanahan!"

"Oh God!" she exclaimed. Then the guilt hit her. *Darn it!* She turned around and saw Eve Chardon jamming a key into the lock. Other than a gash on her chin and a bruised hand, she looked perfectly fine. “Eve! How—”

“Be quiet!” she snapped. “Shut-up or I’ll throw you right back in here, you lousy pig!”

Emily’s smile faded as she stood up, uncertain of what to expect. She could hear a few women snickering behind her.

Eve slid open the door and glared at Emily. “Move,” she brutally commanded.

Emily nervously stepped out into the corridor and waited for her to close the door. Once Eve had locked it, she grabbed her hand and forced her down the corridor. She leaned over to her ear and whispered, “Sorry to be so harsh. We’re being watched so you have to act a little bit like a real prisoner.”

“Where’s my husband?” she demanded. “Is he okay?”

“I’m taking you to him. Now be quiet!” She wanted to stop and tell her everything instead of leaving her worried, but it wasn’t safe. Then again, if she explained the situation, Emily certainly would have a good reason to be anxious.

She opened the doors at the end of the corridor and gestured for Emily to go through. They found themselves in another passage, barely lit with a few bulbs stuck into hanging sockets.

“He’s down here,” Emily said, quickly walking down towards the little door at the end of the hallway. After a quick look to make sure that no one was watching, she unlocked the door and swung the door open.

Emily stepped inside, unprepared for what she was about to see. Her husband lay propped up against the wall. His head was covered with wet, bloodied rags and cold compresses. His face was swollen and cut as numerous abrasions covered the rest of his body. His pants were tattered and torn, soaked with his blood. Even the fresh lab coat Emily had put on him was bled through.

"David!" she cried, running up and throwing her arms around him.

He barely had enough strength to hug her, moaning from the stabbing pain flaring all throughout his body. "Emily," he managed. "I love you. I'm so sorry I let you go."

"It's okay," she reassured him. "You didn't let me go. We passed out from the drugs, remember?"

"All I remember is you calling me a sexy poodle," he said, a bit petulant.

She couldn't help but to giggle a little, gently wiping the hardening stream of blood under his puffed up nostrils. "Who did this to you?"

"Akron. He was asking me about the computer chips and I didn't tell him what he wanted to know."

"What was that?"

Eve gently knelt down beside him. "Me," she glumly said, applying another wet cloth to his head. Then she grabbed a cup of warm tea beside her and delicately slipped two pills into his mouth. "Here," she said, bringing the cup to his lips. "Just swallow those and you'll be feeling better in no time."

She watched as the color started to come back to his weary face as he drank from the ceramic container in her hands. She gazed at his brown eyes, finding herself wondering what it would be like if they were staring back at her in the same way.

A small amount of tea dribbled down the side of his chin. She tenderly brought her hand to his face, feeling the whiskers tickle her fingers as they wiped the tea away. He felt so warm and delicate, yet strong and sheltering. *You poor thing!* she thought. *I just want to hold you in my arms until you're well again!* She smiled at the idea, then remembered Emily kneeling next to her.

"What now?" his wife asked.

Eve bit her lip, trying to pull her mind away from David. "There's a police cruiser in the parking garage just outside. As soon as we can get him on his feet, we're out of here."

"Then let's go," David said, pulling the rags off him and moving to stand up. His head instantly spun with dizziness, but he forced himself up anyway. He managed to stagger a few feet before he was overcome with pain and started to fall.

"David!" Emily shrieked, catching him in her arms and gently lying him back down. "Just stop! I'm not going to leave you!"

"We have to get out of here," he protested.

Eve cleared her throat and stood away. "Wait a little bit for the medication to take effect. You'll be able to function better with the pain gone."

"What pain?" he wearily asked.

"Shh," his wife soothed, gently stroking the side of his face. She kept her eyes focused on his until the panic started to drift away from them. With a tender smile, she suddenly leaned forward and kissed his left cheek, then his right. When she sat back, she saw the longing look in his eyes, helplessly begging her for more. She kissed him again, on the forehead, then the chin, and then upon his lips.

They stayed there for a moment, savoring the feel of each other so close and inseparable. They were entirely oblivious to Eve's presence as they let their hands drift upon each other while their lips remained together, so tight and warm. They found themselves still too far away from one another, even as their bodies were pressed together like magnets, unwilling to part. After a moment, however, reality began to creep back into their minds.

She kissed him harder, planning to retreat at the very next second, only to remain against him. She felt as if her body were turning into a liquid and that the only place that she desired to flow was into him. After a minute, though, she forced herself to face the situation at hand. They were in danger and had to escape. Reluctantly, she took his hand from her breast and squeezed it with a smirk. "We're going to be okay, honey. We're going to be just fine."

"Of course we will," he said, smiling back. "I love you."

"I love you, too," she reminded. Then she turned to Emily and asked, "Did you really mean what you said earlier?"

"About what?" Eve cautiously replied, pretending that she hadn't noticed their short engagement.

She swallowed hard and said, "About us not surviving past this evening."

Eve turned to answer her, but found the confirming words stuck in her throat. *Who am I to break their hopes and dreams?* she asked herself. She suddenly wished that she had never brought it up in the first place as she turned around without answering her.

Emily hung her head in despair. She had started to cry when she felt two fingers touch her cheek. She looked up and smiled at her husband as he wiped her tears aside. "We're going to make it," he said, "One way or another. We'll do it. We'll do it together."

She grabbed his other hand and whispered, "You bet your ass."

Eve grabbed a set off keys off the desk behind her before coming over and touching David's shoulder. "I'm sorry, but we have to do this now. Can you walk yet?"

David groaned as he forced himself up again with Emily's help. He felt just as dizzy as he did before, but managed to stay on his feet.

Eve opened a side door and ushered them out. They walked through and into the garage and breathed in the fresh air. Not a single oil stain was in sight and the only litter to be found was in the trashcans. The two lovers followed Emily over to a gold-painted car, only there were four cylinders with holes at the bottom instead of tires.

"What is this?" Emily asked, watching Eve scramble to open the front door.

"World-One's finest transportation unit for the private sector, the personal hovercraft. The police department here uses them all the time." She unlocked the doors for them and jumped into the driver's seat on the right side. "I've ridden in one of these before so I know how to work it," she said, turning the ignition. The four engines started up with a roar and the vehicle gently rose a few inches above the pavement. "Everybody buckled in?"

Emily and David nervously nodded.

"Okay then. Here we go!" She put the hovercraft in reverse and pressed her foot on the gas pedal. A brief moment passed between the time the engines revved and the back end of the vehicle crashed into another conveyance.

"Opps," she said. She slipped the gear into forward and lightly tapped her foot on the gas pedal. The hovercraft lurched forward, smashing the front end into a pole. "Sorry about that." She gave a nervous laugh, switching back to reverse. The vehicle veered backwards, nearly throwing her passengers out of their seats.

The hovercraft stopped again with a massive crash. Eve looked behind her and saw that she had hit a support pillar. Then she noticed Emily's worried face. "Don't worry. Everything's under control."

"Emily," David moaned.

His wife leaned forward. "I'm right here. We're not going to die." She glanced back at Eve. "Are we?"

She didn't answer, slamming her foot down on the gas pedal once more. The hovercraft hurtled forward, scraping past two other vehicles and clipping off the side-view mirrors.

The passengers let out worried cries as the aircraft burst out of the entrance and descended toward a city street several stories below.

"Now if I know what I'm doing . . ." Eve started, applying more downward thrust. The hovercraft gently nosed up and flew over the traffic below, narrowly missing a double-decker bus as it sped southwards. " . . . We'll be safe in no time."

Emily and David waited for what seemed like an eternity for Eve Chardon to pilot the vehicle away from the towering buildings. Once they were clear of any obstacles, she brought the vehicle a few yards from the desert ground and increased the speed.

"Look at those clouds over there," Emily said, pointing at the dark band stretching across the sky ahead.

"That's where we're going," Eve replied. "And those aren't clouds. They're large smoke billows from burning oil wells."

XLIV

Emily kept her hand on David's shoulder as she yawned and stared out of the window, watching the landscape move by almost as fast as she had seen it on the train into Babylon. The sky above them was black with heavy smoke that covered the mountaintops. To the north was a thinning blue line where the fresh air and modern cities existed, giving the only evidence that day was still in existence. She glanced over at Eve, and then noticed the speedometer reading well over a hundred and fifty miles and hour.

"You said that all of this smoke was from oil wells, right?"

"Mainly," Eve chirped, without taking her eyes off the featureless dirt path ahead of her.

"Then why don't they just put the fires out?"

"They're the ones that set them to punish a group they think are Old World Resistance sympathizers. The Babylonians hate them and want them to suffer."

"Where is this?"

"See that cluster of buildings ahead?" she asked, pointing out the windscreen. All David and Emily could see was a massive pile of rubble that was on fire in several different places. "That's Kuwait City. It's a refugee camp. Though, once it was the diamond of the Persian Gulf that was forced into the World-One Government under the direction of the head of the Iraqi government. When the dictator died and the people rejoiced, the land was punished by the leader, or as you and I know him, the Antichrist."

Emily shivered at the sight ahead. As the vehicle came closer, she could make out the images of people milling back and forth around large fires, trying to keep warm as the cold evening set in. Their clothes were mere rags and their faces full of dirt, yet they didn't appear distraught in their plight.

After drifting into a city street, or what was left of it, Eve set the brakes on the hovercraft. Emily jumped from the vehicle and rushed to help out her husband. With only the light of the fires around her, she could see several of the people in rags move through the piles of rubble to assist them.

"I'm fine," he protested as she put her arm under him.

"No you're not!"

A burly man wearing a turban slipped his arm under his other shoulder. "Listen to what the lady says," he ordered. "You're not well."

"I am so!" He groaned, realizing there was no point in arguing as they were already sitting him on the dusty ground. He brushed his arms off and looked at the massive destruction around him.

Eve carefully maneuvered the craft around, aiming it back towards the north. With the four engines still running and blowing clouds of dirt around them, she stepped out and dashed over to a demolished building. She grabbed a large rock, ran back to the car, and carefully tossed the block on the gas pedal. At once the engines roared and the hovercraft heaved forward with tremendous speed.

"Ha!" Eve shouted, clapping her dirty hands clean.

"Why'd you do that!" Emily cried, a hint of anger in her voice.

"So they can't track us down," she answered with a shrug of her shoulders.

David wasn't paying any attention. He suddenly realized that he couldn't care less as he saw the remains of what used to be a large, flourishing city. Pieces of broken walls stood up out of the rubble, ready to crumble in the wind. Glass, pieces of twisted metal, sharp rocks, and even modern items like coffee-makers and smashed computers were strewn about in the debris. "Unbelievable," he gasped.

The man in the turban sat down next to him. "Yes. It's quite a transition from what it was just a few months ago. But we've managed."

David extended his hand to him. "David Shanahan. Pleased to meet you."

"And the same here," he said, shaking his hand with a friendly grin. He was a jovial man, slightly plump and rounded, but otherwise fit. His tattered garment matched the color of the dirt stuck in his shabby hair. And even though his face was a mess of sweat and dust, there was still so much life beaming from his eyes. "My name's Ershad Novelle. I once owned a major computer company before World-One commandeered it. Now I'm here." He gazed out at the sad images around him. He was familiar with them by now, but it was still heart-wrenching.

"They just took your company and threw you out?" David asked, disgusted. He looked up as he watched his wife tiredly walk over to him and sit down beside him, resting her tired head against his arm.

The man in the turban continued, "I'm a believer in Islam, not the World-One Religion. And I opened my mouth, caused a big ruckus, and barely escaped with my life. And so now I'm here, mingled in with Jews, Muslims, Christians, and even a Buddhist or two. If you want a real unionization of religions, this is it. The real miracle isn't how we all survive here. It's how we manage not to kill each other!" he said, breaking out into laughter.

A voice behind them continued, "And how you scum are allowed to live in this world."

David swallowed hard. He didn't have to turn around to see who it was. He already knew Akron was behind him. He listened to the wind blowing by, wishing that they could be picked up and taken away with it to safety.

"Stand up and turn around so we can see you," Akron ordered.

The two lovers and the Muslim reluctantly obeyed, holding their hands up in surrender. Akron, dressed in his black trench coat, was accompanied by twenty armed soldiers, each with their own little arsenal attached to their bodies. Their faces were as dead as marble as they stood like robots, waiting for a set of commands to control their actions. Their clean, dark uniforms contrasted sharply against the gritty desert sand. If they were fighting a war, they'd be easy targets. But they weren't fighting a war. They were merely exerting their immense power.

With her fists down at her side and her sneer hiding her pretty face, Eve broke through the crowd and stepped toward Akron. "Leave them the hell alone! It's me you want!"

Akron roared, "I couldn't care less about you! Get back and shut-up!"

"How'd you find us?" David demanded.

"We tracked you here with a signal detected from a stolen government hovercraft."

Without warning, a rumble echoed from the desert and a ball of flames ripped up from the ground several miles away.

"What was that?" Akron demanded.

"Just a very expensive hovercraft taken from a Babylon law enforcement center," Eve snapped back. "We didn't think anyone would really miss it."

"You thought wrong," Akron growled, staring at the flames dissipating into black smoke. He looked back at his three fugitives and ordered one of his soldiers to search them.

A young-faced soldier rushed up to the man in the turban and started to pat him down, feeling for any hidden weapons.

Without warning, Ershad lunged at the soldier. Before the armed person could fight back, he had scarfed a gun from their holster and planted the tip of the barrel against his temple. "Stand back or I'll blow his brains out!" Ershad yelled.

"I'm a *her*!" the soldier corrected, barely managing to speak with the tremendously large arm around her throat.

"Oh. Sorry," he quickly whispered. He rolled his eyes. How was he supposed to know? They all looked the same. He looked back at Akron. "Stand back or I'll blow her brains out!"

Akron bit his bottom lip as a barrage of strategies paraded through his mind. "By the command of the World-One Government, I order you to unhand that soldier!"

"Drop your weapons first!" Ershad cried.

"We can not do that!"

"Then I can't let her go. I'm sorry. It's as simple as that." He heard his captive groan in anger. He glanced back at David, Emily, and Eve and gestured for them to move.

Emily and David slowly backed away. The soldiers stared at them with evil glares, but unwilling to fire their weapons and endanger the life of their colleague. The fugitives walked back until they found themselves hidden in the crowd of refugees. Eve followed, wary of the several guns pointed at her. A moment later, they were all safely out Akron's sight.

Ershad glanced back at the twenty soldiers, then down at his squirming hostage.

"He's going to kill me!" she frantically shouted at her colleagues.

Ershad held her tiny neck even tighter. "Be quiet," he snarled into her ear. "I won't hurt you."

"You're hurting me now!" she whined, struggling to free herself from his painful grasp. "Let me go! I don't want to die!" She fought a little more, then relented. She broke down into grievous sobs and said again, "I don't want to die."

"I promise to God and you that I'm not going to hurt you!" he assured.

A sudden fear hit him. *That was kind of loud*, he thought, looking back at Akron who had a smirk on his face. *Shoot!*

"That's what I thought," Akron said, raising his gun at him.

"No!" the female soldier screamed out, the horror piercing her voice and her eyes wide with fear as she stared at Akron's gun. "Don't shoot me! Please don't shoot me!"

Ershad kept hold of her, feeling his heart tearing apart the whole time. She was so desperate and terrified. For a brief moment, he felt as if she was his daughter. As little and defenseless as she was, he wanted to scoop her up in his arms and hug her. Instead, he was holding a gun to her head.

"What's your name?" Akron calmly asked him, the gun still aimed at his head.

"Ershad," the man in the turban replied.

"Very well. Ershad, my good man, kindly release my soldier. You're under a lot of duress. I know. But let her go. I promise you that, whatever trouble you're in, we can get it all worked out in the courts."

Ershad only stared back, not knowing whether or not to trust the man. Then his desperate hostage forlornly begged, "Please let me go. I'm afraid. I just want to go back home."

He let out a sigh, keeping his eyes transfixed on Akron's sincere face. " . . . Okay," he said at last, loosening his grip on her and dropping his weapon.

She bolted from his arms, but suddenly stopped at only a yard away. She turned back to look at him as the warm tears were still running down her cheeks. She mouthed, *Thank you.*

Ershad started to say, "I'm sorry that—"

Akron pulled the trigger.

The female soldier shrieked out in horror.

Ershad felt something hit the center of his chest. He looked down and saw blood oozing out from a hole in his sternum. In disbelief, he gazed back up at Akron's devious smile. "You . . . You s-s-shot me," he stammered.

Akron cocked the hammer back and fired again.

Ershad collapsed to the ground, clutching his hand over the two bullet wounds on his chest. He felt the blood rushing out through his fingers as his head began to feel light and fuzzy.

The female soldier rushed to his side, moved by a sudden consciousness of pity for him. "What can I do?" she asked, her voice quivering.

"Step away!" Akron shouted at her.

She ignored him, grabbing Ershad's arm and looking into his terrified eyes. "Thank you," she said. "I'm so sorry. I'm—"

"Soldier! Get back here now!" Akron commanded.

In a fit of terror, she scrambled back to her feet and rushed back to her position in line. She pretended not to see her commander glaring at her as she stared at the dying man who had let her go.

"There are two fugitives hiding somewhere in this place," Akron said to his team. "They are enemies of the World-One society and they need to be stopped. Find them!"

XLV

Emily, David, and Eve rushed into the foyer of a crumbling museum. The ceiling above them had huge pieces missing, giving a clear view to the sky of smoke above. The walls were spider-webbed with cracks and broken plaster. Elaborate shelves and chests, covered with a heavy layer of dust, lined the room as they exhibited precious artifacts and art work. A small family of four, oblivious to the desperate trio, was huddled together in a corner, praying quietly in the darkness.

David looked ahead. A long corridor filled with display cases extended for hundreds of yards. A large, lengthy item in one of the cases caught his attention. He rushed over to it and slammed his elbow into the transparent pane, sending a sheet of glass shards crashing to the floor. He reached in and pulled an antique elephant gun off its rack. "This might do us some good," he said.

A sudden crash echoed through the hall.

"They're coming!" Eve gulped, grasping David's arm. "Come on! We have to go!" She quickly led them down the corridor. They turned around the corner and entered a large room displaying modern automobiles. A yellow moped stood on a small platform in the center of the room. Eve ran over to it with curious eyes and itching fingers.

A stern voice sounded out from up the hall, shouting, "They're down this way!"

Eve felt her heart fearfully jump inside of her. Finding the key already in the ignition, she switched the motor on. To her surprise, the headlight blinked on and the engine started to run. "Yes! Here we go!" she cried, dragging the vehicle back down on the floor. She jumped on it and said, "Come on!"

Emily straddled herself on the seat and wrapped her arms around Eve's stomach. She glanced back at David, but he was looking away. "David! Hurry!"

He turned back to her. "They're on their way! Get out of here! I'll stall them!"

She jumped up from the seat and cried out, "But—"

"Stay here and go!" David shouted, grabbing her hips and shoving her back down. "I'll find you! I promise!"

"But—"

Eve slammed her foot on the gas pedal and the bike propelled forward. Emily clutched onto her for dear life as they hurtled through the room and down another corridor.

"Stop in there!" a voice ordered from ahead.

David turned back around and looked down the corridor, but it was too dark to see anyone. He could hear approaching footsteps and muffled conversation as he felt a cold sweat break out across his forehead. Still feeling sick and dizzy, he started down the next corridor, holding himself up against the wall for support.

"Show yourselves at once!" the voice ordered. "This is the World-One Military you're dealing with! You can not escape!"

The hell I can't! he thought, moving as fast as he could. He held his aching head with his other hand, feeling squeamish and hazy. He pressed on and suddenly found himself in a large room with the eerie light of the fires shining in through the windows. Several large tanks stood against the walls, each one with a flammability warning.

A devious plan quickly patterned itself inside of his brain as he suddenly remembered the curiosity of being in the chemistry lab at school, so many years ago.

He eagerly rushed over to a tank filled with hydrogen and found a tiny valve at the bottom. He turned the black knob as quickly as he could to open it. Then he moved on to empty several tanks of oxygen. The sound of the gasses pouring out into the room with a shrill whistle made him shiver with nervous excitement. *This is going to be great if I can just make it work!* he thought to himself.

Several corridors away, Emily clung onto Eve with all of her strength, daring not to even think of loosing her grip. "How do we get out of here!" she cried.

"Like this! Hold on!"

"What?"

It was too late to explain. Eve braced herself as they hurtled towards the hole in the wall. She could see the burning sky and land strewn with debris just outside.

"What?" Emily asked again. "I—" She never finished her sentence. She found herself airborne and too terrified to scream. The walls around her vanished, giving way to only air as the bike catapulted out of the building.

A second later, the bike slammed onto the ground and Eve veered to the right, nearly loosing her balance. A cloud of dust drifted up behind them, temporarily blocking them from the sights of Akron's soldiers.

The smoky wind blew across their faces with harsh strength as Eve floored the gas, propelling them faster down the avenue of demolished buildings.

"I have to go back!" Emily cried. "He's my husband!"

"We have to—"

A spray of gunfire shot out from behind.

Eve felt something sharp pierce her leg.

A second later, the back tire blew up.

Eve struggled to steer the bike in the soft dirt, but it was no use. The front tire hit a small depression and the bike fell to the ground, sending the two women flying off into the dirt.

They hit the ground with stunning force. Emily found herself sprawled out on the ground and spitting the dust from her mouth. Eve lay right beside her, dazed and nearly unconscious from hitting her head.

Inside the science laboratory in the museum, David rummaged through the desk drawers, frantically throwing papers out as he desperately searched for an igniter. He came to the middle drawer and found a booklet of matches tucked away in the corner. He ripped it out and held it up to read the label, grinning from ear to ear with his find.

Without warning, a sudden burst of gunfire echoed through the corridors.

He dropped the matches in surprise and ducked underneath the desk.

The shooting guns abruptly stopped. A soldier cried out from the other room, "Where are you! You can't stay hidden forever! Just give yourself up and we'll consider any grievances you have! Please be peaceful!"

Yeah right! David thought, feeling the floor for the matches. He found them again and flipped open the lid. He struck a match and dropped it on the floor, watching the tiny flame grow a little larger as it fed off the carpet fibers. He lit another one and dropped it in one of the desk's open drawers.

"Freeze!" a voice cried.

David didn't move, looking intently under the desk and seeing several pairs of boots on the other side. He swallowed hard, wondering if they knew where he was.

"Come out with your hands where we can see them!" another soldier demanded.

David slowly raised his hands and arose from his hiding place. In the dim light, he could see the dirt scowls on the soldiers' faces as they pointed their lethal weapons at him. "I'm sorry," he explained. "I was just afraid."

A soldier demanded, "Where are the other two!"

"I don't know."

"Sure. Step aside!" he ordered, gesturing him to move with an inclination of his rifle.

David cautiously stepped away from the desk and in front of the picture window, keeping his hands in the air and not taking his eyes off the soldier's brutal eyes. "I'm unarmed and I haven't done anything."

"You've committed treason against the World-One Society!" the soldier screamed. "If I had the authority, I would kill you right now!"

"But you haven't the authority," David said, glancing down and seeing the elephant gun lying on the floor just a foot away. He slowly moved towards it, saying, "The authority all comes from the authority itself. But what's the authority of the authority? Who has the final say in the line of power and order? Huh?"

The soldier thought for a moment, then lowered his weapon as he scowled at him in disgust. "How the bloody hell would I know!"

David snatched the elephant gun back up and pointed it at the soldier. "I think I'm the one with the final say. Wouldn't you agree?"

The soldier raised his gun at him, oblivious to the weapon poised at his head. "Go ahead. I dare you," he sneered.

David smiled and stepped back. He shot a quick glance out of the window, then back at the soldiers.

His heart skipped a beat. *What did I just see!* he suddenly realized. It had been Emily and Eve lying in the street, next to a toppled moped.

He glanced again, just to make sure. *Shit!* he thought, seeing them for sure. Their bodies lay motionless on the desert road as a group of armed soldiers stood several yards away, conversing lightly as if they didn't see the two women—

"What are you waiting for!" the soldier taunted.

David turned back around. He could see the flames underneath the desk growing larger.

Without warning, a tiny flame cloud erupted above one of the flames, then dissipated.

David jumped back, his body pressing against the window as his heart was beating faster than he had ever imagined it possibly could.

"Just drop the gun!" the soldier said, unamused. "I'm tired of playing games!"

David started to say, "So am—"

Another fiery cloud developed over the flames. This time it erupted into a massive ball of fire that instantly enveloped the room.

There was no escape.

The soldiers cried out in pain as the fire surrounded their bodies. They breathed the flames in, singeing the pink flesh of their lungs inside their chests.

David shielded his face and cried out as he felt a hot force push him harder against the window.

The glass shattered and he found himself falling several feet before crashing onto a bed the loose sand. The painful landing momentarily stunned him.

Emily! he remembered. He jumped to his feet, clutching the elephant gun in his bleeding hand. He staggered over to the wrecked bike as quickly as he could, his heart sinking with every inch closer he came to his wife's motionless body. *Oh no! No! This isn't it!* he fearfully thought to himself. "Emily!" he cried out aloud.

"We're all right!" Eve managed to say, forcing herself off the ground as he urgently approached, the terror bleeding from his sad eyes.

"Emily!" he said, grabbing her shoulder. He turned her over, listening to her moan painfully and seeing the abrasions on her face. She looked at him with her big blue eyes, all lost and afraid. She groaned and forced herself to sit up.

"I want to go to sleep," she groggily admitted. "I just want to go to sleep with you."

David kept his hand firmly planted on her shoulder. "It's okay, honey. Everything's going to be okay."

Suddenly, a loud clamor erupted from ahead. He looked up at the crowd and saw a man in a black trench coat moving past them, despite their protests and jeers.

"You're all under arrest!" Akron asserted, storming towards them.

XLVI

David wiped the blood from his lips and raised the elephant gun at the approaching law enforcer. “What! You think that that’s a real gun?” Akron shouted.

David held his ground. “I’ll kill you!” he warned, gripping his weapon with both hands.

Akron wasn’t in the mood for any more games. He reached into his left pocket and pulled out a blood-stained knife. Without an ounce of fear, he marched up to David.

“Fine!” David yelled. “We’ll fight this out!”

Akron swung the blade at him.

He dodged and flung the heavy gun at his head.

Akron caught it with one hand and jammed the knife into his side with the other.

David screamed out in pain and felt his weapon being yanked out of his hands. A moment later, he was being thrown to the ground, across from his wife.

Akron threw the elephant gun onto the ground and pulled out his revolver and pressed it against his head. “Hold the woman down!” he ordered.

Before Emily could react, the tip of a handgun was pressed against her temple. She lay still, pinned to the ground.

He watched her in despair, wishing that he had to power to rescue her from the horrid gun that was gouged against her temple. The glow of the fires around them, their only light, shined off her sweaty face as she stared back at him, her eyes full of bitter sadness.

“This is it,” Akron whispered into his ear.

David recoiled the best he could from Akron's moist, stenchy breath hitting his face. He wanted more than anything to turn around and kill him. He would do it without hesitation. He hated him. He hated him with an ardor.

"Say goodbye to her, Shanahan," Akron continued. "I own her. And I own you. You're both mine."

"No one's yours," David growled back. "She doesn't belong to you. She belongs to me! And I belong to her! We both belong to God!"

"God doesn't exist," he said with an amused chuckle.

"He does so. You've just never let Him inside of you," he snarled back.

Akron grabbed him by the hair and pulled his head off the ground. "You listen to me, you miserable creature, and you listen good! You keep your crazy ideas to yourself! I don't care to hear it!" He slammed his head back against the ground and shoved the tip of his gun against his neck.

"Leave him alone!" Emily screamed.

"What is he to you!" Akron shouted back. "Honestly! What is he to you!"

She gazed sincerely into David's eyes and gently said, "He's my lover. He's my husband. Some day in the future, he will be the father of my children."

"There is no future!" Akron snarled.

She continued, "He's my colleague. He's my playmate . . . He's my best friend. Leave him alone."

Akron thought for a moment, then let out a hearty laugh. "And guess what? He's not your problem anymore. So just shut-up."

David said, "Emily, I love you."

"Stop it!"

She said back, "I love you too."

Akron threw his fist into David's stomach. His victim let out a violent cough and tried to catch his breath as he endured the pain. "I said shut-up!"

Emily glared up at the soldier above her. He wasn't looking.

She had an impulse.

She smacked the soldier's gun away.

David squeezed under Akron's grip and dashed to help her.

Akron fired his revolver.

Searing pain shot up David's thigh as he let out a scream and collapsed to the ground, clutching his wound as the warm blood generously poured out onto the ground.

Emily desperately threw her hands at the soldier, only to be punched in the face and knocked back down. She quickly sat back up in defiance.

"Keep him in place," Akron ordered another soldier. He picked up David's elephant gun and walked up behind Emily. "I want him to see this."

She never realized it was coming.

He slammed the heavy gun against her.

She didn't have a chance to scream before he hit her again, knocking the wind out of her lungs. She gasped for air and said, "Please—"

He brought the gun down on her head, then swiped it across her face. Her body moved with the punches, defenseless to protect herself.

"Stop it!" David screamed, struggling to free himself. He punched the soldier in the face, only to receive triple what he had given.

The pain was grueling. A sharp, stinging sensation ran up her neck and into her head as her back throbbed with blunt pain.

With all his strength, Akron slammed the gun on the top of her head. Then, without a care, he callously kicked her onto the ground.

Aching all over with agonizing pain, she wearily opened her eyes. She could see the dirt beneath her smeared red with her blood. She opened her mouth to let out a sobbing cry of pain, but all that came out was a mixture of blood and saliva.

David crawled over to her, grunting in pain with every move. He raised his trembling finger to her bloodied chin and raised her head. He wanted to tell her how much he loved her and that everything was going to be okay, but he saw the look of pure defeat on her face and felt like dying.

She pulled herself closer to him and buried her face in his arms as she wept.

Akron suddenly stormed forward, grabbed David by his collar, and pulled him back.

"No!" Emily screamed, clutching him by the shoulders and drawing him back with all her strength. "Damn you! Damn you! No!"

Akron raised his fist to strike her. She winced, but held fast to her lover.

"You dare touch her and I'll break your fucking neck!" David screamed, glaring at him with hateful eyes. "Do with me what you want! I don't care anymore! Leave her alone!"

Akron simply stood back with a disgusted sneer on his icy face, crossing his arms as he thought of what to do next. He glanced back at his team, knowing that they were seeing his authority diminish before them. He turned back to the husband and wife and angrily made a pair of fists.

Just then, his pilot approached with her headgear hanging around her neck. "Are you ready to take these two back?"

"You mean this pig and his rotten sow?"

His harsh words only made Emily cry more. Why was this being allowed to happen? She shook her head, throbbing with pain, as she let the tears fall onto his chest. *At least you're here. I'm so glad that it's you with me instead of someone else. Why does it have to end like this?* She glanced over at the crowds of refugees watching them at a distance. They were helpless to save them.

David held onto her as tightly as he could. *I'm supposed to be saving you,* he thought. *I was your protector, and I failed my job. I'm so sorry. So very sorry, sweetheart.* He hung his head in shame, his nose imbedding into her hair and smelling her sweat and blood. "Oh Emily," he said. "I'm sorry."

The pilot growled, "Yes! Of course! Babylon just called and they want these two brought back to face the charges against them as soon as possible."

"I'm ready," he said darkly. "But I want her too." He pointed at Eve. She sneered back at him as two soldiers harshly picked her off the ground.

Emily kept her eyes upon her husband even while being torn away from him by the savage soldiers. They lifted her up and forced her to walk on her feet towards the helicopter. Every step required a massive endurance. She sobbed aloud, her frown open and bent down to the edges of her chin. She didn't care what she looked like anymore. She was drained physically, emotionally, psychologically, and even spiritually. There was nothing more she could possibly do.

She carefully started to climb into the helicopter's storage compartment behind the two front seats as her whole body shook with pain. The impatient soldiers, however, simply shoved her in. She landed on the floor with a moan, but didn't bother to get up. It hurt to much to move anymore. It hurt to even think about it.

David was thrown beside her in the same manner. Eve was more fortunate, being able to climb in on her own despite her wounded leg. The soldiers slammed the compartment doors on them and simply walked away. She sat up against the door and looked down at the two lovers with a grieving heart. She could see the tears silently running down their faces as they lay torn and broken on the metal floor.

"Is it evening yet?" David asked, remembering her earlier opinion on their survival.

"Not yet," she answered. "But I was wrong about what I said. I honestly think that we have more time. They're going to take us back to Babylon. They'll treat us in the hospital and everything will work out. Maybe we can work the courts afterwards. I don't know. We just have to keep trying."

"I don't have much energy left," Emily said, her voice barely above a whisper.

"You'll be okay," Eve said, gently touching her leg. Emily only whimpered. She quickly retreated her hand. "I'm sorry."

"It's okay," she said. "Every time we've moved through time, we've either fallen asleep or gone through mist or a tunnel or something like that. If we stay alive until that happens again, will we end up back home?"

"I don't know," Eve solemnly said. It was the truth. She didn't have any clue. There was only simple logic. They would have to end up somewhere else other than the future. That somewhere else could be anywhere. Even their home.

The front doors suddenly opened as the pilot and Akron jumped in their seats. They switched on the engine and the propellers began to rotate, sending swirls of dust flying around the aircraft.

"Fuel?" the pilot asked.

"Check," Akron announced.

"Avionics?"

"Check."

"Temperature gauge?"

"Everything's fine. Let's just get out of here."

The pilot shrugged and pushed in the throttle. The aircraft began to shake even more as it lifted off the ground. She keyed her microphone and said, "Syphran one eight two alpha foxtrot requesting VFR clearance for Babylon Terminal Control. Over."

She brought the helicopter to the bottom of the massive smoke plumes. The sooty air deposited little grains of carbon on the windscreen, but not enough to impair visibility.

" . . . Clearance granted, Syphran one eight two alpha foxtrot," said a voice over the radio. "Aerial recognizance is on its way to help you in. Advise strong winds to the south of the terminal."

Emily rolled her eyes. She didn't care. She didn't care about anything anymore. She wanted to be cleaned up and left alone in a nice, warm, clean bed. She was tired, hungry, thirsty, and very sick. The last thing she wanted to hear was Akron's voice chattering away in front of her.

"And we're en-route!" the pilot said with a smile as she turned the helicopter northward. "I'll drop you and these prisoners off at the Justice Administration. Then I'm going home."

"Yeah," Akron said, gazing out at the Persian Gulf to the east. The messy waters crashed along the eroded coast with vengeful fury. It was a deadly surf. " . . . Let's take a different route."

"Which one?"

"Go east."

She wanted to protest such a trivial decision, but at the same time, she wasn't about to anger Babylon's elite Law Enforcement Director and run the risk of losing her job. She twisted the yoke to the right and the aircraft banked towards the waters.

Eve suddenly became worried. “I thought that we were going to Babylon.”

“No one asked you!” Akron growled back. He looked back out of the front window. “See that big rock sticking out of the water over there?” he asked. “Bring us there.”

The pilot mumbled something under her breath, but the noise in the cockpit was too loud for him to overhear. She lowered the helicopter towards a massive pillar of rock sticking out above the ocean waters. The entire Persian Gulf coast had been eroded away either by harsh storms or the recent occurrence of severe earthquakes in the region, leaving steep bluffs and protruding rocks all along the coastline. It was a pretty sight from the air. But to actually be on the ground was a different story.

“Now,” Akron said, unbuckling his harness and turning around in his seat. “We’re going to have a little fun here.” He reached over and opened the compartment door.

“What are you doing!” Eve demanded. “You can’t kill us! We’re supposed to have a trial first!”

“Fine! You’re all guilty!” He reached out and grabbed her by the collar.

Emily and David jumped up to grab onto her, but it was too late. Eve Chardon was thrown out of the aircraft.

She watched in horror as the floor disappeared above her.

Her arms hit something.

She grabbed on and found herself hanging on the helicopter’s narrow skid. She looked down and saw a flat rock a few yards beneath her dangling feet. Then she looked back up into the compartment just in time to see David and Emily wrestling Akron’s grip as he forced them towards the opened door.

"Stop!" she screamed, but her voice couldn't be heard over the deafening roar of the propellers. "No!" She watched in horror as Emily and David's bodies helplessly tumbled out of the helicopter by Akron's cruel wrath. Emily's hand slid past the skid, too weak to grab on.

Inside the cockpit, Akron said, "Bring us up." The pilot increased the throttle and hovered even higher. Still, Eve was hanging on. "Can we shake a little?"

"Yep," the pilot said without concern, almost amused. She rocked the craft back and forth in gentle sweeps.

Outside, Eve clung onto the skid for dear life. Using all of her strength and not paying attention to her cramping muscles, she fought to hold on, but to no avail. A moment later, she watched in horror as her arms slowly slipped apart and she lost her grip.

XLVII

The doctor knocked politely on her doorframe before walking into her small office. He could see an evening rain shower ensuing just outside of her window, cooling the city off from the summer heat that had plagued it all day. The hospital president looked up from her desk with a frown. She had a pile of papers before her that needed to be looked at before she could even think of going home. "You've finally decided to show up, I see."

"I'm sorry," Maloney apologized. "I was tied up."

"Yeah. Me too. So much for my kid's birthday party."

The physician sadly hung his head, expecting for the chastisement to begin. A moment later, when he realized that she wasn't going to scold him, he looked back up and asked, "I understand that you wanted me here for a reason?"

She cleared her throat and reached for a glass of water. "You violated the rules. You know that, right?"

"Most certainly."

She took a sip from her glass and stood up. "Don't ever let it happen again. The family signed an agreement not to seek any legal action against us for resuscitating your patient. By the same token, we've agreed to cover all of the further medical costs. We got lucky."

"No we didn't," he sadly said. "Both families agreed a while ago that they would only take this so far. We've reached that limit now. I'm going to have to go in there and turn the machines off on them and I think that we're still going to lose her. We're going to lose them both. And . . . I'm afraid. I've never felt this way before, but I'm afraid."

She suspired and placed her arms akimbo. "We know nothing for a fact. Whatever's happened to those two is unexplainable. They could very well end up coming back, good as new." She frowned again, seeing the skepticism on his face. " . . . Do you believe in God?"

"God?" he asked, giving a light chuckle. "I don't know. At time's like this, I really wish I knew. If he does exist, we could sure use his help now."

She sat there for a moment, thinking over what he had said as she bit her bottom lip and stared at the papers on her desk. "Well," she said, walking out from her desk. "He does exist. And, believe it or not, he is helping us. We just have to figure out how." She strolled over to him and stared at him, face to face. "Are you ready to do what you have to do, doctor?"

Maloney sighed and looked up at the ceiling. "I'm already five minutes late," he admitted. "I hate doing these things."

"It's for the best," she said, placing a hand on his shoulder. "One way or another, it will work out. You'll see. We should go now."

"*We*?" he asked.

"Don't take this personally, but I have to watch you this time. It's in the rule book, section—"

Maloney forced a smile and held up his hand. "I understand," he said. With that, he turned around and headed out of the door with the president right behind him.

The white corridors, as bland in a color scheme as they could possibly be, were filled with the suffocating humidity from the storm outside. He passed patients and other staff members without even a slight nod for a greeting. His mind was too focused on the procedure he was about to perform to care about anything else. After going up a flight of stairs and down another corridor, they found themselves in a waiting area.

The president suddenly stopped and pointed at an old lady sleeping by a magazine rack. "Have you seen that woman there before?" she said.

Maloney scratched his head. "I can't say that I have. Why?"

"I think that someone should look at her. She seems ill. Go take care of your patients. I'll be in as soon as I fetch one of the nurses for her."

The doctor turned around and continued down the hall. When he walked into the small hospital room, he could see that the lights were already on as the evening twilight ruled the sky outside. Maloney could almost smell the sadness when he entered. Not a single eye in the room was dry, except for his. He wondered if he could manage to keep himself composed if everyone else suddenly broke down into sobs. He figured that he could, but it would be hard.

The chief surgeon and a nurse were already waiting for him. Even with their best efforts to be professional, the sadness and consternation was written all over their faces. Maloney exhaled loudly and started to mentally prepare himself by shutting down his emotions. He coldly walked over to David's bedside and gave him one last, thorough examination. His patient was unresponsive. He let his shoulders drop in disappointment as he moved on to check Emily, knowing that he would find the same results.

Sarah huddled against the wall, wiping a tear from her cheek as she stared at her sister's body lying next to her brother-in-law's. *At least they're together*, she thought. She remembered back to a few years ago, hearing her sister once jokingly saying that when she died, she wanted to take her husband down with her. But now it wasn't funny. It was a bitter irony.

The president walked in and stood beside her. She hated the idea of having to monitor her staff, but it was standard procedure after what Maloney had done earlier.

"I know that I'm not ready for this," Sarah said.

"No one ever is," Nathan said, gently stroking the side of her fragile face.

The president said, "But it's time. All they are being made to do is suffer. This is the right thing to do."

The chief of surgery walked over to David's life-support systems and began to prepare them for the shut-down.

Maloney looked out at all of the people in the room. He saw a sea of sadness that in which he was about to drown. *You can do this!* he told himself. *You're a doctor and being a doctor means that you have to do what's best for your patients!* He took a moment to acknowledge his thoughts. They made sense, and yet, meant nothing at all.

Mrs. Dennison wept as she held onto her daughter, as if to keep her from falling into death's grips. Her husband and son stood by, watching helplessly as their loved one was about to pass away.

David's family was equally distraught. His sister was in tears, as well as his mother. His father was trying to hold back and succeeding for the moment, but he would only be able to manage for so long.

The president stepped forward and gently rested her hands on Mrs. Shanahan's shoulders. She forlornly whispered, "It's time,"

She sat back, wiping her tears from her reddened cheeks. "Okay," she whispered in broken defeat. "Okay."

With a heavy heart, Maloney nodded to the other physician. They pushed the levers down and the room fell into still silence.

XLVIII

They hit the rock below with a force that knocked the breath out of their lungs. The pounding of the blades cutting through the air and the sound of the crashing waves below them was deafening to their ears.

Emily turned on her back and watched in horror as the helicopter loomed over them, it's blades slicing the air with vicious force. She could feel her body trembling all over as hot blood ran down the side of her face and dripped onto the ground.

David forced himself up. He wiped the dirt off his mouth, only to find that his lips were bleeding profusely. The large wound on his head had reopened, allowing his warm blood to run freely down his aching body. He glanced over at Eve to make sure she was all right.

His heart forgot to breath as a lump came to his throat. The young woman lay on her chest with her rear slightly elevated. A river of blood trickled out from under her.

"Eve!" Emily screamed. She helped her husband to turn her on her back. They discovered a tiny stalagmite imbedded in her abdomen. Every time she tried to breath out, a tiny stream of blood would squirt out of her.

"Oh, God have mercy," she managed, struggling to breathe.

David picked her up in his arms and held her hand. "Shh. Don't try to talk," he said.

Lost and forlorn, she looked to the right, then to the left. "Where am I? What happened?" She moved her other hand to the stone in her stomach.

"Don't touch it!" Emily warned.

Too late. Eve yanked it out of her body with a piercing scream as the dull pain surged through her. She dropped the bloodied stone and took a moment to recover. Finally, she said, "They got us. Didn't they?"

David sadly looked up at the helicopter hovering over them like a vulture over a dying animal. He was too afraid to tell her the truth. What was the point?

"Everything . . . Everything is so . . . beautiful," she said.

David looked back down at her. She seemed to be smiling, delirious from everything that was happening around her. "You'll go on, now," she said, looking directly at him.

"Go on?" Emily asked.

"You've received the most incredible gift. God let you see yourselves. Who you are as individuals, and who you are as one. You've found the lasting."

"What are you talking about?" David asked.

"You! You and her! You're not two people! You're one! With God's love, you're one! You're one person in two minds! . . . Look around! You've encountered the miracle of the one thing that's remained all along! This is it, your love, the lasting." She smiled and said, "Everything is so beautiful."

David worriedly looked back at Emily. "I think she's hallucinating."

Eve gave him a glare. She knew what she was talking about. But her face let go of the anger as desperation took its place. "Please," she choked, her voice barely audible over the noise of the waves crashing waves and howling wind.

"What is it?" Emily asked.

She looked adoringly into David's eyes, the hope completely gone from her face. There was nothing left for her here now. Nothing but one last favor. "I'm sorry. Kiss me good-bye."

What? David asked in his mind. The simple request had thrown him off guard.

The helicopter, struggling to fly in the wind, swung around and barely managed to hover in place a hundred yards away. The three fugitives on the pillar were completely unaware of what was transpiring in the cockpit.

"Please," Eve begged, then coughing lightly. "You don't have to if . . ."

David gently leaned down and kissed her bloodied lips, tender and swollen with pain that she refused to feel. Using every ounce of energy she had left, she delicately brought her hand up to touch his face, savoring the feel of another human being so intimately close to her. She knew that she was nothing more than a friend in his eyes, but it didn't matter. It was all she needed.

She suddenly pulled her head back and moaned.

"What's wrong? Where are you hurting?" David worried asked.

"Eve!" Emily cried, grabbing her arm. She was unaware of the broken bone protruding out from her punctured skin. She watched in horror as her friend's eyes rolled upwards and her mouth drop open. She moved forward, only to rest her hand in a puddle of warm blood. "Eve! No!"

"God . . . deliver . . . us," she said, exhaling one last time.

"Oh Jesus Christ!" David gasped, feeling her go limp in his arms. He shook her hard, but she didn't stir. Eve Chardon was dead.

"Eve?" Emily cried. She felt her throat knot up as the tears gushed down her cheeks. "Eve!" She clutched onto her lifeless arm in desperation, but the woman did not respond.

He looked up at the black clouds, broken slightly in a few places to reveal a peak at the hundreds of stars in the sky above them. They moved quickly, christened in the orange light of the setting sun, as he yearned for an explanation to all of the madness. "Why!" he screamed. "Where are You in all of this! Are we to just sit here and die while You watch on! Why! Deliver us! Oh Lord, help us!"

Emily grasped his shoulder and hugged him from behind as she sobbed uncontrollably. She knew that she had cried too many tears. The one person who had been there all along for them had been snatched away without mercy. Her heart couldn't take any more of it.

A sudden streak of light fired out from the helicopter's undercarriage. A tremendous ball of fire ripped out from underneath the pillar. The left edge suddenly started to crumble away.

Emily yanked David back just as the rock beneath him disintegrated, but he lost his hold of Eve's body. Her corpse disappeared from view.

The two lovers quickly peered over the edge. They looked just in time to see Eve's body slam into the choppy water. The heavy rocks crashed into the ocean with her, one hitting her head and dragging her from the surface.

"God!" Emily cried in horror. The image below quickly blurred as her tears blinded her. She looked back at David and clutched onto his arms. It was all she could do. The terror had stolen her words right out of her mouth.

Inside the helicopter, Akron let out a pleasant chuckle. "Such a pity, isn't it?" he asked.

"Yes," the pilot mechanically said, fighting with the controls to stay level.

A voice suddenly came over the radio. "Five-three-World-One, aerial recognizance. We have you in our sights at ten o'clock."

She keyed her microphone and growled back, "Keep your distance! The wind is very unstable and I'm having trouble holding."

" . . . Please repeat?"

"Do not come any closer!" she ordered, her spine tingling with fear as she could already hear the approaching helicopter.

Akron kept his eyes transfixed on the two lovers stranded on the rock. "Are we ready to take another shot at them?" he asked.

The pilot glared at him. "This is stupid! I should turn us back to base right now! They're going to die out there anyway!"

"Bring us back home before we finish them off and you're fired," Akron growled.

She let out a frustrated sigh. "Okay. Wait until I get us back into position. Arm the missiles again."

Outside, David clung to his best friend, shielding her from the hellish winds and bitter cold. He watched the helicopter still trying to level itself as another one appeared over the top of the mountain. He felt his heart sink as he helplessly watched their demise being orchestrated before them.

"So this is it!" Emily cried, glaring out at the vast ocean before them, trying to see the beauty Eve had seen in it, but finding none. She realized that she must have meant something else as she watched the white caps of the water violently wash back and forth in the waves. The horizon glowed an orange-red beneath the black clouds. A flash of lightning exploded across the sky with a tremendous crash. She was too scared to feel the wind blowing away the tears on her face. "This is where the world meets Hell and everything between! We're at the end of the world! Here love has no home and no purpose!"

"It has every purpose!" he protested, holding her as close as he could. He looked into her eyes, seemingly lost inside of her forever. He pressed his lips against hers, feeling once more her precious warmth and life. Then he said, "For everything ever done and created, even in this world, it has meaning! God has given us His love and each other! Even if I am to die from life as I know it, here, now, with you and God at my side, it is then the greatest departure that anyone could wish for! We'll go on forever! Love never dies!"

Richard Akron, sitting comfortably in his cozy chair as the pilot guided the helicopter in for another strike, smiled diabolically and readied himself to watch the lovers die in a fiery blast of scorching fire and sharp metal. "Ready?" he asked.

"Just about . . . Shit!" she hollered as another gust of wind forced her a few feet off course. She quickly leveled again. "Fire when ready."

Without warning, the pilot of the other helicopter shouted over the radio. "Go up! Go up!" he frantically screamed.

The pilot keyed her microphone. "Say again?"

Akron flipped the cover off the trigger switch. With deadened eyes, blank of any sign of emotion, he took one last look at his two victims. Then he descended his finger upon the switch.

The pilot slammed her finger back on the key. "Say again! I can't—"

Her words were cut short as a large propeller blade sliced through her window, sending an explosion of glass against her face before it slammed across her throat with indescribable force.

Akron let out a terrified scream as he witnessed her gory decapitation take place in an explosion of hot blood and raw flesh. An instant later, the second propeller crashed into the cockpit and cut through his chest, shattering open his ribcage and allowing him to see his bleeding organs spill out onto his lap and the blood gush out onto the floor.

The two imperiled lovers stayed locked in their embrace.

"I'm glad I'm here with you!" she yelled, the wind blowing her hair in front of her face. "I love you, David Shanahan!"

"Here! Now!" He glanced back out at the unforgiving waters. "And forever!"

A sudden crash made them turn around. The two helicopters, moving towards them, had merged together. The propellers of the second were chipped off as they crashed into the cockpit of the first. A second later, they erupted into massive balls of flames.

"Here! Now! Forever!" she screamed at the top of her lungs.

With their hands together, they jumped.

The burning debris hit the pillar of stone behind them, engulfing it in vicious flames and sending flying rocks and pieces of twisted metal hurtling towards the water.

With terrified shrieks, the two lovers watched the water rushing up to meet them. The white caps bounced up and down, moving like a set of teeth ready to devour them.

XLIX

Nathan hurried out of the elevator and through the waiting room. He glanced towards the magazine rack where a group of nurses and doctors stood around an old lady. Then he turned away in disgust at the sight of the black body bag underneath her feet. *Poor thing*, he thought. *What about her grandchildren?* He decided not to think of such things. There would be plenty of time for that later.

He rushed down the corridor and came to Emily and David's room and stopped in the doorway, taken aback. He had taken too long. The silence in the hospital room was unbearable. No clanking machines or beeping monitors. Just the sound of tears and muffled sobs.

Sarah clung to her sister's arm, the tears silently dripping down her face as she listened to her shallow breathing. The nurse loomed over her with the end of her stethoscope against her sister's chest, listening intently at her heartbeat. "Come on, Em," she whispered. "Come on. You can do it."

Across the room, David's mother and father were in a state of shock. Their son's chest rose slightly, then lowered as he exhaled, and then rose again. "How's his heartbeat?" his father gravely asked.

"It's very faint," Doctor Maloney said. "But it's still there."

"Oh God," David's mother gasped, holding onto her son's arm even harder. "We love you, honey," she said to him. "We're right here."

Nathan Alden stood in the doorway with Frank Klosterman, David's friend and supervisor from work.

Both of them kept their emotions hidden the best they could, but it was everything they could do just to keep the tears from gushing out. Their hopes clung on to what they didn't know. They reminded themselves that anything was always possible, and, at the same time, tried to be realistic.

"Think that they're going to make it?" Frank asked.

" . . . No. I don't," Nathan replied, his eyes shifting over to Sarah. He worried about what he could do for her when the inevitable came. He knew that events like this often changed people forever. It was a part of life. It was a part of growing up.

Frank let out a sigh. "Well, I think that you're wrong."

The nurse listening to Emily's heart frowned. The beat was becoming weaker. *Come back,* she thought. *I'm not losing you! You're my patient! Come back!* She wanted to turn away and cover her face as she frowned, but kept her lips straight and professional. She didn't want to upset the families any more than she had to.

"Emily," Sarah whimpered. "Please don't leave me. I miss you. I've missed you for years now. Please don't go."

Mister Dennison cleared his throat. "Is she going to make it through this?"

The nurse was too concentrated to even hear him. She waited for Emily's next heart beat, but it didn't come. *What! No dying yet! Don't do this!* Then she heard a very soft thump. A moment later, she heard it again. *Good! Still there! Come back! Come on! I know you can do it!*

Doctor Maloney kept his ear on David's heartbeat with a sad frown across his face. He glanced at the young man's handsome face and lamented in the fact that he was too young. And to have his wife go with him was even worse. His heart still clutched on to a hope that perhaps something would reverse itself and his patients would pull through, but his mind reminded him otherwise. He had to keep himself as detached as he could. But hearing his weak heart rhythm didn't help any. He couldn't tell if it was getting any stronger or not.

"Are they going to pull through this?" David's brother asked him.

Maloney didn't answer. He simply didn't know.

L

They crashed feet-first into the cold ocean waters.

Instantaneously, the water broke apart and vanished around them.

The stormy sky above was suddenly transformed into a cloudless dome sprinkled with a trillion twinkling stars. Below them drifted a sea of puffy clouds, rising miles from their bases and caressed in the saffron evening light. The wind was even stronger and it was colder than ever, making them tremble as they descended through the vast abyss towards the clouds.

With their arms outstretched like the wings of an eagle, their hands were held together tighter than diamond rock. The chilly air splashed against their faces with numbing coldness that not even the sun's rays could penetrate, and yet they burned from within.

Oh my God, Emily thought. *It's so beautiful! Your world is unfathomable!*

Deaf from the wailing wind and anesthetized from the cold, all David could sense was the remaining heat of his wife's hand and the miraculous sight below them. *No one has ever seen the world like this before!* he realized.

They gazed at the clouds, enraptured by the question of what lie beneath them. Where would the demise of their journey take them? Another journey? Perhaps it was one of gaining back physical ability and changing the way they lived their lives. Maybe it was something else.

They didn't know. They didn't fear. Feeling God's presence around them, they knew that there was no point in worrying. Emily replayed Eve Chardon's words in her mind. *Everything's going to be okay,* she had said with a peaceful smile.

They were coming closer. The air suddenly turned moist and warm, like the first warm breeze of spring after a harsh winter, melting away any solid coldness. The feeling returned to their skin. Their lungs felt soothed by the soft humidity.

David's eyes stayed transfixed on the gigantic balls of mist. They had less than a minute to travel before they flew through them, descending towards what was below them. He felt a serene warmth inside of him. It was as if he could fall asleep like an infant being held by its mother, even while falling hundreds of yards a second. He turned his head slightly to see her.

The wind blew her hair back from her bloodied face and he could see her joyful grin. She was as radiant as ever. The hope sparkled in her Celtic eyes with a glowing brilliance that he had never seen before. She looked back at him, making him smile in return.

In the time it takes for a photograph to be taken, a heart to beat, an eye to blink and a thought to be pondered and lost, they traversed into the clouds, hand in hand, heart by heart, soul with soul, happily thinking, *Here, now, and forever!*